# EDITH
# WHARTON

# EDITH WHARTON

## THREE COMPLETE WORKS OF LOVE, MORALS, AND MANNERS

*The Age of Innocence*

*Summer*

*Madame de Treymes*

GRAMERCY BOOKS
New York • Avenel

Introduction copyright © 1996 by Random House Value Publishing, Inc.

This 1996 edition is published by Gramercy Books,
a division of Random House Value Publishing, Inc.,
40 Engelhard Avenue, Avenel, New Jersey 07001.

Gramercy Books and colophon are trademarks of
Random House Value Publishing, Inc.

Random House
New York • Toronto • London • Sydney • Auckland

Printed and bound in the United States of America

Library of Congress Cataloging-in-Publication Data
    Wharton, Edith, 1862–1937.
    Edith Wharton: the age of innocence and two other complete works of
love, morals, and manners / Edith Wharton.
        p.     cm. — (Gramercy modern classics)
    Contents: Age of Innocence — Summer — Madame de Treymes.
    ISBN 0–517–12418–1 (hc)
    I. Title.     II. Series.
    PS3545.H16A6     1996
    813'.52—dc20                                                95–49111
                                                                      CIP

8 7 6 5 4 3 2 1

# Contents

INTRODUCTION
vii

THE AGE OF INNOCENCE
1

SUMMER
289

MADAME DE TREYMES
439

# —Introduction—

> It was the old New York way . . . the way of people who
> dreaded scandal more than disease, who placed decency above
> courage, and who considered that nothing was more ill-bred than
> "scenes," except the behavior of those who gave rise to them.
> —*The Age of Innocence*

IN THIS FASHIONABLE SOCIETY, women were ornamental and aimed at
marrying well, men did not need to work, and life was a whirl-
wind of entertaining, travel, sport, and evenings at the opera.
Edith Newbold Jones, born in 1862, was raised in this lofty social
elite, indoctrinated in its requisite manners and morals. She spent
her genteel childhood in New York, Europe, and Newport,
Rhode Island. But Edith was different from the other girls. Possessed of a demanding and hungry intellect, she educated herself
throughout her life in a remarkable range of subjects.

Childhood was a lonely time for Edith in a society that did not
value intellectual pursuits, especially for a woman. From a young
age she showed an interest in writing, but was not encouraged. At
eleven, when she brought her mother the beginnings of a story
that mentioned tidying up a drawing room for a visitor, her
mother sniffed, "Drawing rooms are never untidy." Rebuffed,
Edith turned instead to poetry, and at sixteen she published a
book of verse.

Shy and not quite beautiful, she nonetheless managed, in 1885,
to marry securely within her class: Teddy Wharton was a handsome and congenial Bostonian twelve years older than Edith. Unfortunately the marriage was not to be a happy one: he loved the
outdoors, fishing, amusing repartee; she craved books and intellectual friendships. Edith was unhappy, and her health suffered.

She turned inward, to her imagination, and began to write to fill
the void of "moral solitude" in her marriage. In 1897 she published a how-to book, *The Decoration of Houses,* with the architect
Ogden Codman, Jr. Over the next few years, Edith's health improved as she continued to escape into her writing, but she became increasingly estranged from her husband. Edith Wharton's
first novel, *The Valley of Decision,* was published in 1902, when she
was forty years old. Three years later, another novel, *The House of
Mirth,* was an immediate bestseller, and Wharton's reputation as
chronicler of the world of high society was established.

In 1907 Wharton moved to Paris as her winter home: here at
last was a city of culture and good taste that also encouraged the
exchange and expression of ideas. She met the writer Henry
James, and began to cultivate the kind of intellectual friendships
she desired. That same year, Wharton published the novella
*Madame de Treymes,* considered her most "Jamesian" work. In this
story of thwarted romance, Wharton contrasts French and American society—Paris, with its "look of having been boldly and deliberately planned as a background for the enjoyment of life," and
"lamentable New York." Fanny Frisbee of New York, now the
magnificent Madame Fanny de Malrive of Paris, is seeking a divorce from her aristocratic French husband. John Durham, an
idealistic American who is hopelessly enchanted by Madame de
Malrive's Parisian sophistication, wishes to marry her the moment
she gains her freedom, but when he tries to intervene, he finds
himself entangled in the rigid and formidable code of the
de Malrive family. Fanny's French sister-in-law, Madame
de Treymes, appears to hold the key. In Wharton's ironical ex-
posé, we meet the aristocrats and social climbers, and weigh the
moral dilemma that Durham finally faces.

Edith Wharton settled permanently in Paris in 1910, and over
the next few years she showed her range as a writer, exploring a
variety of subjects. In *Ethan Frome,* for example, one of her best
books, she moved out of the elegant brownstones of the rich and
into a bleak and impoverished town in Massachusetts.

By 1913, Edith and Edward's marriage was over. Edward had
been open about his extramarital sexual exploits, had embezzled
funds, and was suffering increasingly severe mental illness. Then,
a year later, with the advent of World War I, Edith put aside her

writing to focus her considerable energies on the war effort: opening a workshop for women who lost their jobs, organizing hospitals for tubercular patients, creating housing for thousands of French and Belgian refugees—and raising the considerable funds necessary for all of these endeavors. World War I exposed the blue-blooded writer to a harsh new world, far from the privileged realm of her upbringing, and in 1916 Wharton published *Summer,* a novel set in New England, "as remote as possible in setting and subject from the scenes about me." In her 1934 autobiography, *A Backward Glance,* Wharton recalled that *Summer* "was written at a high pitch of creative joy, but amid a thousand interruptions, and while the rest of my being was steeped in the tragic realities of war." As described to her publisher, her intent was to write a "long short story of the dimensions of *Ethan Frome*" that would deal with "the same kind of life in a midsummer landscape," as opposed to the stark wintery setting of the tragic *Ethan Frome.* Wharton was very pleased with *Summer* and considered it one of her best works of fiction, calling it "the Hot Ethan" in a letter to a friend. Sexuality—especially women's sexuality—was a taboo subject in Victorian times, and this story of Charity Royall and her sensual awakening shocked its straitlaced readers and critics. Rich in imagery, *Summer* is set in barren North Dormer, "a weather-beaten sunburned village . . . with no shops, no theaters, no lectures, no 'business block,' only a church . . . and a library for which no books had been bought for twenty years." As a child Charity Royall was "brought down from the Mountain," a place of savage poverty and misery, by lawyer Royall, a somber, lonesome man who has given her a home, although there is no affection between them. Into the life of this discontented, proud, and passionate girl comes Lucius Harney, a visiting architect who sweeps her off her feet. This book contains some of Wharton's most lyrical and evocative descriptions of nature, and some of her most haunting passages. As for the chilling depiction of life on the Mountain, Wharton wrote in her memoirs: "Every detail about the colony of drunken mountain outlaws described in *Summer* was given to me by the rector of the church at Lenox . . . and the lonely peak I have called "the Mountain" was in reality Bear Mountain, an isolated summit not more than twelve miles from our own home. The rector had been fetched there to read the

Burial Service over a woman of evil reputation. . . . Needless to say, when *Summer* appeared, this chapter was received with indignant denial by many reviewers and readers; and not the least vociferous were the New Englanders who for years had sought the reflection of local life in the rose-and-lavender pages of their favorite authoress." As the story crescendos to its surprising conclusion, Charity, Lucius, and Mr. Royall—even in this desolate and impoverished rural setting—are compelled by their own implacable hierarchy of class distinctions and morality.

After the war Wharton moved to the Paris suburbs and returned to the routine of daily writing that she had established years before during her marriage. Every morning she would awaken early, sit in bed, and write, tossing finished pages to the floor for her maid to gather and send out for typing. The next day she would review and revise what she had written, often many times over. By eleven it was time to dress and assume the typical routines of a woman of her social standing—instructing the gardener, entertaining guests, motoring about in her car, dining gracefully with friends.

Now approaching sixty, the expatriate American grew nostalgic. Letting her pen wander back to the old New York of her parents' day, she wrote the immortal *Age of Innocence*. In her memoirs she said, "I found a momentary escape in going back to my childish memories of a long-vanished America. I showed it chapter by chapter to Walter Berry; and when he had finished reading it he said, 'Yes; it's good. But of course you and I are the last people left who can remember New York and Newport as they were then, and nobody else will be interested.'

"I secretly agreed with him as to the chances of my book's success; but it 'had its fate,' and that was—to be one of my rare best-sellers!" Indeed, for *The Age of Innocence*, Edith Wharton won the Pulitzer Prize in 1921. In the book Wharton paints a masterful portrait of the highborn society of old New York as it confronts the changing mores of the newly rich. The reader is transported back to an era of resplendent drawing rooms and exacting social conventions in this story of Newland Archer, a smug, self-assured young man who is engaged to the lovely May Welland. Into this scene of patrician perfection comes May's cousin, the exotic and "Bohemian" Countess Olenska (now estranged from her Polish husband), and all of Archer's lifelong values are thrown into a tailspin.

When the book was published, a reviewer in *The Nation* wrote that Mrs. Wharton described the social rites of old New York "as familiarly as if she loved them and as lucidly as if she hated them." Wharton's story is brimming with wonderful characterizations, like the gossipy Lawrence Lefferts, "the foremost authority on 'form' in New York," the prying Sillerton Jackson, who "applied to the investigation of his friends' affairs the patience of a collector and the science of a naturalist," and the corpulent dowager Catherine Mingott, with her respected social jurisdiction. As Archer and Ellen struggle between propriety and passion, the seriousness with which old New York regarded its social rituals is laid bare in the velvet-draped box at the opera, at the lavish dinner parties and dances, and in the plushly brocaded sitting rooms.

By the early 1920s Edith Wharton was the most renowned American writer of fiction, and in 1923 she received an honorary doctorate from Yale—accepting it on her only trip to the United States in a decade. She lived the rest of her life in her two magnificently decorated homes in France, continuing her prodigious literary output—novels, short stories, including many ghost stories, essays and literary criticism, travel books, and an autobiography—and her lifelong pace of social activity, until her death in 1937 at the age of seventy-five.

This volume contains three of Edith Wharton's finest works of fiction, written at the height of her mature narrative powers. With her mastery of dialogue and characterization, her painterly descriptive detailing, and satirical wit, Edith Wharton is as adept at bringing us into the self-important drawing rooms of high society as she is at depicting the miserable shacks of "the Mountain." On these pages you will meet some of her most memorable characters, rich *and* poor, all trapped in the imposing shadow of society's conventions and mores.

NINA ROSENSTEIN

Westfield, New Jersey
*1996*

# THE AGE
## OF INNOCENCE

# Book One

# 1

On a January evening of the early seventies, Christine Nilsson was singing in Faust at the Academy of Music in New York.

Though there was already talk of the erection, in remote metropolitan distances "above the Forties," of a new opera house which should compete in costliness and splendor with those of the great European capitals, the world of fashion was still content to reassemble every winter in the shabby red and gold boxes of the sociable old Academy. Conservatives cherished it for being small and inconvenient, and thus keeping out the "new people" whom New York was beginning to dread and yet be drawn to; and the sentimental clung to it for its historic associations, and the musical for its excellent acoustics, always so problematic a quality in halls built for the hearing of music.

It was Madame Nilsson's first appearance that winter, and what the daily press had already learned to describe as "an exceptionally brilliant audience" had gathered to hear her, transported through the slippery, snowy streets in private broughams, in the spacious family landau, or in the humbler but more convenient "Brown coupé." To come to the opera in a Brown coupé was almost as honorable a way of arriving as in one's own carriage; and departure by the same means had the immense advantage of enabling one (with a playful allusion to democratic principles) to scramble into the first Brown conveyance in the line, instead of waiting till the cold-and-gin congested nose of one's own coachman gleamed under the portico of the Academy. It was one of the great livery stableman's most masterly intuitions to have discovered that Americans want to get away from amusement even more quickly than they want to get to it.

When Newland Archer opened the door at the back of the club box the curtain had just gone up on the garden scene. There was no reason why the young man should not have come earlier, for he had dined at seven, alone with his mother and sister, and had lingered afterward over a cigar in the Gothic library with glazed black-walnut bookcases and finial-topped chairs, which was the only room in the house where Mrs. Archer allowed smoking. But, in the first place, New York was a metropolis, and perfectly aware that in metropolises it was "not the thing" to arrive early at the opera; and what was or was not "the thing" played a part as important in Newland Archer's New York as the inscrutable to-tem terrors that had ruled the destinies of his forefathers thousands of years ago.

The second reason for his delay was a personal one. He had dawdled over his cigar because he was at heart a dilettante, and thinking over a pleasure to come often gave him a subtler satisfaction than its realization. This was especially the case when the pleasure was a delicate one, as his pleasures mostly were; and on this occasion the moment he looked forward to was so rare and exquisite in quality that—well, if he had timed his arrival in accord with the prima donna's stage manager he could not have entered the Academy at a more significant moment than just as she was singing: "He loves me—he loves me not—*he loves me!*" and sprinkling the falling daisy petals with notes as clear as dew.

She sang, of course, *"M'ama!"* and not "he loves me," since an unalterable and unquestioned law of the musical world required that the German text of French operas sung by Swedish artists should be translated into Italian for the clearer understanding of English-speaking audiences. This seemed as natural to Newland Archer as all the other conventions on which his life was molded: such as the duty of using two silver-backed brushes with his monogram in blue enamel to part his hair, and of never appearing in society without a flower (preferably a gardenia) in his buttonhole.

*"M'ama . . . non m'ama . . ."* the prima donna sang, and *"M'ama!"* with a final burst of love triumphant, as she pressed the disheveled daisy to her lips and lifted her large eyes to the sophisticated countenance of the little brown Faust-Capoul, who was vainly trying, in a tight purple velvet doublet and plumed cap, to look as pure and true as his artless victim.

Newland Archer, leaning against the wall at the back of the

club box, turned his eyes from the stage and scanned the opposite side of the house. Directly facing him was the box of old Mrs. Manson Mingott, whose monstrous obesity had long since made it impossible for her to attend the opera, but who was always represented on fashionable nights by some of the younger members of the family. On this occasion, the front of the box was filled by her daughter-in-law, Mrs. Lovell Mingott, and her daughter, Mrs. Welland; and slightly withdrawn behind these brocaded matrons sat a young girl in white with eyes ecstatically fixed on the stage lovers. As Madame Nilsson's *"M'ama!"* thrilled out above the silent house (the boxes always stopped talking during the Daisy Song) a warm pink mounted to the girl's cheek, mantled her brow to the roots of her fair braids, and suffused the young slope of her breast to the line where it met a modest tulle tucker fastened with a single gardenia. She dropped her eyes to the immense bouquet of lilies-of-the-valley on her knee, and Newland Archer saw her white-gloved fingertips touch the flowers softly. He drew a breath of satisfied vanity and his eyes returned to the stage.

No expense had been spared on the setting, which was acknowledged to be very beautiful even by people who shared his acquaintance with the opera houses of Paris and Vienna. The foreground, to the footlights, was covered with emerald green cloth. In the middle distance symmetrical mounds of woolly green moss bounded by croquet hoops formed the base of shrubs shaped like orange trees but studded with large pink and red roses. Gigantic pansies, considerably larger than the roses, and closely resembling the floral pen wipers made by female parishioners for fashionable clergymen, sprang from the moss beneath the rose trees; and here and there a daisy grafted on a rose branch flowered with a luxuriance prophetic of Mr. Luther Burbank's far-off prodigies.

In the center of this enchanted garden Madame Nilsson, in white cashmere slashed with pale blue satin, a reticule dangling from a blue girdle, and large yellow braids carefully disposed on each side of her muslin chemisette, listened with downcast eyes to M. Capoul's impassioned wooing, and affected a guileless incomprehension of his designs whenever, by word or glance, he persuasively indicated the ground floor window of the neat brick villa projecting obliquely from the right wing.

"The darling!" thought Newland Archer, his glance flitting back to the young girl with the lilies-of-the-valley. "She doesn't even guess what it's all about." And he contemplated her absorbed young face with a thrill of possessorship in which pride in his own masculine initiation was mingled with a tender reverence for her abysmal purity. "We'll read Faust together . . . by the Italian lakes . . ." he thought, somewhat hazily confusing the scene of his projected honeymoon with the masterpieces of literature which it would be his manly privilege to reveal to his bride. It was only that afternoon that May Welland had let him guess that she "cared" (New York's consecrated phrase of maiden avowal), and already his imagination, leaping ahead of the engagement ring, the betrothal kiss, and the march from Lohengrin, pictured her at his side in some scene of old European witchery.

He did not in the least wish the future Mrs. Newland Archer to be a simpleton. He meant her (thanks to his enlightening companionship) to develop a social tact and readiness of wit enabling her to hold her own with the most popular married women of the "younger set," in which it was the recognized custom to attract masculine homage while playfully discouraging it. If he had probed to the bottom of his vanity (as he sometimes nearly did) he would have found there the wish that his wife should be as worldly wise and as eager to please as the married lady whose charms had held his fancy through two mildly agitated years; without, of course, any hint of the frailty which had so nearly marred that unhappy being's life, and had disarranged his own plans for a whole winter.

How this miracle of fire and ice was to be created, and to sustain itself in a harsh world, he had never taken the time to think out; but he was content to hold his view without analyzing it, since he knew it was that of all the carefully brushed, white-waistcoated, buttonhole-flowered gentlemen who succeeded each other in the club box, exchanged friendly greetings with him, and turned their opera glasses critically on the circle of ladies who were the product of the system. In matters intellectual and artistic Newland Archer felt himself distinctly the superior of these chosen specimens of old New York gentility; he had probably read more, thought more, and even seen a good deal more of the world than any other man of the number. Singly they betrayed their inferiority; but grouped together they represented "New York," and the habit of masculine solidarity made him accept their doctrine on all the issues called moral. He instinctively felt that in this respect it would be troublesome—and also rather bad form—to strike out for himself.

"Well—upon my soul!" exclaimed Lawrence Lefferts, turning his opera glass abruptly away from the stage. Lawrence Lefferts was, on the whole, the foremost authority on "form" in New York. He had probably devoted more time than anyone else to the study of this intricate and fascinating question; but study alone could not account for his complete and easy competence. One had only to look at him, from the slant of his bald forehead and the curve of his beautiful fair mustache to the long patent-leather feet at the other end of his lean and elegant person, to feel that the knowledge of "form" must be congenital in anyone who knew how to wear such good clothes so carelessly and carry such height with so much lounging grace. As a young admirer had once said of him: "If anybody can tell a fellow just when to wear a black tie with evening clothes and when not to, it's Larry Lefferts." And on the question of pumps versus patent-leather oxfords his authority had never been disputed.

"My God!" he said, and silently handed his glass to old Sillerton Jackson.

Newland Archer, following Lefferts's glance, saw with surprise that his exclamation had been occasioned by the entry of a new figure into old Mrs. Mingott's box. It was that of a slim young woman, a little less tall than May Welland, with brown hair growing in close curls about her temples and held in place by a narrow band of diamonds. The suggestion of this headdress, which gave her what was then called a "Josephine look," was carried out in the cut of the dark blue velvet gown rather theatrically caught up under her bosom by a girdle with a large old-fashioned clasp. The wearer of this unusual dress, who seemed quite unconscious of the attention it was attracting, stood a moment in the center of the box, discussing with Mrs. Welland the propriety of taking the latter's place in the front right-hand corner; then she yielded with a slight smile, and seated herself in line with Mrs. Welland's sister-in-law, Mrs. Lovell Mingott, who was installed in the opposite corner.

Mr. Sillerton Jackson had returned the opera glass to Lawrence Lefferts. The whole of the club turned instinctively, waiting
to hear what the old man had to say; for old Mr. Jackson was as
great an authority on "family" as Lawrence Lefferts was on
"form." He knew all the ramifications of New York's cousinships
and could not only elucidate such complicated questions as that of
the connection between the Mingotts (through the Thorleys) with
the Dallases of South Carolina, and that of the relationship of the
elder branch of Philadelphia Thorleys to the Albany Chiverses
(on no account to be confused with the Manson Chiverses of University Place), but could also enumerate the leading characteris-
tics of each family: as, for instance, the fabulous stinginess of the
younger lines of Leffertses (the Long Island ones); or the fatal
tendency of the Rushworths to make foolish matches; or the in-
sanity recurring in every second generation of the Albany
Chiverses, with whom their New York cousins had always refused
to intermarry—with the disastrous exception of poor Medora
Manson, who, as everybody knew . . . but then her mother was
a Rushworth.

In addition to this forest of family trees, Mr. Sillerton Jackson
carried between his narrow hollow temples, and under his soft
thatch of silver hair, a register of most of the scandals and mysteries that had smoldered under the unruffled surface of New York
society within the last fifty years. So far indeed did his information extend, and so acutely retentive was his memory, that he was
supposed to be the only man who could have told you who Julius
Beaufort, the banker, really was, and what had become of handsome Bob Spicer, old Mrs. Manson Mingott's father, who had
disappeared so mysteriously (with a large sum of trust money) less
than a year after his marriage, on the very day that a beautiful
Spanish dancer who had been delighting thronged audiences in
the old opera house on the Battery had taken ship for Cuba. But
these mysteries, and many others, were closely locked in Mr. Jackson's breast; for not only did his keen sense of honor forbid his
repeating anything privately imparted, but he was fully aware
that his reputation for discretion increased his opportunities of
finding out what he wanted to know.

The club box, therefore, waited in visible suspense while Mr.
Sillerton Jackson handed back Lawrence Lefferts's opera glass.

For a moment he silently scrutinized the attentive group out of his filmy blue eyes overhung by old veined lids; then he gave his mustache a thoughtful twist, and said simply: "I didn't think the Mingotts would have tried it on."

## 2

NEWLAND ARCHER, during this brief episode, had been thrown into a strange state of embarrassment.

It was annoying that the box which was thus attracting the undivided attention of masculine New York should be that in which his betrothed was seated between her mother and aunt; and for a moment he could not identify the lady in the Empire dress, nor imagine why her presence created such excitement among the initiated. Then light dawned on him, and with it came a momentary rush of indignation. No, indeed; no one would have thought the Mingotts would have tried it on!

But they had; they undoubtedly had; for the low-toned comments behind him left no doubt in Archer's mind that the young woman was May Welland's cousin, the cousin always referred to in the family as "poor Ellen Olenska." Archer knew that she had suddenly arrived from Europe a day or two previously; he had even heard from Miss Welland (not disapprovingly) that she had been to see poor Ellen, who was staying with old Mrs. Mingott. Archer entirely approved of family solidarity, and one of the qualities he most admired in the Mingotts was their resolute championship of the few black sheep that their blameless stock had produced. There was nothing mean or ungenerous in the young man's heart, and he was glad that his future wife should not be restrained by false prudery from being kind (in private) to her unhappy cousin; but to receive Countess Olenska in the family circle was a different thing from producing her in public, at the opera of all places, and in the very box with the young girl whose engagement to him, Newland Archer, was to be announced within a few weeks. No, he felt as old Sillerton Jackson felt; he did not think the Mingotts would have tried it on!

He knew, of course, that whatever man dared (within Fifth Avenue's limits) that old Mrs. Manson Mingott, the matriarch of the line, would dare. He had always admired the high and mighty old lady, who, in spite of having been only Catherine Spicer of Staten Island, with a father mysteriously discredited, and neither money nor position enough to make people forget it, had allied herself with the head of the wealthy Mingott line, married two of her daughters to "foreigners" (an Italian marquis and an English banker), and put the crowning touch to her audacities by building a large house of pale cream-colored stone (when brown sandstone seemed as much the only wear as a frock coat in the afternoon) in an inaccessible wilderness near the Central Park.

Old Mrs. Mingott's foreign daughters had become a legend. They never came back to see their mother, and the latter being, like many persons of active mind and dominating will, sedentary and corpulent in her habit, had philosophically remained at home. But the cream-colored house (supposed to be modeled on the private hotels of the Parisian aristocracy) was there as a visible proof of her moral courage; and she throned in it, among pre-Revolutionary furniture and souvenirs of the Tuileries of Louis Napoleon (where she had shone in her middle age), as placidly as if there were nothing peculiar in living above Thirty-fourth Street, or in having French windows that opened like doors instead of sashes that pushed up.

Everyone (including Mr. Sillerton Jackson) was agreed that old Catherine had never had beauty—a gift which, in the eyes of New York, justified every success, and excused a certain number of failings. Unkind people said that, like her Imperial namesake, she had won her way to success by strength of will and hardness of heart, and a kind of haughty effrontery that was somehow justified by the extreme decency and dignity of her private life. Mr. Manson Mingott had died when she was only twenty-eight, and had "tied up" the money with an additional caution born of the general distrust of the Spicers; but his bold young widow went her way fearlessly, mingled freely in foreign society, married her daughters in heaven knew what corrupt and fashionable circles, hobnobbed with dukes and ambassadors, associated familiarly with papists, entertained opera singers, and was the intimate friend of Mme. Taglioni; and all the while (as Sillerton Jackson was the first to proclaim) there had never been a breath on her reputation; the only respect, he always added, in which she differed from the earlier Catherine.

Mrs. Manson Mingott had long since succeeded in untying her husband's fortune, and had lived in affluence for half a century; but memories of her early straits had made her excessively thrifty, and though, when she bought a dress or a piece of furniture, she took care that it should be of the best, she could not bring herself to spend much on the transient pleasures of the table. Therefore, for totally different reasons, her food was as poor as Mrs. Archer's, and her wines did nothing to redeem it. Her relatives considered that the penury of her table discredited the Mingott name, which had always been associated with good living, but people continued to come to her in spite of the "made dishes" and flat champagne, and in reply to the remonstrances of her son Lovell (who tried to retrieve the family credit by having the best chef in New York) she used to say laughingly: "What's the use of two good cooks in one family, now that I've married the girls and can't eat sauces?"

Newland Archer, as he mused on these things, had once more turned his eyes toward the Mingott box. He saw that Mrs. Welland and her sister-in-law were facing their semicircle of critics with the Mingottian aplomb which old Catherine had inculcated in all her tribe, and that only May Welland betrayed, by a heightened color (perhaps due to the knowledge that he was watching her) a sense of the gravity of the situation. As for the cause of the commotion, she sat gracefully in her corner of the box, her eyes fixed on the stage, and revealing, as she leaned forward, a little more shoulder and bosom than New York was accustomed to seeing, at least in ladies who had reasons for wishing to pass unnoticed.

Few things seemed to Newland Archer more awful than an offence against "Taste," that far-off divinity of whom "Form" was the mere visible representative and vicegerent. Madame Olenska's pale and serious face appealed to his fancy as suited to the occasion and to her unhappy situation, but the way her dress (which had no tucker) sloped away from her thin shoulders shocked and troubled him. He hated to think of May Welland's being exposed to the influence of a young woman so careless of the dictates of Taste.

"After all," he heard one of the younger men begin behind

him (everybody talked through the Mephistopheles-and-Martha scenes), "after all, just *what* happened?"

"Well—she left him; nobody attempts to deny that."

"He's an awful brute, isn't he?" continued the young inquirer, a candid Thorley, who was evidently preparing to enter the lists as the lady's champion.

"The very worst; I knew him at Nice," said Lawrence Lefferts with authority. "A half-paralyzed white sneering fellow—rather handsome head, but eyes with a lot of lashes. Well, I'll tell you the sort: when he wasn't with women he was collecting china. Paying any price for both, I understand."

There was a general laugh, and the young champion said: "Well, then—?"

"Well, then; she bolted with his secretary."

"Oh, I see." The champion's face fell.

"It didn't last long, though: I heard of her a few months later living alone in Venice. I believe Lovell Mingott went out to get her. He said she was desperately unhappy. That's all right—but this parading her at the opera's another thing."

"Perhaps," young Thorley hazarded, "she's too unhappy to be left at home."

This was greeted with an irreverent laugh, and the youth blushed deeply, and tried to look as if he had meant to insinuate what knowing people called a "double entendre."

"Well—it's queer to have brought Miss Welland, anyhow," someone said in a low tone, with a side glance at Archer.

"Oh, that's part of the campaign: Granny's orders, no doubt," Lefferts laughed. "When the old lady does a thing she does it thoroughly."

The act was ending, and there was a general stir in the box. Suddenly Newland Archer felt himself impelled to decisive action. The desire to be the first man to enter Mrs. Mingott's box, to proclaim to the waiting world his engagement to May Welland, and to see her through whatever difficulties her cousin's anomalous situation might involve her in; this impulse had abruptly overruled all scruples and hesitations, and sent him hurrying through the red corridors to the farther side of the house.

As he entered the box his eyes met Miss Welland's, and he saw that she had instantly understood his motive, though the family dignity which both considered so high a virtue would not permit her to tell him so. The persons of their world lived in an atmosphere of faint implications and pale delicacies, and the fact that he and she understood each other without a word seemed to the young man to bring them nearer than any explanation would have done. Her eyes said: "You see why Mamma brought me," and his answered: "I would not for the world have had you stay away."

"You know my niece Countess Olenska?" Mrs. Welland inquired as she shook hands with her future son-in-law. Archer bowed without extending his hand, as was the custom on being introduced to a lady; and Ellen Olenska bent her head slightly, keeping her own pale-gloved hands clasped on her huge fan of eagle feathers. Having greeted Mrs. Lovell Mingott, a large blond lady in creaking satin, he sat down beside his betrothed, and said in a low tone: "I hope you've told Madame Olenska that we're engaged? I want everybody to know—I want you to let me announce it this evening at the ball."

Miss Welland's face grew rosy as the dawn, and she looked at him with radiant eyes. "If you can persuade Mamma," she said, "but why should we change what is already settled?" He made no answer but that which his eyes returned, and she added, still more confidently smiling: "Tell my cousin yourself: I give you leave. She says she used to play with you when you were children."

She made way for him by pushing back her chair, and promptly, and a little ostentatiously, with the desire that the whole house should see what he was doing, Archer seated himself at the Countess Olenska's side.

"We *did* use to play together, didn't we?" she asked, turning her grave eyes to his. "You were a horrid boy, and kissed me once behind a door; but it was your cousin Vandie Newland, who never looked at me, that I was in love with." Her glance swept the horseshoe curve of boxes. "Ah, how this brings it all back to me—I see everybody here in knickerbockers and pantalettes," she said with her trailing slightly foreign accent, her eyes returning to his face.

Agreeable as their expression was, the young man was shocked that they should reflect so unseemly a picture of the august tribunal before which, at that very moment, her case was being tried. Nothing could be in worse taste than misplaced flippancy; and he answered somewhat stiffly: "Yes, you have been away a very long time."

"Oh, centuries and centuries, so long," she said, "that I'm sure I'm dead and buried, and this dear old place is heaven"; which, for reasons he could not define, struck Newland Archer as an even more disrespectful way of describing New York society.

# —— 3 ——

*It invariably* happened in the same way.

Mrs. Julius Beaufort, on the night of her annual ball, never failed to appear at the opera; indeed, she always gave her ball on an opera night in order to emphasize her complete superiority to household cares, and her possession of a staff of servants competent to organize every detail of the entertainment in her absence.

The Beauforts' house was one of the few in New York that possessed a ballroom (it antedated even Mrs. Manson Mingott's and the Headly Chiverses'); and at a time when it was beginning to be thought "provincial" to put a "crash" over the drawing-room floor and move the furniture upstairs, the possession of a ballroom that was used for no other purpose, and left for three hundred and sixty-four days of the year to shuttered darkness, with its gilt chairs stacked in a corner and its chandelier in a bag; this undoubted superiority was felt to compensate for whatever was regrettable in the Beaufort past.

Mrs. Archer, who was fond of coining her social philosophy into axioms, had once said: "We all have our pet common people—" and though the phrase was a daring one, its truth was secretly admitted in many an exclusive bosom. But the Beauforts were not exactly common; some people said they were even worse. Mrs. Beaufort belonged indeed to one of America's most honored families; she had been the lovely Regina Dallas (of the South Carolina branch), a penniless beauty introduced to New York society by her cousin, the imprudent Medora Manson, who was always doing the wrong thing from the right motive. When one was related to the Mansons and the Rushworths one had a *"droit de cité"* (as Mr. Sillerton Jackson, who had frequented the Tuileries, called it) in New York society; but did one not forfeit it in marrying Julius Beaufort?

The question was: who *was* Beaufort? He passed for an Englishman, was agreeable, handsome, ill-tempered, hospitable, and witty. He had come to America with letters of recommendation from old Mrs. Manson Mingott's English son-in-law, the banker, and had speedily made himself an important position in the world of affairs; but his habits were dissipated, his tongue was bitter, his antecedents were mysterious; and when Medora Manson announced her cousin's engagement to him it was felt to be one more act of folly in poor Medora's long record of imprudences.

But folly is as often justified of her children as wisdom, and two years after young Mrs. Beaufort's marriage it was admitted that she had the most distinguished house in New York. No one knew exactly how the miracle was accomplished. She was indolent, passive, the caustic even called her dull; but dressed like an idol, hung with pearls, growing younger and blonder and more beautiful each year, she throned in Mr. Beaufort's heavy brownstone palace, and drew all the world there without lifting her jeweled little finger. The knowing people said it was Beaufort himself who trained the servants, taught the chef new dishes, told the gardeners what hothouse flowers to grow for the dinner table and the drawing rooms, selected the guests, brewed the after-dinner punch, and dictated the little notes his wife wrote to her friends. If he did, these domestic activities were privately performed, and he presented to the world the appearance of a careless and hospitable millionaire strolling into his own drawing room with the detachment of an invited guest, and saying: "My wife's gloxinias are a marvel, aren't they? I believe she gets them out from Kew."

Mr. Beaufort's secret, people were agreed, was the way he carried things off. It was all very well to whisper that he had been "helped" to leave England by the international banking house in which he had been employed; he carried off that rumor as easily as the rest—though New York's business conscience was no less sensitive than its moral standard—he carried everything before him, and all New York into his drawing rooms, and for over twenty years now people had said they were "going to the Beauforts'" with the same tone of security as if they had said they were going to Mrs. Manson Mingott's, and with the added satisfaction of knowing they would get hot canvasback ducks and vintage wines, instead of tepid Veuve Clicquot without a year and warmed-up croquettes from Philadelphia.

Mrs. Beaufort, then, had as usual appeared in her box just before the Jewel Song; and when, again as usual, she rose at the end of the third act, drew her opera cloak about her lovely shoulders, and disappeared, New York knew that meant that half an hour later the ball would begin.

The Beaufort house was one that New Yorkers were proud to show to foreigners, especially on the night of the annual ball. The Beauforts had been among the first people in New York to own their own red velvet carpet and have it rolled down the steps by their own footmen, under their own awning, instead of hiring it with the supper and the ballroom chairs. They had also inaugurated the custom of letting the ladies take their cloaks off in the hall, instead of shuffling up to the hostess's bedroom and recurling their hair with the aid of the gas burner; Beaufort was understood to have said that he supposed all his wife's friends had maids who saw to it that they were properly *coiffées* when they left home.

Then the house had been boldly planned with a ballroom, so that, instead of squeezing through a narrow passage to get to it (as at the Chiverses') one marched solemnly down a vista of enfiladed drawing rooms (the sea green, the crimson, and the *bouton d'or*), seeing from afar the many-candled lusters reflected in the polished parquetry, and beyond that the depths of a conservatory where camellias and tree ferns arched their costly foliage over seats of black and gold bamboo.

Newland Archer, as became a young man of his position, strolled in somewhat late. He had left his overcoat with the silk-stockinged footmen (the stockings were one of Beaufort's few fatuities), had dawdled awhile in the library hung with Spanish leather and furnished with Buhl and malachite, where a few men were chatting and putting on their dancing gloves, and had finally joined the line of guests whom Mrs. Beaufort was receiving on the threshold of the crimson drawing room.

Archer was distinctly nervous. He had not gone back to his club after the opera (as the young bloods usually did), but, the night being fine, had walked for some distance up Fifth Avenue before turning back in the direction of the Beauforts' house. He was definitely afraid that the Mingotts might be going too far;

that, in fact, they might have Granny Mingott's orders to bring the Countess Olenska to the ball.

From the tone of the club box he had perceived how grave a mistake that would be; and, though he was more than ever determined to "see the thing through," he felt less chivalrously eager to champion his betrothed's cousin than before their brief talk at the opera.

Wandering on to the *bouton d'or* drawing room (where Beaufort had had the audacity to hang "Love Victorious," the much-discussed nude of Bouguereau) Archer found Mrs. Welland and her daughter standing near the ballroom door. Couples were already gliding over the floor beyond: the light of the wax candles fell on revolving tulle skirts, on girlish heads wreathed with modest blossoms, on the dashing aigrettes and ornaments of the young married women's coiffures, and on the glitter of highly glazed shirtfronts and fresh glacé gloves.

Miss Welland, evidently about to join the dancers, hung on the threshold, her lilies-of-the-valley in her hand (she carried no other bouquet), her face a little pale, her eyes burning with a candid excitement. A group of young men and girls were gathered about her, and there was much hand clasping, laughing, and pleasantry on which Mrs. Welland, standing slightly apart, shed the beam of a qualified approval. It was evident that Miss Welland was in the act of announcing her engagement, while her mother affected the air of parental reluctance considered suitable to the occasion.

Archer paused a moment. It was at his express wish that the announcement had been made, and yet it was not thus that he would have wished to have his happiness known. To proclaim it in the heat and noise of a crowded ballroom was to rob it of the fine bloom of privacy which should belong to things nearest the heart. His joy was so deep that this blurring of the surface left its essence untouched, but he would have liked to keep the surface pure too. It was something of a satisfaction to find that May Welland shared this feeling. Her eyes fled to his beseechingly, and their look said: "Remember, we're doing this because it's right."

No appeal could have found a more immediate response in Archer's breast; but he wished that the necessity of their action had been represented by some ideal reason, and not simply by poor Ellen Olenska. The group about Miss Welland made way for him with significant smiles, and after taking his share of the felicitations he drew his betrothed into the middle of the ballroom floor and put his arm about her waist.

"Now we shan't have to talk," he said, smiling into her candid eyes as they floated away on the soft waves of the Blue Danube.

She made no answer. Her lips trembled into a smile, but the eyes remained distant and serious, as if bent on some ineffable vision. "Dear," Archer whispered, pressing her to him: it was borne in on him that the first hours of being engaged, even if spent in a ballroom, had in them something grave and sacramental. What a new life it was going to be, with this whiteness, radiance, goodness at one's side!

The dance over, the two, as became an affianced couple, wandered into the conservatory; and sitting behind a tall screen of tree ferns and camellias Newland pressed her gloved hand to his lips.

"You see I did as you asked me to," she said.

"Yes. I couldn't wait," he answered, smiling. After a moment he added: "Only I wish it hadn't had to be at a ball."

"Yes, I know." She met his glance comprehendingly. "But after all—even here we're alone together, aren't we?"

"Oh, dearest—always!" Archer cried.

Evidently she was always going to understand; she was always going to say the right thing. The discovery made the cup of his bliss overflow, and he went on gaily: "The worst of it is that I want to kiss you and I can't." As he spoke he took a swift glance about the conservatory, assured himself of their momentary privacy, and catching her to him laid a fugitive pressure on her lips. To counteract the audacity of this proceeding he led her to a bamboo sofa in a less secluded part of the conservatory, and sitting down beside her broke a lily-of-the-valley from her bouquet. She sat silent, and the world lay like a sunlit valley at their feet.

"Did you tell my cousin Ellen?" she asked presently, as if she spoke through a dream.

He roused himself, and remembered that he had not done so. Some invincible repugnance to speak of such things to the strange foreign woman had checked the words on his lips.

"No—I hadn't the chance after all," he said, fibbing hastily.

"Ah." She looked disappointed, but gently resolved on gaining her point. "You must, then, for I didn't either; and I shouldn't like her to think—"

"Of course not. But aren't you, after all, the person to do it?"

She pondered on this. "If I'd done it at the right time, yes: but now that there's been a delay I think you must explain that I'd asked you to tell her at the opera, before our speaking about it to everybody here. Otherwise she might think I had forgotten her. You see, she's one of the family, and she's been away so long that she's rather—sensitive."

Archer looked at her glowingly. "Dear and great angel! Of course I'll tell her." He glanced a trifle apprehensively toward the crowded ballroom. "But I haven't seen her yet. Has she come?"

"No; at the last minute she decided not to."

"At the last minute?" he echoed, betraying his surprise that she should ever have considered the alternative possible.

"Yes. She's awfully fond of dancing," the young girl answered simply. "But suddenly she made up her mind that her dress wasn't smart enough for a ball, though we thought it so lovely; and so my aunt had to take her home."

"Oh, well—" said Archer with happy indifference. Nothing about his betrothed pleased him more than her resolute determination to carry to its utmost limit that ritual of ignoring the "unpleasant" in which they had both been brought up.

"She knows as well as I do," he reflected, "the real reason of her cousin's staying away; but I shall never let her see by the least sign that I am conscious of there being a shadow of a shade on poor Ellen Olenska's reputation."

# ——— 4 ———

🌿 IN THE COURSE of the next day the first of the usual betrothal visits were exchanged. The New York ritual was precise and inflexible in such matters; and in conformity with it Newland Archer first went his mother and sister to call on Mrs. Welland, after which he and Mrs. Welland and May drove out to old Mrs. Manson Mingott's to receive that venerable ancestress's blessing.

A visit to Mrs. Manson Mingott was always an amusing episode to the young man. The house in itself was already an historic document, though not, of course, as venerable as certain other old family houses in University Place and lower Fifth Avenue. Those were of the purest 1830, with a grim harmony of cabbage-rose-garlanded carpets, rosewood consoles, round-arched fireplaces with black marble mantels, and immense glazed bookcases of mahogany; whereas old Mrs. Mingott, who had built her house later, had bodily cast out the massive furniture of her prime, and mingled with the Mingott heirlooms the frivolous upholstery of the Second Empire. It was her habit to sit in a window of her sitting room on the ground floor, as if watching calmly for life and fashion to flow northward to her solitary doors. She seemed in no hurry to have them come, for her patience was equaled by her confidence. She was sure that presently the hoardings, the quarries, the one-story saloons, the wooden greenhouses in ragged gardens, and the rocks from which goats surveyed the scene, would vanish before the advance of residences as stately as her own—perhaps (for she was an impartial woman) even statelier; and that the cobblestones over which the old clattering omnibuses bumped would be replaced by smooth asphalt, such as people reported having seen in Paris. Meanwhile, as everyone she cared to see came to *her* (and she could fill her rooms as easily as the Beauforts, and without adding a single item to the menu of her suppers), she did not suffer from her geographic isolation.

The immense accretion of flesh which had descended on her in

24

middle life like a flood of lava on a doomed city had changed her from a plump active little woman with a neatly turned foot and ankle into something as vast and august as a natural phenomenon. She had accepted this submergence as philosophically as all her other trials, and now, in extreme old age, was rewarded by presenting to her mirror an almost unwrinkled expanse of firm pink and white flesh, in the center of which the traces of a small face survived as if awaiting excavation. A flight of smooth double chins led down to the dizzy depths of a still-snowy bosom veiled in snowy muslins that were held in place by a miniature portrait of the late Mr. Mingott; and around and below, wave after wave of black silk surged away over the edges of a capacious armchair, with two tiny white hands poised like gulls on the surface of the billows.

The burden of Mrs. Manson Mingott's flesh had long since made it impossible for her to go up and down stairs, and with characteristic independence she had made her reception rooms upstairs and established herself (in flagrant violation of all the New York proprieties) on the ground floor of her house; so that, as you sat in her sitting-room window with her, you caught (through a door that was always open, and a looped-back yellow damask portière) the unexpected vista of a bedroom with a huge low bed upholstered like a sofa, and a toilet table with frivolous lace flounces and a gilt-framed mirror.

Her visitors were startled and fascinated by the foreignness of this arrangement, which recalled scenes in French fiction, and architectural incentives to immorality such as the simple American had never dreamed of. That was how women with lovers lived in the wicked old societies, in apartments with all the rooms on one floor, and all the indecent propinquities that their novels described. It amused Newland Archer (who had secretly situated the love scenes of "Monsieur de Camors" in Mrs. Mingott's bedroom) to picture her blameless life led in the stage setting of adultery; but he said to himself, with considerable admiration, that if a lover had been what she wanted, the intrepid woman would have had him too.

To the general relief the Countess Olenska was not present in her grandmother's drawing room during the visit of the betrothed couple. Mrs. Mingott said she had gone out; which, on a day of such glaring sunlight, and at the "shopping hour," seemed in itself an indelicate thing for a compromised woman to do. But at any rate it spared them the embarrassment of her presence, and the faint shadow that her unhappy past might seem to shed on their radiant future. The visit went off successfully, as was to have been expected. Old Mrs. Mingott was delighted with the engagement, which, being long foreseen by watchful relatives, had been carefully passed upon in family council; and the engagement ring, a large thick sapphire set in invisible claws, met with her unqualified admiration.

"It's the new setting: of course it shows the stone beautifully, but it looks a little bare to old-fashioned eyes," Mrs. Welland had explained, with a conciliatory side glance at her future son-in-law.

"Old-fashioned eyes? I hope you don't mean mine, my dear? I like all the novelties," said the ancestress, lifting the stone to her small bright orbs, which no glasses had ever disfigured. "Very handsome," she added, returning the jewel; "very liberal. In my time a cameo set in pearls was thought sufficient. But it's the hand that sets off the ring, isn't it, my dear Mr. Archer?" and she waved one of her tiny hands, with small pointed nails and rolls of aged fat encircling the wrist like ivory bracelets. "Mine was modeled in Rome by the great Ferrigiani. You should have May's done: no doubt he'll have it done, my child. Her hand is large—it's these modern sports that spread the joints—but the skin is white. And when's the wedding to be?" she broke off, fixing her eyes on Archer's face.

"Oh—" Mrs. Welland murmured, while the young man, smiling at his betrothed, replied: "As soon as ever it can, if only you'll back me up, Mrs. Mingott."

"We must give them time to get to know each other a little better, Mamma," Mrs. Welland interposed, with the proper affectation of reluctance; to which the ancestress rejoined: "Know each other? Fiddlesticks! Everybody in New York has always known everybody. Let the young man have his way, my dear; don't wait till the bubble's off the wine. Marry them before Lent; I may catch pneumonia any winter now, and I want to give the wedding breakfast."

These successive statements were received with the proper expressions of amusement, incredulity, and gratitude; and the visit was breaking up in a vein of mild pleasantry when the door opened to admit the Countess Olenska, who entered in bonnet and mantle followed by the unexpected figure of Julius Beaufort.

There was a cousinly murmur of pleasure between the ladies, and Mrs. Mingott held out Ferrigiani's model to the banker. "Ha! Beaufort, this is a rare favor!" (She had an odd foreign way of addressing men by their surnames.)

"Thanks. I wish it might happen oftener," said the visitor in his easy arrogant way. "I'm generally so tied down; but I met the Countess Ellen in Madison Square, and she was good enough to let me walk home with her."

"Ah—I hope the house will be gayer, now that Ellen's here!" cried Mrs. Mingott with a glorious effrontery. "Sit down—sit down, Beaufort: push up the yellow armchair; now I've got you I want a good gossip. I hear your ball was magnificent; and I understand you invited Mrs. Lemuel Struthers? Well—I've a curiosity to see the woman myself."

She had forgotten her relatives, who were drifting out into the hall under Ellen Olenska's guidance. Old Mrs. Mingott had always professed a great admiration for Julius Beaufort, and there was a kind of kinship in their cool domineering way and their shortcuts through the conventions. Now she was eagerly curious to know what had decided the Beauforts to invite (for the first time) Mrs. Lemuel Struthers, the widow of Struthers's Shoe Polish, who had returned the previous year from a long initiatory sojourn in Europe to lay siege to the tight little citadel of New York. "Of course if you and Regina invite her the thing is settled. Well, we need new blood and new money—and I hear she's still very good-looking," the carnivorous old lady declared.

In the hall, while Mrs. Welland and May drew on their furs, Archer saw that the Countess Olenska was looking at him with a faintly questioning smile.

"Of course you know already—about May and me," he said, answering her look with a shy laugh. "She scolded me for not giving you the news last night at the opera: I had her orders to tell you that we were engaged—but I couldn't, in that crowd."

The smile passed from Countess Olenska's eyes to her lips: she looked younger, more like the bold brown Ellen Mingott of his boyhood. "Of course I know; yes. And I'm so glad. But one doesn't tell such things first in a crowd." The ladies were on the threshold and she held out her hand.

"Good-bye; come and see me someday," she said, still looking at Archer.

In the carriage, on the way down Fifth Avenue, they talked pointedly of Mrs. Mingott, of her age, her spirit, and all her wonderful attributes. No one alluded to Ellen Olenska, but Archer knew that Mrs. Welland was thinking: "It's a mistake for Ellen to be seen, the very day after her arrival, parading up Fifth Avenue at the crowded hour with Julius Beaufort—" and the young man himself mentally added: "And she ought to know that a man who's just engaged doesn't spend his time calling on married women. But I daresay in the set she'd lived in they do—they never do anything else." And, in spite of the cosmopolitan views on which he prided himself, he thanked heaven that he was a New Yorker, and about to ally himself with one of his own kind.

# 5

THE NEXT EVENING old Mr. Sillerton Jackson came to dine with the Archers.

Mrs. Archer was a shy woman and shrank from society, but she liked to be well informed as to its doings. Her old friend Mr. Sillerton Jackson applied to the investigation of his friends' affairs the patience of a collector and the science of a naturalist; and his sister, Miss Sophy Jackson, who lived with him, and was entertained by all the people who could not secure her much-sought-after brother, brought home bits of minor gossip that filled out usefully the gaps in his picture.

Therefore, whenever anything happened that Mrs. Archer wanted to know about, she asked Mr. Jackson to dine; and as she honored few people with her invitations, and as she and her daughter Janey were an excellent audience, Mr. Jackson usually came himself instead of sending his sister. If he could have dictated all the conditions, he would have chosen the evenings when Newland was out; not because the young man was uncongenial to him (the two got on capitally at their club) but because the old anecdotist sometimes felt, on Newland's part, a tendency to weigh his evidence that the ladies of the family never showed.

Mr. Jackson, if perfection had been attainable on earth, would also have asked that Mrs. Archer's food should be a little better. But then New York, as far back as the mind of man could travel, had been divided into the two great fundamental groups of the Mingotts and Mansons and all their clan, who cared about eating and clothes and money, and the Archer-Newland-van-der-Luyden tribe, who were devoted to travel, horticulture, and the best fiction, and looked down on the grosser forms of pleasure.

You couldn't have everything, after all. If you dined with the Lovell Mingotts you got canvasback and terrapin and vintage wines; at Adeline Archer's you could talk about Alpine scenery and "The Marble Faun"; and luckily the Archer Madeira had gone round the Cape. Therefore when a friendly summons came from Mrs. Archer, Mr. Jackson, who was a true eclectic, would usually say to his sister: "I've been a little gouty since my last dinner at the Lovell Mingotts'—it will do me good to diet at Adeline's."

Mrs. Archer, who had long been a widow, lived with her son and daughter in West Twenty-eighth Street. An upper floor was dedicated to Newland, and the two women squeezed themselves into narrower quarters below. In an unclouded harmony of tastes and interests they cultivated ferns in Wardian cases, made macramé lace and wool embroidery on linen, collected American revolutionary glazed ware, subscribed to *Good Words,* and read Ouida's novels for the sake of the Italian atmosphere. (They preferred those about peasant life, because of the descriptions of scenery and the pleasanter sentiments, though in general they liked novels about people in society, whose motives and habits were more comprehensible, spoke severely of Dickens, who "had never drawn a gentleman," and considered Thackeray less at home in the great world than Bulwer—who, however, was beginning to be thought old-fashioned.)

Mrs. and Miss Archer were both great lovers of scenery. It was what they principally sought and admired on their occasional travels abroad; considering architecture and painting as subjects for men, and chiefly for learned persons who read Ruskin. Mrs. Archer had been born a Newland, and mother and daughter, who were as like as sisters, were both, as people said, "true Newlands"; tall, pale, and slightly round-shouldered, with long noses, sweet smiles and a kind of drooping distinction like that in certain faded Reynolds portraits. Their physical resemblance would have been complete if an elderly *embonpoint* had not stretched Mrs. Archer's black brocade, while Miss Archer's brown and purple poplins hung, as the years went on, more and more slackly on her virgin frame.

Mentally, the likeness between them, as Newland was aware, was less complete than their identical mannerisms often made it appear. The long habit of living together in mutually dependent intimacy had given them the same vocabulary, and the same habit of beginning their phrases "Mother thinks" or "Janey thinks," according as one or the other wished to advance an opinion of her own; but in reality, while Mrs. Archer's serene unimaginative-ness rested easily in the accepted and familiar, Janey was subject to starts and aberrations of fancy welling up from springs of sup-pressed romance.

Mother and daughter adored each other and revered their son and brother; and Archer loved them with a tenderness made compunctious and uncritical by the sense of their exaggerated admiration, and by his secret satisfaction in it. After all, he thought it a good thing for a man to have his authority respected in his own house, even if his sense of humor sometimes made him question the force of his mandate.

On this occasion the young man was very sure that Mr. Jackson would rather have had him dine out, but he had his own reasons for not doing so.

Of course old Jackson wanted to talk about Ellen Olenska, and of course Mrs. Archer and Janey wanted to hear what he had to tell. All three would be slightly embarrassed by Newland's pres-ence, now that his prospective relation to the Mingott clan had been made known; and the young man waited with an amused curiosity to see how they would turn the difficulty.

They began, obliquely, by talking about Mrs. Lemuel Struthers.

"It's a pity the Beauforts asked her," Mrs. Archer said gently. "But then Regina always does what he tells her, and *Beaufort*—"

"Certain *nuances* escape Beaufort," said Mr. Jackson, cau-tiously inspecting the broiled shad, and wondering for the thou-sandth time why Mrs. Archer's cook always burned the roe to a cinder. (Newland, who had long shared his wonder, could always detect it in the older man's expression of melancholy disap-proval.)

"Oh, necessarily. Beaufort is a vulgar man," said Mrs. Archer. "My grandfather Newland always used to say to my mother: 'Whatever you do, don't let that fellow Beaufort be introduced to the girls.' But at least he's had the advantage of associating with gentlemen; in England too, they say. It's all very mysterious—" She glanced at Janey and paused. She and Janey knew every fold of the Beaufort mystery, but in public Mrs. Archer continued to assume that the subject was not one for the unmarried.

"But this Mrs. Struthers," Mrs. Archer continued, "what did you say *she* was, Sillerton?"

"Out of a mine: or rather out of the saloon at the head of the pit. Then with Living Waxworks, touring New England. After the police broke *that* up, they say she lived—" Mr. Jackson in his turn glanced at Janey, whose eyes began to bulge from under her prominent lids. There were still hiatuses for her in Mrs. Struthers's past.

"Then," Mr. Jackson continued (and Archer saw he was wondering why no one had told the butler never to slice cucumbers with a steel knife), "then Lemuel Struthers came along. They say his advertizer used the girl's head for the shoe-polish posters; her hair's intensely black, you know—the Egyptian style. Anyhow, he—eventually—married her." There were volumes of innuendo in the way the "eventually" was spaced, and each syllable given its due stress.

"Oh, well—at the pass we've come to nowadays, it doesn't matter," said Mrs. Archer indifferently. The ladies were not really interested in Mrs. Struthers just then; the subject of Ellen Olenska was too fresh and too absorbing to them. Indeed, Mrs. Struthers's name had been introduced by Mrs. Archer only that she might presently be able to say: "And Newland's new cousin— Countess Olenska? Was *she* at the ball too?"

There was a faint touch of sarcasm in the reference to her son, and Archer knew it and had expected it. Even Mrs. Archer, who was seldom unduly pleased with human events, had been altogether glad of her son's engagement. ("Especially after that silly business with Mrs. Rushworth," as she had remarked to Janey, alluding to what had once seemed to Newland a tragedy of which his soul would always bear the scar.) There was no better match in New York than May Welland, look at the question from whatever point you chose. Of course such a marriage was only what Newland was entitled to; but young men are so foolish and incalculable—and some women so ensnaring and unscrupulous—that it was nothing short of a miracle to see one's only son safe past the Siren Isle and in the haven of a blameless domesticity.

All this Mrs. Archer felt, and her son knew she felt; but he knew also that she had been perturbed by the premature announcement of his engagement, or rather by its cause; and it was

for that reason—because on the whole he was a tender and indulgent master—that he had stayed at home that evening. "It's not
that I don't approve of the Mingotts' *esprit de corps;* but why Newland's engagement should be mixed up with that Olenska
woman's comings and goings I don't see," Mrs. Archer grumbled
to Janey, the only witness of her slight lapses from perfect sweetness.

She had behaved beautifully—and in beautiful behavior she
was unsurpassed—during the call on Mrs. Welland, but Newland
knew (and his betrothed doubtless guessed) that all through the
visit she and Janey were nervously on the watch for Madame
Olenska's possible intrusion; and when they left the house together she had permitted herself to say to her son: "I'm thankful
that Augusta Welland received us alone."

These indications of inward disturbance moved Archer the
more that he too felt that the Mingotts had gone a little too far.
But, as it was against all the rules of their code that the mother
and son should ever allude to what was uppermost in their
thoughts, he simply replied: "Oh, well, there's always a phase of
family parties to be gone through when one gets engaged, and
the sooner it's over the better." At which his mother merely
pursed her lips under the lace veil that hung down from her gray
velvet bonnet trimmed with frosted grapes.

Her revenge, he felt—her lawful revenge—would be to "draw"
Mr. Jackson that evening on the Countess Olenska; and, having
publicly done his duty as a future member of the Mingott clan,
the young man had no objection to hearing the lady discussed in
private—except that the subject was already beginning to bore
him.

Mr. Jackson had helped himself to a slice of the tepid filet
which the mournful butler had handed him with a look as scepti-
cal as his own, and had rejected the mushroom sauce after a
scarcely perceptible sniff. He looked baffled and hungry, and
Archer reflected that he would probably finish his meal on Ellen
Olenska.

Mr. Jackson leaned back in his chair, and glanced up at the
candlelit Archers, Newlands, and van der Luydens hanging in
dark frames on the dark walls.

"Ah, how your grandfather Archer loved a good dinner, my

dear Newland!" he said, his eyes on the portrait of a plump full-chested young man in a stock and a blue coat, with a view of a white-columned country house behind him, "Well—well—well . . . I wonder what he would have said to all these foreign marriages!"

Mrs. Archer ignored the allusion to the ancestral cuisine and Mr. Jackson continued with deliberation: "No, she was *not* at the ball."

"Ah—" Mrs. Archer murmured, in a tone that implied: "She had that decency."

"Perhaps the Beauforts don't know her," Janey suggested with her artless malice.

Mr. Jackson gave a faint sip, as if he had been tasting invisible Madeira. "Mrs. Beaufort may not—but Beaufort certainly does, for she was seen walking up Fifth Avenue this afternoon with him by the whole of New York."

"Mercy—" moaned Mrs. Archer, evidently perceiving the uselessness of trying to ascribe the actions of foreigners to a sense of delicacy.

"I wonder if she wears a round hat or a bonnet in the afternoon," Janey speculated. "At the opera I know she had on dark blue velvet, perfectly plain and flat—like a nightgown."

"Janey!" said her mother, and Miss Archer blushed and tried to look audacious.

"It was, at any rate, in better taste not to go to the ball," Mrs. Archer continued.

A spirit of perversity moved her son to rejoin: "I don't think it was a question of taste with her. May said she meant to go, and then decided that the dress in question wasn't smart enough."

Mrs. Archer smiled at this confirmation of her inference. "Poor Ellen," she simply remarked; adding compassionately: "We must always bear in mind what an eccentric bringing up Medora Manson gave her. What can you expect of a girl who was allowed to wear black satin at her coming-out ball?"

"Ah—don't I remember her in it!" said Mr. Jackson, adding: "Poor girl!" in the tone of one who, while enjoying the memory, had fully understood at the time what the sight portended.

"It's odd," Janey remarked, "that she should have kept such an ugly name as Ellen. I should have changed it to Elaine." She glanced about the table to see the effect of this.

Her brother laughed. "Why Elaine?"

"I don't know; it sounds more—more Polish," said Janey, blushing.

"It sounds more conspicuous, and that can hardly be what she wishes," said Mrs. Archer distantly.

"Why not?" broke in her son, growing suddenly argumentative. "Why shouldn't she be conspicuous if she chooses? Why should she slink about as if it were she who had disgraced herself? She's 'poor Ellen' certainly, because she had the bad luck to make a wretched marriage, but I don't see that that's a reason for hiding her head as if she were the culprit."

"That, I suppose," said Mr. Jackson speculatively, "is the line the Mingotts mean to take."

The young man reddened. "I didn't have to wait for their cue, if that's what you mean, sir. Madame Olenska has had an unhappy life: that doesn't make her an outcast."

"There are rumors," began Mr. Jackson, glancing at Janey.

"Oh, I know: the secretary," the young man took him up. "Nonsense, Mother; Janey's grown up. They say, don't they," he went on, "that the secretary helped her to get away from her brute of a husband, who kept her practically a prisoner? Well, what if he did? I hope there isn't a man among us who wouldn't have done the same in such a case."

Mr. Jackson glanced over his shoulder to say to the sad butler: "Perhaps . . . that sauce . . . just a little, after all—"; then, having helped himself, he remarked: "I'm told she's looking for a house. She means to live here."

"I hear she means to get a divorce," said Janey boldly.

"I hope she will!" Archer exclaimed.

The word had fallen like a bombshell in the pure and tranquil atmosphere of the Archer dining room. Mrs. Archer raised her delicate eyebrows in the particular curve that signified: "The butler—" and the young man, himself mindful of the bad taste of discussing such intimate matters in public, hastily branched off into an account of his visit to old Mrs. Mingott.

After dinner, according to immemorial custom. Mrs. Archer and Janey trailed their long silk draperies up to the drawing room, where, while the gentlemen smoked below stairs, they sat beside a Carcel lamp with an engraved globe, facing each other across a rosewood worktable with a green silk bag under it, and stitched at the two ends of a tapestry band of field flowers destined to adorn an "occasional" chair in the drawing room of young Mrs. Newland Archer.

While this rite was in progress in the drawing room, Archer settled Mr. Jackson in an armchair near the fire in the Gothic library and handed him a cigar. Mr. Jackson sank into the armchair with satisfaction, lit his cigar with perfect confidence (it was Newland who bought them), and stretching his thin old ankles to the coals, said: "You say the secretary merely helped her to get away, my dear fellow? Well, he was still helping her a year later, then; for somebody met 'em living at Lausanne together."

Newland reddened. "Living together? Well, why not? Who had the right to make her life over if she hadn't? I'm sick of the hypocrisy that would bury alive a woman of her age if her husband prefers to live with harlots."

He stopped and turned away angrily to light his cigar. "Women ought to be free—as free as we are," he declared, making a discovery of which he was too irritated to measure the terrific consequences.

Mr. Sillerton Jackson stretched his ankles nearer the coals and emitted a sardonic whistle.

"Well," he said after a pause, "apparently Count Olenski takes your view; for I never heard of his having lifted a finger to get his wife back."

# ——6——

THAT EVENING, after Mr. Jackson had taken himself away, and the ladies had retired to their chintz-curtained bedroom, Newland Archer mounted thoughtfully to his own study. A vigilant hand had, as usual, kept the fire alive and the lamp trimmed; and the room, with its rows and rows of books, its bronze and steel statuettes of "The Fencers" on the mantelpiece and its many photographs of famous pictures, looked singularly homelike and welcoming.

As he dropped into his armchair near the fire his eyes rested on a large photograph of May Welland, which the young girl had given him in the first days of their romance, and which had now displaced all the other portraits on the table. With a new sense of awe he looked at the frank forehead, serious eyes, and gay innocent mouth of the young creature whose soul's custodian he was to be. That terrifying product of the social system he belonged to and believed in, the young girl who knew nothing and expected everything, looked back at him like a stranger through May Welland's familiar features; and once more it was borne in on him that marriage was not the safe anchorage he had been taught to think, but a voyage on uncharted seas.

The case of the Countess Olenska had stirred up old settled convictions and set them drifting dangerously through his mind. His own exclamation: "Women should be free—as free as we are," struck to the root of a problem that it was agreed in his world to regard as nonexistent. "Nice" women, however wronged, would never claim the kind of freedom he meant, and generous-minded men like himself were therefore—in the heat of argument—the more chivalrously ready to concede it to them. Such verbal generosities were in fact only a humbugging disguise of the inexorable conventions that tied things together and bound people down to the old pattern. But here he was pledged to defend, on the part of his betrothed's cousin, conduct that, on his own wife's part, would justify him in calling down on her all the thunders of Church and State. Of course the dilemma was purely hypothetical; since he wasn't a blackguard Polish nobleman, it was absurd to speculate what his wife's rights would be if he *were*. But Newland Archer was too imaginative not to feel that, in his case and May's, the tie might gall for reasons far less gross and palpable. What could he and she really know of each other, since it was his duty, as a "decent" fellow, to conceal his past from her, and hers, as a marriageable girl, to have no past to conceal? What if, for some one of the subtler reasons that would tell with both of them, they should tire of each other, misunderstand or irritate each other? He reviewed his friends' marriages—the supposedly happy ones—and saw none that answered, even remotely, to the passionate and tender comradeship which he pictured as his permanent relation with May Welland. He perceived that such a picture presupposed, on her part, the experience, the versatility, the freedom of judgment, which she had been carefully trained not to possess; and with a shiver of foreboding he saw his marriage becoming what most of the other marriages about him were; a dull association of material and social interests held together by ignorance on the one side and hypocrisy on the other. Lawrence Lefferts occurred to him as the husband who had most completely realized this enviable ideal. As became the high priest of form, he had formed a wife so completely to his own convenience that, in the most conspicuous moments of his frequent love affairs with other men's wives, she went about in smiling unconsciousness, saying that "Lawrence was so frightfully strict"; and had been known to blush indignantly, and avert her gaze, when someone alluded in her presence to the fact that Julius Beaufort (as became a "foreigner" of doubtful origin) had what was known in New York as "another establishment."

Archer tried to console himself with the thought that he was not quite such an ass as Larry Lefferts, nor May such a simpleton as poor Gertrude; but the difference was after all one of intelligence and not of standards. In reality they all lived in a kind of hieroglyphic world, where the real thing was never said or done or even thought, but only represented by a set of arbitrary signs; as when Mrs. Welland, who knew exactly why Archer had pressed her to announce her daughter's engagement at the Beaufort ball (and had indeed expected him to do no less), yet felt obliged to simulate reluctance, and the air of having had her hand forced, quite as, in the books on Primitive Man that people of advanced culture were beginning to read, the savage bride is dragged with shrieks from her parents' tent.

The result, of course, was that the young girl who was the center of this elaborate system of mystification remained the more inscrutable for her very frankness and assurance. She was frank, poor darling, because she had nothing to conceal, assured because she knew of nothing to be on her guard against; and with no better preparation than this, she was to be plunged overnight into what people evasively called "the facts of life."

The young man was sincerely but placidly in love. He delighted in the radiant good looks of his betrothed, in her health, her horsemanship, her grace and quickness at games, and the shy interest in books and ideas that she was beginning to develop under his guidance. (She had advanced far enough to join him in ridiculing the *Idylls of the King*, but not to feel the beauty of "Ulysses" and "The Lotos-Eaters.") She was straightforward, loyal, and brave; she had a sense of humor (chiefly proved by her laughing at *his* jokes); and he suspected, in the depths of her innocently gazing soul, a glow of feeling that it would be a joy to waken. But when he had gone the brief round of her he returned discouraged by the thought that all this frankness and innocence were only an artificial product. Untrained human nature was not frank and innocent; it was full of the twists and defenses of an instinctive guile. And he felt himself oppressed by this creation of factitious purity, so cunningly manufactured by a conspiracy of mothers and aunts and grandmothers and long-dead ancestresses, because it was supposed to be what he wanted, what he had a right to, in order that he might exercise his lordly pleasure in smashing it like an image made of snow.

There was a certain triteness in these reflections: they were those habitual to young men on the approach of their wedding day. But they were generally accompanied by a sense of compunction and self-abasement of which Newland Archer felt no trace. He could not deplore (as Thackeray's heroes so often exasperated him by doing) that he had not a blank page to offer his bride in exchange for the unblemished one she was to give to

him. He could not get away from the fact that if he had been
brought up as she had they would have been no more fit to find
their way about than the Babes in the Wood; nor could he, for all
his anxious cogitations, see any honest reason (any, that is, unconnected with his own momentary pleasure, and the passion of masculine vanity) why his bride should not have been allowed the
same freedom of experience as himself.

Such questions, at such an hour, were bound to drift through
his mind; but he was conscious that their uncomfortable persis-
tence and precision were due to the inopportune arrival of the
Countess Olenska. Here he was, at the very moment of his betrothal—a moment for pure thoughts and cloudless hopes—
pitchforked into a coil of scandal which raised all the special problems he would have preferred to let lie. "Hang Ellen Olenska!" he
grumbled, as he covered his fire and began to undress. He could
not really see why her fate should have the least bearing on his;
yet he dimly felt that he had only just begun to measure the risks
of the championship which his engagement had forced upon
him.

A few days later the bolt fell.

The Lovell Mingotts had sent out cards for what was known as
"a formal dinner" (that is, three extra footmen, two dishes for
each course, and a Roman punch in the middle) and had headed
their invitations with the words "To meet the Countess Olenska,"
in accordance with the hospitable American fashion, which treats
strangers as if they were royalties, or at least as their ambassadors.

The guests had been selected with a boldness and discrimination in which the initiated recognized the firm hand of Catherine
the Great. Associated with such immemorial standbys as the Selfridge Merrys, who were asked everywhere because they always
had been, the Beauforts, on whom there was a claim of relationship, and Mr. Sillerton Jackson and his sister Sophy (who went
wherever her brother told her to), were some of the most fashionable and yet most irreproachable of the dominant "young married" set; the Lawrence Leffertses, Mrs. Lefferts Rushworth (the
lovely widow), the Harry Thorleys, the Reggie Chiverses, and
young Morris Dagonet and his wife (who was a van der Luyden).
The company indeed was perfectly assorted, since all the mem-

bers belonged to the little inner group of people who, during the long New York season, disported themselves together daily and nightly with apparently undiminished zest.

Forty-eight hours later the unbelievable had happened; everyone had refused the Mingotts' invitation except the Beauforts and old Mr. Jackson and his sister. The intended slight was emphasized by the fact that even the Reggie Chiverses, who were of the Mingott clan, were among those inflicting it; and by the uniform wording of the notes, in all of which the writers "regretted that they were unable to accept," without the mitigating plea of a "previous engagement" that ordinary courtesy prescribed.

New York society was, in those days, far too small, and too scant in its resources, for everyone in it (including livery-stable-keepers, butlers, and cooks) not to know exactly on which evenings people were free; and it was thus possible for the recipients of Mrs. Lovell Mingott's invitations to make cruelly clear their determination not to meet the Countess Olenska.

The blow was unexpected; but the Mingotts, as their way was, met it gallantly. Mrs. Lovell Mingott confided the case to Mrs. Welland, who confided it to Newland Archer; who, aflame at the outrage, appealed passionately and authoritatively to his mother; who, after a painful period of inward resistance and outward temporizing, succumbed to his instances (as she always did), and immediately embracing his cause with an energy redoubled by her previous hesitations, put on her gray velvet bonnet and said: "I'll go and see Louisa van der Luyden."

The New York of Newland Archer's day was a small and slippery pyramid, in which, as yet, hardly a fissure had been made or a foothold gained. At its base was a firm foundation of what Mrs. Archer called "plain people"; an honorable but obscure majority of respectable families who (as in the case of the Spicers or the Leffertses or the Jacksons) had been raised above their level by marriage with one of the ruling clans. People, Mrs. Archer always said, were not as particular as they used to be; and with old Catherine Spicer ruling one end of Fifth Avenue, and Julius Beaufort the other, you couldn't expect the old traditions to last much longer.

Firmly narrowing upward from this wealthy but inconspicuous substratum was the compact and dominant group which the

Mingotts, Newlands, Chiverses, and Mansons so actively represented. Most people imagined them to be the very apex of the
pyramid; but they themselves (at least those of Mrs. Archer's generation) were aware that, in the eyes of the professional genealo-
gist, only a still smaller number of families could lay claim to that
eminence.

"Don't tell me," Mrs. Archer would say to her children, "all this
modern newspaper rubbish about a New York aristocracy. If
there is one, neither the Mingotts nor the Mansons belong to it;
no, nor the Newlands or the Chiverses either. Our grandfathers
and great-grandfathers were just respectable English or Dutch
merchants, who came to the colonies to make their fortune, and
stayed here because they did so well. One of your great-grandfathers signed the Declaration, and another was a general on Washington's staff, and received General Burgoyne's sword after the
battle of Saratoga. These are things to be proud of, but they have
nothing to do with rank or class. New York has always been a
commercial community, and there are not more than three families in it who can claim an aristocratic origin in the real sense of
the word."

Mrs. Archer and her son and daughter, like everyone else in
New York, knew who these privileged beings were: the Dagonets
of Washington Square, who came of an old English country family
allied with the Pitts and Foxes; the Lannings, who had intermar-
ried with the descendants of Count de Grasse, and the van der
Luydens, direct descendants of the first Dutch governor of Man-
hattan, and related by pre-Revolutionary marriages to several
members of the French and British aristocracy.

The Lannings survived only in the person of two very old but
lively Miss Lannings, who lived cheerfully and reminiscently
among family portraits and Chippendale; the Dagonets were a
considerable clan, allied to the best names in Baltimore and Philadelphia; but the van der Luydens, who stood above all of them,
had faded into a kind of superterrestrial twilight from which only
two figures impressively emerged; those of Mr. and Mrs. Henry
van der Luyden.

Mrs. Henry van der Luyden had been Louisa Dagonet, and
her mother had been the granddaughter of Colonel du Lac, of an
old Channel Island family, who had fought under Cornwallis and

had settled in Maryland, after the war, with his bride, Lady Angelica Trevenna, fifth daughter of the Earl of St. Austrey. The tie between the Dagonets, the du Lacs of Maryland, and their aristocratic Cornish kinsfolk, the Trevennas, had always remained close and cordial. Mr. and Mrs. van der Luyden had more than once paid long visits to the present head of the house of Trevenna, the Duke of St. Austrey, at his country seat in Cornwall and at St. Austrey in Gloucestershire; and his Grace had frequently announced his intention of someday returning their visit (without the Duchess, who feared the Atlantic).

Mr. and Mrs. van der Luyden divided their time between Trevenna, their place in Maryland, and Skuytercliff, the great estate on the Hudson which had been one of the colonial grants of the Dutch government to the famous first Governor, and of which Mr. van der Luyden was still "Patroon." Their large solemn house in Madison Avenue was seldom opened, and when they came to town they received in it only their most intimate friends.

"I wish you would go with me, Newland," his mother said, suddenly pausing at the door of the Brown coupé. "Louisa is fond of you; and of course it's on account of dear May that I'm taking this step—and also because, if we don't all stand together, there'll be no such thing as Society left."

# ——— 7 ———

✿ Mrs. HENRY VAN DER LUYDEN listened in silence to her cousin Mrs. Archer's narrative.

It was all very well to tell yourself in advance that Mrs. van der Luyden was always silent, and that, though noncommittal by nature and training, she was very kind to the people she really liked. Even personal experience of these facts was not always a protection from the chill that descended on one in the high-ceilinged white-walled Madison Avenue drawing room, with the pale brocaded armchairs so obviously uncovered for the occasion, and the gauze still veiling the ormolu mantel ornaments and the beautiful old carved frame of Gainsborough's *Lady Angelica du Lac*.

Mrs. van der Luyden's portrait by Huntington (in black velvet and Venetian point) faced that of her lovely ancestress. It was generally considered "as fine as a Cabanel," and, though twenty years had elapsed since its execution, was still "a perfect likeness." Indeed the Mrs. van der Luyden who sat beneath it listening to Mrs. Archer might have been the twin sister of the fair and still youngish woman drooping against a gilt armchair before a green rep curtain. Mrs. van der Luyden still wore black velvet and Venetian point when she went into society—or rather (since she never dined out) when she threw open her own doors to receive it. Her fair hair, which had faded without turning gray, was still parted in flat overlapping points on her forehead, and the straight nose that divided her pale blue eyes was only a little more pinched about the nostrils than when the portrait had been painted. She always, indeed, struck Newland Archer as having been rather gruesomely preserved in the airless atmosphere of a perfectly irreproachable existence, as bodies caught in glaciers keep for years a rosy life-in-death.

Like all his family, he esteemed and admired Mrs. van der Luyden; but he found her gentle bending sweetness less approachable than the grimness of some of his mother's old aunts, fierce spinsters who said "No" on principle before they knew what they were going to be asked.

Mrs. van der Luyden's attitude said neither yes nor no, but always appeared to incline to clemency till her thin lips, wavering into the shadow of a smile, made the almost invariable reply: "I shall first have to talk this over with my husband."

She and Mr. van der Luyden were so exactly alike that Archer often wondered how, after forty years of the closest conjugality, two such merged identities ever separated themselves enough for anything as controversial as a talking-over. But as neither had ever reached a decision without prefacing it by this mysterious conclave, Mrs. Archer and her son, having set forth their case, waited resignedly for the familiar phrase.

Mrs. van der Luyden, however, who had seldom surprised anyone, now surprised them by reaching her long hand toward the bell rope.

"I think," she said, "I should like Henry to hear what you have told me."

A footman appeared, to whom she gravely added: "If Mr. van der Luyden has finished reading the newspaper, please ask him to be kind enough to come."

She said "reading the newspaper" in the tone in which a Minister's wife might have said: "Presiding at a Cabinet meeting"—not from any arrogance of mind, but because the habit of a lifetime, and the attitude of her friends and relations, had led her to consider Mr. van der Luyden's least gesture as having an almost sacerdotal importance.

Her promptness of action showed that she considered the case as pressing as Mrs. Archer; but, lest she should be thought to have committed herself in advance, she added, with the sweetest look: "Henry always enjoys seeing you, dear Adeline, and he will wish to congratulate Newland."

The double doors had solemnly reopened and between them appeared Mr. Henry van der Luyden, tall, spare and frock-coated, with faded fair hair, a straight nose like his wife's, and the same look of frozen gentleness in eyes that were merely pale gray instead of pale blue.

Mr. van der Luyden greeted Mrs. Archer with cousinly affabil-ity, proffered to Newland low-voiced congratulations couched in the same language as his wife's, and seated himself in one of the brocade armchairs with the simplicity of a reigning sovereign.

"I had just finished reading the *Times,*" he said, laying his long fingertips together. "In town my mornings are so much occupied that I find it more convenient to read the newspapers after luncheon."

"Ah, there's a great deal to be said for that plan—indeed I think my Uncle Egmont used to say he found it less agitating not to read the morning papers till after dinner," said Mrs. Archer responsively.

"Yes: my good father abhorred hurry. But now we live in a constant rush," said Mr. van der Luyden in measured tones, looking with pleasant deliberation about the large shrouded room which to Archer was so complete an image of its owners.

"But I hope you *had* finished your reading, Henry?" his wife interposed.

"Quite—quite," he reassured her.

"Then I should like Adeline to tell you—"

"Oh, it's really Newland's story," said his mother smiling: and proceeded to rehearse once more the monstrous tale of the affront inflicted on Mrs. Lovell Mingott.

"Of course," she ended, "Augusta Welland and Mary Mingott both felt that, especially in view of Newland's engagement, you and Henry *ought to know.*"

"Ah—" said Mr. van der Luyden, drawing a deep breath.

There was a silence during which the tick of the monumental ormolu clock on the white marble mantelpiece grew as loud as the boom of a minute gun. Archer contemplated with awe the two slender faded figures, seated side by side in a kind of viceregal rigidity, mouthpieces of some remote ancestral authority which fate compelled them to wield, when they would so much rather have lived in simplicity and seclusion, digging invisible weeds out of the perfect lawns of Skuytercliff, and playing Patience together in the evenings.

Mr. van der Luyden was the first to speak.

"You really think this is due to some—some intentional interference of Lawrence Lefferts's?" he inquired, turning to Archer.

"I'm certain of it, sir. Larry has been going it rather harder than usual lately—if cousin Louisa won't mind my mentioning it—having rather a stiff affair with the postmaster's wife in their village, or someone of that sort; and whenever poor Gertrude Lefferts begins to suspect anything, and he's afraid of trouble, he gets up a fuss of this kind, to show how awfully moral he is, and talks at the top of his voice about the impertinence of inviting his wife to meet people he doesn't wish her to know. He's simply using Madame Olenska as a lightning rod; I've seen him try the same thing often before."

"The *Leffertses!*—" said Mrs. van der Luyden.

"The *Leffertses!*—" echoed Mrs. Archer. "What would Uncle Egmont have said of Lawrence Lefferts's pronouncing on anybody's social position? It shows what Society has come to."

"We'll hope it has not quite come to that," said Mr. van der Luyden firmly.

"Ah, if only you and Louisa went out more!" sighed Mrs. Archer.

But instantly she became aware of her mistake. The van der Luydens were morbidly sensitive to any criticism of their secluded existence. They were the arbiters of fashion, the Court of last Appeal, and they knew it, and bowed to their fate. But being shy and retiring persons, with no natural inclination for their part, they lived as much as possible in the sylvan solitude of Skuytercliff, and when they came to town, declined all invitations on the plea of Mrs. van der Luyden's health.

Newland Archer came to his mother's rescue. "Everybody in New York knows what you and cousin Louisa represent. That's why Mrs. Mingott felt she ought not allow this slight on Countess Olenska to pass without consulting you."

Mrs. van der Luyden glanced at her husband, who glanced back at her.

"It is the principle that I dislike," said Mr. van der Luyden. "As long as a member of a well-known family is backed up by that family it should be considered—final."

"It seems so to me," said his wife, as if she were producing a new thought.

"I had no idea," Mr. van der Luyden continued, "that things had come to such a pass." He paused, and looked at his wife again. "It occurs to me, my dear, that the Countess Olenska is already a sort of relation—through Medora Manson's first husband. At any rate, she will be when Newland marries." He turned toward the young man. "Have you read this morning's *Times*, Newland?"

"Why, yes, sir," said Archer, who usually tossed off half a dozen papers with his morning coffee.

Husband and wife looked at each other again. Their pale eyes clung together in prolonged and serious consultation; then a faint smile fluttered over Mrs. van der Luyden's face. She had evidently guessed and approved.

Mr. van der Luyden turned to Mrs. Archer. "If Louisa's health allowed her to dine out—I wish you would say to Mrs. Lovell Mingott—she and I would have been happy to—er—fill the places of the Lawrence Leffertses at her dinner." He paused to let the irony of this sink in. "As you know, this is impossible." Mrs. Archer sounded a sympathetic assent. "But Newland tells me he has read this morning's *Times;* therefore he has probably seen that Louisa's relative, the Duke of St. Austrey, arrives next week on the *Russia*. He is coming to enter his new sloop, the *Guinevere,* in next summer's International Cup Race; and also to have a little canvasback shooting at Trevenna." Mr. van der Luyden paused again, and continued with increasing benevolence: "Before taking him down to Maryland we are inviting a few friends to meet him here—only a little dinner—with a reception afterward. I am sure Louisa will be as glad as I am if Countess Olenska will let us include her among our guests." He got up, bent his long body with a stiff friendliness toward his cousin, and added: "I think I have Louisa's authority for saying that she will herself leave the invitation to dine when she drives out presently: with our cards— of course with our cards."

Mrs. Archer, who knew this to be a hint that the seventeen-hand chestnuts which were never kept waiting were at the door, rose with a hurried murmur of thanks. Mrs. van der Luyden beamed on her with the smile of Esther interceding with Ahasuerus, but her husband raised a protesting hand.

"There is nothing to thank me for, dear Adeline; nothing whatever. This kind of thing must not happen in New York; it shall not, as long as I can help it," he pronounced with sovereign gentleness as he steered his cousins to the door.

Two hours later, everyone knew that the great C-spring barouche in which Mrs. van der Luyden took the air at all seasons had been seen at old Mrs. Mingott's door, where a large square envelope was handed in; and that evening at the opera Mr. Sillerton Jackson was able to state that the envelope contained a card inviting the Countess Olenska to the dinner which the van der Luydens were giving the following week for their cousin, the Duke of St. Austrey.

Some of the younger men in the club box exchanged a smile at this announcement, and glanced sideways at Lawrence Lefferts, who sat carelessly in the front of the box, pulling his long fair mustache, and who remarked with authority, as the soprano paused: "No one but Patti ought to attempt the Sonnambula."

# ——8——

It was generally agreed in New York that the Countess Olenska had "lost her looks."

She had appeared there first, in Newland Archer's boyhood, as a brilliantly pretty little girl of nine or ten, of whom people said that she "ought to be painted." Her parents had been continental wanderers, and after a roaming babyhood she had lost them both, and been taken in charge by her aunt, Medora Manson, also a wanderer, who was herself returning to New York to "settle down."

Poor Medora, repeatedly widowed, was always coming home to settle down (each time in a less expensive house), and bringing with her a new husband or an adopted child; but after a few months she invariably parted from her husband or quarreled with her ward, and, having got rid of her house at a loss, set out again on her wanderings. As her mother had been a Rushworth, and her last unhappy marriage had linked her to one of the crazy Chiverses, New York looked indulgently on her eccentricities; but when she returned with her little orphaned niece, whose parents had been popular in spite of their regrettable taste for travel, people thought it a pity that the pretty child should be in such hands.

Everyone was disposed to be kind to little Ellen Mingott, though her dusky red cheeks and tight curls gave her an air of gaiety that seemed unsuitable in a child who should still have been in black for her parents. It was one of the misguided Medora's many peculiarities to flout the unalterable rules that regulated American mourning, and when she stepped from the steamer her family were scandalized to see that the crape veil she wore for her own brother was seven inches shorter than those of her sisters-in-law, while little Ellen was in crimson merino and amber beads, like a gypsy foundling.

But New York had so long resigned itself to Medora that only a

few old ladies shook their heads over Ellen's gaudy clothes, while
her other relations fell under the charm of her high color and
high spirits. She was a fearless and familiar little thing, who asked
disconcerting questions, made precocious comments, and possessed outlandish arts, such as dancing a Spanish shawl dance and
singing Neapolitan love songs to a guitar. Under the direction of
her aunt (whose real name was Mrs. Thorley Chivers, but who,
having received a papal title, had resumed her first husband's
patronymic, and called herself the Marchioness Manson, because
in Italy she could turn it into Manzoni) the little girl received an
expensive but incoherent education, which included "drawing
from the model," a thing never dreamed of before, and playing
the piano in quintets with professional musicians.

Of course no good could come of this; and when, a few years
later, poor Chivers finally died in a madhouse, his widow (draped
in strange weeds) again pulled up stakes and departed with Ellen,
who had grown into a tall bony girl with conspicuous eyes. For
some time no more was heard of them; then news came of Ellen's
marriage to an immensely rich Polish nobleman of legendary
fame, whom she had met at a ball at the Tuileries, and who was
said to have princely establishments in Paris, Nice, and Florence,
a yacht at Cowes, and many square miles of shooting in Transylva-
nia. She disappeared in a kind of sulfurous apotheosis, and when
a few years later Medora again came back to New York, subdued,
impoverished, mourning a third husband, and in quest of a still
smaller house, people wondered that her rich niece had not been
able to do something for her. Then came the news that Ellen's
own marriage had ended in disaster, and that she was herself
returning home to seek rest and oblivion among her kinsfolk.

These things passed through Newland Archer's mind a week
later as he watched the Countess Olenska enter the van der
Luyden drawing room on the evening of the momentous dinner.
The occasion was a solemn one, and he wondered a little nervously how she would carry it off. She came rather late, one hand
still ungloved, and fastening a bracelet about her wrist; yet she
entered without any appearance of haste or embarrassment the
drawing room in which New York's most chosen company was
somewhat awfully assembled.

In the middle of the room she paused, looking about her with a grave mouth and smiling eyes; and in that instant Newland Archer rejected the general verdict on her looks. It was true that her early radiance was gone. The red cheeks had paled; she was thin, worn, a little older-looking than her age, which must have been nearly thirty. But there was about her the mysterious authority of beauty, a sureness in the carriage of the head, the movement of the eyes, which, without being in the least theatrical, struck his as highly trained and full of a conscious power. At the same time she was simpler in manner than most of the ladies present, and many people (as he heard afterward from Janey) were disappointed that her appearance was not more "stylish"— for stylishness was what New York most valued. It was, perhaps, Archer reflected, because her early vivacity had disappeared; because she was so quiet—quiet in her movements, her voice, and the tones of her low-pitched voice. New York had expected something a good deal more reasonant in a young woman with such a history.

The dinner was a somewhat formidable business. Dining with the van der Luydens was at best no light matter, and dining there with a duke who was their cousin was almost a religious solemnity. It pleased Archer to think that only an old New Yorker could perceive the shade of difference (to New York) between being merely a duke and being the van der Luydens' duke. New York took stray noblemen calmly, and even (except in the Struthers set) with a certain distrustful *hauteur;* but when they presented such credentials as these they were received with an old-fashioned cordiality that they would have been greatly mistaken in ascribing solely to their standing in Debrett. It was for just such distinctions that the young man cherished his old New York even while he smiled at it.

The van der Luydens had done their best to emphasise the importance of the occasion. The du Lac Sèvres and the Trevenna George II plate were out; so was the van der Luyden "Lowestoft" (East India Company) and the Dagonet Crown Derby. Mrs. van der Luyden looked more than ever like a Cabanel, and Mrs. Archer, in her grandmother's seed pearls and emeralds, reminded her son of an Isabey miniature. All the ladies had on their handsomest jewels, but it was characteristic of the house and the occasion that these were mostly in rather heavy old-fashioned settings; and old Miss Lanning, who had been persuaded to come, actually wore her mother's cameos and a Spanish blond shawl.

The Countess Olenska was the only young woman at the dinner; yet, as Archer scanned the smooth plump elderly faces between their diamond necklaces and towering ostrich feathers, they struck him as curiously immature compared with hers. It frightened him to think what must have gone to the making of her eyes.

The Duke of St. Austrey, who sat at his hostess's right, was naturally the chief figure of the evening. But if the Countess Olenska was less conspicuous than had been hoped, the duke was almost invisible. Being a well-bred man he had not (like another recent ducal visitor) come to the dinner in a shooting jacket; but his evening clothes were so shabby and baggy, and he wore them with such an air of their being homespun, that (with his stooping way of sitting, and the vast beard spreading over his shirtfront) he hardly gave the appearance of being in dinner attire. He was short, round-shouldered, sunburned, with a thick nose, small eyes, and a sociable smile; but he seldom spoke, and when he did it was in such low tones that, despite the frequent silences of expectation about the table, his remarks were lost to all but his neighbors.

When the men joined the ladies after dinner the duke went straight up to the Countess Olenska, and they sat down in a corner and plunged into animated talk. Neither seemed aware that the duke should first have paid his respects to Mrs. Lovell Mingott and Mrs. Headly Chivers, and the countess have conversed with that amiable hypochondriac, Mr. Urban Dagonet of Washington Square, who, in order to have the pleasure of meeting her, had broken through his fixed rule of not dining out between January and April. The two chatted together for nearly twenty minutes; then the countess rose and, walking alone across the wide drawing room, sat down at Newland Archer's side.

It was not the custom in New York drawing rooms for a lady to get up and walk away from one gentleman in order to seek the company of another. Etiquette required that she should wait, immovable as an idol, while the men who wished to converse with her succeeded each other at her side. But the countess was appar-

ently unaware of having broken any rule; she sat at perfect ease in
a corner of the sofa beside Archer, and looked at him with the
kindest eyes.

"I want you to talk to me about May," she said.

Instead of answering her he asked: "You knew the duke before?"

"Oh, yes—we used to see him every winter at Nice. He's very
fond of gambling—he used to come to the house a great deal."
She said it in the simplest manner, as if she had said: "He's fond
of wildflowers"; and after a moment she added candidly: "I think
he's the dullest man I ever met."

This pleased her companion so much that he forgot the slight
shock her previous remark had caused him. It was undeniably
exciting to meet a lady who found the van der Luydens' duke
dull, and dared to utter the opinion. He longed to question her,
to hear more about the life of which her careless words had given
him so illuminating a glimpse; but he feared to touch on distress-
ing memories, and before he could think of anything to say she
had strayed back to her original subject.

"May is a darling; I've seen no young girl in New York so
handsome and so intelligent. Are you very much in love with
her?"

Newland Archer reddened and laughed. "As much as a man
can be."

She continued to consider him thoughtfully, as if not to miss
any shade of meaning in what he said, "Do you think, then, there
is a limit?"

"To being in love? If there is, I haven't found it!"

She glowed with sympathy. "Ah—it's really and truly a romance?"

"The most romantic of romances!"

"How delightful! And you found it all out for yourselves—it
was not in the least arranged for you?"

Archer looked at her incredulously. "Have you forgotten," he
asked with a smile, "that in our country we don't allow our marriages to be arranged for us?"

A dusky blush rose to her cheek, and he instantly regretted his
words.

"Yes," she answered, "I'd forgotten. You must forgive me if I sometimes make these mistakes. I don't always remember that everything here is good that was—that was bad where I've come from." She looked down at her Viennese fan of eagle feathers, and he saw that her lips trembled.

"I'm so sorry," he said impulsively; "but you *are* among friends here, you know."

"Yes—I know. Wherever I go I have that feeling. That's why I came home. I want to forget everything else, to become a complete American again, like the Mingotts and Wellands, and you and your delightful mother, and all the other good people here tonight. Ah, here's May arriving, and you will want to hurry away to her," she added, but without moving; and her eyes turned back from the door to rest on the young man's face.

The drawing rooms were beginning to fill up with after-dinner guests, and following Madame Olenska's glance Archer saw May Welland entering with her mother. In her dress of white and silver, with a wreath of silver blossoms in her hair, the tall girl looked like a Diana just alight from the chase.

"Oh," said Archer, "I have so many rivals; you see she's already surrounded. There's the duke being introduced."

"Then stay with me a little longer," Madame Olenska said in a low tone, just touching his knee with her plumed fan. It was the lightest touch, but it thrilled him like a caress.

"Yes, let me stay," he answered in the same tone, hardly knowing what he said; but just then Mr. van der Luyden came up, followed by old Mr. Urban Dagonet. The countess greeted them with her grave smile, and Archer, feeling his host's admonitory glance on him, rose and surrendered his seat.

Madame Olenska held out her hand as if to bid him good-bye.

"Tomorrow, then, after five—I shall expect you," she said; and then turned back to make room for Mr. Dagonet.

"Tomorrow—" Archer heard himself repeating, though there had been no engagement, and during their talk she had given him no hint that she wished to see him again.

As he moved away he saw Lawrence Lefferts, tall and resplendent, leading his wife up to be introduced; and heard Gertrude Lefferts say, as she beamed on the countess with her large unperceiving smile: "But I think we used to go to dancing school together when we were children—." Behind her, waiting their turn to name themselves to the countess, Archer noticed a number of the recalcitrant couples who had declined to meet her at Mrs. Lovell Mingott's. As Mrs. Archer remarked: when the van der Luydens chose, they knew how to give a lesson. The wonder was that they chose so seldom.

The young man felt a touch on his arm and saw Mrs. van der Luyden looking down on him from the pure eminence of black velvet and the family diamonds. "It was good of you, dear Newland, to devote yourself so unselfishly to Madame Olenska. I told your cousin Henry he must really come to the rescue."

He was aware of smiling at her vaguely, and she added, as if condescending to his natural shyness: "I've never seen May looking lovelier. The duke thinks her the handsomest girl in the room."

# 9

THE COUNTESS OLENSKA had said "after five"; and at half after the hour Newland Archer rang the bell of the peeling stucco house with a giant wisteria throttling its feeble cast-iron balcony, which she had hired, far down West Twenty-third Street, from the vagabond Medora.

It was certainly a strange quarter to have settled in. Small dressmakers, bird stuffers, and "people who wrote" were her nearest neighbors; and further down the disheveled street Archer recognized a dilapidated wooden house, at the end of a paved path, in which a writer and journalist called Winsett, whom he used to come across now and then, had mentioned that he lived. Winsett did not invite people to his house; but he had once pointed it out to Archer in the course of a nocturnal stroll, and the latter had asked himself, with a little shiver, if the humanities were so meanly housed in other capitals.

Madame Olenska's own dwelling was redeemed from the same appearance only by a little more paint about the window frames; and as Archer mustered its modest front he said to himself that the Polish count must have robbed her of her fortune as well as of her illusions.

The young man had spent an unsatisfactory day. He had lunched with the Wellands, hoping afterward to carry off May for a walk in the park. He wanted to have her to himself, to tell her how enchanting she had looked the night before, and how proud he was of her, and to press her to hasten their marriage. But Mrs. Welland had firmly reminded him that the round of family visits was not half over, and, when he hinted at advancing the date of the wedding, had raised reproachful eyebrows and sighed out: "Twelve dozen of everything—hand-embroidered—"

Packed in the family landau they rolled from one tribal door-step to another, and Archer, when the afternoon's round was over, parted from his betrothed with the feeling that he had been

shown off like a wild animal cunningly trapped. He supposed that
his readings in anthropology caused him to take such a coarse
view of what was after all a simple and natural demonstration of
family feeling; but when he remembered that the Wellands did
not expect the wedding to take place till the following autumn,
and pictured what his life would be till then, a dampness fell upon
his spirit.

"Tomorrow," Mrs. Welland called after him, "we'll do the
Chiverses and the Dallases"; and he perceived that she was going
through their two families alphabetically, and that they were only
in the first quarter of the alphabet.

He had meant to tell May of the Countess Olenska's request—
her command, rather—that he should call on her that afternoon;
but in the brief moments when they were alone he had had more
pressing things to say. Besides, it struck him as a little absurd to
allude to the matter. He knew that May most particularly wanted
him to be kind to her cousin; was it not that wish which had
hastened the announcement of their engagement? It gave him an
odd sensation to reflect that, but for the countess's arrival, he
might have been, if not still a free man, at least a man less irrevo-
cably pledged. But May had willed it so, and he felt himself somehow relieved of further responsibility—and therefore at liberty, if
he chose, to call on her cousin without telling her.

As he stood on Madame Olenska's threshold curiosity was his
uppermost feeling. He was puzzled by the tone in which she had
summoned him; he concluded that she was less simple than she
seemed.

The door was opened by a swarthy foreign-looking maid, with
a prominent bosom under a gay neckerchief, whom he vaguely
fancied to be Sicilian. She welcomed him with all her white teeth,
and answering his inquiries by a head shake of incomprehension
led him through the narrow hall into a low firelit drawing room.
The room was empty, and she left him, for an appreciable time, to
wonder whether she had gone to find her mistress, or whether
she had not understood what he was there for, and thought it
might be to wind the clocks—of which he perceived that the only
visible specimen had stopped. He knew that the southern races
communicated with each other in the language of pantomime,
and was mortified to find her shrugs and smiles so unintelligible.

At length she returned with a lamp; and Archer, having mean-while put together a phrase out of Dante and Petrarch, evoked the answer: *"La signora è fuori; ma verrà subito";* which he took to mean: "She's out—but you'll soon see."

What he saw, meanwhile, with the help of the lamp, was the faded shadowy charm of a room unlike any room he had known. He knew that the Countess Olenska had brought some of her possessions with her—bits of wreckage, she called them—and these, he supposed, were represented by some small slender ta-bles of dark wood, a delicate little Greek bronze on the chimney-piece, and a stretch of red damask nailed on the discolored wallpaper behind a couple of Italian-looking pictures in old frames.

Newland Archer prided himself on his knowledge of Italian art. His boyhood had been saturated with Ruskin, and he had read all the latest books: John Addington Symonds, Vernon Lee's *Euphorion,* the essays of P. G. Hamerton, and a wonderful new volume called *The Renaissance* by Walter Pater. He talked easily of Botticelli, and spoke of Fra Angelico with a faint condescension. But these pictures bewildered him, for they were like nothing that he was accustomed to look at (and therefore able to see) when he traveled in Italy; and perhaps, also, his powers of observation were impaired by the oddness of finding himself in this strange empty house, where apparently no one expected him. He was sorry that he had not told May Welland of Countess Olenska's request, and a little disturbed by the thought that his betrothed might come in to see her cousin. What would she think if she found him sitting there with the air of intimacy implied by waiting alone in the dusk at a lady's fireside?

But since he had come he meant to wait, and he sank into a chair and stretched his feet to the logs.

It was odd to have summoned him in that way, and then for-gotten him; but Archer felt more curious than mortified. The atmosphere of the room was so different from any he had ever breathed that self-consciousness vanished in the sense of adven-ture. He had been before in drawing rooms hung with red dam-ask, with pictures "of the Italian school"; what struck him was the way in which Medora Manson's shabby hired house, with its blighted background of pampas grass and Rogers statuettes, had, by a turn of the hand, and the skillfull use of a few properties, been transformed into something intimate, "foreign," subtly suggestive of old romantic scenes and sentiments. He tried to analyze the trick, to find a clue to it in the way the chairs and tables were grouped, in the fact that only two Jacqueminot roses (of which nobody ever bought less than a dozen) had been placed in the slender vase at his elbow, and in vague pervading perfume that was not what one put on handkerchiefs, but rather like the scent of some far-off bazaar, a smell made up of Turkish coffee and ambergris and dried roses.

His mind wandered away to the question of what May's drawing room would look like. He knew that Mr. Welland, who was behaving "very handsomely," already had his eye on a newly built house in East Thirty-ninth Street. The neighborhood was thought remote, and the house was built in a ghastly greenish-yellow stone that the younger architects were beginning to employ as a protest against the brownstone of which the uniform hue coated New York like a cold chocolate sauce; but the plumbing was perfect. Archer would have liked to travel, to put off the housing question; but, though the Wellands approved of an extended European honeymoon (perhaps even a winter in Egypt), they were firm as to the need of a house for the returning couple. The young man felt that his fate was sealed: for the rest of his life he would go up every evening between the cast-iron railings of that greenish-yellow doorstep, and pass through a Pompeian vestibule into a hall with a wainscoting of varnished yellow wood. But beyond that his imagination could not travel. He knew the drawing room above had a bay window, but he could not fancy how May would deal with it. She submitted cheerfully to the purple satin and yellow tuftings of the Welland drawing room, to its sham Buhl tables and gilt vitrines full of modern Saxe. He saw no reason to suppose that she would want anything different in her own house; and his only comfort was to reflect that she would probably let him arrange his library as he pleased—which would be, of course, with "sincere" Eastlake furniture, and the plain new bookcases without glass doors.

The round-bosomed maid came in, drew the curtains, pushed back a log, and said consolingly: *"Verrà—verrà."* When she had gone Archer stood up and began to wander about. Should he wait any longer? His position was becoming rather foolish. Perhaps he had misunderstood Madame Olenska—perhaps she had not invited him after all.

Down the cobblestones of the quiet street came the ring of a stepper's hoofs; they stopped before the house, and he caught the opening of a carriage door. Parting the curtains he looked out into the early dusk. A streetlamp faced him, and in its light he saw Julius Beaufort's compact English brougham, drawn by a big roan, and the banker descending from it, and helping out Madame Olenska.

Beaufort stood, hat in hand, saying something which his companion seemed to negative; then they shook hands, and he jumped into his carriage while she mounted the steps.

When she entered the room she showed no surprise at seeing Archer there; surprise seemed the emotion that she was least addicted to.

"How do you like my funny house?" she asked. "To me it's like heaven."

As she spoke she untied her little velvet bonnet and tossing it away with her long cloak stood looking at him with meditative eyes.

"You've arranged it delightfully," he rejoined, alive to the flatness of the words, but imprisoned in the conventional by his consuming desire to be simple and striking.

"Oh, it's a poor little place. My relations despise it. But at any rate it's less gloomy than the van der Luydens'."

The words gave him an electric shock, for few were the rebellious spirits who would have dared to call the stately home of the van der Luydens gloomy. Those privileged to enter it shivered there, and spoke of it as "handsome." But suddenly he was glad that she had given voice to the general shiver.

"It's delicious—what you've done here," he repeated.

"I like the little house," she admitted, "but I suppose what I like is the blessedness of its being here, in my own country and my own town; and then, of being alone in it." She spoke so low that he hardly heard the last phrase; but in his awkwardness he took it up.

"You like so much to be alone?"

"Yes, as long as my friends keep me from feeling lonely." She sat down near the fire, said: "Nastasia will bring the tea presently," and signed to him to return to his armchair, adding: "I see you've already chosen your corner."

Leaning back, she folded her arms behind her head, and looked at the fire under drooping lids.

"This is the hour I like best—don't you?"

A proper sense of his dignity caused him to answer: "I was afraid you'd forgotten the hour. Beaufort must have been very engrossing."

She looked amused. "Why—have you waited long? Mr. Beaufort took me to see a number of houses—since it seems I'm not to be allowed to stay in this one." She appeared to dismiss both Beaufort and himself from her mind, and went on: "I've never been in a city where there seems to be such a feeling against living in *des quartiers excentriques*. What does it matter where one lives? I'm told this street is respectable."

"It's not fashionable."

"Fashionable! Do you all think so much of that? Why not make one's own fashions? But I suppose I've lived too independently; at any rate, I want to do what you all do—I want to feel cared for and safe."

He was touched, as he had been the evening before when she spoke of her need of guidance.

"That's what your friends want you to feel. New York's an awfully safe place," he added with a flash of sarcasm.

"Yes, isn't it? One feels that," she cried, missing the mockery. "Being here is like—like—being taken on a holiday when one has been a good little girl and done all one's lessons."

The analogy was well meant, but did not altogether please him. He did not mind being flippant about New York, but disliked to hear anyone else take the same tone. He wondered if she did not begin to see what a powerful engine it was, and how nearly it had crushed her. The Lovell Mingotts' dinner, patched up *in extremis* out of all sorts of social odds and ends, ought to have taught her the narrowness of her escape; but either she had been all along unaware of having skirted disaster, or else she had lost sight of it in the triumph of the van der Luyden evening. Archer inclined to the former theory; he fancied that her New York was still completely undifferentiated, and the conjecture nettled him.

"Last night," he said, "New York laid itself out for you. The van der Luydens do nothing by halves."

"No: how kind they are! It was such a nice party. Everyone seems to have such an esteem for them."

The terms were hardly adequate; she might have spoken in that way of a tea party at the dear old Miss Lannings'.

"The van der Luydens," said Archer, feeling himself pompous as he spoke, "are the most powerful influence in New York society. Unfortunately—owing to her health—they receive very seldom."

She unclasped her hands from behind her head, and looked at him meditatively.

"Isn't that perhaps the reason?"

"The reason—?"

"For their great influence; that they make themselves so rare."

He colored a little, stared at her—and suddenly felt the penetration of the remark. At a stroke she had pricked the van der Luydens and they collapsed. He laughed, and sacrificed them.

Nastasia brought the tea, with handleless Japanese cups and little covered dishes, placing the tray on a low table.

"But you'll explain these things to me—you'll tell me all I ought to know," Madame Olenska continued, leaning forward to hand him his cup.

"It's you who are telling me; opening my eyes to things I'd looked at so long that I'd ceased to see them."

She detached a small gold cigarette case from one of her bracelets, held it out to him, and took a cigarette herself. On the chimney were long spills for lighting them.

"Ah, then we can both help each other. But I want help so much more. You must tell me just what to do."

It was on the tip of his tongue to reply: "Don't be seen driving about the streets with Beaufort—" but he was being too deeply drawn into the atmosphere of the room, which was her atmosphere, and to give advice of that sort would have been like telling someone who was bargaining for atta-of-roses in Samarkand that one should always be provided with arctics for a New York winter. New York seemed much farther off than Samarkand, and if they were indeed to help each other she was rendering what might prove the first of their mutual services by making him look at his native city objectively. Viewed thus, as through the wrong end of a telescope, it looked disconcertingly small and distant; but then from Samarkand it would.

A flame darted from the logs and she bent over the fire, stretching her thin hands so close to it that a faint halo shone about the oval nails. The light touched to russet the rings of dark hair escaping from her braids, and made her pale face paler.

"There are plenty of people to tell you what to do," Archer rejoined, obscurely envious of them.

"Oh—all my aunts? And my dear old Granny?" She considered the idea impartially. "They're all a little vexed with me for setting up for myself—poor Granny especially. She wanted to keep me with her; but I had to be free—" He was impressed by this light way of speaking of the formidable Catherine, and moved by the thought of what must have given Madame Olenska this thirst for even the loneliest kind of freedom. But the idea of Beaufort gnawed him.

"I think I understand how you feel," he said. "Still, your family can advise you; explain differences; show you the way."

She lifted her thin black eyebrows. "Is New York such a labyrinth? I thought it so straight up and down—like Fifth Avenue. And with all the cross streets numbered!" She seemed to guess his faint disapproval of this, and added, with the rare smile that enchanted her whole face: "If you knew how I like it for just *that*—the straight-up-and-downness, and the big honest labels on everything!"

He saw his chance. "Everything may be labeled—but everybody is not."

"Perhaps. I may simplify too much—but you'll warn me if I do." She turned from the fire to look at him. "There are only two people here who make me feel as if they understood what I mean and could explain things to me: you and Mr. Beaufort."

Archer winced at the joining of the names, and then, with a quick readjustment, understood, sympathized, and pitied. So close to the powers of evil she must have lived that she still breathed more freely in their air. But since she felt that he understood her also, his business would be to make her see Beaufort as he really was, with all he represented—and abhor it.

He answered gently: "I understand. But just at first don't let go of your old friends' hands: I mean the older women, your Granny Mingott, Mrs. Welland, Mrs. van der Luyden. They like and admire you—they want to help you."

She shook her head and sighed. "Oh, I know—I know! But on condition that they don't hear anything unpleasant. Aunt Welland put it in those very words when I tried. . . . Does no one want to know the truth here, Mr. Archer? The real loneliness is living among all these kind people who only ask one to pretend!" She lifted her hands to her face, and he saw her thin shoulders shaken by a sob.

"Madame Olenska!—Oh, don't, Ellen," he cried, starting up and bending over her. He drew down one of her hands, clasping and chafing it like a child's while he murmured reassuring words; but in a moment she freed herself, and looked up at him with wet lashes.

"Does no one cry here, either? I suppose there's no need to, in heaven," she said, straightening her loosened braids with a laugh, and bending over the teakettle. It was burned into his consciousness that he had called her "Ellen"—called her so twice; and that she had not noticed it. Far down the inverted telescope he saw the faint white figure of May Welland—in New York.

Suddenly Nastasia put her head in to say something in her rich Italian.

Madame Olenska, again with a hand at her hair, uttered an exclamation of assent—a flashing *"Già—già"*—and the Duke of St. Austrey entered, piloting a tremendous black-wigged and red-plumed lady in overflowing furs.

"My dear Countess, I've brought an old friend of mine to see you—Mrs. Struthers. She wasn't asked to the party last night, and she wants to know you."

The duke beamed on the group, and Madame Olenska advanced with a murmur of welcome toward the queer couple. She seemed to have no idea how oddly matched they were, nor what a liberty the duke had taken in bringing his companion—and to do him justice, as Archer perceived, the duke seemed as unaware of it himself.

"Of course I want to know you, my dear," cried Mrs. Struthers in a round rolling voice that matched her bold feathers and her brazen wig. "I want to know everybody who's young and interesting and charming. And the duke tells me you like music—didn't you, Duke? You're a pianist yourself, I believe? Well, do you want to hear Sarasate play tomorrow evening at my house? You know I've something going on every Sunday evening—it's the day when New York doesn't know what to do with itself, and so I say to it: 'Come and be amused.' And the duke thought you'd be tempted by Sarasate. You'll find a number of your friends."

Madame Olenska's face grew brilliant with pleasure. "How kind! How good of the duke to think of me!" She pushed a chair up to the tea table and Mrs. Struthers sank into it delectably. "Of course I shall be too happy to come."

"That's all right, my dear. And bring your young gentleman with you." Mrs. Struthers extended a hail-fellow hand to Archer. "I can't put a name to you—but I'm sure I've met you—I've met everybody, here, or in Paris or London. Aren't you in diplomacy? All the diplomatists come to me. You like music too? Duke, you must be sure to bring him."

The duke said "Rather" from the depths of his beard, and Archer withdrew with a stiffly circular bow that made him feel as full of spine as a self-conscious schoolboy among careless and unnoticing elders.

He was not sorry for the dénouement of his visit: he only wished it had come sooner, and spared him a certain waste of emotion. As he went out into the wintry night, New York again became vast and imminent, and May Welland the loveliest woman in it. He turned into his florist's to send her the daily box of lilies-of-the-valley which, to his confusion, he found he had forgotten that morning.

As he wrote a word on his card and waited for an envelope he glanced about the embowered shop, and his eye lit on a cluster of yellow roses. He had never seen any as sun-golden before, and his first impulse was to send them to May instead of the lilies. But they did not look like her—there was something too rich, too strong, in their fiery beauty. In a sudden revulsion of mood, and almost without knowing what he did, he signed to the florist to lay the roses in another long box, and slipped his card into a second envelope, on which he wrote the name of the Countess Olenska;

then, just as he was turning away, he drew the card out again, and left the empty envelope on the box.

"They'll go at once?" he inquired, pointing to the roses.

The florist assured him that they would.

# —— 10 ——

THE NEXT DAY he persuaded May to escape for a walk in the park after luncheon. As was the custom in old-fashioned Episcopalian New York, she usually accompanied her parents to church on Sunday afternoons; but Mrs. Welland condoned her truancy, having that very morning won her over to the necessity of a long engagement, with time to prepare a hand-embroidered trousseau containing the proper number of dozens.

The day was delectable. The bare vaulting of trees along the mall was ceiled with lapis lazuli, and arched above snow that shone like splintered crystals. It was the weather to call out May's radiance, and she burned like a young maple in the frost. Archer was proud of the glances turned on her, and the simple joy of possessorship cleared away his underlying perplexities.

"It's so delicious—waking every morning to smell lilies-of-the-valley in one's room!" she said.

"Yesterday they came late. I hadn't time in the morning—"

"But your remembering each day to send them makes me love them so much more than if you'd given a standing order, and they came every morning on the minute, like one's music teacher—as I know Gertrude Lefferts's did, for instance, when she and Lawrence were engaged."

"Ah—they would!" laughed Archer, amused at her keenness. He looked sideways at her fruitlike cheek and felt rich and secure enough to add: "When I sent your lilies yesterday afternoon I saw some rather gorgeous yellow roses and packed them off to Madame Olenska. Was that right?"

"How dear of you! Anything of that kind delights her. It's odd she didn't mention it: she lunched with us today, and spoke of Mr. Beaufort's having sent her wonderful orchids, and cousin Henry van der Luyden a whole hamper of carnations from Skuytercliff. She seems so surprised to receive flowers. Don't people send them in Europe? She thinks it such a pretty custom."

"Oh, well, no wonder mine were overshadowed by Beaufort's," said Archer irritably. Then he remembered that he had not put a card with the roses, and was vexed at having spoken of them. He wanted to say: "I called on your cousin yesterday," but hesitated. If Madame Olenska had not spoken of his visit it might seem awkward that he should. Yet not to do so gave the affair an air of mystery that he disliked. To shake off the question he began to talk of their own plans, their future, and Mrs. Welland's insistence on a long engagement.

"If you call it long! Isabel Chivers and Reggie were engaged for two years: Grace and Thorley for nearly a year and a half. Why aren't we very well off as we are?"

It was the traditional maidenly interrogation, and he felt ashamed of himself for finding it singularly childish. No doubt she simply echoed what was said for her; but she was nearing her twenty-second birthday, and he wondered at what age "nice" women began to speak for themselves.

"Never, if we won't let them, I suppose," he mused, and re-called his mad outburst to Mr. Sillerton Jackson: "Women ought to be as free as we are—"

It would presently be his task to take the bandage from this young woman's eyes, and bid her look forth on the world. But how many generations of the women who had gone to her making had descended bandaged to the family vault? He shivered a little, remembering some of the new ideas in his scientific books, and the much-cited instance of the Kentucky cave fish, which had ceased to develop eyes because they had no use for them. What if, when he had bidden May Welland to open hers, they could only look out blankly at blankness?

"We might be much better off. We might be altogether to-gether—we might travel."

Her face lit up. "That would be lovely," she owned: she would love to travel. But her mother would not understand their want-ing to do things so differently.

"As if the mere 'differently' didn't account for it!" the wooer insisted.

"Newland! You're so original!" she exulted.

His heart sank, for he saw that he was saying all the things that young men in the same situation were expected to say, and that she was making the answers that instinct and tradition taught her to make—even to the point of calling him original.

"Original! We're all as like each other as those dolls cut out of the same folded paper. We're like patterns stenciled on a wall. Can't you and I strike out for ourselves, May?"

He had stopped and faced her in the excitement of their discussion, and her eyes rested on him with a bright unclouded admiration.

"Mercy—shall we elope?" she laughed.

"If you would—"

"You *do* love me, Newland! I'm so happy."

"But then—why not be happier?"

"We can't behave like people in novels, though, can we?"

"Why not—why not—why not?"

She looked a little bored by his insistence. She knew very well that they couldn't, but it was troublesome to have to produce a reason. "I'm not clever enough to argue with you. But that kind of thing is rather—vulgar, isn't it?" she suggested, relieved to have hit on a word that would assuredly extinguish the whole subject.

"Are you so much afraid, then, of being vulgar?"

She was evidently staggered by this. "Of course I should hate it—so would you," she rejoined, a trifle irritably.

He stood silent, beating his stick nervously against his boot top; and feeling that she had indeed found the right way of closing the discussion, she went on lightheartedly: "Oh, did I tell you that I showed Ellen my ring? She thinks it the most beautiful setting she ever saw. There's nothing like it in the rue de la Paix, she said. I do love you, Newland, for being so artistic!"

The next afternoon, as Archer, before dinner, sat smoking sullenly in his study, Janey wandered in on him. He had failed to stop at his club on the way up from the office where he exercised the profession of law in the leisurely manner common to well-to-do New Yorkers of his class. He was out of spirits and slightly out of temper, and a haunting horror of doing the same thing every day at the same hour besieged his brain.

"Sameness—sameness!" he muttered, the word running through his head like a persecuting tune as he saw the familiar tall-hatted figures lounging behind the plate glass; and because he usually dropped in at the club at that hour he had gone home instead. He knew not only what they were likely to be talking about, but the part each one would take in the discussion. The duke of course would be their principal theme; though the appearance in Fifth Avenue of a golden-haired lady in a small canary-colored brougham with a pair of black cobs (for which Beaufort was generally thought responsible) would also doubtless be thoroughly gone into. Such "women" (as they were called) were few in New York, those driving their own carriages still fewer, and the appearance of Miss Fanny Ring in Fifth Avenue at the fashionable hour had profoundly agitated society. Only the day before, her carriage had passed Mrs. Lovell Mingott's, and the latter had instantly rung the little bell at her elbow and ordered the coachman to drive her home. "What if it had happened to Mrs. van der Luyden?" people asked each other with a shudder. Archer could hear Lawrence Lefferts, at that very hour, holding forth on the disintegration of society.

He raised his head irritably when his sister Janey entered, and then quickly bent over his book (Swinburne's *Chastelard*—just out) as if he had not seen her. She glanced at the writing table heaped with books, opened a volume of the *Contes Drôlatiques,* made a wry face over the archaic French, and sighed: "What learned things you read!"

"Well—?" he asked, as she hovered Cassandra-like before him.

"Mother's very angry."

"Angry? With whom? About what?"

"Miss Sophy Jackson has just been here. She brought word that her brother would come in after dinner: she couldn't say very much, because he forbade her to: he wishes to give all the details himself. He's with cousin Louisa van der Luyden now."

"For heaven's sake, my dear girl, try a fresh start. It would take an omniscient deity to know what you're talking about."

"It's not a time to be profane, Newland. . . . Mother feels badly enough about your not going to church . . ."

With a groan he plunged back into his book.

*"Newland!* Do listen. Your friend Madame Olenska was at Mrs. Lemuel Struther's party last night: she went there with the duke and Mr. Beaufort."

At the last clause of this announcement a senseless anger swelled the young man's breast. To smother it he laughed, "Well, what of it? I knew she meant to."

Janey paled and her eyes began to project. "You knew she meant to—and you didn't try to stop her? To warn her?"

"Stop her? Warn her?" He laughed again. "I'm not engaged to be married to the Countess Olenska!" The words had a fantastic sound in his own ears.

"You're marrying into her family."

"Oh, family—family!" he jeered.

"Newland—don't you care about Family?"

"Not a brass farthing."

"Nor about what cousin Louisa van der Luyden will think?"

"Not the half of one—if she thinks such old maid's rubbish."

"Mother is not an old maid," said his virgin sister with pinched lips.

He felt like shouting back: "Yes, she is, and so are the van der Luydens, and so we all are, when it comes to being so much as brushed by the wingtip of Reality." But he saw her long gentle face puckering into tears, and felt ashamed of the useless pain he was inflicting.

"Hang Countess Olenska! Don't be a goose, Janey—I'm not her keeper."

"No; but you *did* ask the Wellands to announce your engagement sooner so that we might all back her up; and if it hadn't been for that cousin Louisa would never have invited her to the dinner for the duke."

"Well—what harm was there in inviting her? She was the best-looking woman in the room; she made the dinner a little less funereal than the usual van der Luyden banquet."

"You know cousin Henry asked her to please you: he persuaded cousin Louisa. And now they're so upset that they're going back to Skuytercliff tomorrow. I think, Newland, you'd better come down. You don't seem to understand how Mother feels."

In the drawing room Newland found his mother. She raised a troubled brow from her needlework to ask: "Has Janey told you?"

"Yes." He tried to keep his tone as measured as her own. "But I can't take it very seriously."

"Not the fact of having offended cousin Louisa and cousin Henry?"

"The fact that they can be offended by such a trifle as Countess Olenska's going to the house of a woman they consider common."

"*Consider—!*"

"Well, who is; but who has good music, and amuses people on Sunday evenings, when the whole of New York is dying of inanition."

"Good music? All I know is, there was a woman who got up on a table and sang the things they sing at the places you go to in Paris. There was smoking and champagne."

"Well—that kind of thing happens in other places, and the world still goes on."

"I don't suppose, dear, you're really defending the French Sunday?"

"I've heard you often enough, Mother, grumble at the English Sunday when we've been in London."

"New York is neither Paris nor London."

"Oh, no, it's not!" her son groaned.

"You mean, I suppose, that society here is not as brilliant? You're right, I daresay; but we belong here, and people should respect our ways when they come among us. Ellen Olenska especially: she came back to get away from the kind of life people lead in brilliant societies."

Newland made no answer, and after a moment his mother ventured: "I was going to put on my bonnet and ask you to take me to see cousin Louisa for a moment before dinner." He frowned, and she continued: "I thought you might explain to her what you've just said: that society abroad is different . . . that people are not as particular, and that Madame Olenska may not have realized how we feel about such things. It would be, you know, dear," she added with an innocent adroitness, "in Madame Olenska's interest if you did."

"Dearest Mother, I really don't see how we're concerned in the matter. The duke took Madame Olenska to Mrs. Struthers's—in fact he brought Mrs. Struthers to call on her. I was there when they came. If the van der Luydens want to quarrel with anybody, the real culprit is under their own roof."

"Quarrel? Newland, did you ever know of cousin Henry's

quarreling? Besides, the duke's his guest; and a stranger too. Strangers don't discriminate: how should they? Countess Olenska is a New Yorker, and should have respected the feelings of New York."

"Well, then, if they must have a victim, you have my leave to throw Madame Olenska to them," cried her son, exasperated. "I don't see myself—or you either—offering ourselves up to expiate her crimes."

"Oh, of course you see only the Mingott side," his mother answered in the sensitive tone that was her nearest approach to anger.

The sad butler drew back the drawing-room portières and announced: "Mr. Henry van der Luyden."

Mrs. Archer dropped her needle and pushed her chair back with an agitated hand.

"Another lamp," she cried to the retreating servant, while Janey bent over to straighten her mother's cap.

Mr. van der Luyden's figure loomed on the threshold, and Newland Archer went forward to greet his cousin.

"We were just talking about you, sir," he said.

Mr. van der Luyden seemed overwhelmed by the announcement. He drew off his glove to shake hands with the ladies, and smoothed his tall hat shyly, while Janey pushed an armchair forward, and Archer continued: "And the Countess Olenska."

Mrs. Archer paled.

"Ah—a charming woman. I have just been to see her," said Mr. van der Luyden, complacency restored to his brow. He sank into the chair, laid his hat and gloves on the floor beside him in the old-fashioned way, and went on: "She has a real gift for arranging flowers. I had sent her a few carnations from Skuytercliff, and I was astonished. Instead of massing them in big bunches as our head gardener does, she had scattered them about loosely, here and there . . . I can't say how. The duke had told me: he said: 'Go and see how cleverly she's arranged her drawing room.' And she has. I should really like to take Louisa to see her, if the neighborhood were not so—unpleasant."

A dead silence greeted this unusual flow of words from Mr. van der Luyden. Mrs. Archer drew her embroidery out of the basket into which she had nervously tumbled it, and Newland, leaning against the chimneyplace and twisting a hummingbird-feather screen in his hand, saw Janey's gaping countenance lit up by the coming of the second lamp.

"The fact is," Mr. van der Luyden continued, stroking his long gray leg with a bloodless hand weighed down by the patroon's great signet ring, "the fact is, I dropped in to thank her for the very pretty note she wrote me about my flowers; and also—but this is between ourselves, of course—to give her a friendly warning about allowing the duke to carry her off to parties with him. I don't know if you've heard—"

Mrs. Archer produced an indulgent smile. "Has the duke been carrying her off to parties?"

"You know what these English grandees are. They're all alike. Louisa and I are very fond of our cousin—but it's hopeless to expect people who are accustomed to the European courts to trouble themselves about our little republican distinctions. The duke goes where he's amused." Mr. van der Luyden paused, but no one spoke. "Yes—it seems he took her with him last night to Mrs. Lemuel Struthers's. Sillerton Jackson has just been to us with the foolish story, and Louisa was rather troubled. So I thought the shortest way was to go straight to Countess Olenska and explain—by the merest hint, you know—how we feel in New York about certain things. I felt I might, without indelicacy, because the evening she dined with us she rather suggested . . . rather let me see that she would be grateful for guidance. And she *was*."

Mr. van der Luyden looked about the room with what would have been self-satisfaction on features less purged of the vulgar passions. On his face it became a mild benevolence which Mrs. Archer's countenance dutifully reflected.

"How kind you both are, dear Henry—always! Newland will particularly appreciate what you have done because of dear May and his new relations."

She shot an admonitory glance at her son, who said: "Immensely, sir. But I was sure you'd like Madame Olenska."

Mr. van der Luyden looked at him with extreme gentleness. "I never ask to my house, my dear Newland," he said, "anyone whom I do not like. And so I have just told Sillerton Jackson."

With a glance at the clock he rose and added: "But Louisa will be waiting. We are dining early, to take the duke to the opera."

After the portières had solemnly closed behind their visitor a silence fell upon the Archer family.

"Gracious—how romantic!" at last broke explosively from Janey. No one knew exactly what inspired her elliptic comments, and her relations had long since given up trying to interpret them.

Mrs. Archer shook her head with a sigh. "Provided it all turns out for the best," she said, in the tone of one who knows how surely it will not. "Newland, you must stay and see Sillerton Jackson when he comes this evening: I really shan't know what to say to him."

"Poor Mother! But he won't come—" he son laughed, stooping to kiss away her frown.

# ——11——

**SOME TWO WEEKS LATER,** Newland Archer, sitting in abstracted idleness in his private compartment of the office of Letterblair, Lamson, and Low, attorneys at law, was summoned by the head of the firm.

Old Mr. Letterblair, the accredited legal adviser of three generations of New York gentility, throned behind his mahogany desk in evident perplexity. As he stroked his close-clipped white whiskers and ran his hand through the rumpled gray locks above his jutting brows, his disrespectful junior partner thought how much he looked like the Family Physician annoyed with a patient whose symptoms refuse to be classified.

"My dear sir—" he always addressed Archer as "sir"—"I have sent for you to go into a little matter; a matter which, for the moment, I prefer not to mention either to Mr. Skipworth or Mr. Redwood." The gentlemen he spoke of were the other senior partners of the firm; for, as was always the case with legal associations of old standing in New York, all the partners named on the office letterhead were long since dead; and Mr. Letterblair, for example, was, professionally speaking, his own grandson.

He leaned back in his chair with a furrowed brow. "For family reasons—" he continued.

Archer looked up.

"The Mingott family," said Mr. Letterblair with an explanatory smile and bow. "Mrs. Manson Mingott sent for me yesterday. Her granddaughter the Countess Olenska wishes to sue her husband for divorce. Certain papers have been placed in my hands." He paused and drummed on his desk. "In view of your prospective alliance with the family I should like to consult you—to consider the case with you—before taking any farther steps."

Archer felt the blood in his temples. He had seen the Countess Olenska only once since his visit to her, and then at the opera, in the Mingott box. During this interval she had become a less vivid and importunate image, receding from his foreground as May Welland resumed her rightful place in it. He had not heard her divorce spoken of since Janey's first random allusion to it, and had dismissed the tale as unfounded gossip. Theoretically, the idea of divorce was almost as distasteful to him as to his mother; and he was annoyed that Mr. Letterblair (no doubt prompted by old Catherine Mingott) should be so evidently planning to draw him into the affair. After all, there were plenty of Mingott men for such jobs, and as yet he was not even a Mingott by marriage.

He waited for the senior partner to continue. Mr. Letterblair unlocked a drawer and drew out a packet. "If you will run your eye over these papers—"

Archer frowned. "I beg your pardon, sir; but just because of the prospective relationship, I should prefer your consulting Mr. Skipworth or Mr. Redwood."

Mr. Letterblair looked surprised and slightly offended. It was unusual for a junior to reject such an opening.

He bowed. "I respect your scruple, sir; but in this case I believe true delicacy requires you to do as I ask. Indeed, the suggestion is not mine but Mrs. Manson Mingott's and her son's. I have seen Lovell Mingott; and also Mr. Welland. They all named you."

Archer felt his temper rising. He had been somewhat languidly drifting with events for the last fortnight, and letting May's fair looks and radiant nature obliterate the rather importunate pressure of the Mingott claims. But this behest of old Mrs. Mingott's roused him to a sense of what the clan thought they had the right to exact from a prospective son-in-law; and he chafed at the role.

"Her uncles ought to deal with this," he said.

"They have. The matter has been gone into by the family. They are opposed to the countess's idea; but she is firm, and insists on a legal opinion."

The young man was silent: he had not opened the packet in his hand.

"Does she want to marry again?"

"I believe it is suggested; but she denies it."

"Then—"

"Will you oblige me, Mr. Archer, by first looking through these papers? Afterward, when we have talked the case over, I will give you my opinion."

Archer withdrew reluctantly with the unwelcome documents. Since their last meeting he had half-unconsciously collaborated with events in ridding himself of the burden of Madame Olenska. His hour alone with her by the firelight had drawn them into a momentary intimacy on which the Duke of St. Austrey's intrusion with Mrs. Lemuel Struthers, and the countess's joyous greeting of them, had rather providentially broken. Two days later Archer had assisted at the comedy of her reinstatement in the van der Luydens' favor, and had said to himself, with a touch of tartness, that a lady who knew how to thank all-powerful elderly gentlemen to such good purpose for a bunch of flowers did not need either the private consolations or the public championship of a young man of his small compass. To look at the matter in this light simplified his own case and surprisingly furbished up all the dim domestic virtues. He could not picture May Welland, in whatever conceivable emergency, hawking about her private difficulties and lavishing her confidences on strange men; and she had never seemed to him finer or fairer than in the week that followed. He had even yielded to her wish for a long engagement, since she had found the one disarming answer to his plea for haste.

"You know, when it comes to the point, your parents have always let you have your way ever since you were a little girl," he argued; and she had answered, with her clearest look: "Yes, and that's what makes it so hard to refuse the very last thing they'll ever ask of me as a little girl."

That was the old New York note; that was the kind of answer he would like always to be sure of his wife's making. If one had habitually breathed the New York air there were times when anything less crystalline seemed stifling.

The papers he had retired to read did not tell him much in fact; but they plunged him into an atmosphere in which he choked and spluttered. They consisted mainly of an exchange of letters between Count Olenski's solicitors and a French legal firm to whom the countess had applied for the settlement of her financial situation. There was also a short letter from the count to his wife: after reading it, Newland Archer rose, jammed the papers back into their envelope, and reentered Mr. Letterblair's office.

"Here are the letters, sir. If you wish, I'll see Madame Olenska," he said in a constrained voice.

"Thank you—thank you, Mr. Archer. Come and dine with me
tonight if you're free, and we'll go into the matter afterward: in
case you wish to call on our client tomorrow."

Newland Archer walked straight home again that afternoon. It
was a winter evening of transparent clearness, with an innocent
young moon above the housetops; and he wanted to fill his soul's
lungs with the pure radiance, and not exchange a word with
anyone till he and Mr. Letterblair were closeted together after
dinner. It was impossible to decide otherwise than he had done:
he must see Madame Olenska himself rather than let her secrets
be bared to other eyes. A great wave of compassion had swept
away his indifference and impatience: she stood before him as an
exposed and pitiful figure, to be saved at all costs from farther
wounding herself in her mad plunges against fate.

He remembered what she had told him of Mrs. Welland's request to be spared whatever was "unpleasant" in her history, and
winced at the thought that it was perhaps this attitude of mind
which kept the New York air so pure. "Are we only Pharisees after
all?" he wondered, puzzled by the effort to reconcile his instinctive disgust at human vileness with his equally instinctive pity for
human frailty.

For the first time he perceived how elementary his own principles had always been. He passed for a young man who had not
been afraid of risks, and he knew that his secret love affair with
poor silly Mrs. Thorley Rushworth had not been too secret to
invest him with a becoming air of adventure. But Mrs. Rushworth
was "that kind of woman"; foolish, vain, clandestine by nature,
and far more attracted by the secrecy and peril of the affair than
by such charms and qualities as he possessed. When the fact
dawned on him it nearly broke his heart, but now it seemed the
redeeming feature of the case. The affair, in short, had been of
the kind that most of the young men of his age had been through,
and emerged from with calm consciences and an undisturbed
belief in the abysmal distinction between the women one loved
and respected and those one enjoyed—and pitied. In this view
they were sedulously abetted by their mothers, aunts, and other
elderly female relatives, who all shared Mrs. Archer's belief that

when "such things happened" it was undoubtedly foolish of the man, but somehow always criminal of the woman. All the elderly ladies whom Archer knew regarded any woman who loved imprudently as necessarily unscrupulous and designing, and mere simple-minded man as powerless in her clutches. The only thing to do was to persuade him, as early as possible, to marry a nice girl, and then trust to her to look after him.

In the complicated old European communities, Archer began to guess, love problems might be less simple and less easily classified. Rich and idle and ornamental societies must produce many more such situations; and there might even be one in which a woman naturally sensitive and aloof would yet, from the force of circumstances, from sheer defenselessness and loneliness, be drawn into a tie inexcusable by conventional standards.

On reaching home he wrote a line to the Countess Olenska, asking at what hour of the next day she could receive him, and despatched it by a messenger boy, who returned presently with a word to the effect that she was going to Skuytercliff the next morning to stay over Sunday with the van der Luydens, but that he would find her alone that evening after dinner. The note was written on a rather untidy half-sheet, without date or address, but her hand was firm and free. He was amused at the idea of her weekending in the stately solitude of Skuytercliff, but immediately afterward felt that there, of all places, she would most feel the chill of minds rigorously averted from the "unpleasant."

He was at Mr. Letterblair's punctually at seven, glad of the pretext for excusing himself soon after dinner. He had formed his own opinion from the papers entrusted to him, and did not especially want to go into the matter with his senior partner. Mr. Letterblair was a widower, and they dined alone, copiously and slowly, in a dark shabby room hung with yellowing prints of *The Death of Chatham* and *The Coronation of Napoleon*. On the sideboard, between fluted Sheraton knife cases, stood a decanter of Haut Brion, and another of the old Lanning port (the gift of a client), which the wastrel Tom Lanning had sold off a year or two before his mysterious and discreditable death in San Francisco—an incident less publicly humiliating to the family than the sale of the cellar.

After a velvety oyster soup came shad and cucumbers, then a young broiled turkey with corn fritters, followed by a canvasback with currant jelly and a celery mayonnaise. Mr. Letterblair, who lunched on a sandwich and tea, dined deliberately and deeply, and insisted on his guest's doing the same. Finally, when the closing rites had been accomplished, the cloth was removed, cigars were lit, and Mr. Letterblair, leaning back in his chair and pushing the port westward, said, spreading his back agreeably to the coal fire behind him "The whole family are against a divorce. And I think rightly."

Archer instantly felt himself on the other side of the argument. "But why, sir? If there ever was a case—"

"Well—what's the use? *She's* here—he's there; the Atlantic's between them. She'll never get back a dollar more of her money than what he's voluntarily returned to her: their damned heathen marriage settlements take precious good care of that. As things go over there, Olenski's acted generously; he might have turned her out without a penny."

The young man knew this and was silent.

"I understand, though," Mr. Letterblair continued, "that she attaches no importance to the money. Therefore, as the family say, why not let well enough alone?"

Archer had gone to the house an hour earlier in full agreement with Mr. Letterblair's view; but put into words by this selfish, well-fed, and supremely indifferent old man it suddenly became the Pharisaic voice of a society wholly absorbed in barricading itself against the unpleasant.

"I think that's for her to decide."

"H'm—have you considered the consequences if she decides for divorce?"

"You mean the threat in her husband's letter? What weight would that carry? It's no more than the vague charge of an angry blackguard."

"Yes, but it might make some unpleasant talk if he really defends the suit."

"Unpleasant—!" said Archer explosively.

Mr. Letterblair looked at him from under inquiring eyebrows, and the young man, aware of the uselessness of trying to explain what was in his mind, bowed acquiescently while his senior continued: "Divorce is always unpleasant."

"You agree with me?" Mr. Letterblair resumed, after a waiting silence.

"Naturally," said Archer.

"Well, then, I may count on you; the Mingotts may count on you; to use your influence against the idea?"

Archer hesitated. "I can't pledge myself till I've seen the Countess Olenska," he said at length.

"Mr. Archer, I don't understand you. Do you want to marry into a family with a scandalous divorce suit hanging over it?"

"I don't think that has anything to do with the case."

Mr. Letterblair put down his glass of port and fixed on his young partner a cautious and apprehensive gaze.

Archer understood that he ran the risk of having his mandate withdrawn, and for some obscure reason he disliked the prospect. Now that the job had been thrust on him he did not propose to relinquish it; and, to guard against the possibility, he saw that he must reassure the unimaginative old man who was the legal conscience of the Mingotts.

"You may be sure, sir, that I shan't commit myself till I've reported to you; what I meant was that I'd rather not give an opinion till I've heard what Madame Olenska has to say."

Mr. Letterblair nodded approvingly at an excess of caution worthy of the best New York tradition, and the young man, glancing at his watch, pleaded an engagement and took leave.

# —— 12 ——

OLD-FASHIONED New York dined at seven, and the habit of after-dinner calls, though derided in Archer's set, still generally prevailed. As the young man strolled up Fifth Avenue from Waverley Place, the long thoroughfare was deserted but for a group of carriages standing before the Reggie Chiverses' (where there was a dinner for the duke), and the occasional figure of an elderly gentleman in heavy overcoat and muffler ascending a brownstone doorstep and disappearing into a gaslit hall. Thus, as Archer crossed Washington Square, he remarked that old Mr. du Lac was calling on his cousins the Dagonets, and turning down the corner of West Tenth Street he saw Mr. Skipworth, of his own firm, obviously bound on a visit to the Miss Lannings. A little farther up Fifth Avenue, Beaufort appeared on his doorstep, darkly projected against a blaze of light, descended to his private brougham, and rolled away to a mysterious and probably unmentionable destination. It was not an opera night, and no one was giving a party, so that Beaufort's outing was undoubtedly of a clandestine nature Archer connected it in his mind with a little house beyond Lexington Avenue in which beribboned window curtains and flowerboxes had recently appeared, and before whose newly painted door the canary-colored brougham of Miss Fanny Ring was frequently seen to wait.

Beyond the small and slippery pyramid which composed Mrs. Archer's world lay the almost unmapped quarter inhabited by artists, musicians, and "people who wrote." These scattered fragments of humanity had never shown any desire to be amalgamated with the social structure. In spite of odd ways, they were said to be, for the most part, quite respectable, but they preferred to keep to themselves. Medora Manson, in her prosperous days, had inaugurated a "literary salon"; but it had soon died out owing to the reluctance of the literary to frequent it.

Others had made the same attempt, and there was a household

of Blenkers—an intense and voluble mother, and three blowsy daughters who imitated her—where one met Edwin Booth and Patti and William Winter, and the new Shakespearean actor George Rignold, and some of the magazine editors and musical and literary critics.

Mrs. Archer and her group felt a certain timidity concerning these persons. They were odd, they were uncertain, they had things one didn't know about in the background of their lives and minds. Literature and art were deeply respected in the Archer set, and Mrs. Archer was always at pains to tell her children how much more agreeable and cultivated society had been when it included such figures as Washington Irving, Fitz-Greene Halleck, and the poet of *The Culprit Fay*. The most celebrated authors of that generation had been "gentlemen"; perhaps the unknown persons who succeeded them had gentlemanly sentiments, but their origin, their appearance, their hair, their intimacy with the stage and the opera, made any old New York criterion inapplicable to them.

"When I was a girl," Mrs. Archer used to say, "we knew everybody between the Battery and Canal Street; and only the people one knew had carriages. It was perfectly easy to place anyone then; now one can't tell, and I prefer not to try."

Only old Catherine Mingott, with her absence of moral prejudices and almost *parvenu* indifference to the subtler distinctions, might have bridged the abyss; but she had never opened a book or looked at a picture, and cared for music only because it reminded her of gala nights at the *Italiens,* in the days of her triumph at the Tuileries. Possibly Beaufort, who was her match in daring, would have succeeded in bringing about a fusion; but his grand house and silk-stockinged footmen were an obstacle to informal sociability. Moreover, he was as illiterate as old Mrs. Mingott, and considered "fellows who wrote" as the mere paid purveyors of rich men's pleasures; and no one rich enough to influence his opinion had ever questioned it.

Newland Archer had been aware of these things ever since he could remember, and had accepted them as part of the structure of his universe. He knew that there were societies where painters and poets and novelists and men of science, and even great actors, were as sought after as dukes; he had often pictured to

himself what it would have been to live in the intimacy of drawing
rooms dominated by the talk of Mérimée (whose *Lettres à une
Inconnue* was one of his inseparables), of Thackeray, Browning, or
William Morris. But such things were inconceivable in New York,
and unsettling to think of. Archer knew most of the "fellows who
wrote," the musicians and the painters: he met them at the Century, or at the little musical and theatrical clubs that were beginning to come into existence. He enjoyed them there, and was
bored with them at the Blenkers', where they were mingled with
fervid and dowdy women who passed them about like captured
curiosities; and even after his most exciting talks with Ned Winsett he always came away with the feeling that if his world was
small, so was theirs, and that the only way to enlarge either was to
reach a stage of manners where they would naturally merge.

He was reminded of this by trying to picture the society in
which the Countess Olenska had lived and suffered, and also—
perhaps—tasted mysterious joys. He remembered with what
amusement she had told him that her grandmother Mingott and
the Wellands objected to her living in a "Bohemian" quarter
given over to "people who wrote." It was not the peril but the
poverty that her family disliked; but that shade escaped her, and
she supposed they considered literature compromising.

She herself had no fears of it, and the books scattered about
her drawing room (a part of the house in which books were usually supposed to be "out of place"), though chiefly works of fiction, had whetted Archer's interest with such new names as those
of Paul Bourget, Huysmans, and the Goncourt brothers. Rumi-
nating on these things as he approached her door, he was once
more conscious of the curious way in which she reversed his values, and of the need of thinking himself into conditions incredibly
different from any that he knew if he were to be of use in her
present difficulty.

Nastasia opened the door, smiling mysteriously. On the bench in
the hall lay a sable-lined overcoat, a folded opera hat of dull silk
with a gold J. B. on the lining, and a white silk muffler: there was
no mistaking the fact that these costly articles were the property
of Julius Beaufort.

Archer was angry: so angry that he came near scribbling a

word on his card and going away; then he remembered that in writing to Madame Olenska he had been kept by excess of discretion from saying that he wished to see her privately. He had therefore no one but himself to blame if she had opened her doors to other visitors; and he entered the drawing room with the dogged determination to make Beaufort feel himself in the way, and to outstay him.

The banker stood leaning against the mantelshelf, which was draped with an old embroidery held in place by brass candelabra containing church candles of yellowish wax. He had thrust his chest out, supporting his shoulders against the mantel and resting his weight on one large patent-leather foot. As Archer entered he was smiling and looking down on his hostess, who sat on a sofa placed at right angles to the chimney. A table banked with flowers formed a screen behind it, and against the orchids and azaleas which the young man recognised as tributes from the Beaufort hothouses, Madame Olenska sat half-reclined, her head propped on a hand and her wide sleeve leaving the arm bare to the elbow.

It was usual for ladies who received in the evenings to wear what were called "simple dinner dresses": a close-fitting armor of whale-boned silk, slightly open in the neck, with lace ruffles filling in the crack, and tight sleeves with a flounce uncovering just enough wrist to show an Etruscan gold bracelet or a velvet band. But Madame Olenska, heedless of tradition, was attired in a long robe of red velvet bordered about the chin and down the front with glossy black fur. Archer remembered, on his last visit to Paris, seeing a portrait by the new painter, Carolus Duran, whose pictures were the sensation of the Salon, in which the lady wore one of these bold sheathlike robes with her chin nestling in fur. There was something perverse and provocative in the notion of fur worn in the evening in a heated drawing room, and in the combination of a muffled throat and bare arms; but the effect was undeniably pleasing.

"Lord love us—three whole days at Skytercliff!" Beaufort was saying in his loud sneering voice as Archer entered. "You'd better take all your furs, and a hot-water bottle."

"Why? Is the house so cold?" she asked, holding out her left hand to Archer in a way mysteriously suggesting that she expected him to kiss it.

"No, but the missus is," said Beaufort, nodding carelessly to the young man.

"But I thought her so kind. She came herself to invite me. Granny says I must certainly go."

"Granny would, of course. And *I* say it's a shame you're going to miss the little oyster supper I'd planned for you at Delmonico's next Sunday, with Campanini and Scalchi and a lot of jolly people."

She looked doubtfully from the banker to Archer.

"Ah—that does tempt me! Except the other evening at Mrs. Struthers's I've not met a single artist since I've been here."

"What kind of artists? I know one or two painters, very good fellows, that I could bring to see you if you'd allow me," said Archer boldly.

"Painters? Are there painters in New York?" asked Beaufort in a tone implying that there could be none since he did not buy their pictures; and Madame Olenska said to Archer, with her grave smile: "That would be charming. But I was really thinking of dramatic artists, singers, actors, musicians. My husband's house was always full of them."

She said the words "my husband" as if no sinister associations were connected with them, and in a tone that seemed almost to sigh over the lost delights of her married life. Archer looked at her perplexedly, wondering if it were lightness or dissimulation that enabled her to touch so easily on the past at the very moment when she was risking her reputation in order to break with it.

"I do think," she went on, addressing both men, "that the *imprévu* adds to one's enjoyment. It's perhaps a mistake to see the same people every day."

"It's confoundedly dull, anyhow; New York is dying of dullness," Beaufort grumbled. "And when I try to liven it up for you, you go back on me. Come—think better of it! Sunday is your last chance, for Campanini leaves next week for Baltimore and Philadelphia; and I've a private room, and a Steinway, and they'll sing all night for me."

"How delicious! May I think it over, and write to you tomorrow morning?"

She spoke amiably, yet with the least hint of dismissal in her voice. Beaufort evidently felt it, and being unused to dismissals, stood staring at her with an obstinate line between his eyes.

"Why not now?"

"It's too serious a question to decide at this late hour."

"Do you call it late?"

She returned his glance coolly. "Yes, because I have still to talk business with Mr. Archer for a little while."

"Ah," Beaufort snapped. There was no appeal from her tone, and with a slight shrug he recovered his composure, took her hand, which he kissed with a practiced air, and calling out from the threshold: "I say, Newland, if you can persuade the countess to stop in town of course you're included in the supper," left the room with his heavy important step.

For a moment Archer fancied that Mr. Letterblair must have told her of his coming; but the irrelevance of her next remark made him change his mind.

"You know painters, then? You live in their milieu?" she asked, her eyes full of interest.

"Oh, not exactly. I don't know that the arts have a milieu here, any of them; they're more like a very thinly settled outskirt."

"But you care for such things?"

"Immensely. When I'm in Paris or London I never miss an exhibition. I try to keep up."

She looked down at the tip of the little satin boot that peeped from her long draperies.

"I used to care immensely too: my life was full of such things. But now I want to try not to."

"You want to try not to?"

"Yes. I want to cast off all my old life, to become just like everybody else here."

Archer reddened. "You'll never be like everybody else," he said.

She raised her straight eyebrows a little. "Ah, don't say that. If you knew how I hate to be different!"

Her face had grown as somber as a tragic mask. She leaned forward, clasping her knee in her thin hands, and looking away from him into remote dark distances.

"I want to get away from it all," she insisted.

He waited a moment and cleared his throat. "I know, Mr. Letterblair has told me."

"Ah?"

"That's the reason I've come. He asked me to—you see I'm in the firm."

She looked slightly surprised, and then her eyes brightened. "You mean you can manage it for me? I can talk to you instead of Mr. Letterblair? Oh, that will be so much easier!"

Her tone touched him, and his confidence grew with his self-satisfaction. He perceived that she had spoken of business to Beaufort simply to get rid of him; and to have routed Beaufort was something of a triumph.

"I am here to talk about it," he repeated.

She sat silent, her head still propped by the arm that rested on the back of the sofa. Her face looked pale and extinguished, as if dimmed by the rich red of her dress. She struck Archer, of a sudden, as a pathetic and even pitiful figure.

"Now we're coming to hard facts," he thought, conscious in himself of the same instinctive recoil that he had so often criticized in his mother and her contemporaries. How little practice he had had in dealing with unusual situations! Their very vocabulary was unfamiliar to him, and seemed to belong to fiction and the stage. In face of what was coming he felt as awkward and embarrassed as a boy.

After a pause Madame Olenska broke out with unexpected vehemence: "I want to be free; I want to wipe out all the past."

"I understand that."

Her face warmed. "Then you'll help me?"

"First—" he hesitated—"perhaps I ought to know a little more."

She seemed surprised. "You know about my husband—my life with him?"

He made a sign of assent.

"Well—then—what more is there? In this country are such things tolerated? I'm a Protestant—our church does not forbid divorce in such cases."

"Certainly not."

They were both silent again, and Archer felt the specter of Count Olenski's letter grimacing hideously between them. The letter filled only half a page, and was just what he had described it to be in speaking of it to Mr. Letterblair: the vague charge of an angry blackguard. But how much truth was behind it? Only Count Olenski's wife could tell.

"I've looked through the papers you gave to Mr. Letterblair," he said at length.

"Well—can there be anything more abominable?"

"No."

She changed her position slightly, screening her eyes with her lifted hand.

"Of course you know," Archer continued, "that if your husband chooses to fight the case—as he threatens to—"

"Yes—?"

"He can say things—things that might be unpl—might be disagreeable to you: say them publicly, so that they would get about, and harm you even if—"

"If—?"

"I mean: no matter how unfounded they were."

She paused for a long interval; so long that, not wishing to keep his eyes on her shaded face, he had time to imprint on his mind the exact shape of her other hand, the one on her knee, and every detail of the three rings on her fourth and fifth fingers; among which, he noticed, a wedding ring did not appear.

"What harm could such accusations, even if he made them publicly, do me here?"

It was on his lips to exclaim: "My poor child—far more harm than anywhere else!" Instead, he answered, in a voice that sounded in his ears like Mr. Letterblair's: "New York society is a very small world compared with the one you've lived in. And it's ruled, in spite of appearances, by a few people with—well, rather old-fashioned ideas."

She said nothing, and he continued: "Our ideas about marriage and divorce are particularly old-fashioned. Our legislation favors divorce—our social customs don't."

"Never?"

"Well—not if the woman, however injured, however irreproachable, has appearances in the least degree against her, has exposed herself by any unconventional action to—to offensive insinuations—"

She drooped her head a little lower, and he waited again, intensely hoping for a flash of indignation, or at least a brief cry of denial. None came.

A little traveling clock ticked purringly at her elbow, and a log broke in two and sent up a shower of sparks. The whole hushed and brooding room seemed to be waiting silently with Archer.

"Yes," she murmured at length, "that's what my family tell me."

He winced a little. "It's not unnatural—"

"*Our* family," she corrected herself, and Archer colored. "For you'll be my cousin soon," she continued gently.

"I hope so."

"And you take their view?"

He stood up at this, wandered across the room, stared with void eyes at one of the pictures against the old red damask, and came back irresolutely to her side. How could he say, "Yes, if what your husband hints is true, or if you've no way of disproving it?"

"Sincerely—" she interjected, as he was about to speak.

He looked down into the fire. "Sincerely, then—what should you gain that would compensate for the possibility—the certainty—of a lot of beastly talk?"

"But my freedom—is that nothing?"

It flashed across him at that instant that the charge in the letter was true, and that she hoped to marry the partner of her guilt. How was he to tell her that, if she really cherished such a plan, the laws of the State were inexorably opposed to it? The mere suspicion that the thought was in her mind made him feel harshly and impatiently toward her. "But aren't you as free as air as it is?" he returned. "Who can touch you? Mr. Letterblair tells me the financial question has been settled—"

"Oh, yes," she said indifferently.

"Well, then: is it worthwhile to risk what may be infinitely disagreeable and painful? Think of the newspapers—their vileness! It's all stupid and narrow and unjust—but one can't make over society."

"No," she acquiesced, and her tone was so faint and desolate that he felt a sudden remorse for his own hard thoughts.

"The individual, in such cases, is nearly always sacrificed to what is supposed to be the collective interest: people cling to any convention that keeps the family together—protects the children, if there are any," he rambled on, pouring out all the stock phrases that rose to his lips in his intense desire to cover over the ugly reality which her silence seemed to have laid bare. Since she would not or could not say the one word that would have cleared the air, his wish was not to let her feel that he was trying to probe into her secret. Better keep on the surface, in the prudent old New York way, than risk uncovering a wound he could not heal.

"It's my business, you know," he went on, "to help you to see these things as the people who are fondest of you see them. The Mingotts, the Wellands, the van der Luydens, all your friends and relations: if I didn't show you honestly how they judge such questions, it wouldn't be fair of me, would it?" He spoke insistently, almost pleading with her in his eagerness to cover up that yawning silence.

She said slowly: "No, it wouldn't be fair."

The fire had crumbled down to grayness, and one of the lamps made a gurgling appeal for attention. Madame Olenska rose, wound it up, and returned to the fire, but without resuming her seat.

Her remaining on her feet seemed to signify that there was nothing more for either of them to say, and Archer stood up also.

"Very well. I will do what you wish," she said abruptly. The blood rushed to his forehead; and, taken aback by the suddenness of her surrender, he caught her two hands awkwardly in his.

"I—I do want to help you," he said.

"You do help me. Good night, my cousin."

He bent and laid his lips on her hands, which were cold and lifeless. She drew them away, and he turned to the door, found his coat and hat under the faint gaslight of the hall, and plunged out into the winter night bursting with the belated eloquence of the inarticulate.

# ——13——

It was a crowded night at Wallack's theater.

The play was *The Shaughraun,* with Dion Boucicault in the title role and Harry Montague and Ada Dyas as the lovers. The popularity of the admirable English company was at its height, and *The Shaughraun* always packed the house. In the galleries the enthusiasm was unreserved; in the stalls and boxes, people smiled a little at the hackneyed sentiments and claptrap situations, and enjoyed the play as much as the galleries did.

There was one episode, in particular, that held the house from floor to ceiling. It was that in which Harry Montague, after a sad, almost monosyllabic scene of parting with Miss Dyas, bade her good-bye, and turned to go. The actress, who was standing near the mantelpiece and looking down into the fire, wore a gray cashmere dress without fashionable loopings or trimmings, molded to her tall figure and flowing in long lines about her feet. Around her neck was a narrow black velvet ribbon with the ends falling down her back.

When her wooer turned from her she rested her arms against the mantelshelf and bowed her face in her hands. On the threshold he paused to look at her; then he stole back, lifted one of the ends of velvet ribbon, kissed it, and left the room without her hearing him or changing her attitude. And on this silent parting the curtain fell.

It was always for the sake of that particular scene that Newland Archer went to see *The Shaughraun.* He thought the adieux of Montague and Ada Dyas as fine as anything he had ever seen Croisette and Bressant do in Paris, or Madge Robertson and Kendal in London; in its reticence, its dumb sorrow, it moved him more than the most famous histrionic outpourings.

On the evening in question the little scene acquired an added poignancy by reminding him—he could not have said why—of his leave-taking from Madame Olenska after their confidential talk a week or ten days earlier.

It would have been as difficult to discover any resemblance between the two situations as between the appearance of the persons concerned. Newland Archer could not pretend to anything approaching the young English actor's romantic good looks, and Miss Dyas was a tall red-haired woman of monumental build whose pale and pleasantly ugly face was utterly unlike Ellen Olenska's vivid countenance. Nor were Archer and Madame Olenska two lovers parting in heartbroken silence; they were client and lawyer separating after a talk which had given the lawyer the worst possible impression of the client's case. Wherein, then, lay the resemblance that made the young man's heart beat with a kind of retrospective excitement? It seemed to be in Madame Olenska's mysterious faculty of suggesting tragic and moving possibilities outside the daily run of experience. She had hardly ever said a word to him to produce this impression, but it was a part of her, either a projection of her mysterious and outlandish background or of something inherently dramatic, passionate and unusual in herself. Archer had always been inclined to think that chance and circumstance played a small part in shaping people's lots compared with their innate tendency to have things happen to them. This tendency he had felt from the first in Madame Olenska. The quiet, almost passive young woman struck him as exactly the kind of person to whom things were bound to happen, no matter how much she shrank from them and went out of her way to avoid them. The exciting fact was her having lived in an atmosphere so thick with drama that her own tendency to provoke it had apparently passed unperceived. It was precisely the odd absence of surprise in her that gave him the sense of her having been plucked out of a very maelstrom: the things she took for granted gave the measure of those she had rebelled against.

Archer had left her with the conviction that Count Olenski's accusation was not unfounded. The mysterious person who figured in his wife's past as "the secretary" had probably not been unrewarded for his share in her escape. The conditions from which she had fled were intolerable, past speaking of, past believing: she was young, she was frightened, she was desperate—what more natural than that she should be grateful to her rescuer? The pity was that her gratitude put her, in the law's eyes and the world's, on a par with her abominable husband. Archer had made her understand this, as he was bound to do; he had also made her understand that simple-hearted kindly New York, on whose larger charity she had apparently counted, was precisely the place where she could least hope for indulgence.

To have to make this fact plain to her—and to witness her resigned acceptance of it—had been intolerably painful to him. He felt himself drawn to her by obscure feelings of jealousy and pity, as if her dumbly confessed error had put her at his mercy, humbling yet endearing her. He was glad it was to him she had revealed her secret, rather than to the cold scrutiny of Mr. Letterblair, or the embarrassed gaze of her family. He immediately took it upon himself to assure them both that she had given up her idea of seeking a divorce, basing her decision on the fact that she had understood the uselessness of the proceeding; and with infinite relief they had all turned their eyes from the "unpleasantness" she had spared them.

"I was sure Newland would manage it," Mrs. Welland had said proudly of her future son-in-law; and old Mrs. Mingott, who had summoned him for a confidential interview, had congratulated him on his cleverness, and added impatiently: "Silly goose! I told her myself what nonsense it was. Wanting to pass herself off as Ellen Mingott and an old maid, when she has the luck to be a married woman and a countess!"

These incidents had made the memory of his last talk with Madame Olenska so vivid to the young man that as the curtain fell on the parting of the two actors his eyes filled with tears, and he stood up to leave the theater.

In doing so, he turned to the side of the house behind him, and saw the lady of whom he was thinking seated in a box with the Beauforts, Lawrence Lefferts, and one or two other men. He had not spoken with her alone since their evening together, and had tried to avoid being with her in company, but now their eyes met, and as Mrs. Beaufort recognized him at the same time, and made her languid little gesture of invitation, it was impossible not to go into the box.

Beaufort and Lefferts made way for him, and after a few words with Mrs. Beaufort, who always preferred to look beautiful and not have to talk, Archer seated himself behind Madame Olenska. There was no one else in the box but Mr. Sillerton Jackson, who was telling Mrs. Beaufort in a confidential undertone about Mrs. Lemuel Struthers's last Sunday reception (where some people reported that there had been dancing). Under cover of this circumstantial narrative, to which Mrs. Beaufort listened with her perfect smile, and her head at just the right angle to be seen in profile from the stalls, Madame Olenska turned and spoke in a low voice.

"Do you think," she asked, glancing toward the stage, "he will send her a bunch of yellow roses tomorrow morning?"

Archer reddened, and his heart gave a leap of surprise. He had called only twice on Madame Olenska, and each time he had sent her a box of yellow roses, and each time without a card. She had never before made any allusion to the flowers, and he supposed she had never thought of him as the sender. Now her sudden recognition of the gift, and her associating it with the tender leave-taking on the stage, filled him with an agitated pleasure.

"I was thinking of that too—I was going to leave the theater in order to take the picture away with me," he said.

To his surprise her color rose, reluctantly and duskily. She looked down at the mother-of-pearl opera glass in her smoothly gloved hands, and said, after a pause: "What do you do while May is away?"

"I stick to my work," he answered, faintly annoyed by the question.

In obedience to a long-established habit, the Wellands had left the previous week for St. Augustine, where, out of regard for the supposed susceptibility of Mr. Welland's bronchial tubes, they always spent the latter part of the winter. Mr. Welland was a mild and silent man, with no opinions but with many habits. With these habits none might interfere; and one of them demanded that his wife and daughter should always go with him on his annual journey to the south. To preserve an unbroken domesticity was essential to his peace of mind; he would not have known where his hairbrushes were, or how to provide stamps for his letters, if Mrs. Welland had not been there to tell him.

As all the members of the family adored each other, and as Mr. Welland was the central object of their idolatry, it never occurred to his wife and May to let him go to St. Augustine alone; and his sons, who were both in the law, and could not leave New York during the winter, always joined him for Easter and traveled back with him.

It was impossible for Archer to discuss the necessity of May's accompanying her father. The reputation of the Mingotts' family physician was largely based on the attack of pneumonia which Mr. Welland had never had; and his insistence on St. Augustine was therefore inflexible. Originally, it had been intended that May's engagement should not be announced till her return from Florida, and the fact that it had been made known sooner could not be expected to alter Mr. Welland's plans. Archer would have liked to join the travelers and have a few weeks of sunshine and boating with his betrothed; but he too was bound by custom and conventions. Little arduous as his professional duties were, he would have been convicted of frivolity by the whole Mingott clan if he had suggested asking for a holiday in midwinter; and he accepted May's departure with the resignation which he perceived would have to be one of the principal constituents of married life.

He was conscious that Madame Olenska was looking at him under lowered lids. "I have done what you wished—what you advised," she said abruptly.

"Ah—I'm glad," he returned, embarrassed by her broaching the subject at such a moment.

"I understand—that you were right," she went on a little breathlessly; "but sometimes life is difficult . . . perplexing . . ."

"I know."

"And I wanted to tell you that I *do* feel you were right, and that I'm grateful to you," she ended, lifting her opera glass quickly to her eyes as the door of the box opened and Beaufort's resonant voice broke in on them.

Archer stood up, and left the box and the theater.

Only the day before he had received a letter from May Welland in which, with characteristic candor, she had asked him to "be kind to Ellen" in their absence. "She likes you and admires you so much—and you know, though she doesn't show it, she's still very lonely and unhappy. I don't think Granny understands her, or

Uncle Lovell Mingott either; they really think she's much world-lier and fonder of society than she is. And I can quite see that New York must seem dull to her, though the family won't admit it. I think she's been used to lots of things we haven't got; wonderful music, and picture shows, and celebrities—artists and authors and all the clever people you admire. Granny can't understand her wanting anything but lots of dinners and clothes—but I can see that you're almost the only person in New York who can talk to her about what she really cares for."

His wise May—how he had loved her for that letter! But he had not meant to act on it; he was too busy, to begin with, and he did not care, as an engaged man, to play too conspicuously the part of Madame Olenska's champion. He had an idea that she knew how to take care of herself a good deal better than the ingenuous May imagined. She had Beaufort at her feet, Mr. van der Luyden hovering above her like a protecting deity, and any number of candidates (Lawrence Lefferts among them) waiting their opportunity in the middle distance. Yet he never saw her, or exchanged a word with her, without feeling that, after all, May's ingenuousness almost amounted to a gift of divination. Ellen Olenska was lonely and she was unhappy.

# —14—

As he came out into the lobby Archer ran across his friend Ned Winsett, the only one among what Janey called his "clever people" with whom he cared to probe into things a little deeper than the average level of club and chophouse banter.

He had caught sight, across the house, of Winsett's shabby round-shouldered back, and had once noticed his eyes turned toward the Beaufort box. The two men shook hands, and Winsett proposed a bock at a little German restaurant around the corner. Archer, who was not in the mood for the kind of talk they were likely to get there, declined on the plea that he had work to do at home; and Winsett said: "Oh, well so have I for that matter, and I'll be the Industrious Apprentice too."

They strolled along together, and presently Winsett said: "Look here, what I'm really after is the name of the dark lady in that swell box of yours—with the Beauforts, wasn't she? The one your friend Lefferts seems so smitten by."

Archer, he could not have said why, was slightly annoyed. What the devil did Ned Winsett want with Ellen Olenska's name? And above all, why did he couple it with Lefferts's? It was unlike Winsett to manifest such curiosity; but after all, Archer remembered, he was a journalist.

"It's not for an interview, I hope?" he laughed.

"Well—not for the press; just for myself," Winsett rejoined. "The fact is she's a neighbor of mine—queer quarter for such a beauty to settle in—and she's been awfully kind to my little boy, who fell down her area chasing his kitten, and gave himself a nasty cut. She rushed in bareheaded, carrying him in her arms, with his knee all beautifully bandaged, and was so sympathetic and beautiful that my wife was too dazzled to ask her name."

A pleasant glow dilated Archer's heart. There was nothing extraordinary in the tale: any woman would have done as much for a neighbor's child. But it was just like Ellen, he felt, to have rushed in bareheaded, carrying the boy in her arms, and to have dazzled poor Mrs. Winsett into forgetting to ask who she was.

"That is the Countess Olenska—a granddaughter of old Mrs. Mingott's."

"Whew—a countess!" whistled Ned Winsett. "Well, I didn't know countesses were so neighborly. Mingotts ain't."

"They would be, if you'd let them."

"Ah, well—" It was their old interminable argument as to the obstinate unwillingness of the "clever people" to frequent the fashionable, and both men knew that there was no use in prolonging it.

"I wonder," Winsett broke off, "how a countess happens to live in our slum?"

"Because she doesn't care a hang about where she lives—or about any of our little social signposts," said Archer, with a secret pride in his own picture of her.

"H'm—been in bigger places, I suppose," the other commented. "Well, here's my corner."

He slouched off across Broadway, and Archer stood looking after him and musing on his last words.

Ned Winsett had those flashes of penetration; they were the most interesting thing about him, and always made Archer wonder why they had allowed him to accept failure so stolidly at any age when most men are still struggling.

Archer had known that Winsett had a wife and child, but he had never seen them. The two men always met at the Century, or at some haunt of journalists and theatrical people, such as the restaurant where Winsett had proposed to go for a bock. He had given Archer to understand that his wife was an invalid; which might be true of the poor lady, or might merely mean that she was lacking in social gifts or in evening clothes, or in both. Winsett himself had a savage abhorrence of social observances: Archer, who dressed in the evening because he thought it cleaner and more comfortable to do so, and who had never stopped to consider that cleanliness and comfort are two of the costliest items in a modest budget, regarded Winsett's attitude as part of the boring "Bohemian" pose that always made fashionable people, who changed their clothes without talking about it, and were not forever harping on the number of servants one kept, seem so much simpler and less self-conscious than the others. Nevertheless, he was always stimulated by Winsett, and whenever he caught sight of the journalist's lean bearded face and melancholy eyes he would rout him out of his corner and carry him off for a long talk.

Winsett was not a journalist by choice. He was a pure man of letters, untimely born in a world that had no need of letters; but after publishing one volume of brief and exquisite literary appreciations, of which one hundred and twenty copies were sold, thirty given away, and the balance eventually destroyed by the publishers (as per contract) to make room for more marketable material, he had abandoned his real calling, and taken a subeditorial job on a women's weekly, where fashionplates and paper patterns alternated with New England love stories and advertisements of temperance drinks.

On the subject of "Hearth-fires" (as the paper was called) he was inexhaustibly entertaining; but beneath his fun lurked the sterile bitterness of the still young man who has tried and given up. His conversation always made Archer take the measure of his own life, and feel how little it contained; but Winsett's, after all, contained still less, and though their common fund of intellectual interests and curiosities made their talks exhilarating, their exchange of views usually remained within the limits of a pensive dilettantism.

"The fact is, life isn't much a fit for either of us," Winsett had once said. "I'm down and out; nothing to be done about it. I've got only one ware to produce, and there's no market for it here, and won't be in my time. But you're free and you're well-off. Why don't *you* get into touch? There's only one way to do it: to go into politics."

Archer threw his head back and laughed. There one saw at a flash the unbridgeable difference between men like Winsett and the others—Archer's kind. Everyone in polite circles knew that, in America, "a gentleman couldn't go into politics." But, since he could hardly put it in that way to Winsett, he answered evasively: "Look at the career of the honest man in American politics! They don't want us."

"Who's 'they'? Why don't you all get together and be 'they' yourselves?"

Archer's laugh lingered on his lips in a slightly condescending smile. It was useless to prolong the discussion: everybody knew the melancholy fate of the few gentlemen who had risked their clean linen in municipal or state politics in New York. The day was past when that sort of thing was possible: the country was in possession of the bosses and the emigrant, and decent people had to fall back on sport or culture.

"Culture! Yes—if we had it! But there are just a few little local patches, dying out here and there for lack of—well, hoeing and cross-fertilizing: the last remnants of the old European tradition that your forebears brought with them. But you're in a pitiful little minority: you've got no center, no competition, no audience. You're like the pictures on the walls of a deserted house: 'The Portrait of a Gentleman.' You'll never amount to anything, any of you, till you roll up your sleeves and get right down into the muck. That, or emigrate . . . God! If I could emigrate . . ."

Archer mentally shrugged his shoulders and turned the conversation back to books, where Winsett, if uncertain, was always interesting. Emigrate! As if a gentleman could abandon his own country! One could no more do that than one could roll up one's sleeves and go down into the muck. A gentleman simply stayed at home and abstained. But you couldn't make a man like Winsett see that; and that was why the New York of literary clubs and exotic restaurants, though a first shake made it seem more of a kaleidoscope, turned out, in the end, to be a smaller box, with a more monotonous pattern, than the assembled atoms of Fifth Avenue.

The next morning Archer scoured the town in vain for more yellow roses. In consequence of this search he arrived late at the office, perceived that his doing so made no difference whatever to anyone, and was filled with sudden exasperation at the elaborate futility of his life. Why should he not be, at that moment, on the sands of St. Augustine with May Welland? No one was deceived by his pretense of professional activity. In old-fashioned legal firms like that of which Mr. Letterblair was the head, and which were mainly engaged in the management of large estates and "conservative" investments, there were always two or three young men, fairly well-off, and without professional ambition, who, for a certain number of hours each day, sat at their desks accomplishing trivial tasks, or simply reading the newspapers. Though it was supposed to be proper for them to have an occupation, the crude fact of moneymaking was still regarded as derogatory, and the law, being a profession, was accounted a more gentlemanly pursuit than business. But none of these young men had much hope of really advancing in his profession, or any earnest desire to do so; and over many of them the green mold of the perfunctory was already perceptibly spreading.

It made Archer shiver to think that it might be spreading over him too. He had, to be sure, other tastes and interests; he spent his vacations in European travel, cultivated the "clever people" May spoke of, and generally tried to "keep up," as he had somewhat wistfully put it to Madame Olenska. But once he was married, what would become of this narrow margin of life in which his real experiences were lived? He had seen enough of other young men who had dreamed his dream, though perhaps less ardently, and who had gradually sunk into the placid and luxurious routine of their elders.

From the office he sent a note by messenger to Madame Olenska, asking if he might call that afternoon, and begging her to let him find a reply at his club; but at the club he found nothing, nor did he receive any letter the following day. This unexpected silence mortified him beyond reason, and though the next morning he saw a glorious cluster of yellow roses behind a florist's windowpane, he left it there. It was only on the third morning that he received a line by post from the Countess Olenska. To his surprise it was dated from Skuytercliff, whither the van der Luydens had promptly retreated after putting the duke on board his steamer.

"I ran away," the writer began abruptly (without the usual preliminaries), "the day after I saw you at the play, and these kind friends have taken me in. I wanted to be quiet, and think things over. You were right in telling me how kind they were. I feel myself so safe here. I wish that you were with us." She ended with a conventional "Yours sincerely," and without any allusion to the date of her return.

The tone of the note surprised the young man. What was Madame Olenska running away from, and why did she feel the need to be safe? His first thought was of some dark menace from abroad; then he reflected that he did not know her epistolary style, and that it might run to picturesque exaggeration. Women always exaggerated; and moreover she was not wholly at her ease in English, which she often spoke as if she were translating from the French. *"Je me suis évadée—"* put in that way, the opening sentence immediately suggested that she might merely have wanted to escape from a boring round of engagements; which was very likely true, for he judged her to be capricious, and easily wearied of the pleasure of the moment.

It amused him to think of the van der Ludyens' having carried her off to Skuytercliff on a second visit, and this time for an indefinite period. The doors of Skuytercliff were rarely and grudgingly opened to visitors, and a chilly weekend was the most ever offered to the few thus privileged. But Archer had seen, on his last visit to Paris, the delicious play of Labiche, *Le Voyage de M. Perrichon,* and he remembered M. Perrichon's dogged and undiscouraged attachment to the young man whom he had pulled out of the glacier. The van der Luydens had rescued Madame Olenska from a doom almost as icy; and though there were many other reasons for being attracted to her, Archer knew that beneath them all lay the gentle and obstinate determination to go on rescuing her.

He felt a distinct disappointment on learning that she was away; and almost immediately remembered that, only the day before, he had refused an invitation to spend the following Sunday with the Reggie Chiverses at their house on the Hudson, a few miles below Skuytercliff.

He had had his fill long ago of the noisy friendly parties at Highbank, with coasting, iceboating, sleighing, long tramps in the snow, and a general flavor of mild flirting and milder practical jokes. He had just received a box of new books from his London bookseller, and had preferred the prospect of a quiet Sunday at home with his spoils. But he now went into the club writing room, wrote a hurried telegram, and told the servant to send it immediately. He knew that Mrs. Reggie didn't object to her visitors' suddenly changing their minds, and that there was always a room to spare in her elastic house.

# ——15——

NEWLAND ARCHER arrived at the Chiverses' on Friday evening, and on Saturday went conscientiously through all the rites appertaining to a weekend at Highbank.

In the morning he had a spin in the iceboat with his hostess and a few of the hardier guests; in the afternoon he "went over the farm" with Reggie, and listened, in the elaborately appointed stables, to long and impressive disquisitions on the horse; after tea he talked in a corner of the firelit hall with a young lady who had professed herself brokenhearted when his engagement was announced, but was now eager to tell him of her own matrimonial hopes; and finally, about midnight, he assisted in putting a goldfish in one visitor's bed, dressed up a burglar in the bathroom of a nervous aunt, and saw in the small hours by joining in a pillow fight that ranged from the nurseries to the basement. But on Sunday after luncheon he borrowed a cutter, and drove over to Skuytercliff.

People had always been told that the house at Skuytercliff was an Italian villa. Those who had never been to Italy believed it; so did some who had. The house had been built by Mr. van der Luyden in his youth, on his return from the "grand tour," and in anticipation of his approaching marriage with Miss Louisa Dagonet. It was a large square wooden structure, with tongued and grooved walls painted pale green and white, a Corinthian portico, and fluted pilasters between the windows. From the high ground on which it stood a series of terraces bordered by balustrades and urns descended in the steel-engraving style to a small irregular lake with an asphalt edge overhung by rare weeping conifers. To the right and left, the famous weedless lawns studded with "specimen" trees (each of a different variety) rolled away to long ranges of grass crested with elaborate cast-iron ornaments; and below, in a hollow, lay the four-roomed stone house which the first patroon had built on the land granted him in 1612.

Against the uniform sheet of snow and the grayish winter sky the Italian villa loomed up rather grimly; even in summer it kept its distance, and the boldest coleus bed had never ventured nearer than thirty feet from its awful front. Now, as Archer rang the bell, the long tinkle seemed to echo through a mausoleum; and the surprise of the butler who at length responded to the call was as great as though he had been summoned from his final sleep.

Happily Archer was of the family, and therefore, irregular though his arrival was, entitled to be informed that the Countess Olenska was out, having driven to afternoon service with Mrs. van der Luyden exactly three quarters of an hour earlier.

"Mr. van der Luyden," the butler continued, "is in, sir; but my impression is that he is either finishing his nap or else reading yesterday's *Evening Post*. I heard him say, sir, on his return from church this morning, that he intended to look through the *Evening Post* after luncheon; if you like, sir, I might go to the library door and listen—"

But Archer, thanking him, said that he would go and meet the ladies; and the butler, obviously relieved, closed the door on him majestically.

A groom took the cutter to the stables, and Archer struck through the park to the highroad. The village of Skuytercliff was only a mile and a half away, but he knew that Mrs. van der Luyden never walked, and that he must keep to the road to meet the carriage. Presently, however, coming down a footpath that crossed the highway, he caught sight of a slight figure in a red cloak, with a big dog running ahead. He hurried forward, and Madame Olenska stopped short with a smile of welcome.

"Ah, you've come!" she said, and drew her hand from her muff.

The red cloak made her look gay and vivid, like the Ellen Mingott of old days; and he laughed as he took her hand, and answered: "I came to see what you were running away from."

Her face clouded over, but she answered: "Ah, well—you will see, presently."

The answer puzzled him. "Why—do you mean that you've been overtaken?"

She shrugged her shoulders, with a little movement like Nastasia's, and rejoined in a lighter tone: "Shall we walk on? I'm so cold after the sermon. And what does it matter, now you're here to protect me?"

The blood rose to his temples and he caught a fold of her cloak. "Ellen—what is it? You must tell me."

"Oh, presently—let's run a race first: my feet are freezing to the ground," she cried; and gathering up the cloak she fled away across the snow, the dog leaping about her with challenging barks. For a moment Archer stood watching, his gaze delighted by the flash of the red meteor against the snow, then he started after her, and they met, panting and laughing, at a wicket that led into the park.

She looked up at him and smiled. "I knew you'd come!"

"That shows you wanted me to," he returned, with a dispro-portionate joy in their nonsense. The white glitter of the trees filled the air with its own mysterious brightness, and as they walked on over the snow the ground seemed to sing under their feet.

"Where did you come from?" Madame Olenska asked.

He told her, and added: "It was because I got your note."

After a pause she said, with a just perceptible chill in her voice: "May asked you to take care of me."

"I didn't need any asking."

"You mean—I'm so evidently helpless and defenseless? What a poor thing you must all think me! But women here seem not—seem never to feel the need: any more than the blessed in heaven."

He lowered his voice to ask: "What sort of a need?"

"Ah, don't ask me! I don't speak your language," she retorted petulantly.

The answer smote him like a blow, and he stood still in the path, looking down at her.

"What did I come for, if I don't speak yours?"

"Oh, my friend—!" She laid her hand lightly on his arm, and he pleaded earnestly: "Ellen—why won't you tell me what's hap-pened?"

She shrugged again. "Does anything ever happen in heaven?"

He was silent, and they walked on a few yards without ex-changing a word. Finally she said: "I will tell you—but where,

where, where? One can't be alone for a minute in that great semi-
nary of a house, with all the doors wide open, and always a servant bringing tea, or a log for the fire, or the newspaper! Is there
nowhere in an American house where one may be by one's self?
You're so shy, and yet you're so public. I always feel as if I were in
the convent again—or on the stage, before a dreadfully polite
audience that never applauds."

"Ah, you don't like us!" Archer exclaimed.

They were walking past the house of the old Patroon, with its
squat walls and small square windows compactly grouped about a
central chimney. The shutters stood wide, and through one of the
newly washed windows Archer caught the light of a fire.

"Why—the house is open!" he said.

She stood still. "No, only for today, at least. I wanted to see it,
and Mr. van der Luyden had the fire lit and the windows opened,
so that we might stop there on the way back from church this
morning." She ran up the steps and tried the door. "It's still
unlocked—what luck! Come in and we can have a quiet talk. Mrs.
van der Luyden has driven over to see her old aunts at Rhinebeck
and we shan't be missed at the house for another hour."

He followed her into the narrow passage. His spirits, which
had dropped at her last words, rose with an irrational leap. The
homely little house stood there, its panels and brasses shining in
the firelight, as if magically created to receive them. A big bed of
embers still gleamed in the kitchen chimney, under an iron pot
hung from an ancient crane. Rush-bottomed armchairs faced
each other across the tiled hearth, and rows of Delft plates stood
on shelves against the walls. Archer stooped over and threw a log
upon the embers.

Madame Olenska, dropping her cloak, sat down in one of the
chairs. Archer leaned against the chimney and looked at her.

"You're laughing now, but when you wrote me you were unhappy," he said.

"Yes." She paused. "But I can't feel unhappy when you're
here."

"I shan't be here long," he rejoined, his lips stiffening with the
effort to say just so much and no more.

"No, I know. But I'm improvident: I live in the moment when
I'm happy."

The words stole through him like a temptation, and to close his senses to it he moved away from the hearth and stood gazing out at the black tree boles against the snow. But it was as if she too had shifted her place, and he still saw her, between himself and the trees, drooping over the fire with her indolent smile. Archer's heart was beating insubordinately. What if it were from him that she had been running away, and if she had waited to tell him so till they were here alone together in this secret room?

"Ellen, if I'm really a help to you—if you really wanted me to come—tell me what's wrong, tell me what it is you're running away from," he insisted.

He spoke without shifting his position, without even turning to look at her: if the thing was to happen, it was to happen in this way, with the whole width of the room between them, and his eyes still fixed on the outer snow.

For a long moment she was silent; and in that moment Archer imagined her, almost heard her, stealing up behind him to throw her light arms about his neck. While he waited, soul and body throbbing with the miracle to come, his eyes mechanically received the image of a heavily coated man with his fur collar turned up who was advancing along the path to the house. The man was Julius Beaufort.

"Ah—!" Archer cried, bursting into a laugh.

Madame Olenska had sprung up and moved to his side, slipping her hand into his, but after a glance through the window her face paled and she shrank back.

"So that was it?" Archer said derisively.

"I didn't know he was here," Madame Olenska murmured. Her hand still clung to Archer's; but he drew away from her, and walking out into the passage threw open the door of the house.

"Hallo, Beaufort—this way! Madame Olenska was expecting you," he said.

During his journey back to New York the next morning, Archer relived with a fatiguing vividness his last moments at Skuytercliff.

Beaufort, though clearly annoyed at finding him with Madame Olenska, had, as usual, carried off the situation highhandedly. His way of ignoring people whose presence inconvenienced him actually gave them, if they were sensitive to it, a feeling of invisibility, of nonexistence. Archer, as the three strolled back through the park, was aware of this odd sense of disembodiment; and humbling as it was to his vanity it gave him the ghostly advantage of observing unobserved.

Beaufort had entered the little house with his usual easy assurance; but he could not smile away the vertical line between his eyes. It was fairly clear that Madame Olenska had not known that he was coming, though her words to Archer had hinted at the possibility; at any rate, she had evidently not told him where she was going when she left New York, and her unexplained departure had exasperated him. The ostensible reason of his appearance was the discovery, the very night before, of a "perfect little house," not in the market, which was really just the thing for her, but would be snapped up instantly if she didn't take it; and he was loud in mock reproaches for the dance she had led him in running away just as he had found it.

"If only this new dodge for talking along a wire had been a little bit nearer perfection I might have told you all this from town, and been toasting my toes before the club fire at this minute, instead of tramping after you through the snow," he grumbled, disguising a real irritation under the pretense of it; and at this opening Madame Olenska twisted the talk away to the fantastic possibility that they might one day actually converse with each other from street to street, or even—incredible dream!—from one town to another. This struck from all three allusions to Edgar Poe and Jules Verne, and such platitudes as naturally rise to the lips of the most intelligent when they are talking against time, and dealing with a new invention in which it would seem ingenuous to believe too soon; and the question of the telephone carried them safely back to the big house.

Mrs. van der Luyden had not yet returned; and Archer took his leave and walked off to fetch the cutter, while Beaufort followed the Countess Olenska indoors. It was probable that, little as the van der Luydens encouraged unannounced visits, he could count on being asked to dine, and sent back to the station to catch the nine o'clock train; but more than that he would certainly not get, for it would be inconceivable to his hosts that a gentleman traveling without luggage should wish to spend the night, and distasteful to them to propose it to a person with whom they were on terms of such limited cordiality as Beaufort.

Beaufort knew all this, and must have foreseen it; and his taking the long journey for so small a reward gave the measure of his impatience. He was undeniably in pursuit of the Countess Olenska; and Beaufort had only one object in view in his pursuit of pretty women. His dull and childless home had long since palled on him; and in addition to more permanent consolations he was always in quest of amorous adventures in his own set. This was the man from whom Madame Olenska was avowedly flying: the question was whether she had fled because his importunities displeased her, or because she did not wholly trust herself to resist them; unless, indeed, all her talk of flight had been a blind, and her departure no more than a maneuver.

Archer did not really believe this. Little as he had actually seen of Madame Olenska, he was beginning to think that he could read her face, and if not her face, her voice; and both had betrayed annoyance, and even dismay, at Beaufort's sudden appearance. But, after all, if this were the case, was it not worse than if she had left New York for the express purpose of meeting him? If she had done that, she ceased to be an object of interest, she threw in her lot with the vulgarest of dissemblers: a woman engaged in a love affair with Beaufort "classed" herself irretrievably.

No, it was worse a thousand times if, judging Beaufort, and probably despising him, she was yet drawn to him by all that gave him an advantage over the other men about her: his habit of two continents and two societies, his familiar association with artists and actors and people generally in the world's eye, and his careless contempt for local prejudices. Beaufort was vulgar, he was uneducated, he was purse-proud; but the circumstances of his life, and a certain native shrewdness, made him better worth talking to than many men, morally and socially his betters, whose horizon was bounded by the Battery and the Central Park. How should anyone coming from a wider world not feel the difference and be attracted by it?

Madame Olenska, in a burst of irritation, had said to Archer that he and she did not talk the same language; and the young man knew that in some respects this was true. But Beaufort understood every turn of her dialect, and spoke it fluently: his view

of life, his tone, his attitude, were merely a coarser reflection of
those revealed in Count Olenski's letter. This might seem to be to
his disadvantage with Count Olenski's wife; but Archer was too
intelligent to think that a young woman like Ellen Olenska would
necessarily recoil from everything that reminded her of her past.
She might believe herself wholly in revolt against it; but what had
charmed her in it would still charm her, even though it were
against her will.

Thus, with a painful impartiality, did the young man make out
the case for Beaufort, and for Beaufort's victim. A longing to
enlighten her was strong in him; and there were moments when
he imagined that all she asked was to be enlightened.

That evening he unpacked his books from London. The box
was full of things he had been waiting for impatiently; a new
volume of Herbert Spencer, another collection of the prolific Al-
phonse Daudet's brilliant tales, and a novel called *Middlemarch*, as
to which there had lately been interesting things said in the re-
views. He had declined three dinner invitations in favor of this
feast; but though he turned the pages with the sensuous joy of the
book lover, he did not know what he was reading, and one book
after another dropped from his hand. Suddenly, among them, he
lit on a small volume of verse which he had ordered because the
name had attracted him: *The House of Life*. He took it up, and
found himself plunged in an atmosphere unlike any he had ever
breathed in books; so warm, so rich, and yet so ineffably tender,
that it gave a new and haunting beauty to the most elementary of
human passions. All through the night he pursued through those
enchanted pages the vision of a woman who had the face of Ellen
Olenska; but when he woke the next morning, and looked out at
the brownstone houses across the street, and thought of his desk
in Mr. Letterblair's office, and the family pew in Grace Church,
his hour in the park of Skuytercliff became as far outside the pale
of probability as the visions of the night.

"Mercy, how pale you look, Newland!" Janey commented over
the coffee cups at breakfast; and his mother added: "Newland,
dear, I've noticed lately that you've been coughing; I do hope
you're not letting yourself be overworked?" For it was the conviction of both ladies that, under the iron despotism of his senior
partners, the young man's life was spent in the most exhausting

professional labors—and he had never thought it necessary to undeceive them.

The next two or three days dragged by heavily. The taste of the usual was like cinders in his mouth, and there were moments when he felt as if he were being buried alive under his future. He heard nothing of the Countess Olenska, or of the perfect little house, and though he met Beaufort at the club they merely nodded at each other across the whist tables. It was not till the fourth evening that he found a note awaiting him on his return home. "Come late tomorrow: I must explain to you. Ellen." These were the only words it contained.

The young man, who was dining out, thrust the note into his pocket, smiling a little at the Frenchness of the "to you." After dinner he went to a play; and it was not until his return home, after midnight, that he drew Madame Olenska's missive out again and reread it slowly a number of times. There were several ways of answering it, and he gave considerable thought to each one during the watches of an agitated night. That on which, when morning came, he finally decided was to pitch some clothes into a portmanteau and jump on board a boat that was leaving that very afternoon for St. Augustine.

# —16—

WHEN ARCHER walked down the sandy main street of St. Augustine to the house which had been pointed out to him as Mr. Welland's, and saw May Welland standing under a magnolia with the sun in her hair, he wondered why he had waited so long to come.

Here was the truth, here was reality, here was the life that belonged to him; and he, who fancied himself so scornful of arbitrary restraints, had been afraid to break away from his desk because of what people might think of his stealing a holiday!

Her first exclamation was: "Newland—has anything happened?" and it occurred to him that it would have been more "feminine" if she had instantly read in his eyes why he had come. But when he answered: "Yes—I found I had to see you," her happy blushes took the chill from her surprise, and he saw how easily he would be forgiven, and how soon even Mr. Letterblair's mild disapproval would be smiled away by a tolerant family.

Early as it was, the main street was no place for any but formal greetings, and Archer longed to be alone with May, and to pour out all his tenderness and his impatience. It still lacked an hour to the late Welland breakfast time, and instead of asking him to come in she proposed that they should walk out to an old orange garden beyond the town. She had just been for a row on the river, and the sun that netted the little waves with gold seemed to have caught her in its meshes. Across the warm brown of her cheek her blown hair glittered like silver wire; and her eyes too looked lighter, almost pale in their youthful limpidity. As she walked beside Archer with her long swinging gait her face wore the vacant serenity of a young marble athlete.

To Archer's strained nerves the vision was as soothing as the sight of the blue sky and the lazy river. They sat down on a bench under the orange trees and he put his arm about her and kissed her. It was like drinking at a cold spring with the sun on it; but his pressure may have been more vehement than he had intended, for the blood rose to her face and she drew back as if he had startled her.

"What is it?" he asked, smiling; and she looked at him with surprise, and answered: "Nothing."

A slight embarrassment fell on them, and her hand slipped out of his. It was the only time that he had kissed her on the lips except for their fugitive embrace in the Beaufort conservatory, and he saw that she was disturbed, and shaken out of her cool boyish composure.

"Tell me what you do all day," he said, crossing his arms under his tilted-back head, and pushing his hat forward to screen the sun dazzle. To let her talk about familiar and simple things was the easiest way of carrying on his own independent train of thought; and he sat listening to her simple chronicle of swimming, sailing, and riding, varied by an occasional dance at the primitive inn when a man-of-war came in. A few pleasant people from Philadelphia and Baltimore were picnicking at the inn, and the Selfridge Merrys had come down for three weeks because Kate Merry had had bronchitis. They were planning to lay out a lawn tennis court on the sands; but no one but Kate and May had racquets, and most of the people had not even heard of the game.

All this kept her very busy, and she had not had time to do more than look at the little vellum book that Archer had sent her the week before (the *Sonnets from the Portuguese*); but she was learning by heart "How they brought the Good News from Ghent to Aix," because it was one of the first things he had ever read to her; and it amused her to be able to tell him that Kate Merry had never even heard of a poet called Robert Browning.

Presently she started up, exclaiming that they would be late for breakfast; and they hurried back to the tumbledown house with its paintless porch and unpruned hedge of plumbago and pink geraniums where the Wellands were installed for the winter. Mr. Welland's sensitive domesticity shrank from the discomforts of the slovenly southern hotel, and at immense expense, and in face of almost insuperable difficulties, Mrs. Welland was obliged, year after year, to improvise an establishment partly made up of discontented New York servants and partly drawn from the local African supply.

"The doctors want my husband to feel that he is in his own home; otherwise he would be so wretched that the climate would not do him any good," she explained, winter after winter, to the sympathizing Philadelphians and Baltimoreans; and Mr. Welland, beaming across a breakfast table miraculously supplied with the most varied delicacies, was presently saying to Archer: "You see, my dear fellow, we camp—we literally camp. I tell my wife and May that I want to teach them how to rough it."

Mr. and Mrs. Welland had been as much surprised as their daughter by the young man's sudden arrival; but it had occurred to him to explain that he had felt himself on the verge of a nasty cold, and this seemed to Mr. Welland an all-sufficient reason for abandoning any duty.

"You can't be too careful, especially toward spring," he said, heaping his plate with straw-colored griddlecakes and drowning them in golden syrup. "If I'd only been as prudent at your age May would have been dancing at the Assemblies now, instead of spending her winters in a wilderness with an old invalid."

"Oh, but I love it here, Papa; you know I do. If only Newland could stay I should like it a thousand times better than New York."

"Newland must stay till he has quite thrown off his cold," said Mrs. Welland indulgently; and the young man laughed, and said he supposed there was such a thing as one's profession.

He managed, however, after an exchange of telegrams with the firm, to make his cold last a week; and it shed an ironic light on the situation to know that Mr. Letterblair's indulgence was partly due to the satisfactory way in which his brilliant young junior partner had settled the troublesome matter of the Olenski divorce. Mr. Letterblair had let Mrs. Welland know that Mr. Archer had "rendered an invaluable service" to the whole family, and that old Mrs. Manson Mingott had been particularly pleased; and one day when May had gone for a drive with her father in the only vehicle the place produced Mrs. Welland took occasion to touch on a topic which she always avoided in her daughter's presence.

"I'm afraid Ellen's ideas are not at all like ours. She was barely eighteen when Medora Manson took her back to Europe—you remember the excitement when she appeared in black at her coming-out ball? Another of Medora's fads—really this time it was almost prophetic! That must have been at least twelve years ago; and since then Ellen has never been to America. No wonder she is completely Europeanized."

"But European society is not given to divorce: Countess Olenska thought she would be conforming to American ideas in asking for her freedom." It was the first time that the young man had pronounced her name since he had left Skuytercliff, and he felt the color rise to his cheek.

Mrs. Welland smiled compassionately. "That is just like the extraordinary things that foreigners invent about us. They think we dine at two o'clock and countenance divorce! That is why it seems to me so foolish to entertain them when they come to New York. They accept our hospitality, and then they go home and repeat the same stupid stories."

Archer made no comment on this, and Mrs. Welland continued: "But we do most thoroughly appreciate your persuading Ellen to give up the idea. Her grandmother and her Uncle Lovell could do nothing with her; both of them have written that her changing her mind was entirely due to your influence—in fact she said so to her grandmother. She has an unbounded admiration for you. Poor Ellen—she was always a wayward child. I wonder what her fate will be?"

"What we've all contrived to make it," he felt like answering. "If you'd all of you rather she should be Beaufort's mistress than some decent fellow's wife you've certainly gone the right way about it."

He wondered what Mrs. Welland would have said if he had uttered the words instead of merely thinking them. He could picture the sudden decomposure of her firm placid features, to which a lifelong mastery over trifles had given an air of factitious authority. Traces still lingered on them of a fresh beauty like her daughter's; and he asked himself if May's face was doomed to thicken into the same middle-aged image of invincible innocence.

Ah, no, he did not want May to have that kind of innocence, the innocence that seals the mind against imagination and the heart against experience!

"I verily believe," Mrs. Welland continued, "that if the horrible business had come out in the newspapers it would have been my husband's deathblow. I don't know any of the details; I only ask not to, as I told poor Ellen when she tried to talk to me about it. Having an invalid to care for, I have to keep my mind bright and happy. But Mr. Welland was terribly upset; he had a slight temperature every morning while we were waiting to hear what had been decided. It was the horror of his girl's learning that such things were possible—but of course, dear Newland, you felt that too. We all knew that you were thinking of May."

"I'm always thinking of May," the young man rejoined, rising to cut short the conversation.

He had meant to seize the opportunity of his private talk with Mrs. Welland to urge her to advance the date of his marriage. But he could think of no arguments that would move her, and with a sense of relief he saw Mr. Welland and May driving up to the door.

His only hope was to plead again with May, and on the day before his departure he walked with her to the ruinous garden of the Spanish Mission. The background lent itself to allusions to European scenes; and May, who was looking her loveliest under a wide-brimmed hat that cast a shadow of mystery over her too-clear eyes, kindled into eagerness as he spoke of Granada and the Alhambra.

"We might be seeing it all this spring—even the Easter ceremonies at Seville," he urged, exaggerating his demands in the hope of a larger concession.

"Easter in Seville? And it will be Lent next week!" she laughed.

"Why shouldn't we be married in Lent?" he rejoined, but she looked so shocked that he saw his mistake.

"Of course I didn't mean that, dearest, but soon after Easter—so that we could sail at the end of April. I know I could arrange it at the office."

She smiled dreamily upon the possibility; but he perceived that to dream of it sufficed her. It was like hearing him read aloud out of his poetry books the beautiful things that could not possibly happen in real life.

"Oh, do go on, Newland. I do love your descriptions."

"But why should they be only descriptions? Why shouldn't we make them real?"

"We shall, dearest, of course; next year." Her voice lingered over it.

"Don't you want them to be real sooner? Can't I persuade you to break away now?"

She bowed her head, vanishing from him under her conniving hat brim.

"Why should we dream away another year? Look at me, dear! Don't you understand how I want you for my wife?"

For a moment she remained motionless; then she raised on him eyes of such despairing clearness that he half-released her waist from his hold. But suddenly her look changed and deepened inscrutably. "I'm not sure if I *do* understand," she said. "Is it—is it because you're not certain of continuing to care for me?"

Archer sprang up from his seat. "My God—perhaps—I don't know," he broke out angrily.

May Welland rose also; as they faced each other she seemed to grow in womanly stature and dignity. Both were silent for a moment, as if dismayed by the unforeseen trend of their words: then she said in a low voice: "If that is it—is there someone else?"

"Someone else—between you and me?" He echoed her words slowly, as though they were only half-intelligible and he wanted time to repeat the question to himself. She seemed to catch the uncertainty of his voice, for she went on in a deepening tone: "Let us talk frankly, Newland. Sometimes I've felt a difference in you; especially since our engagement has been announced."

"Dear—what madness!" he recovered himself to exclaim.

She met his protest with a faint smile. "If it is, it won't hurt us to talk about it." She paused, and added, lifting her head with one of her noble movements: "Or even if it's true: why shouldn't we speak of it? You might so easily have made a mistake."

He lowered his head, staring at the black leaf pattern on the sunny path at their feet. "Mistakes are always easy to make; but if I had made one of the kind you suggest, is it likely that I should be imploring you to hasten our marriage?"

She looked downward too, disturbing the pattern with the point of her sunshade while she struggled for expression. "Yes," she said at length. "You might want—once for all—to settle the question: it's one way."

Her quiet lucidity startled him, but did not mislead him into thinking her insensible. Under her hat brim he saw the pallor of her profile, and a slight tremor of the nostril above her resolutely steadied lips.

"Well—?" he questioned, sitting down on the bench and looking up at her with a frown that he tried to make playful.

She dropped back into her seat and went on: "You mustn't think that a girl knows as little as her parents imagine. One hears and one notices—one has one's feelings and ideas. And of course, long before you told me that you cared for me, I'd known that there was someone else you were interested in; everyone was talking about it two years ago at Newport. And once I saw you sitting together on the verandah at a dance—and when she came back into the house her face was sad, and I felt sorry for her; I remembered it afterward, when we were engaged."

Her voice had sunk almost to a whisper, and she sat clasping and unclasping her hands about the handle of her sunshade. The young man laid his upon them with a gentle pressure; his heart dilated with an inexpressible relief.

"My dear child—was *that* it? If you only knew the truth!"

She raised her head quickly. "Then there is a truth I don't know?"

He kept his hand over hers. "I meant, the truth about the old story you speak of."

"But that's what I want to know, Newland—what I ought to know. I couldn't have my happiness made out of a wrong—an unfairness—to somebody else. And I want to believe that it would be the same with you. What sort of a life could we build on such foundations?"

Her face had taken on a look of such tragic courage that he felt like bowing himself down at her feet. "I've wanted to say this for a long time," she went on. "I've wanted to tell you that, when two people really love each other, I understand that there may be situations which make it right that they should—should go against public opinion. And if you feel yourself in any way pledged . . . pledged to the person we've spoken of . . . and if there is any way . . . any way in which you can fulfill your pledge . . . even by her getting a divorce . . . Newland, don't give her up because of me!"

His surprise at discovering that her fears had fastened upon an

episode so remote and so completely of the past as his love affair
with Mrs. Thorley Rushworth gave way to wonder at the generosity of her view. There was something superhuman in an attitude
so recklessly unorthodox, and if other problems had not pressed
on him he would have been lost in wonder at the prodigy of the
Wellands' daughter urging him to marry his former mistress. But
he was still dizzy with the glimpse of the precipice they had
skirted, and full of a new awe at the mystery of young girlhood.

For a moment he could not speak; then he said: "There is no
pledge—no obligation whatever—of the kind you think. Such
cases don't always—present themselves quite as simply as . . .
But that's no matter . . . I love your generosity, because I feel as
you do about those things . . . I feel that each case must be
judged individually, on its own merits . . . irrespective of stupid
conventionalities . . . I mean, each woman's right to her liberty—" He pulled himself up, startled by the turn his thoughts
had taken, and went on, looking at her with a smile: "Since you
understand so many things, dearest, can't you go a little farther,
and understand the uselessness of our submitting to another
form of the same foolish conventionalities? If there's no one and
nothing between us, isn't that an argument for marrying quickly,
rather than for more delay?"

She flushed with joy and lifted her face to his; as he bent to it
he saw that her eyes were full of happy tears. But in another
moment she seemed to have descended from her womanly eminence to helpless and timorous girlhood; and he understood that
her courage and initiative were all for others, and that she had
none for herself. It was evident that the effort of speaking had
been much greater than her studied composure betrayed, and
that at his first word of reassurance she had dropped back into
the usual, as a too-adventurous child takes refuge in its mother's
arms.

Archer had no heart to go on pleading with her; he was too
much disappointed at the vanishing of the new being who had
cast that one deep look at him from her transparent eyes. May
seemed to be aware of his disappointment, but without knowing
how to alleviate it; and they stood up and walked silently home.

# —17—

"YOUR COUSIN the countess called on Mother while you were away," Janey Archer announced to her brother on the evening of his return.

The young man, who was dining alone with his mother and sister, glanced up in surprise and saw Mrs. Archer's gaze demurely bent on her plate. Mrs. Archer did not regard her seclusion from the world as a reason for being forgotten by it; and Newland guessed that she was slightly annoyed that he should be surprised by Madame Olenska's visit.

"She had on a black velvet polonaise with jet buttons, and a tiny green monkey muff. I never saw her so stylishly dressed," Janey continued. "She came alone, early on Sunday afternoon; luckily the fire was lit in the drawing room. She had one of those new card cases. She said she wanted to know us because you'd been so good to her."

Newland laughed. "Madame Olenska always takes that tone about her friends. She's very happy at being among her own people again."

"Yes, so she told us," said Mrs. Archer. "I must say she seems thankful to be here."

"I hope you liked her, Mother."

Mrs. Archer drew her lips together. "She certainly lays herself out to please, even when she is calling on an old lady."

"Mother doesn't think her simple," Janey interjected, her eyes screwed upon her brother's face.

"It's just my old-fashioned feeling; dear May is my ideal," said Mrs. Archer.

"Ah," said her son, "they're not alike."

Archer had left St. Augustine charged with many messages for old Mrs. Mingott; and a day or two after his return to town he called on her.

The old lady received him with unusual warmth; she was grateful to him for persuading the Countess Olenska to give up the idea of a divorce; and when he told her that he had deserted the office without leave, and rushed down to St. Augustine simply because he wanted to see May, she gave an adipose chuckle and patted his knee with her puffball hand.

"Ah, ah—so you kicked over the traces, did you? And I suppose Augusta and Welland pulled long faces, and behaved as if the end of the world had come? But little May—she knew better, I'll be bound?"

"I hoped she did; but after all she wouldn't agree to what I'd gone down to ask for."

"Wouldn't she indeed? And what was that?"

"I wanted to get her to promise that we should be married in April. What's the use of our wasting another year?"

Mrs. Manson Mingott screwed up her little mouth into a grimace of mimic prudery and twinkled at him through malicious lids. " 'Ask Mamma,' I suppose—the usual story. Ah, these Mingotts—all alike! Born in a rut, and you can't root 'em out of it. When I built this house you'd have thought I was moving to California! Nobody ever *had* built above Fortieth Street—no, says I, nor above the Battery either, before Christopher Columbus discovered America. No, no; not one of them wants to be different; they're as scared of it as the smallpox. Ah, my dear Mr. Archer, I thank my stars I'm nothing but a vulgar Spicer; but there's not one of my own children that takes after me but my little Ellen." She broke off, still twinkling at him, and asked, with the casual irrelevance of old age: "Now, why in the world didn't you marry my little Ellen?"

Archer laughed. "For one thing, she wasn't there to be married."

"No—to be sure; more's the pity. And now it's too late; her life is finished." She spoke with the cold-blooded complacency of the aged throwing earth into the grave of young hopes. The young man's heart grew chill, and he said hurriedly: "Can't I persuade you to use your influence with the Wellands, Mrs. Mingott? I wasn't made for long engagements."

Old Catherine beamed on him approvingly. "No, I can see that. You've got a quick eye. When you were a little boy I've no doubt you liked to be helped first." She threw back her head with a laugh that made her chins ripple like little waves. "Ah, here's my Ellen now!" she exclaimed as the portières parted behind her.

Madame Olenska came forward with a smile. Her face looked vivid and happy, and she held out her hand gaily to Archer while she stooped to her grandmother's kiss.

"I was just saying to him, my dear: 'Now, why didn't you marry my little Ellen?' "

Madame Olenska looked at Archer, still smiling. "And what did he answer?"

"Oh, my darling, I leave you to find that out! He's been down to Florida to see his sweetheart."

"Yes, I know." She still looked at him. "I went to see your mother, to ask where you'd gone. I sent a note that you never answered, and I was afraid you were ill."

He muttered something about leaving unexpectedly, in a great hurry, and having intended to write to her from St. Augustine.

"And of course once you were there you never thought of me again!" She continued to beam on him with a gaiety that might have been a studied assumption of indifference.

"If she still needs me, she's determined not to let me see it," he thought, stung by her manner. He wanted to thank her for having been to see his mother, but under the ancestress's malicious eye he felt himself tongue-tied and constrained.

"Look at him—in such hot haste to get married that he took French leave and rushed down to implore the silly girl on his knees! That's something like a lover—that's the way handsome Bob Spicer carried off my poor mother; and then got tired of her before I was weaned—though they only had to wait eight months for me! But there—you're not a Spicer, young man; luckily for you and for May. It's only my poor Ellen that has kept any of their wicked blood; the rest of them are all model Mingotts," cried the old lady scornfully.

Archer was aware that Madame Olenska, who had seated herself at her grandmother's side, was still thoughtfully scrutinizing him. The gaiety had faded from her eyes, and she said with great gentleness: "Surely, Granny, we can persuade them between us to do as he wishes."

Archer rose to go, and as his hand met Madame Olenska's he

felt that she was waiting for him to make some allusion to her unanswered letter.

"When can I see you?" he asked as she walked with him to the door of the room.

"Whenever you like, but it must be soon if you want to see the little house again. I am moving next week."

A pang shot through him at the memory of his lamplit hours in the low-studded drawing room. Few as they had been, they were thick with memories.

"Tomorrow evening?"

She nodded. "Tomorrow, yes, but early. I'm going out."

The next day was a Sunday, and if she were "going out" on a Sunday evening it could, of course, be only to Mrs. Lemuel Struthers's. He felt a slight movement of annoyance, not so much at her going there (for he rather liked her going where she pleased in spite of the van der Luydens), but because it was the kind of house at which she was sure to meet Beaufort, where she must have known beforehand that she would meet him—and where she was probably going for that purpose.

"Very well, tomorrow evening," he repeated, inwardly resolved that he would not go early, and that by reaching her door late he would either prevent her from going to Mrs. Struthers's, or else arrive after she had started—which, all things considered, would no doubt be the simplest solution.

It was only half-past eight, after all, when he rang the bell under the wisteria; not as late as he had intended by half an hour—but a singular restlessness had driven him to her door. He reflected, however, that Mrs. Struthers's Sunday evenings were not like a ball, and that her guests, as if to minimize their delinquency, usually went early.

The one thing he had not counted on, in entering Madame Olenska's hall, was to find hats and overcoats there. Why had she bidden him to come early if she was having people to dine? On a closer inspection of the garments besides which Nastasia was laying his own, his resentment gave way to curiosity. The overcoats were in fact the very strangest he had ever seen under a polite roof; and it took but a glance to assure himself that neither of them belonged to Julius Beaufort. One was a shaggy yellow ulster of "reach-me-down" cut, the other a very old and rusty cloak with a cape—something like what the French called a "Macfarlane." This garment, which appeared to be made for a person of prodigious size, had evidently seen long and hard wear, and its greenish-black folds gave out a moist sawdusty smell suggestive of prolonged sessions against barroom walls. On it lay a ragged gray scarf and an odd felt hat of semiclerical shape.

Archer raised his eyebrows inquiringly at Nastasia, who raised hers in return with a fatalistic *"Già!"* as she threw open the drawing-room door.

The young man saw at once that his hostess was not in the room; then, with surprise, he discovered another lady standing by the fire. This lady, who was long, lean, and loosely put together, was clad in raiment intricately looped and fringed, with plaids and stripes and bands of plain color disposed in a design to which the clue seemed missing. Her hair, which had tried to turn white and only succeeded in fading, was surmounted by a Spanish comb and black lace scarf, and silk mittens, visibly darned, covered her rheumatic hands.

Beside her, in a cloud of cigar smoke, stood the owners of the two overcoats, both in morning clothes that they had evidently not taken off since morning. In one of the two, Archer, to his surprise, recognized Ned Winsett; the other and older, who was unknown to him, and whose gigantic frame declared him to be the wearer of the "Macfarlane," had a feebly leonine head with crumpled gray hair, and moved his arms with large pawing gestures, as though he were distributing lay blessings to a kneeling multitude.

These three persons stood together on the hearth rug, their eyes fixed on an extraordinarily large bouquet of crimson roses, with a knot of purple pansies at their base, that lay on the sofa where Madame Olenska usually sat.

"What they must have cost at this season—though of course it's the sentiment one cares about!" the lady was saying in a sighing staccato as Archer came in.

The three turned with surprise at his appearance, and the lady, advancing, held out her hand.

"Dear Mr. Archer—almost my cousin Newland!" she said. "I am the Marchioness Manson."

Archer bowed, and she continued: "My Ellen has taken me in for a few days. I came from Cuba, where I have been spending the winter with Spanish friends—such delightful distinguished people: the highest nobility of old Castile—how I wish you could know them! But I was called away by our dear great friend here, Dr. Carver. You don't know Dr. Agathon Carver, founder of the Valley of Love Community?"

Dr. Carver inclined his leonine head, and the marchioness continued: "Ah, New York—New York—how little the life of the spirit has reached it! But I see you do know Mr. Winsett."

"Oh, yes—*I* reached him some time ago, but not by that route," Winsett said with his dry smile.

The marchioness shook her head reprovingly. "How do you know, Mr. Winsett? The spirit bloweth where it listeth."

"List—oh, list!" interjected Dr. Carver in a stentorian murmur.

"But do sit down, Mr. Archer. We four have been having a delightful little dinner together, and my child has gone up to dress. She expects you; she will be down in a moment. We were just admiring these marvelous flowers, which will surprise her when she reappears."

Winsett remained on his feet. "I'm afraid I must be off. Please tell Madame Olenska that we shall all feel lost when she abandons our street. This house has been an oasis."

"Ah, but she won't abandon *you*. Poetry and art are the breath of life to her. It *is* poetry you write, Mr. Winsett?"

"Well, no, but I sometimes read it," said Winsett, including the group in a general nod and slipping out of the room.

"A caustic spirit—*un peu sauvage*. But so witty; Dr. Carver, you *do* think him witty?"

"I never think of wit," said Dr. Carver severely.

"Ah—ah—you never think of wit! How merciless he is to us weak mortals, Mr. Archer! But he lives only in the life of the spirit; and tonight he is mentally preparing the lecture he is to deliver presently at Mrs. Blenker's. Dr. Carver, would there be time, before you start for the Blenkers' to explain to Mr. Archer your illuminating discovery of the Direct Contact? But no, I see it is nearly nine o'clock, and we have no right to detain you while so many are waiting for your message."

Dr. Carver looked slightly disappointed at this conclusion, but, having compared his ponderous gold timepiece with Madame Olenska's little traveling clock, he reluctantly gathered up his mighty limbs for departure.

"I shall see you later, dear friend?" he suggested to the marchioness, who replied with a smile: "As soon as Ellen's carriage comes I will join you; I do hope the lecture won't have begun."

Dr. Carver looked thoughtfully at Archer. "Perhaps, if this young gentleman is interested in my experiences, Mrs. Blenker might allow you to bring him with you?"

"Oh, dear friend, if it were possible—I am sure she would be too happy. But I fear my Ellen counts on Mr. Archer herself."

"That," said Dr. Carver, "is unfortunate—but here is my card." He handed it to Archer, who read on it, in Gothic characters:

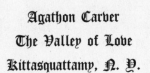

Agathon Carver
The Valley of Love
Kittasquattamy, N. Y.

Dr. Carver bowed himself out, and Mrs. Manson, with a sigh that might have been either of regret or relief, again waved Archer to a seat.

"Ellen will be down in a moment; and before she comes, I am so glad of this quiet moment with you."

Archer murmured his pleasure at their meeting, and the marchioness continued, in her low sighing accents: "I know everything, dear Mr. Archer—my child has told me all you have done for her. Your wise advice: your courageous firmness—thank heaven it was not too late!"

The young man listened with considerable embarrassment. Was there anyone, he wondered, to whom Madame Olenska had not proclaimed his intervention in her private affairs?

"Madame Olenska exaggerates. I simply gave her a legal opinion, as she asked me to."

"Ah, but in doing it—in doing it you were the unconscious

instrument of—of—what word have we moderns for Providence, Mr. Archer?" cried the lady, tilting her head on one side and drooping her lids mysteriously. "Little did you know that at that very moment I was being appealed to: being approached, in fact—from the other side of the Atlantic!"

She glanced over her shoulder, as though fearful of being overheard, and then, drawing her chair nearer, and raising a tiny ivory fan to her lips, breathed behind it: "By the count himself— my poor, mad, foolish Olenski, who asks only to take her back on her own terms."

"Good God!" Archer exclaimed, springing up.

"You are horrified? Yes, of course, I understand. I don't defend poor Stanislas, though he has always called me his best friend. He does not defend himself—he casts himself at her feet: in my person." She tapped her emaciated bosom. "I have his letter here."

"A letter?— Has Madame Olenska seen it?" Archer stammered, his brain whirling with the shock of the announcement.

The Marchioness Manson shook her head softly. "Time—time. I must have time. I know my Ellen—haughty, intractable; shall I say, just a shade unforgiving?"

"But, good heavens, to forgive is one thing; to go back into that hell—"

"Ah, yes," the marchioness acquiesced. "So she describes it— my sensitive child! But on the material side, Mr. Archer, if one may stoop to consider such things; do you know what she is giving up? Those roses there on the sofa—acres like them, under glass and in the open, in his matchless terraced gardens at Nice! Jewels—historic pearls: the Sobieski emeralds—sables—but she cares nothing for all these! Art and beauty, those she does care for, she lives for, as I always have, and those also surrounded her. Pictures, priceless furniture, music, brilliant conversation—ah, that, my dear young man, if you'll excuse me, is what you've no conception of here! And she had it all, and the homage of the greatest. She tells me she is not thought handsome in New York— good heavens! Her portrait has been painted nine times; the greatest artists in Europe have begged for the privilege. Are these things nothing? And the remorse of an adoring husband?"

As the Marchioness Manson rose to her climax her face assumed an expression of ecstatic retrospection which would have moved Archer's mirth had he not been numb with amazement.

He would have laughed if anyone had foretold to him that his first sight of poor Medora Manson would have been in the guise of a messenger of Satan; but he was in no mood for laughing now, and she seemed to him to come straight out of the hell from which Ellen Olenska had just escaped.

"She knows nothing yet—of all this?" he asked abruptly.

Mrs. Manson laid a purple finger on her lips. "Nothing directly—but does she suspect? Who can tell? The truth is, Mr. Archer, I have been waiting to see you. From the moment I heard of the firm stand you had taken, and of your influence over her, I hoped it might be possible to count on your support—to convince you . . ."

"That she ought to go back? I would rather see her dead!" cried the young man violently.

"Ah," the Marchioness murmured, without visible resentment. For a while she sat in her armchair, opening and shutting the absurd ivory fan between her mittened fingers, but suddenly she lifted her head and listened.

"Here she comes," she said in a rapid whisper, and then, pointing to the bouquet on the sofa: "Am I to understand that you prefer *that*, Mr. Archer? After all, marriage is marriage . . . and my niece is still a wife. . . ."

# ——18——

**W**HAT ARE you two plotting together, Aunt Medora?" Madame Olenska cried as she came into the room.

She was dressed as if for a ball. Everything about her shimmered and glimmered softly, as if her dress had been woven out of candle beams; and she carried her head high, like a pretty woman challenging a roomful of rivals.

"We were saying, my dear, that here was something beautiful to surprise you with," Mrs. Manson rejoined, rising to her feet and pointing archly to the flowers.

Madame Olenska stopped short and looked at the bouquet. Her color did not change, but a sort of white radiance of anger ran over her like summer lightning. "Ah," she exclaimed, in a shrill voice that the young man had never heard, "who is ridiculous enough to send me a bouquet? Why a bouquet? And why tonight of all nights? I am not going to a ball; I am not a girl engaged to be married. But some people are always ridiculous."

She turned back to the door, opened it, and called out: "Nastasia!"

The ubiquitous handmaiden promptly appeared, and Archer heard Madame Olenska say, in an Italian that she seemed to pronounce with intentional deliberateness in order that he might follow it: "Here—throw this into the dustbin!" and then, as Nastasia stared protestingly: "But no—it's not the fault of the poor flowers. Tell the boy to carry them to the house three doors away, the house of Mr. Winsett, the dark gentleman who dined here. His wife is ill—they may give her pleasure. . . . The boy is out, you say? Then, my dear one, run yourself; here, put my cloak over you and fly. I want the thing out of the house immediately! And, as you live, don't say they come from me!"

She flung her velvet opera cloak over the maid's shoulders and turned back into the drawing room, shutting the door sharply. Her bosom was rising high under its lace, and for a moment

Archer thought she was about to cry; but she burst into a laugh instead, and looking from the marchioness to Archer, asked abruptly: "And you two—have you made friends!"

"It's for Mr. Archer to say, darling; he has waited patiently while you were dressing."

"Yes—I gave you time enough: my hair wouldn't go," Madame Olenska said, raising her hand to the heaped-up curls of her chignon. "But that reminds me: I see Dr. Carver is gone, and you'll be late at the Blenkers'. Mr. Archer, will you put my aunt in the carriage?"

She followed the marchioness into the hall, saw her fitted into a miscellaneous heap of overshoes, shawls, and tippets, and called from the doorstep: "Mind, the carriage is to be back for me at ten!" Then she returned to the drawing room, where Archer, on reentering it, found her standing by the mantelpiece, examining herself in the mirror. It was not usual, in New York society, for a lady to address her parlormaid as "my dear one," and send her out on an errand wrapped in her own opera cloak; and Archer, through all his deeper feelings, tasted the pleasurable excitement of being in a world where action followed on emotion with such Olympian speed.

Madame Olenska did not move when he came up behind her, and for a second their eyes met in the mirror; then she turned, threw herself into her sofa corner, and sighed out: "There's time for a cigarette."

He handed her the box and lit a spill for her; and as the flame flashed up into her face she glanced at him with laughing eyes and said: "What do you think of me in a temper?"

Archer paused a moment; then he answered with sudden resolution: "It makes me understand what your aunt has been saying about you."

"I knew she'd been talking about me. Well?"

"She said you were used to all kinds of things—splendors and amusements and excitements—that we could never hope to give you here."

Madame Olenska smiled faintly into the circle of smoke about her lips.

"Medora is incorrigibly romantic. It has made up to her for so many things!"

Archer hesitated again, and again took his risk. "Is your aunt's romanticism always consistent with accuracy?"

"You mean: does she speak the truth?" Her niece considered. "Well, I'll tell you: in almost everything she says, there's something true and something untrue. But why do you ask? What has she been telling you?"

He looked away into the fire, and then back at her shining presence. His heart tightened with the thought that this was their last evening by that fireside, and that in a moment the carriage would come to carry her away.

"She says—she pretends that Count Olenski has asked her to persuade you to go back to him."

Madame Olenska made no answer. She sat motionless, holding her cigarette in her half-lifted hand. The expression of her face had not changed, and Archer remembered that he had before noticed her apparent incapacity for surprise.

"You knew, then?" he broke out.

She was silent for so long that the ash dropped from her cigarette. She brushed it to the floor. "She has hinted about a letter: poor darling! Medora's hints—"

"Is it at your husband's request that she has arrived here suddenly?"

Madame Olenska seemed to consider this question also. "There again: one can't tell. She told me she had had a 'spiritual summons,' whatever that is, from Dr. Carver. I'm afraid she's going to marry Dr. Carver . . . poor Medora, there's always someone she wants to marry. But perhaps the people in Cuba just got tired of her! I think she was with them as a sort of paid companion. Really, I don't know why she came."

"But you do believe she has a letter from your husband?"

Again Madame Olenska brooded silently; then she said: "After all, it was to be expected."

The young man rose and went to lean against the fireplace. A sudden restlessness possessed him, and he was tongue-tied by the sense that their minutes were numbered, and that at any moment he might hear the wheels of the returning carriage.

"You know that your aunt believes you will go back?"

Madame Olenska raised her head quickly. A deep blush rose to her face and spread over her neck and shoulders. She blushed seldom and painfully, as if it hurt her like a burn.

"Many cruel things have been believed of me," she said.

"Oh, Ellen—forgive me; I'm a fool and a brute!"

She smiled a little. "You are horribly nervous; you have your own troubles. I know you think the Wellands are unreasonable about your marriage, and of course I agree with you. In Europe people don't understand our long American engagements; I suppose they are not as calm as we are." She pronounced the "we" with a faint emphasis that gave it an ironic sound.

Archer felt the irony but did not dare to take it up. After all, she had perhaps purposely deflected the conversation from her own affairs, and after the pain his last words had evidently caused her he felt that all he could do was to follow her lead. But the sense of the waning hour made him desperate: he could not bear the thought that a barrier of words should drop between them again.

"Yes," he said abruptly. "I went south to ask May to marry me after Easter. There's no reason why we shouldn't be married then."

"And May adores you—and yet you couldn't convince her? I thought her too intelligent to be the slave of such absurd superstitions."

"She *is* too intelligent—she's not their slave."

Madame Olenska looked at him. "Well, then—I don't understand."

Archer reddened, and hurried on with a rush. "We had a frank talk—almost the first. She thinks my impatience a bad sign."

"Merciful heavens—a bad sign?"

"She thinks it means that I can't trust myself to go on caring for her. She thinks, in short, I want to marry her at once to get away from someone that I—care for more."

Madame Olenska examined this curiously. "But if she thinks that—why isn't she in a hurry too?"

"Because she's not like that: she's so much nobler. She insists all the more on the long engagement, to give me time—"

"Time to give her up for the other woman?"

"If I want to."

Madame Olenska leaned toward the fire and gazed into it with fixed eyes. Down the quiet street Archer heard the approaching trot of her horses.

"That *is* noble," she said, with a slight break in her voice.

"Yes. But it's ridiculous."

"Ridiculous? Because you don't care for anyone else?"

"Because I don't mean to marry anyone else."

"Ah." There was another long interval. At length she looked up at him and asked: "This other woman—does she love you?"

"Oh, there's no other woman. I mean, the person that May was thinking of is—was never—"

"Then, why, after all, are you in such haste?"

"There's your carriage," said Archer.

She half-rose and looked about her with absent eyes. Her fan and gloves lay on the sofa beside her and she picked them up mechanically.

"Yes, I suppose I must be going."

"You're going to Mrs. Struther's?"

"Yes." She smiled and added: "I must go where I am invited, or I should be too lonely. Why not come with me?"

Archer felt that at any cost he must keep her beside him, must make her give him the rest of her evening. Ignoring her question, he continued to lean against the chimneypiece, his eyes fixed on the hand in which she held her gloves and fan, as if watching to see if he had the power to make her drop them.

"May guessed the truth," he said. "There is another woman— but not the one she thinks."

Ellen Olenska made no answer, and did not move. After a moment he sat down beside her, and, taking her hand, softly unclasped it, so that the gloves and fan fell on the sofa between them.

She started up, and freeing herself from him moved away to the other side of the hearth. "Ah, don't make love to me! Too many people have done that," she said, frowning.

Archer, changing color, stood up also: it was the bitterest rebuke she could have given him. "I have never made love to you," he said, "and I never shall. But you are the woman I would have married if it had been possible for either of us."

"Possible for either of us?" She looked at him with unfeigned astonishment. "And you say that—when it's you who've made it impossible?"

He stared at her, groping in a blackness through which a single arrow of light tore its blinding way.

"*I've* made it impossible—?"

"You, you, *you!*" she cried, her lip trembling like a child's on the verge of tears. "Isn't it you who made me give up divorcing—give it up because you showed me how selfish and wicked it was, how one must sacrifice one's self to preserve the dignity of marriage . . . and to spare one's family the publicity, the scandal? And because my family was going to be your family—for May's sake and for yours—I did what you told me, what you proved to me that I ought to do. Ah," she broke out with a sudden laugh, "I've made no secret of having done it for you!"

She sank down on the sofa again, crouching among the festive ripples of her dress like a stricken masquerader; and the young man stood by the fireplace and continued to gaze at her without moving.

"Good God," he groaned. "When I thought—"

"You thought?"

"Ah, don't ask me what I thought!"

Still looking at her, he saw the same burning flush creep up her neck to her face. She sat upright, facing him with a rigid dignity.

"I do ask you."

"Well, then: there were things in that letter you asked me to read—"

"My husband's letter?"

"Yes."

"I had nothing to fear from that letter: absolutely nothing! All I feared was to bring notoriety, scandal, on the family—on you and May."

"Good God," he groaned again, bowing his face in his hands.

The silence that followed lay on them with the weight of things final and irrevocable. It seemed to Archer to be crushing him down like his own gravestone; in all the wide future he saw nothing that would ever lift that load from his heart. He did not move from his place, or raise his head from his hands; his hidden eyeballs went on staring into utter darkness.

"At least I loved you—" he brought out.

On the other side of the hearth, from the sofa corner where he supposed that she still crouched, he heard a faint stifled crying like a child's. He started up and came to her side.

"Ellen! What madness! Why are you crying? Nothing's done that can't be undone. I'm still free, and you're going to be." He had her in his arms, her face like a wet flower at his lips, and all their vain terrors shriveling up like ghosts at sunrise. The one thing that astonished him now was that he should have stood for five minutes arguing with her across the width of the room, when just touching her made everything so simple.

She gave him back all his kiss, but after a moment he felt her stiffening in his arms, and she put him aside and stood up.

"Ah, my poor Newland—I suppose this had to be. But it doesn't in the least alter things," she said, looking down at him in her turn from the hearth.

"It alters the whole of life for me."

"No, no—it mustn't, it can't. You're engaged to May Welland, and I'm married."

He stood up too, flushed and resolute. "Nonsense! It's too late for that sort of thing. We've no right to lie to other people or to ourselves. We won't talk of your marriage, but do you see me marrying May after this?"

She stood silent, resting her thin elbows on the mantelpiece, her profile reflected in the glass behind her. One of the locks of her chignon had become loosened and hung on her neck; she looked haggard and almost old.

"I don't see you," she said at length, "putting that question to May. Do you?"

He gave a reckless shrug. "It's too late to do anything else."

"You say that because it's the easiest thing to say at this moment—not because it's true. In reality it's too late to do anything but what we'd both decided on."

"Ah, I don't understand you!"

She forced a pitiful smile that pinched her face instead of smoothing it. "You don't understand because you haven't yet guessed how you've changed things for me: oh, from the first— long before I knew all you'd done."

"All I'd done?"

"Yes. I was perfectly unconscious at first that people here were shy of me—that they thought I was a dreadful sort of person. It seems they had even refused to meet me at dinner. I found that out afterward; and how you'd made your mother go with you to the van der Luydens'; and how you'd insisted on announcing your engagement at the Beaufort ball, so that I might have two families to stand by me instead of one—"

At that he broke into a laugh.

"Just imagine," she said, "how stupid and unobservant I was! I knew nothing of all this till Granny blurted it out one day. New York simply meant peace and freedom to me: it was coming home. And I was so happy at being among my own people that everyone I met seemed kind and good, and glad to see me. But from the very beginning," she continued, "I felt there was no one as kind as you; no one who gave me reasons that I understood for doing what at first seemed so hard and—unnecessary. The very good people didn't convince me; I felt they'd never been tempted. But you knew, you understood; you had felt the world outside tugging at one with all its golden hands—and yet you hated the things it asks of one; you hated happiness bought by disloyalty and cruelty and indifference. That was what I'd never known before—and it's better than anything I've known."

She spoke in a low even voice, without tears or visible agitation; and each word, as it dropped from her, fell into his breast like burning lead. He sat bowed over, his head between his hands, staring at the hearth rug, and at the tip of the satin shoe that showed under her dress. Suddenly he knelt down and kissed the shoe.

She bent over him, laying her hands on his shoulders, and looking at him with eyes so deep that he remained motionless under her gaze.

"Ah, don't let us undo what you've done!" she cried. "I can't go back now to that other way of thinking. I can't love you unless I give you up."

His arms were yearning up to her; but she drew away, and they remained facing each other, divided by the distance that her words had created. Then, abruptly, his anger overflowed.

"And Beaufort? Is he to replace me?"

As the words sprang out he was prepared for an answering

flare of anger; and he would have welcomed it as fuel for his own. But Madame Olenska only grew a shade paler, and stood with her arms hanging down before her, and her head slightly bent, as her way was when she pondered a question.

"He's waiting for you now at Mrs. Struthers's; why don't you go to him?" Archer sneered.

She turned to ring the bell. "I shall not go out this evening; tell the carriage to go and fetch the Signora Marchesa," she said when the maid came.

After the door had closed again Archer continued to look at her with bitter eyes. "Why this sacrifice? Since you tell me that you're lonely I've no right to keep you from your friends."

She smiled a little under her wet lashes. "I shan't be lonely now. I *was* lonely; I *was* afraid. But the emptiness and the darkness are gone; when I turn back into myself now I'm like a child going at night into a room where there's always a light."

Her tone and her look still enveloped her in a soft inaccessibility, and Archer groaned out again: "I don't understand you!"

"Yet you understand May!"

He reddened under the retort, but kept his eyes on her. "May is ready to give me up."

"What! Three days after you've entreated her on your knees to hasten your marriage?"

"She's refused; that gives me the right—"

"Ah, you've taught me what an ugly word that is," she said.

He turned away with a sense of utter weariness. He felt as though he had been struggling for hours up the face of a steep precipice, and now, just as he had fought his way to the top, his hold had given way and he was pitching down headlong into darkness.

If he could have got her in his arms again he might have swept away her arguments, but she still held him at a distance by something inscrutably aloof in her look and attitude, and by his own awed sense of her sincerity. At length he began to plead again.

"If we do this now it will be worse afterward—worse for everyone—"

"No—no—no!" she almost screamed, as if he frightened her.

At that moment the bell sent a long tinkle through the house.

They had heard no carriage stopping at the door, and they stood motionless, looking at each other with startled eyes.

Outside, Nastasia's step crossed the hall, the outer door opened, and a moment later she came in carrying a telegram which she handed to the Countess Olenska.

"The lady was very happy at the flowers," Nastasia said, smoothing her apron. "She thought it was her *signor marito* who had sent them, and she cried a little and said it was a folly."

Her mistress smiled and took the yellow envelope. She tore it open and carried it to the lamp; then, when the door had closed again, she handed the telegram to Archer.

It was dated from St. Augustine, and addressed to the Countess Olenska. In it he read: "Granny's telegram successful. Papa and Mamma agree marriage after Easter. Am telegraphing Newland. Am too happy for words and love you dearly. Your grateful May."

Half an hour later, when Archer unlocked his own front door, he found a similar envelope on the hall table on top of his pile of notes and letters. The message inside the envelope was also from May Welland, and ran as follows: "Parents consent wedding Tuesday after Easter at twelve Grace Church eight bridesmaids please see Rector so happy love May."

Archer crumpled up the yellow sheet as if the gesture could annihilate the news it contained. Then he pulled out a small pocket diary and turned over the pages with trembling fingers; but he did not find what he wanted, and cramming the telegram into his pocket he mounted the stairs.

A light was shining through the door of the little hall room which served Janey as a dressing room and boudoir, and her brother rapped impatiently on the panel. The door opened, and his sister stood before him in her immemorial purple flannel dressing gown, with her hair "on pins." Her face looked pale and apprehensive.

"Newland! I hope there's no bad news in that telegram? I waited on purpose, in case—" (No item of his correspondence was safe from Janey.)

He took no notice of her question. "Look here—what day is Easter this year?"

She looked shocked at such unchristian ignorance. "Easter? Newland! Why, of course, the first week in April. Why?"

"The first week?" He turned again to the pages of his diary, calculating rapidly under his breath. "The first week, did you say?" He threw back his head with a long laugh.

"For mercy's sake what's the matter?"

"Nothing's the matter, except that I'm going to be married in a month."

Janey fell upon his neck and pressed him to her purple flannel breast. "Oh Newland, how wonderful! I'm so glad! But, dearest, why do you keep on laughing? Do hush, or you'll wake Mamma."

# Book Two

---

# —— 19 ——

THE DAY was fresh, with a lively spring wind full of dust. All the old ladies in both families had got out their faded sables and yellowing ermines, and the smell of camphor from the front pews almost smothered the faint spring scent of the lilies banking the altar.

Newland Archer, at a signal from the sexton, had come out of the vestry and placed himself with his best man on the chancel step of Grace Church.

The signal meant that the brougham bearing the bride and her father was in sight, but there was sure to be a considerable interval of adjustment and consultation in the lobby, where the bridesmaids were already hovering like a cluster of Easter blossoms. During this unavoidable lapse of time the bridegroom, in proof of his eagerness, was expected to expose himself alone to the gaze of the assembled company; and Archer had gone through this formality as resignedly as through all the others which made of a nineteenth-century New York wedding a rite that seemed to belong to the dawn of history. Everything was equally easy—or equally painful, as one chose to put it—in the path he was committed to tread, and he had obeyed the flurried injunctions of his best man as piously as other bridegrooms had obeyed his own, in the days when he had guided them through the same labyrinth.

So far he was reasonably sure of having fulfilled all his obligations. The bridesmaids' eight bouquets of white lilac and lilies-of-the-valley had been sent in due time, as well as the gold and sapphire sleevelinks of the eight ushers and the best man's cat's-eye scarf pin. Archer had sat up half the night trying to vary the wording of his thanks for the last batch of presents from men friends and ex-lady loves; the fees for the bishop and the rector were safely in the pocket of his best man; his own luggage was already at Mrs. Manson Mingott's, where the wedding breakfast was to take place, and so were the traveling clothes into which he was to change; and a private compartment had been engaged in the train that was to carry the young couple to their unknown destination—concealment of the spot in which the bridal night was to be spent being one of the most sacred taboos of the prehistoric ritual.

"Got the ring all right?" whispered young van der Luyden Newland, who was inexperienced in the duties of a best man and awed by the weight of his responsibility.

Archer made the gesture which he had seen so many bridegrooms make: with his ungloved right hand he felt in the pocket of his dark gray waistcoat and assured himself that the little gold circlet (engraved inside: *Newland to May, April —, 187–*) was in its place; then, resuming his former attitude, his tall hat and pearl-gray gloves with black stitchings grasped in his left hand, he stood looking at the door of the church.

Overhead, Handel's *March* swelled pompously through the imitation stone vaulting, carrying on its waves the faded drift of the many weddings at which, with cheerful indifference, he had stood on the same chancel step watching other brides float up the nave toward other bridegrooms.

"How like a first night at the opera!" he thought, recognizing all the same faces in the same boxes (no, pews), and wondering if, when the Last Trump sounded, Mrs. Selfridge Merry would be there with the same towering ostrich feathers in her bonnet, and Mrs. Beaufort with the same diamond earrings and the same smile—and whether suitable proscenium seats were already prepared for them in another world.

After that there was still time to review, one by one, the familiar countenances in the first rows; the women's sharp with curiosity and excitement, the men's sulky with the obligation of having to put on their frock coats before luncheon and fight for food at the wedding breakfast.

"Too bad the breakfast is at old Catherine's," the bridegroom could fancy Reggie Chivers saying. "But I'm told that Lovell Mingott insisted on its being cooked by his own chef, so it ought to be good if one can only get at it." And he could imagine Sillerton Jackson adding with authority: "My dear fellow, haven't you heard? It's to be served at small tables, in the new English fashion."

Archer's eyes lingered a moment on the left-hand pew, where his mother, who had entered the church on Mr. Henry van der Luyden's arm, sat weeping softly under her Chantilly veil, her hands in her grandmother's ermine muff.

"Poor Janey!" he thought, looking at his sister. "Even by screwing her head around she can see only the people in the few front pews, and they're mostly dowdy Newlands and Dagonets."

On the hither side of the white ribbon dividing off the seats reserved for the families he saw Beaufort, tall and red-faced, scrutinizing the women with his arrogant stare. Beside him sat his wife, all silvery chinchilla and violets, and on the far side of the ribbon, Lawrence Lefferts's sleekly brushed head seemed to mount guard over the invisible deity of "Good Form" who presided at the ceremony.

Archer wondered how many flaws Lefferts's keen eyes would discover in the ritual of his divinity; then he suddenly recalled that he too had once thought such questions important. The things that had filled his days seemed now like a nursery parody of life, or like the wrangles of medieval schoolmen over metaphysical terms that nobody had ever understood. A stormy discussion as to whether the wedding presents should be "shown" had darkened the last hours before the wedding; and it seemed inconceivable to Archer that grown-up people should work themselves into a state of agitation over such trifles, and that the matter should have been decided (in the negative) by Mrs. Welland's saying, with indignant tears: "I should as soon turn the reporters loose in my house." Yet there was a time when Archer had had definite and rather aggressive opinions on all such problems, and when everything concerning the manners and customs of his little tribe had seemed to him fraught with worldwide significance.

"And all the while, I suppose," he thought, "real people were living somewhere, and real things happening to them . . ."

*"There they come!"* breathed the best man excitedly, but the bridegroom knew better.

The cautious opening of the door of the church meant only that Mr. Brown the livery-stable keeper (gowned in black in his intermittent character of sexton) was taking a preliminary survey of the scene before marshaling his forces. The door was softly shut again; then after another interval it swung majestically open, and a murmur ran through the church: "The family!"

Mrs. Welland came first, on the arm of her eldest son. Her large pink face was appropriately solemn, and her plum-colored satin with pale blue side panels, and blue ostrich plumes in a small satin bonnet, met with general approval; but before she had settled herself with a stately rustle in the pew opposite Mrs. Archer's the spectators were craning their necks to see who was coming after her. Wild rumors had been abroad the day before to the effect that Mrs. Manson Mingott, in spite of her physical disabilities, had resolved on being present at the ceremony; and the idea was so much in keeping with her sporting character that bets ran high at the clubs as to her being able to walk up the nave and squeeze into a seat. It was known that she had insisted on sending her own carpenter to look into the possibility of taking down the end panel of the front pew, and to measure the space between the seat and the front, but the result had been discouraging, and for one anxious day her family had watched her dallying with the plan of being wheeled up the nave in her enormous bath chair and sitting enthroned in it at the foot of the chancel.

The idea of this monstrous exposure of her person was so painful to her relations that they could have covered with gold the ingenious person who suddenly discovered that the chair was too wide to pass between the iron uprights of the awning which extended from the church door to the curbstone. The idea of doing away with this awning, and revealing the bride to the mob of dressmakers and newspaper reporters who stood outside fighting to get near the joints of the canvas, exceeded even old Catherine's courage, though for a moment she had weighed the possibility. "Why, they might take a photograph of my child *and put it in the papers!*" Mrs. Welland exclaimed when her mother's last plan was hinted to her; and from this unthinkable indecency the clan recoiled with a collective shudder. The ancestress had had to give in, but her concession was bought only by the promise that the wedding breakfast should take place under her roof, though (as the Washington Square connection said) with the Wellands' house in easy reach it was hard to have to make a special price with Brown to drive one to the other end of nowhere.

Though all these transactions had been widely reported by the

Jacksons, a sporting minority still clung to the belief that old Catherine would appear in church, and there was a distinct lowering of the temperature when she was found to have been replaced by her daughter-in-law. Mrs. Lovell Mingott had the high color and glassy stare induced in ladies of her age and habit by the effort of getting into a new dress; but once the disappointment occasioned by her mother-in-law's nonappearance had subsided, it was agreed that her black Chantilly over lilac satin, with a bonnet of Parma violets, formed the happiest contrast to Mrs. Welland's blue and plum color. Far different was the impression produced by the gaunt and mincing lady who followed on Mr. Mingott's arm, in a wild dishevelment of stripes and fringes and floating scarves; and as this last apparition glided into view Archer's heart contracted and stopped beating.

He had taken it for granted that the Marchioness Manson was still in Washington, where she had gone some four weeks previously with her niece, Madame Olenska. It was generally understood that their abrupt departure was due to Madame Olenska's desire to remove her aunt from the baleful eloquence of Dr. Agathon Carver, who had nearly succeeded in enlisting her as a recruit for the Valley of Love; and in the circumstances no one had expected either of the ladies to return for the wedding. For a moment Archer stood with his eyes fixed on Medora's fantastic figure, straining to see who came behind her; but the little procession was at an end, for all the lesser members of the family had taken their seats, and the eight tall ushers, gathering themselves together like birds or insects preparing for some migratory maneuver, were already slipping through the side doors into the lobby.

"Newland—I say: *she's here!*" the best man whispered.

Archer roused himself with a start.

A long time had apparently passed since his heart had stopped beating, for the white and rosy procession was in fact halfway up the nave, the bishop, the rector and two white-winged assistants were hovering about the flower-banked altar, and the first chords of the Spohr symphony were strewing their flowerlike notes before the bride.

Archer opened his eyes (but could they really have been shut, as he imagined?), and felt his heart beginning to resume its usual task. The music, the scent of the lilies on the altar, the vision of the cloud of tulle and orange blossoms floating nearer and nearer, the sight of Mrs. Archer's face suddenly convulsed with happy sobs, the low benedictory murmur of the rector's voice, the ordered evolutions of the eight pink bridesmaids and the eight black ushers: all these sights, sounds, and sensations, so familiar in themselves, so unutterably strange and meaningless in his new relation to them, were confusedly mingled in his brain.

"My God," he thought, *"have* I got the ring?"—and once more he went through the bridegroom's convulsive gesture.

Then, in a moment, May was beside him, such radiance streaming from her that it sent a faint warmth through his numbness, and he straightened himself and smiled into her eyes.

"Dearly beloved, we are gathered together here," the rector began . . .

The ring was on her hand, the bishop's benediction had been given, the bridesmaids were a-poise to resume their place in the procession, and the organ was showing preliminary symptoms of breaking out into the Mendelssohn *March,* without which no newly wedded couple had ever emerged upon New York.

"Your arm—*I say, give her your arm!*" young Newland nervously hissed, and once more Archer became aware of having been adrift far off in the unknown. What was it that had sent him there, he wondered? Perhaps the glimpse, among the anonymous spectators in the transept, of a dark coil of hair under a hat which, a moment later, revealed itself as belonging to an unknown lady with a long nose, so laughably unlike the person whose image she had evoked that he asked himself if he were becoming subject to hallucinations.

And now he and his wife were pacing slowly down the nave, carried forward on the light Mendelssohn ripples, the spring day beckoning to them through widely opened doors, and Mrs. Welland's chestnuts, with big white favors on their frontlets, curvetting and showing off at the far end of the canvas tunnel.

The footman, who had a still bigger white favor on his lapel, wrapped May's white cloak about her, and Archer jumped into the brougham at her side. She turned to him with a triumphant smile and their hands clasped under her veil.

"Darling!" Archer said—and suddenly the same black abyss

yawned before him and he felt himself sinking into it, deeper and deeper, while his voice rambled on smoothly and cheerfully: "Yes, of course I thought I'd lost the ring; no wedding would be complete if the poor devil of a bridegroom didn't go through that. But you *did* keep me waiting, you know! I had time to think of every horror that might possibly happen."

She surprised him by turning, in full Fifth Avenue, and flinging her arms about his neck. "But none ever *can* happen now, can it, Newland, as long as we two are together?"

Every detail of the day had been so carefully thought out that the young couple, after the wedding breakfast, had ample time to put on their traveling clothes, descend the wide Mingott stairs between laughing bridesmaids and weeping parents, and get into the brougham under the traditional shower of rice and satin slippers; and there was still half an hour left in which to drive to the station, buy the last weeklies at the bookstall with the air of seasoned travelers, and settle themselves in the reserved compartment in which May's maid had already placed her dove-colored traveling cloak and glaringly new dressing bag from London.

The old du Lac aunts at Rhinebeck had put their house at the disposal of the bridal couple, with a readiness inspired by the prospect of spending a week in New York with Mrs. Archer; and Archer, glad to escape the usual "bridal suite" in a Philadelphia or Baltimore hotel, had accepted with an equal alacrity.

May was enchanted at the idea of going to the country, and childishly amused at the vain efforts of the eight bridesmaids to discover where their mysterious retreat was situated. It was thought "very English" to have a country house lent to one, and the fact gave a last touch of distinction to what was generally conceded to be the most brilliant wedding of the year, but where the house was no one was permitted to know, except the parents of bride and groom, who, when taxed with the knowledge, pursed their lips and said mysteriously: "Ah, they didn't tell us—" which was manifestly true, since there was no need to.

Once they were settled in their compartment, and the train, shaking off the endless wooden suburbs, had pushed out into the pale landscape of spring, talk became easier than Archer had expected. May was still, in look and tone, the simple girl of yester-

day, eager to compare notes with him as to the incidents of the
wedding, and discussing them as impartially as a bridesmaid talking it all over with an usher. At first Archer had fancied that
this detachment was the disguise of an inward tremor; but her
clear eyes revealed only the most tranquil unawareness. She was
alone for the first time with her husband, but her husband was
only the charming comrade of yesterday. There was no one
whom she liked as much, no one whom she trusted as completely,
and the culminating "lark" of the whole delightful adventure of
engagement and marriage was to be off with him alone on a
journey, like a grown-up person, like a "married woman," in
fact.

It was wonderful that—as he had learned in the Mission garden at St. Augustine—such depths of feeling could coexist with
such absence of imagination. But he remembered how, even
then, she had surprised him by dropping back to inexpressive
girlishness as soon as her conscience had been eased of its burden, and he saw that she would probably go through life dealing
to the best of her ability with each experience as it came, but
never anticipating any by so much as a stolen glance.

Perhaps that faculty of unawareness was what gave her eyes
their transparency, and her face the look of representing a type
rather than a person; as if she might have been chosen to pose for
a Civic Virtue or a Greek goddess. The blood that ran so close to
her fair skin might have been a preserving fluid rather than a
ravaging element; yet her look of indestructible youthfulness
made her seem neither hard nor dull, but only primitive and
pure. In the thick of this meditation Archer suddenly felt himself
looking at her with the startled gaze of a stranger, and plunged
into a reminiscence of the wedding breakfast and of Granny
Mingott's immense and triumphant pervasion of it.

May settled down to frank enjoyment of the subject. "I was
surprised, though—weren't you?—that Aunt Medora came after
all. Ellen wrote that they were neither of them well enough to
take the journey. I do wish it had been she who had recovered!
Did you see the exquisite old lace she sent me?"

He had known that the moment must come sooner or later,
but he had somewhat imagined that by force of willing he might
hold it at bay.

"Yes—I—no: yes, it was beautiful," he said, looking at her blindly, and wondering if, whenever he heard those two syllables, all his carefully built-up world would tumble about him like a house of cards.

"Aren't you tired? It will be good to have some tea when we arrive—I'm sure the aunts have got everything beautifully ready," he rattled on, taking her hand in his, and her mind rushed away instantly to the magnificent tea and coffee service of Baltimore silver which the Beauforts had sent, and which "went" so perfectly with Uncle Lovell Mingott's trays and side dishes.

In the spring twilight the train stopped at the Rhinebeck station, and they walked along the platform to the waiting carriage.

"Ah, how awfully kind of the van der Luydens—they've sent their man over from Skuytercliff to meet us," Archer exclaimed, as a sedate person out of livery approached them and relieved the maid of her bags.

"I'm extremely sorry, sir," said this emissary, "that a little accident has occurred at the Miss du Lacs': a leak in the water tank. It happened yesterday, and Mr. van der Luyden, who heard of it this morning, sent a housemaid up by the early train to get the patroon's house ready. It will be quite comfortable, I think you'll find, sir; and the Miss du Lacs have sent their cook over, so that it will be exactly the same as if you'd been at Rhinebeck."

Archer stared at the speaker so blankly that he repeated in still more apologetic accents: "It'll be exactly the same, sir, I do assure you—" and May's eager voice broke out, covering the embarrassed silence: "The same as Rhinebeck? The patroon's house? But it will be a hundred thousand times better—won't it, Newland? It's too dear and kind of Mr. van der Luyden to have thought of it."

And as they drove off, with the maid beside the coachman, and their shining bridal bags on the seat before them, she went on excitedly: "Only fancy, I've never been inside it—have you? The van der Luydens show it to so few people. But they opened it for Ellen, it seems, and she told me what a darling little place it was: she says it's the only house she's seen in America that she could imagine being perfectly happy in."

"Well—that's what we're going to be, isn't it?" cried her husband gaily, and she answered with her boyish smile: "Ah, it's just our luck beginning—the wonderful luck we're always going to have together!"

# ──20──

"OF COURSE we must dine with Mrs. Carfry, dearest," Archer said, and his wife looked at him with an anxious frown across the monumental Britannia ware of their lodging house breakfast table.

In all the rainy desert of autumnal London there were only two people whom the Newland Archers knew, and these two they had sedulously avoided, in conformity with the old New York tradition that it was not "dignified" to force one's self on the notice of one's acquaintances in foreign countries.

Mrs. Archer and Janey, in the course of their visits to Europe, had so unflinchingly lived up to this principle, and met the friendly advances of their fellow travelers with an air of such impenetrable reserve, that they had almost achieved the record of never having exchanged a word with a "foreigner" other than those employed in hotels and railway stations. Their own compatriots—save those previously known or properly accredited—they treated with an even more pronounced disdain; so that, unless they ran across a Chivers, a Dagonet, or a Mingott, their months abroad were spent in an unbroken tête-à-tête. But the utmost precautions are sometimes unavailing; and one night at Botzen one of the two English ladies in the room across the passage (whose names, dress, and social situation were already intimately known to Janey) had knocked on the door and asked if Mrs. Archer had a bottle of liniment. The other lady—the intruder's sister, Mrs. Carfry—had been seized with a sudden attack of bronchitis, and Mrs. Archer, who never traveled without a complete family pharmacy, was fortunately able to produce the required remedy.

Mrs. Carfry was very ill, and as she and her sister Miss Harle were traveling alone they were profoundly grateful to the Archer ladies, who supplied them with ingenious comforts and whose efficient maid helped to nurse the invalid back to health.

When the Archers left Botzen they had no idea of ever seeing
Mrs. Carfry and Miss Harle again. Nothing, to Mrs. Archer's
mind, would have been more "undignified" than to force one's
self on the notice of a "foreigner" to whom one had happened to
render an accidental service. But Mrs. Carfry and her sister, to
whom this point of view was unknown, and who would have
found it utterly incomprehensible, felt themselves linked by an
eternal gratitude to the "delightful Americans" who had been so
kind at Botzen. With touching fidelity they seized every chance of
meeting Mrs. Archer and Janey in the course of their continental
travels, and displayed a supernatural acuteness in finding out
when they were to pass through London on their way to or from
the States. The intimacy became indissoluble, and Mrs. Archer
and Janey, whenever they alighted at Brown's Hotel, found
themselves awaited by two affectionate friends who, like themselves, cultivated ferns in Wardian cases, made macramé lace,
read the memoirs of the Baroness Bunsen and had views about
the occupants of the leading London pulpits. As Mrs. Archer said,
it made "another thing of London" to know Mrs. Carfry and Miss
Harle, and by the time that Newland became engaged the tie
between the families was so firmly established that it was thought
"only right" to send a wedding invitation to the two English ladies, who sent, in return, a pretty bouquet of pressed Alpine flowers under glass. And on the dock, when Newland and his wife
sailed for England, Mrs. Archer's last word had been: "You must
take May to see Mrs. Carfry."

Newland and his wife had had no idea of obeying this injunction; but Mrs. Carfry, with her usual acuteness, had run them
down and sent them an invitation to dine; and it was over this
invitation that May Archer was wrinkling her brows across the tea
and muffins.

"It's all very well for you, Newland; you *know* them. But I shall
feel so shy among a lot of people I've never met. And what shall I
wear?"

Newland leaned back in his chair and smiled at her. She
looked handsomer and more Diana-like than ever. The moist
English air seemed to have deepened the bloom of her cheeks
and softened the slight hardness of her virginal features, or else it

was simply the inner glow of happiness, shining through like a light under ice.

"Wear, dearest? I thought a trunkful of things had come from Paris last week."

"Yes, of course. I meant to say that I shan't know *which* to wear." She pouted a little. "I've never dined out in London, and I don't want to be ridiculous."

He tried to enter into her perplexity. "But don't English women dress just like everybody else in the evening?"

"Newland! How can you ask such funny questions? When they go to the theater in old ball dresses and bare heads."

"Well, perhaps they wear new ball dresses at home, but at any rate Mrs. Carfry and Miss Harle won't. They'll wear caps like my mother's—and shawls, very soft shawls."

"Yes, but how will the other women be dressed?"

"Not as well as you, dear," he rejoined, wondering what had suddenly developed in her Janey's morbid interest in clothes.

She pushed back her chair with a sigh. "That's dear of you, Newland, but it doesn't help me much."

He had an inspiration. "Why not wear your wedding dress? That can't be wrong, can it?"

"Oh, dearest! If I only had it here! But it's gone to Paris to be made over for next winter, and Worth hasn't sent it back."

"Oh, well—" said Archer, getting up. "Look here—the fog's lifting. If we made a dash for the National Gallery we might manage to catch a glimpse of the pictures."

The Newland Archers were on their way home, after a three months' wedding tour which May, in writing to her girl friends, vaguely summarized as "blissful."

They had not gone to the Italian Lakes: on reflection, Archer had not been able to picture his wife in that particular setting. Her own inclination (after a month with the Paris dressmakers) was for mountaineering in July and swimming in August. This plan they punctually fulfilled, spending July at Interlaken and Grindelwald, and August at a little place called Etretat, on the Normandy coast, which someone had recommended as quaint and quiet. Once or twice, in the mountains, Archer had pointed southward and said: "There's Italy"; and May, her feet in a gentian bed, had smiled cheerfully, and replied: "It would be lovely to go there next winter, if only you didn't have to be in New York."

But in reality traveling interested her even less than he had expected. She regarded it (once her clothes were ordered) as merely an enlarged opportunity for walking, riding, swimming, and trying her hand at the fascinating new game of lawn tennis, and when they finally got back to London (where they were to spend a fortnight while he ordered *his* clothes) she no longer concealed the eagerness with which she looked forward to sailing.

In London nothing interested her but the theaters and the shops, and she found the theaters less exciting than the Paris *cafés chantants* where, under the blossoming horse chestnuts of the Champs Élysées, she had had the novel experience of looking down from the restaurant terrace on an audience of "cocottes," and having her husband interpret to her as much of the songs as he thought suitable for bridal ears.

Archer had reverted to all his old inherited ideas about marriage. It was less trouble to conform with the tradition and treat May exactly as all his friends treated their wives than to try to put into practice the theories with which his untrammeled bachelorhood had dallied. There was no use in trying to emancipate a wife who had not the dimmest notion that she was not free, and he had long since discovered that May's only use of the liberty she supposed herself to possess would be to lay it on the altar of her wifely adoration. Her innate dignity would always keep her from making the gift abjectly, and a day might even come (as it once had) when she would find strength to take it altogether back if she thought she were doing it for his own good. But with a conception of marriage so uncomplicated and incurious as hers such a crisis could be brought about only by something visibly outrageous in his own conduct; and the fineness of her feeling for him made that unthinkable. Whatever happened, he knew, she would always be loyal, gallant, and unresentful, and that pledged him to the practice of the same virtues.

All this tended to draw him back into his old habits of mind. If her simplicity had been the simplicity of pettiness he would have chafed and rebelled, but since the lines of her character, though so few, were on the same fine mold as her face, she became the tutelary divinity of all his old traditions and reverences.

Such qualities were scarcely of the kind to enliven foreign travel, though they made her so easy and pleasant a companion, but he saw at once how they would fall into place in their proper setting. He had no fear of being oppressed by them, for his artistic and intellectual life would go on, as it always had, outside the domestic circle; and within it there would be nothing small and stifling—coming back to his wife would never be like entering a stuffy room after a tramp in the open. And when they had children the vacant corners in both their lives would be filled.

All these things went through his mind during their long slow drive from Mayfair to South Kensington, where Mrs. Carfry and her sister lived. Archer too would have preferred to escape their friends' hospitality: in conformity with the family tradition he had always traveled as a sightseer and looker-on, affecting a haughty unconsciousness of the presence of his fellow beings. Once only, just after Harvard, he had spent a few gay weeks at Florence with a band of queer Europeanized Americans, dancing all night with titled ladies in palaces, and gambling half the day with the rakes and dandies of the fashionable club; but it had all seemed to him, though the greatest fun in the world, as unreal as a carnival. These queer cosmopolitan women, deep in complicated love affairs which they appeared to feel the need of retailing to everyone they met, and the magnificent young officers and elderly dyed wits who were the subjects or the recipients of their confidences, were too different from the people Archer had grown up among, too much like expensive and rather malodorous hothouse exotics, to detain his imagination long. To introduce his wife into such a society was out of the question, and in the course of his travels no other had shown any marked eagerness for his company.

Not long after their arrival in London he had run across the Duke of St. Austrey, and the duke, instantly and cordially recognizing him, had said: "Look me up, won't you?"—but no proper-spirited American would have considered that a suggestion to be acted on, and the meeting was without a sequel. They had even managed to avoid May's English aunt, the banker's wife, who was still in Yorkshire; in fact, they had purposely postponed going to London till the autumn in order that their arrival during the season might not appear pushing and snobbish to these unknown relatives.

"Probably there'll be nobody at Mrs. Carfry's—London's a desert at this season, and you've made yourself much too beautiful," Archer said to May, who sat at his side in the handsom so spotlessly splendid in her sky-blue cloak edged with swansdown that it seemed wicked to expose her to the London grime.

"I don't want them to think that we dress like savages," she replied, with a scorn that Pocahontas might have resented, and he was struck again by the religious reverence of even the most unworldly American women for the social advantages of dress.

"It's their armor," he thought, "their defense against the unknown, and their defiance of it." And he understood for the first time the earnestness with which May, who was incapable of tying a ribbon in her hair to charm him, had gone through the solemn rite of selecting and ordering her extensive wardrobe.

He had been right in expecting the party at Mrs. Carfry's to be a small one. Besides their hostess and her sister, they found, in the long chilly drawing room, only another shawled lady, a genial vicar who was her husband, a silent lad whom Mrs. Carfry named as her nephew, and a small dark gentleman with lively eyes whom she introduced as his tutor, pronouncing a French name as she did so.

Into this dimly lit and dim-featured group May Archer floated like a swan with the sunset on her: she seemed larger, fairer, more voluminously rustling than her husband had ever seen her, and he perceived that the rosiness and rustlingness were the tokens of an extreme and infantile shyness.

"What on earth will they expect me to talk about?" her helpless eyes implored him at the very moment that her dazzling apparition was calling forth the same anxiety in their own bosoms. But beauty, even when distrustful of itself, awakens confidence in the manly heart, and the vicar and the French-named tutor were soon manifesting to May their desire to put her at her ease.

In spite of their best efforts, however, the dinner was a languishing affair. Archer noticed that his wife's way of showing herself at her ease with foreigners was to become more uncompromisingly local in her references, so that, though her loveliness was an encouragement to admiration, her conversation was a chill to repartee. The vicar soon abandoned the struggle; but the tutor, who spoke the most fluent and accomplished English, gallantly continued to pour it out to her until the ladies, to the manifest relief of all concerned, went up to the drawing room.

The vicar, after a glass of port, was obliged to hurry away to a meeting, and the shy nephew, who appeared to be an invalid, was packed off to bed. But Archer and the tutor continued to sit over their wine, and suddenly Archer found himself talking as he had not done since his last symposium with Ned Winsett. The Carfry nephew, it turned out, had been threatened with consumption, and had had to leave Harrow for Switzerland, where he had spent two years in the milder air of Lake Leman. Being a bookish youth, he had been entrusted to M. Rivière, who had brought him back to England, and was to remain with him till he went up to Oxford the following spring; and M. Rivière added with simplicity that he should then have to look out for another job.

It seemed impossible, Archer thought, that he should be long without one, so varied were his interests and so many his gifts. He was a man of about thirty, with a thin ugly face (May would certainly have called him common-looking) to which the play of his ideas gave an intense expressiveness, but there was nothing frivolous or cheap in his animation.

His father, who had died young, had filled a small diplomatic post, and it had been intended that the son should follow the same career; but an insatiable taste for letters had thrown the young man into journalism, then into authorship (apparently unsuccessful), and at length—after other experiments and vicissitudes which he spared his listener—into tutoring English youths in Switzerland. Before that, however, he had lived much in Paris, frequented the Goncourt *grenier,* been advised by Maupassant not to attempt to write (even that seemed to Archer a dazzling honor!), and had often talked with Mérimée in his mother's house. He had obviously always been desperately poor and anxious (having a mother and an unmarried sister to provide for), and it was apparent that his literary ambitions had failed. His situation, in fact, seemed, materially speaking, no more brilliant than Ned Winsett's; but he had lived in a world in which, as he said, no one who loved ideas need hunger mentally. As it was precisely of that love that poor Winsett was starving to death,

Archer looked with a sort of vicarious envy at this eager impecu-
nious young man who had fared so richly in his poverty.

"You see, Monsieur, it's worth everything, isn't it, to keep one's
intellectual liberty, not to enslave one's powers of appreciation,
one's critical independence? It was because of that that I abandoned journalism, and took to so much duller work: tutoring and
private secretaryship. There is a good deal of drudgery, of
course; but one preserves one's moral freedom, what we call in
French one's *quant à soi.* And when one hears good talk one can
join in it without compromising any opinions but one's own; or
one can listen, and answer it inwardly. Ah, good conversation—
there's nothing like it, is there? The air of ideas is the only air
worth breathing. And so I have never regretted giving up either
diplomacy or journalism—two different forms of the same self-
abdication." He fixed his vivid eyes on Archer as he lit another
cigarette. "*Voyez-vous,* Monsieur, to be able to look life in the face:
that's worth living in a garret for, isn't it? But, after all, one must
earn enough to pay for the garret; and I confess that to grow old
as a private tutor—or a 'private' anything—is almost as chilling to
the imagination as a second secretaryship at Bucharest. Sometimes I feel I must make a plunge: an immense plunge. Do you
suppose, for instance, there would be any opening for me in
America—in New York?"

Archer looked at him with startled eyes. New York, for a young
man who had frequented the Goncourts and Flaubert, and who
thought the life of ideas the only one worth living! He continued
to stare at M. Rivière perplexedly, wondering how to tell him that
his very superiorities and advantages would be the surest hin-
drance to success.

"New York—New York—but must it be especially New York?"
he stammered, utterly unable to imagine what lucrative opening
his native city could offer to a young man to whom good conversation appeared to be the only necessity.

A sudden flush rose under M. Rivière's sallow skin. "I—I
thought it your metropolis: is not the intellectual life more active
there?" he rejoined; then, as if fearing to give his hearer the
impression of having asked a favor, he went on hastily: "One
throws out random suggestions—more to one's self than to others. In reality, I see no immediate prospect—" and rising from his

seat he added, without a trace of constraint: "But Mrs. Carfry will think that I ought to be taking you upstairs."

During the homeward drive Archer pondered deeply on this episode. His hour with M. Rivière had put new air into his lungs, and his first impulse had been to invite him to dine the next day, but he was beginning to understand why married men did not always immediately yield to their first impulses.

"That young tutor is an interesting fellow: we had some awfully good talk after dinner about books and things," he threw out tentatively in the hansom.

May roused herself from one of the dreamy silences into which he had read so many meanings before six months of marriage had given him the key to them.

"The little Frenchman? Wasn't he dreadfully common?" she questioned coldly, and he guessed that she nursed a secret disappointment at having been invited out in London to meet a clergyman and a French tutor. The disappointment was not occasioned by the sentiment ordinarily defined as snobbishness, but by old New York's sense of what was due to it when it risked its dignity in foreign lands. If May's parents had entertained the Carfrys in Fifth Avenue they would have offered them something more substantial than a parson and a schoolmaster.

But Archer was on edge, and took her up.

"Common—common *where?*" he queried, and she returned with unusual readiness: "Why, I should say anywhere but in his schoolroom. Those people are always awkward in society. But then" she added disarmingly, "I suppose I shouldn't have known if he was clever."

Archer disliked her use of the word "clever" almost as much as her use of the word "common," but he was beginning to fear his tendency to dwell on the things he disliked in her. After all, her point of view had always been the same. It was that of all the people he had grown up among, and he had always regarded it as necessary but negligible. Until a few months ago he had never known a "nice" woman who looked at life differently, and if a man married it must necessarily be among the nice.

"Ah—then I won't ask him to dine!" he concluded with a laugh, and May echoed, bewildered: "Goodness—ask the Carfrys' tutor?"

"Well, not on the same day with the Carfrys, if you prefer I shouldn't. But I did rather want another talk with him. He's looking for a job in New York."

Her surprise increased with her indifference: he almost fancied that she suspected him of being tainted with "foreignness."

"A job in New York? What sort of a job? People don't have French tutors. What does he want to do?"

"Chiefly to enjoy good conversation, I understand," her husband retorted perversely, and she broke into an appreciative laugh. "Oh, Newland, how funny! Isn't that *French?*"

On the whole, he was glad to have the matter settled for him by her refusing to take seriously his wish to invite M. Rivière. Another after-dinner talk would have made it difficult to avoid the question of New York, and the more Archer considered it the less he was able to fit M. Rivière into any conceivable picture of New York as he knew it.

He perceived with a flash of chilling insight that in future many problems would be thus negatively solved for him, but as he paid the hansom and followed his wife's long train into the house he took refuge in the comforting platitude that the first six months were always the most difficult in marriage. "After that I suppose we shall have pretty nearly finished rubbing off each other's angles," he reflected, but the worst of it was that May's pressure was already bearing on the very angles whose sharpness he most wanted to keep.

# — 21 —

❧ THE SMALL BRIGHT LAWN stretched away smoothly to the big bright sea.

The turf was hemmed with an edge of scarlet geranium and coleus, and cast-iron vases painted in chocolate color, standing at intervals along the winding path that led to the sea, looped their garlands of petunia and ivy geranium above the neatly raked gravel.

Halfway between the edge of the cliff and the square wooden house (which was also chocolate-colored, but with the tin roof of the verandah striped in yellow and brown to represent an awning) two large targets had been placed against a background of shrubbery. On the other side of the lawn, facing the targets, was pitched a real tent, with benches and garden seats about it. A number of ladies in summer dresses and gentlemen in gray frock coats and tall hats stood on the lawn or sat upon the benches, and every now and then a slender girl in starched muslin would step from the tent, bow in hand, and speed her shaft at one of the targets, while the spectators interrupted their talk to watch the result.

Newland Archer, standing on the verandah of the house, looked curiously down upon this scene. On each side of the shiny painted steps was a large blue china flowerpot on a bright yellow china stand. A spiky green plant filled each pot, and below the verandah ran a wide border of blue hydrangeas edged with more red geraniums. Behind him, the French windows of the drawing rooms through which he had passed gave glimpses, between swaying lace curtains, of glassy parquet floors islanded with chintz poufs, dwarf armchairs, and velvet tables covered with trifles in silver.

The Newport Archery Club always held its August meeting at the Beauforts'. The sport, which had hitherto known no rival but croquet, was beginning to be discarded in favor of lawn tennis, but the latter game was still considered too rough and inelegant for social occasions, and as an opportunity to show off pretty dresses and graceful attitudes the bow and arrow held their own.

Archer looked down with wonder at the familiar spectacle. It surprised him that life should be going on in the old way when his own reactions to it had so completely changed. It was Newport that had first brought home to him the extent of the change. In New York, during the previous winter, after he and May had settled down in the new greenish-yellow house with the bow window and the Pompeian vestibule, he had dropped back with relief into the old routine of the office, and the renewal of this daily activity had served as a link with his former self. Then there had been the pleasurable excitement of choosing a showy gray stepper for May's brougham (the Wellands had given the carriage), and the abiding occupation and interest of arranging his new library, which, in spite of family doubts and disapprovals, had been carried out as he had dreamed, with a dark embossed paper, Eastlake bookcases and "sincere" armchairs and tables. At the Century he had found Winsett again, and at the Knickerbocker the fashionable young men of his own set; and what with the hours dedicated to the law and those given to dining out or entertaining friends at home, with an occasional evening at the opera or the play, the life he was living had still seemed a fairly real and inevitable sort of business.

But Newport represented the escape from duty into an atmosphere of unmitigated holiday-making. Archer had tried to persuade May to spend the summer on a remote island off the coast of Maine (called, appropriately enough, Mount Desert), where a few hardy Bostonians and Philadelphians were camping in "native" cottages, and whence came reports of enchanting scenery and a wild, almost trapperlike existence amid woods and waters.

But the Wellands always went to Newport, where they owned one of the square boxes on the cliffs, and their son-in-law could adduce no good reason why he and May should not join them there. As Mrs. Welland rather tartly pointed out, it was hardly worthwhile for May to have worn herself out trying on summer clothes in Paris if she was not to be allowed to wear them; and this argument was of a kind to which Archer had as yet found no answer.

May herself could not understand his obscure reluctance to fall in with so reasonable and pleasant a way of spending the summer. She reminded him that he had always liked Newport in his bachelor days, and as this was indisputable he could only profess that he was sure he was going to like it better than ever now that they were to be there together. But as he stood on the Beaufort verandah and looked out on the brightly peopled lawn it came home to him with a shiver that he was not going to like it at all.

It was not May's fault, poor dear. If, now and then, during their travels, they had fallen slightly out of step, harmony had been restored by their return to the conditions she was used to. He had always foreseen that she would not disappoint him, and he had been right. He had married (as most young men did) because he had met a perfectly charming girl at the moment when a series of rather aimless sentimental adventures were ending in premature disgust; and she had represented peace, stability, comradeship, and the steadying sense of an unescapable duty.

He could not say that he had been mistaken in his choice, for she had fulfilled all that he had expected. It was undoubtedly gratifying to be the husband of one of the handsomest and most popular young married women in New York, especially when she was also one of the sweetest-tempered and most reasonable of wives; and Archer had never been insensible to such advantages. As for the momentary madness which had fallen upon him on the eve of his marriage, he had trained himself to regard it as the last of his discarded experiments. The idea that he could ever, in his senses, have dreamed of marrying the Countess Olenska had become almost unthinkable, and she remained in his memory simply as the most plaintive and poignant of a line of ghosts.

But all these abstractions and eliminations made of his mind a rather empty and echoing place, and he supposed that was one of the reasons why the busy animated people on the Beaufort lawn shocked him as if they had been children playing in a graveyard.

He heard a murmur of skirts beside him, and the Marchioness Manson fluttered out of the drawing-room window. As usual, she was extraordinarily festooned and bedizened, with a limp Leghorn hat anchored to her head by many windings of faded gauze, and a little black velvet parasol on a carved ivory handle absurdly balanced over her much larger hat brim.

"My dear Newland, I had no idea that you and May had arrived! You yourself came only yesterday, you say? Ah, business—business—professional duties . . . I understand. Many husbands, I know, find it impossible to join their wives here except for the weekend." She cocked her head on one side and languished at him through screwed-up eyes. "But marriage is one long sacrifice, as I used often to remind my Ellen—"

Archer's heart stopped with the queer jerk which it had given once before, and which seemed suddenly to slam a door between himself and the outer world; but this break of continuity must have been of the briefest, for he presently heard Medora answering a question he had apparently found voice to put.

"No, I am not staying here, but with the Blenkers, in their delicious solitude at Portsmouth. Beaufort was kind enough to send his famous trotters for me this morning, so that I might have at least a glimpse of one of Regina's garden parties; but this evening I go back to rural life. The Blenkers, dear original beings, have hired a primitive old farmhouse at Portsmouth where they gather about them representative people . . ." She drooped slightly beneath her protecting brim, and added with a faint blush: "This week Dr. Agathon Carver is holding a series of Inner Thought meetings there. A contrast indeed to this gay scene of worldly pleasure—but then I have always lived on contrasts! To me the only death is monotony. I always say to Ellen: Beware of monotony; it's the mother of all the deadly sins. But my poor child is going through a phase of exaltation, of abhorrence of the world. You know, I suppose, that she has declined all invitations to stay at Newport, even with her grandmother Mingott? I could hardly persuade her to come with me to the Blenkers', if you will believe it! The life she leads is morbid, unnatural. Ah, if she had only listened to me when it was still possible . . . when the door was still open. . . . But shall we go down and watch this absorbing match? I hear your May is one of the competitors."

Strolling toward them from the tent Beaufort advanced over the lawn, tall, heavy, too tightly buttoned into a London frock coat, with one of his own orchids in its buttonhole. Archer, who had not seen him for two or three months, was struck by the change in his appearance. In the hot summer light his floridness seemed heavy and bloated, and but for his erect square-shouldered walk he would have looked like an overfed and over-dressed old man.

There were all sorts of rumors afloat about Beaufort. In the spring he had gone off on a long cruise to the West Indies in his new steam yacht, and it was reported that, at various points where he had touched, a lady resembling Miss Fanny Ring had been seen in his company. The steam yacht, built in the Clyde, and fitted with tiled bathrooms and other unheard-of luxuries, was said to have cost him half a million; and the pearl necklace which he had presented to his wife on his return was as magnificent as such expiatory offerings are apt to be. Beaufort's fortune was substantial enough to stand the strain; and yet the disquieting rumors persisted, not only in Fifth Avenue but in Wall Street. Some people said he had speculated unfortunately in railways, others that he was being bled by one of the most insatiable members of her profession; and to every report of threatened insolvency Beaufort replied by a fresh extravagance: the building of a new row of orchid houses, the purchase of a new string of race-horses, or the addition of a new Meissonnier or Cabanel to his picture gallery.

He advanced toward the marchioness and Newland with his usual half-sneering smile. "Hullo, Medora! Did the trotters do their business? Forty minutes, eh? . . . Well, that's not so bad, considering your nerves had to be spared." He shook hands with Archer, and then, turning back with them, placed himself on Mrs. Manson's other side, and said, in a low voice, a few words which their companion did not catch.

The marchioness replied by one of her queer foreign jerks, and a *"Que voulez-vous?"* which deepened Beaufort's frown; but he produced a good semblance of a congratulatory smile as he glanced at Archer to say: "You know May's going to carry off the first prize."

"Ah, then it remains in the family," Medora rippled, and at that moment they reached the tent and Mrs. Beaufort met them in a girlish cloud of mauve muslin and floating veils.

May Welland was just coming out of the tent. In her white dress, with a pale green ribbon about the waist and a wreath of ivy on her hat, she had the same Diana-like aloofness as when she had entered the Beaufort ballroom on the night of her engagement. In the interval not a thought seemed to have passed behind her eyes or a feeling through her heart; and though her husband knew that she had the capacity for both he marveled afresh at the way in which experience dropped away from her.

She had her bow and arrow in her hand, and placing herself on the chalkmark traced on the surf she lifted the bow to her shoulder and took aim. The attitude was so full of a classic grace that a murmur of appreciation followed her appearance, and Archer felt the glow of proprietorship that so often cheated him into momentary well-being. Her rivals—Mrs. Reggie Chivers, the Merry girls, and divers rosy Thorleys, Dagonets, and Mingotts, stood behind her in a lovely anxious group, brown heads and golden bent above the scores, and pale muslins and flower-wreathed hats mingled in a tender rainbow. All were young and pretty, and bathed in summer bloom; but not one had the nymphlike ease of his wife, when, with tense muscles and happy frown, she bent her soul upon some feat of strength.

"Gad," Archer heard Lawrence Lefferts say, "not one of the lot holds the bow as she does," and Beaufort retorted: "Yes, but that's the only kind of target she'll ever hit."

Archer felt irrationally angry. His host's contemptuous tribute to May's "niceness" was just what a husband should have wished to hear said of his wife. The fact that a coarse-minded man found her lacking in attraction was simply another proof of her quality, yet the words sent a faint shiver through his heart. What if "niceness" carried to that supreme degree were only a negation, the curtain dropped before an emptiness? As he looked at May, returning flushed and calm from her final bull's-eye, he had the feeling that he had never yet lifted that curtain.

She took the congratulations of her rivals and of the rest of the company with the simplicity that was her crowning grace. No one could ever be jealous of her triumphs because she managed to give the feeling that she would have been just as serene if she had missed them. But when her eyes met her husband's her face glowed with the pleasure she saw in his.

Mrs. Welland's basketwork pony carriage was waiting for them, and they drove off among the dispersing carriages, May handling the reins and Archer sitting at her side.

The afternoon sunlight still lingered upon the bright lawns

and shrubberies, and up and down Bellevue Avenue rolled a double line of victorias, dogcarts, landaus, and "vis-à-vis," carrying well-dressed ladies and gentlemen away from the Beaufort garden party, or homeward from their daily afternoon turn along the Ocean Drive.

"Shall we go to see Granny?" May suddenly proposed. "I should like to tell her myself that I've won the prize. There's lots of time before dinner."

Archer acquiesced, and she turned the ponies down Narragansett Avenue, crossed Spring Street, and drove out toward the rocky moorland beyond. In this unfashionable region Catherine the Great, always indifferent to precedent and thrifty of purse, had built herself in her youth a many peaked and crossbeamed *cottage-orné* on a bit of cheap land overlooking the bay. Here, in a thicket of stunted oaks, her verandahs spread themselves above the island-dotted waters. A winding drive led up between iron stags and blue glass balls embedded in mounds of geraniums to a front door of highly varnished walnut under a striped verandah roof, and behind it ran a narrow hall with a black and yellow star-patterned parquet floor, upon which opened four small square rooms with heavy flock papers under ceilings on which an Italian housepainter had lavished all the divinities of Olympus. One of these rooms had been turned into a bedroom by Mrs. Mingott when the burden of flesh descended on her, and in the adjoining one she spent her days, enthroned in a large armchair between the open door and window, and perpetually waving a palm-leaf fan which the prodigious projection of her bosom kept so far from the rest of her person that the air it set in motion stirred only the fringe of the antimacassars on the chair arms.

Since she had been the means of hastening his marriage old Catherine had shown to Archer the cordiality which a service rendered excites toward the person served. She was persuaded that irrepressible passion was the cause of his impatience, and being an ardent admirer of impulsiveness (when it did not lead to the spending of money) she always received him with a genial twinkle of complicity and a play of allusion to which May seemed fortunately impervious.

She examined and appraised with much interest the diamond-tipped arrow which had been pinned on May's bosom at the conclusion of the match, remarking that in her day a filigree brooch would have been thought enough, but that there was no denying that Beaufort did things handsomely.

"Quite an heirloom, in fact, my dear," the old lady chuckled. "You must leave it in fee to your eldest girl." She pinched May's white arm and watched the color flood her face. "Well, well, what have I said to make you shake out the red flag? Ain't there going to be any daughters—only boys, eh? Good gracious, look at her blushing again all over her blushes! What—can't I say that either? Mercy me—when my children beg me to have all those gods and goddesses painted out overhead I always say I'm too thankful to have somebody about me that *nothing* can shock!"

Archer burst into a laugh, and May echoed it, crimson to the eyes.

"Well, now tell me all about the party, please, my dears, for I shall never get a straight word about it out of that silly Medora," the ancestress continued, and, as May exclaimed: "Cousin Medora? But I thought she was going back to Portsmouth?" she answered placidly: "So she is—but she's got to come here first to pick up Ellen. Ah—you didn't know Ellen had come to spend the day with me? Such folderol, her not coming for the summer, but I gave up arguing with young people about fifty years ago. Ellen—*Ellen!*" she cried in her shrill old voice, trying to bend forward far enough to catch a glimpse of the lawn beyond the verandah.

There was no answer, and Mrs. Mingott rapped impatiently with her stick on the shiny floor. A mulatto maidservant in a bright turban, replying to the summons, informed her mistress that she had seen "Miss Ellen" going down the path to the shore, and Mrs. Mingott turned to Archer.

"Run down and fetch her, like a good grandson; this pretty lady will describe the party to me," she said, and Archer stood up as if in a dream.

He had heard the Countess Olenska's name pronounced often enough during the year and a half since they had last met, and was even familiar with the main incidents of her life in the interval. He knew that she had spent the previous summer at Newport, where she appeared to have gone a great deal into society, but that in the autumn she had suddenly sublet the "perfect house" which Beaufort had been at such pains to find for her, and decided to establish herself in Washington. There, during the winter, he had heard of her (as one always heard of pretty women in Washington) as shining in the "brilliant diplomatic society" that was supposed to make up for the social shortcomings of the Administration. He had listened to these accounts, and to various contradictory reports on her appearance, her conversation, her point of view, and her choice of friends, with the detachment with which one listens to reminiscences of someone long since dead; not till Medora suddenly spoke her name at the archery match had Ellen Olenska become a living presence to him again. The marchioness's foolish lisp had called up a vision of the little firelit drawing room and the sound of the carriage wheels returning down the deserted street. He thought of a story he had read, of some peasant children in Tuscany lighting a bunch of straw in a wayside cavern, and revealing old silent images in their painted tomb . . .

The way to the shore descended from the bank on which the house was perched to a walk above the water planted with weeping willows. Through their veil Archer caught the glint of the Lime Rock, with its whitewashed turret and the tiny house in which the heroic lighthouse keeper, Ida Lewis, was living her last venerable years. Beyond it lay the flat reaches and ugly government chimneys of Goat Island, the bay spreading northward in a shimmer of gold to Prudence Island with its low growth of oaks, and the shores of Conanicut faint in the sunset haze.

From the willow walk projected a slight wooden pier ending in a sort of pagodalike summerhouse; and in the pagoda a lady stood, leaning against the rail, her back to the shore. Archer stopped at the sight as if he had waked from sleep. That vision of the past was a dream, and the reality was what awaited him in the house on the bank overhead: was Mrs. Welland's pony carriage circling around and around the oval at the door, was May sitting under the shameless Olympians and glowing with secret hopes, was the Welland villa at the far end of Bellevue Avenue, and Mr. Welland, already dressed for dinner, and pacing the drawing-room floor, watch in hand, with dyspeptic impatience—for it was one of the houses in which one always knew exactly what is happening at a given hour.

"What am I? A son-in-law—" Archer thought.

The figure at the end of the pier had not moved. For a long moment the young man stood halfway down the bank, gazing at the bay furrowed with the coming and going of sailboats, yacht launches, fishing craft, and the trailing black coal barges hauled by noisy tugs. The lady in the summerhouse seemed to be held by the same sight. Beyond the gray bastions of Fort Adams a long-drawn sunset was splintering up into a thousand fires, and the radiance caught the sail of a cat boat as it beat out through the channel between the Lime Rock and the shore. Archer, as he watched, remembered the scene in *The Shaughraun*, and Montague lifting Ada Dyas's ribbon to his lips without her knowing that he was in the room.

"She doesn't know—she hasn't guessed. Shouldn't I know if she came up behind me, I wonder?" he mused, and suddenly he said to himself: "If she doesn't turn before that sail crosses the Lime Rock light I'll go back."

The boat was gliding out on the receding tide. It slid before the Lime Rock, blotted out Ida Lewis's little house, and passed across the turret in which the light was hung. Archer waited till a wide space of water sparkled between the last reef of the island and the stern of the boat, but still the figure in the summerhouse did not move.

He turned and walked up the hill.

"I'm sorry you didn't find Ellen—I should have liked to see her again," May said as they drove home through the dusk. "But perhaps she wouldn't have cared—she seems so changed."

"Changed?" echoed her husband in a colorless voice, his eyes fixed on the ponies' twitching ears.

"So indifferent to her friends, I mean; giving up New York and her house, and spending her time with such queer people. Fancy how hideously uncomfortable she must be at the Blenkers'! She says she does it to keep cousin Medora out of mischief: to prevent her marrying dreadful people. But I sometimes think we've always bored her."

Archer made no answer, and she continued, with a tinge of hardness that he had never before noticed in her frank fresh voice: "After all, I wonder if she wouldn't be happier with her husband."

He burst into a laugh. *"Sancta simplicitas!"* he exclaimed, and as she turned a puzzled frown on him he added: "I don't think I ever heard you say a cruel thing before."

"Cruel?"

"Well—watching the contortions of the damned is supposed to be a favorite sport of the angels, but I believe even they don't think people happier in hell."

"It's a pity she ever married abroad then," said May in the placid tone with which her mother met Mr. Welland's vagaries, and Archer felt himself gently relegated to the category of unreasonable husbands.

They drove down Bellevue Avenue and turned in between the chamfered wooden gateposts surmounted by cast-iron lamps which marked the approach to the Welland villa. Lights were already shining through its windows, and Archer, as the carriage stopped, caught a glimpse of his father-in-law, exactly as he had pictured him, pacing the drawing room, watch in hand and wearing the pained expression that he had long since found to be much more efficacious than anger.

The young man, as he followed his wife into the hall, was conscious of a curious reversal of mood. There was something about the luxury of the Welland house and the density of the Welland atmosphere, so charged with minute observances and exactions, that always stole into his system like a narcotic. The heavy carpets, the watchful servants, the perpetually reminding tick of disciplined clocks, the perpetually renewed stack of cards and invitations on the hall table, the whole chain of tyrannical trifles binding one hour to the next, and each member of the household to all the others, made any less systematized and affluent existence seem unreal and precarious. But now it was the Welland house, and the life he was expected to lead in it, that had become unreal and irrelevant, and the brief scene on the shore, when he had stood irresolute, halfway down the bank, was as close to him as the blood in his veins.

All night he lay awake in the big chintz bedroom at May's side, watching the moonlight slant along the carpet, and thinking of Ellen Olenska driving home across the gleaming beaches behind Beaufort's trotters.

A PARTY for the Blenkers—the Blenkers?"

Mr. Welland laid down his knife and fork and looked anxiously and incredulously across the luncheon table at his wife, who, adjusting her gold eyeglasses, read aloud in the tone of high comedy: "Professor and Mrs. Emerson Sillerton request the pleasure of Mr. and Mrs. Welland's company at the meeting of the Wednesday Afternoon Club on August 25th at 3 o'clock punctually. To meet Mrs. and the Misses Blenker.

"Red Gables, Catherine Street.                                    R.S.V.P."

"Good gracious—" Mr. Welland gasped, as if a second reading had been necessary to bring the monstrous absurdity of the thing home to him.

"Poor Amy Sillerton—you never can tell what her husband will do next," Mrs. Welland sighed. "I suppose he's just discovered the Blenkers."

Professor Emerson Sillerton was a thorn in the side of Newport society; and a thorn that could not be plucked out, for it grew on a venerable and venerated family tree. He was, as people said, a man who had had "every advantage." His father was Sillerton Jackson's uncle, his mother a Pennilow of Boston; on each side there was wealth and position, and mutual suitability. Nothing— as Mrs. Welland had often remarked—nothing on earth obliged Emerson Sillerton to be an archeologist, or indeed a professor of any sort, or to live in Newport in winter, or do any of the other revolutionary things that he did. But at least, if he was going to break with tradition and flout society in the face, he need not have married poor Amy Dagonet, who had a right to expect "something different," and money enough to keep her own carriage.

No one in the Mingott set could understand why Amy Sillerton had submitted so tamely to the eccentricities of a husband who filled the house with long-haired men and short-haired women, and, when he traveled, took her to explore tombs in Yucatan instead of going to Paris or Italy. But there they were, set in their ways, and apparently unaware that they were different from other people, and when they gave one of their dreary annual garden parties every family on the Cliffs, because of the Sillerton-Pennilow-Dagonet connection, had to draw lots and send an unwilling representative.

"It's a wonder," Mrs. Welland remarked, "that they didn't choose the Cup Race day! Do you remember, two years ago, their giving a party for a black man on the day of Julia Mingott's *thé dansant?* Luckily this time there's nothing else going on that I know of—for of course some of us will have to go."

Mr. Welland sighed nervously. " 'Some of us,' my dear—more than one? Three o'clock is such a very awkward hour. I have to be here at half-past three to take my drops: it's really no use trying to follow Bencomb's new treatment if I don't do it systematically; and if I join you later, of course I shall miss my drive." At the thought he laid down his knife and fork again, and a flush of anxiety rose to his finely wrinkled cheek.

"There's no reason why you should go at all, my dear," his wife answered with a cheerfulness that had become automatic. "I have some cards to leave at the other end of Bellevue Avenue, and I'll drop in at about half-past three and stay long enough to make poor Amy feel that she hasn't been slighted." She glanced hesitatingly at her daughter. "And if Newland's afternoon is provided for perhaps May can drive you out with the ponies, and try their new russet harness."

It was a principle in the Welland family that people's days and hours should be what Mrs. Welland called "provided for." The melancholy possibility of having to "kill time" (especially for those who did not care for whist or solitaire) was a vision that haunted her as the specter of the unemployed haunts the philanthropist. Another of her principles was that parents should never (at least visibly) interfere with the plans of their married children; and the difficulty of adjusting this respect for May's independence with the exigency of Mr. Welland's claims could be overcome only by the exercise of an ingenuity which left not a second of Mrs. Welland's own time unprovided for.

"Of course I'll drive with Papa—I'm sure Newland will find

something to do," May said, in a tone that gently reminded her husband of his lack of response. It was a cause of constant distress to Mrs. Welland that her son-in-law showed so little foresight in planning his days. Often already, during the fortnight that he had passed under her roof, when she inquired how he meant to spend his afternoon, he had answered paradoxically: "Oh, I think for a change I'll just save it instead of spending it—" and once, when she and May had had to go on a long-postponed round of afternoon calls, he had confessed to having lain all the afternoon under a rock on the beach below the house.

"Newland never seems to look ahead," Mrs. Welland once ventured to complain to her daughter, and May answered serenely: "No, but you see it doesn't matter, because when there's nothing particular to do he reads a book."

"Ah, yes—like his father!" Mrs. Welland agreed, as if allowing for an inherited oddity, and after that the question of Newland's unemployment was tacitly dropped.

Nevertheless, as the day for the Sillerton reception approached, May began to show a natural solicitude for his welfare, and to suggest a tennis match at the Chiverses', or a sail on Julius Beaufort's cutter, as a means of atoning for her temporary desertion. "I shall be back by six, you know, dear: Papa never drives later than that—" and she was not reassured till Archer said that he thought of hiring a runabout and driving up the island to a stud farm to look at a second horse for her brougham. They had been looking for this horse for some time, and the suggestion was so acceptable that May glanced at her mother as if to say: "You see he knows how to plan out his time as well as any of us."

The idea of the stud farm and the brougham horse had germinated in Archer's mind on the very day when the Emerson Sillerton invitation had first been mentioned, but he had kept it to himself as if there were something clandestine in the plan, and discovery might prevent its execution. He had, however, taken the precaution to engage in advance a runabout with a pair of old livery-stable trotters that could still do their eighteen miles on level roads; and at two o'clock, hastily deserting the luncheon table, he sprang into the light carriage and drove off.

The day was perfect. A breeze from the north drove little puffs of white cloud across an ultramarine sky, with a bright sea running under it. Bellevue Avenue was empty at that hour, and after dropping the stable lad at the corner of Mill Street Archer turned down the Old Beach Road and drove across Eastman's Beach.

He had the feeling of unexplained excitement with which, on half-holidays at school, he used to start off into the unknown. Taking his pair at an easy gait, he counted on reaching the stud farm, which was not far beyond Paradise Rocks, before three o'clock; so that, after looking over the horse (and trying him if he seemed promising) he would still have four golden hours to dispose of.

As soon as he heard of the Sillerton's party he had said to himself that the Marchioness Manson would certainly come to Newport with the Blenkers, and that Madame Olenska might again take the opportunity of spending the day with her grandmother. At any rate, the Blenker habitation would probably be deserted, and he would be able, without indiscretion, to satisfy a vague curiosity concerning it. He was not sure that he wanted to see the Countess Olenska again, but ever since he had looked at her from the path above the bay he had wanted, irrationally and indescribably, to see the place she was living in, and to follow the movements of her imagined figure as he had watched the real one in the summerhouse. The longing was with him day and night, an incessant undefinable craving, like the sudden whim of a sick man for food or drink once tasted and long since forgotten. He could not see beyond the craving, or picture what it might lead to, for he was not conscious of any wish to speak to Madame Olenska or to hear her voice. He simply felt that if he could carry away the vision of the spot of earth she walked on, and the way the sky and sea enclosed it, the rest of the world might seem less empty.

When he reached the stud farm a glance showed him that the horse was not what he wanted; nevertheless he took a turn behind it in order to prove to himself that he was not in a hurry. But at three o'clock he shook out the reins over the trotters and turned into the byroads leading to Portsmouth. The wind had dropped and a faint haze on the horizon showed that a fog was waiting to steal up the Saconnet on the turn of the tide; but all about him fields and woods were steeped in golden light.

He drove past gray-shingled farmhouses in orchards, past hay fields and groves of oak, past villages with white steeples rising sharply into the fading sky; and at last, after stopping to ask the way of some men at work in a field, he turned down a lane between high banks of goldenrod and brambles. At the end of the lane was the blue glimmer of the river; to the left, standing in front of a clump of oaks and maples, he saw a long tumble-down house with white paint peeling from its clapboards.

On the roadside facing the gateway stood one of the open sheds in which the New Englander shelters his farming implements and visitors "hitch" their "teams." Archer, jumping down, led his pair into the shed, and after tying them to a post turned toward the house. The patch of lawn before it had relapsed into a hay field, but to the left an overgrown box garden full of dahlias and rusty rosebushes encircled a ghostly summerhouse of trelliswork that had once been white, surmounted by a wooden Cupid who had lost his bow and arrow but continued to take ineffectual aim.

Archer leaned for a while against the gate. No one was in sight, and not a sound came from the open windows of the house: a grizzled Newfoundland dozing before the door seemed as ineffectual a guardian as the arrowless Cupid. It was strange to think that this place of silence and decay was the home of the turbulent Blenkers, yet Archer was sure that he was not mistaken.

For a long time he stood there, content to take in the scene, and gradually falling under its drowsy spell; but at length he roused himself to the sense of the passing time. Should he look his fill and then drive away? He stood irresolute, wishing suddenly to see the inside of the house, so that he might picture the room that Madame Olenska sat in. There was nothing to prevent his walking up to the door and ringing the bell; if, as he supposed, she was away with the rest of the party, he could easily give his name, and ask permission to go into the sitting room to write a message.

But instead, he crossed the lawn and turned toward the box garden. As he entered it he caught sight of something bright-colored in the summerhouse, and presently made it out to be a pink parasol. The parasol drew him like a magnet: he was sure it was hers. He went into the summerhouse, and sitting down on the rickety seat picked up the silken thing and looked at its carved handle, which was made of some rare wood that gave out an aromatic scent. Archer lifted the handle to his lips.

He heard a rustle of skirts against the box, and sat motionless, leaning on the parasol handle with clasped hands, and letting the rustle come nearer without lifting his eyes. He had always known that this must happen . . .

"Oh, Mr. Archer!" exclaimed a loud young voice, and looking up he saw before him the youngest and largest of the Blenker girls, blond and blowsy, in bedraggled muslin. A red blotch on one of her cheeks seemed to show that it had recently been pressed against a pillow, and her half-awakened eyes stared at him hospitably but confusedly.

"Gracious—where did you drop from? I must have been sound asleep in the hammock. Everybody else has gone to Newport. Did you ring?" she incoherently inquired.

Archer's confusion was greater than hers. "I—no—that is, I was just going to. I had to come up the island to see about a horse, and I drove over on a chance of finding Mrs. Blenker and your visitors. But the house seemed empty—so I sat down to wait."

Miss Blenker, shaking off the fumes of sleep, looked at him with increasing interest. "The house *is* empty. Mother's not here, or the marchioness—or anybody but me." Her glance became faintly reproachful. "Didn't you know that Professor and Mrs. Sillerton are giving a garden party for mother and all of us this afternoon? It was too unlucky that I couldn't go; but I've had a sore throat, and mother was afraid of the drive home this evening. Did you ever know anything so disappointing? Of course," she added gaily, "I shouldn't have minded half as much if I'd known you were coming."

Symptoms of a lumbering coquetry became visible in her, and Archer found the strength to break in: "But Madame Olenska—has she gone to Newport too?"

Miss Blenker looked at him with surprise. "Madame Olenska—didn't you know she'd been called away?"

"Called away?—"

"Oh, my best parasol! I lent it to that goose of a Katie, because it matched her ribbons, and the careless thing must have dropped it here. We Blenkers are all like that . . . real Bohemians!" Recovering the sunshade with a powerful hand she unfurled it and suspended its rosy dome above her head. "Yes, Ellen was called away yesterday: she lets us call her Ellen, you know. A telegram came from Boston: she said she might be gone for two days. I do *love* the way she does her hair, don't you?" Miss Blenker rambled on.

Archer continued to stare through her as though she had been transparent. All he saw was the trumpery parasol that arched its pinkness above her giggling head.

After a moment he ventured: "You don't happen to know why Madame Olenska went to Boston? I hope it was not on account of bad news?"

Miss Blenker took this with a cheerful incredulity. "Oh, I don't believe so. She didn't tell us what was in the telegram. I think she didn't want the marchioness to know. She's so romantic-looking, isn't she? Doesn't she remind you of Mrs. Scott-Siddons when she reads *Lady Geraldine's Courtship*? Did you never hear her?"

Archer was dealing hurriedly with crowding thoughts. His whole future seemed suddenly to be unrolled before him; and passing down its endless emptiness he saw the dwindling figure of a man to whom nothing was ever to happen. He glanced about him at the unpruned garden, the tumble-down house, and the oak grove under which the dusk was gathering. It had seemed so exactly the place in which he ought to have found Madame Olenska; and she was far away, and even the pink sunshade was not hers . . .

He frowned and hesitated. "You don't know, I suppose—I shall be in Boston tomorrow. If I could manage to see her—"

He felt that Miss Blenker was losing interest in him, though her smile persisted. "Oh, of course; how lovely of you! She's staying at the Parker House; it must be horrible there in this weather."

After that Archer was but intermittently aware of the remarks they exchanged. He could only remember stoutly resisting her entreaty that he should await the returning family and have high tea with them before he drove home. At length, with his hostess still at his side, he passed out of range of the wooden Cupid, unfastened his horse, and drove off. At the turn of the lane he saw Miss Blenker standing at the gate and waving the pink parasol.

THE NEXT MORNING, when Archer got out of the Fall River train, he emerged upon a steaming midsummer Boston. The streets near the station were full of the smell of beer and coffee and decaying fruit and a shirtsleeved populace moved through them with the intimate abandon of boarders going down the passage to the bathroom.

Archer found a cab and drove to the Somerset Club for breakfast. Even the fashionable quarters had the air of untidy domesticity to which no excess of heat ever degrades the European cities. Caretakers in calico lounged on the doorsteps of the wealthy, and the Common looked like a pleasure ground on the morrow of a Masonic picnic. If Archer had tried to imagine Ellen Olenska in improbable scenes he could not have called up any into which it was more difficult to fit her than this heat-prostrated and deserted Boston.

He breakfasted with appetite and method, beginning with a slice of melon, and studying a morning paper while he waited for his toast and scrambled eggs. A new sense of energy and activity had possessed him ever since he had announced to May the night before that he had business in Boston, and should take the Fall River boat that night and go on to New York the following evening. It had always been understood that he would return to town early in the week, and when he got back from his expedition to Portsmouth a letter from the office, which fate had conspicuously placed on a corner of the hall table, sufficed to justify his sudden change of plan. He was even ashamed of the ease with which the whole thing had been done: it reminded him, for an uncomfortable moment, of Lawrence Lefferts's masterly contrivances for securing his freedom. But this did not long trouble him, for he was not in an analytic mood.

After breakfast he smoked a cigarette and glanced over the *Commercial Advertiser*. While he was thus engaged two or three men he knew came in, and the usual greetings were exchanged: it was the same world after all, though he had such a queer sense of having slipped through the meshes of time and space.

He looked at his watch, and finding that it was half-past nine got up and went into the writing room. There he wrote a few lines, and ordered a messenger to take a cab to the Parker House and wait for the answer. He then sat down behind another newspaper and tried to calculate how long it would take a cab to get to the Parker House.

"The lady was out, sir," he suddenly heard a waiter's voice at his elbow; and he stammered: "Out?—" as if it were a word in a strange language.

He got up and went into the hall. It must be a mistake: she could not be out at that hour. He flushed with anger at his own stupidity: why had he not sent the note as soon as he arrived?

He found his hat and stick and went forth into the street. The city had suddenly become as strange and vast and empty as if he were a traveler from distant lands. For a moment he stood on the doorstep hesitating; then he decided to go to the Parker House. What if the messenger had been misinformed, and she were still there?

He started to walk across the Common, and on the first bench, under a tree, he saw her sitting. She had a gray silk sunshade over her head—how could he ever have imagined her with a pink one? As he approached he was struck by her listless attitude: she sat there as if she had nothing else to do. He saw her drooping profile, and the knot of hair fastened low in the neck under her dark hat, and the long wrinkled glove on the hand that held the sunshade. He came a step or two nearer, and she turned and looked at him.

"Oh"—she said, and for the first time he noticed a startled look on her face; but in another moment it gave way to a slow smile of wonder and contentment.

"Oh"—she murmured again, on a different note, as he stood looking down at her, and without rising she made a place for him on the bench.

"I'm here on business—just got here," Archer explained, and, without knowing why, he suddenly began to feign astonishment at seeing her. "But what on earth are *you* doing in this wilderness?" He had really no idea what he was saying: he felt as if he were shouting at her across endless distances, and she might vanish again before he could overtake her.

"I? Oh, I'm here on business too," she answered, turning her head toward him so that they were face to face. The words hardly reached him: he was aware only of her voice, and of the startling fact that not an echo of it had remained in his memory. He had not even remembered that it was low-pitched, with a faint roughness on the consonants.

"You do your hair differently," he said, his heart beating as if he had uttered something irrevocable.

"Differently? No—it's only that I do it as best I can when I'm without Nastasia."

"Nastasia; but isn't she with you?"

"No, I'm alone. For two days it was not worthwhile to bring her."

"You're alone—at the Parker House?"

She looked at him with a flash of her old malice. "Does it strike you as dangerous?"

"No, not dangerous—"

"But unconventional? I see, I suppose it is." She considered a moment. "I hadn't thought of it, because I've just done something so much more unconventional." The faint tinge of irony lingered in her eyes. "I've just refused to take back a sum of money—that belonged to me."

Archer sprang up and moved a step or two away. She had furled her parasol and sat absently drawing patterns on the gravel. Presently he came back and stood before her.

"Someone—has come here to meet you?"

"Yes."

"With this offer?"

She nodded.

"And you refused—because of the conditions?"

"I refused," she said after a moment.

He sat down by her again. "What were the conditons?"

"Oh, they were not onerous: just to sit at the head of his table now and then."

There was another interval of silence. Archer's heart had

slammed itself shut in the queer way it had, and he sat vainly groping for a word.

"He wants you back—at any price?"

"Well—a considerable price. At least the sum is considerable for me."

He paused again, beating about the question he felt he must put.

"It was to meet him here that you came?"

She stared, and then burst into a laugh. "Meet him—my husband? *Here?* At this season he's always at Cowes or Baden."

"He sent someone?"

"Yes."

"With a letter?"

She shook her head. "No, just a message. He never writes. I don't think I've had more than one letter from him." The allusion brought the color to her cheek, and it reflected itself in Archer's vivid blush.

"Why does he never write?"

"Why should he? What does one have secretaries for?"

The young man's blush deepened. She had pronounced the word as if it had no more significance than any other in her vocabulary. For a moment it was on the tip of his tongue to ask: "Did he send his secretary, then?" But the remembrance of Count Olenski's only letter to his wife was too present to him. He paused again, and then took another plunge.

"And the person?"

"The emissary? The emissary," Madame Olenska rejoined, still smiling, "might, for all I care, have left already; but he has insisted on waiting till this evening . . . in case . . . on the chance . . ."

"And you came out here to think the chance over?"

"I came out to get a breath of air. The hotel's too stifling. I'm taking the afternoon train back to Portsmouth."

They sat silent, not looking at each other, but straight ahead at the people passing along the path. Finally she turned her eyes again to his face and said: "You're not changed."

He felt like answering: "I was, till I saw you again," but instead he stood up abruptly and glanced about him at the untidy sweltering park.

"This is horrible. Why shouldn't we go out a little on the bay? There's a breeze, and it will be cooler. We might take the steamboat down to Point Arley." She glanced up at him hesitatingly and he went on: "On a Monday morning there won't be anybody on the boat. My train doesn't leave till evening: I'm going back to New York. Why shouldn't we?" he insisted, looking down at her, and suddenly he broke out: "Haven't we done all we could?"

"Oh"—she murmured again. She stood up and reopened her sunshade, glancing about her as if to take counsel of the scene, and assure herself of the impossibility of remaining in it. Then her eyes returned to his face. "You mustn't say things like that to me," she said.

"I'll say anything you like, or nothing. I won't open my mouth unless you tell me to. What harm can it do to anybody? All I want is to listen to you," he stammered.

She drew out a little gold-faced watch on an enameled chain. "Oh, don't calculate," he broke out. "Give me the day! I want to get you away from that man. At what time was he coming?"

Her color rose again. "At eleven."

"Then you must come at once."

"You needn't be afraid—if I don't come."

"Nor you either—if you do. I swear I only want to hear about you, to know what you've been doing. It's a hundred years since we've met—it may be another hundred before we meet again."

She still wavered, her anxious eyes on his face. "Why didn't you come down to the beach to fetch me, the day I was at Granny's?" she asked.

"Because you didn't look round—because you didn't know I was there. I swore I wouldn't unless you looked round." He laughed as the childishness of the confession struck him.

"But I didn't look round on purpose."

"On purpose?"

"I knew you were there; when you drove in I recognized the ponies. So I went down to the beach."

"To get away from me as far as you could?"

She repeated in a low voice: "To get away from you as far as I could."

He laughed out again, this time in boyish satisfaction. "Well, you see it's no use. I may as well tell you," he added, "that the business I came here for was just to find you. But, look here, we must start or we shall miss our boat."

"Our boat?" She frowned perplexedly, and then smiled. "Oh, but I must go back to the hotel first: I must leave a note—"

"As many notes as you please. You can write here." He drew out a note case and one of the new stylographic pens. "I've even got an envelope—you see how everything's predestined! There— steady the thing on your knee, and I'll get the pen going in a second. They have to be humored; wait—" He banged the hand that held the pen against the back of the bench. "It's like jerking down the mercury in a thermometer: just a trick. Now try—"

She laughed, and bending over the sheet of paper which he had laid on his note case, began to write. Archer walked away a few steps, staring with radiant unseeing eyes at the passersby, who, in their turn, paused to stare at the unwonted sight of a fashionably dressed lady writing a note on her knee on a bench in the Common.

Madame Olenska slipped the sheet into the envelope, wrote a name on it, and put it into her pocket. Then she too stood up.

They walked back toward Beacon Street, and near the club Archer caught sight of the plush-lined "herdic" which had carried his note to the Parker House, and whose driver was reposing from this effort by bathing his brow at the corner hydrant.

"I told you everything was predestined! Here's a cab for us. You see!" They laughed, astonished at the miracle of picking up a public conveyance at that hour, and in that unlikely spot, in a city where cab stands were still a "foreign" novelty.

Archer, looking at his watch, saw that there was time to drive to the Parker House before going to the steamboat landing. They rattled through the hot streets and drew up at the door of the hotel.

Archer held out his hand for the letter. "Shall I take it in?" he asked, but Madame Olenska, shaking her head, sprang out and disappeared through the glazed doors. It was barely half-past ten; but what if the emissary, impatient for her reply, and not knowing how else to employ his time, were already seated among the travelers with cooling drinks at their elbows of whom Archer had caught a glimpse as she went in?

He waited, pacing up and down before the herdic. A Sicilian

youth with eyes like Nastasia's offered to shine his boots, and an Irish matron to sell him peaches; and every few moments the doors opened to let out hot men with straw hats tilted far back, who glanced at him as they went by. He marveled that the door should open so often, and that all the people it let out should look so like each other, and so like all the other hot men who, at that hour, through the length and breadth of the land, were passing continuously in and out of the swinging doors of hotels.

And then, suddenly, came a face that he could not relate to the other faces. He caught but a flash of it, for his pacings had carried him to the farthest point of his beat, and it was in turning back to the hotel that he saw, in a group of typical countenances—the lank and weary, the round and surprised, the lantern-jawed and mild—this other face that was so many more things at once, and things so different. It was that of a young man, pale too, and half-extinguished by the heat, or worry, or both, but somehow, quicker, vivider, more conscious; or perhaps seeming so because he was so different. Archer hung a moment on a thin thread of memory, but it snapped and floated off with the disappearing face—apparently that of some foreign businessman, looking doubly foreign in such a setting. He vanished in the stream of passersby, and Archer resumed his patrol.

He did not care to be seen watch in hand within view of the hotel, and his unaided reckoning of the lapse of time led him to conclude that, if Madame Olenska was so long in reappearing, it could only be because she had met the emissary and been waylaid by him. At the thought Archer's apprehension rose to anguish.

"If she doesn't come soon I'll go in and find her," he said.

The doors swung open again and she was at his side. They got into the herdic, and as it drove off he took out his watch and saw that she had been absent just three minutes. In the clatter of loose windows that made talk impossible they bumped over the disjointed cobblestones to the wharf.

Seated side by side on a bench of the half-empty boat they found that they had hardly anything to say to each other, or rather that what they had to say communicated itself best in the blessed silence of their release and their isolation.

As the paddle wheels began to turn, and wharves and shipping

to recede through the veil of heat, it seemed to Archer that everything in the old familiar world of habit was receding also. He
longed to ask Madame Olenska if she did not have the same
feeling: the feeling that they were starting on some long voyage
from which they might never return. But he was afraid to say it,
or anything else that might disturb the delicate balance of her
trust in him. In reality he had no wish to betray that trust. There
had been days and nights when the memory of their kiss had
burned and burned on his lips; the day before even, on the drive
to Portsmouth, the thought of her had run through him like fire;
but now that she was beside him, and they were drifting forth into
this unknown world, they seemed to have reached the kind of
deeper nearness that a touch may sunder.

As the boat left the harbor and turned seaward a breeze stirred
about them and the bay broke up into long oily undulations, then
into ripples tipped with spray. The fog of sultriness still hung
over the city, but ahead lay a fresh world of ruffled waters, and
distant promontories with lighthouses in the sun. Madame Olenska, leaning back against the boat rail, drank in the coolness between parted lips. She had wound a long veil about her hat, but it
left her face uncovered, and Archer was struck by the tranquil
gaiety of her expression. She seemed to take their adventure as a
matter of course, and to be neither in fear of unexpected en-
counters, nor (what was worse) unduly elated by their possibility.

In the bare dining room of the inn, which he had hoped they
would have to themselves, they found a strident party of inno-
cent-looking young men and women—schoolteachers on a holiday, the landlord told them—and Archer's heart sank at the idea
of having to talk through their noise.

"This is hopeless—I'll ask for a private room," he said, and
Madame Olenska, without offering any objection, waited while he
went in search of it. The room opened on a long wooden verandah, with the sea coming in at the windows. It was bare and cool,
with a table covered with a coarse checkered cloth and adorned
by a bottle of pickles and a blueberry pie under a cage. No more
guileless-looking *cabinet particulier* ever offered its shelter to a
clandestine couple: Archer fancied he saw the sense of its reassurance in the faintly amused smile with which Madame Olenska sat
down opposite to him. A woman who had run away from her

husband—and reputedly with another man—was likely to have mastered the art of taking things for granted, but something in the quality of her composure took the edge from his irony. By being so quiet, so unsurprised and so simple she had managed to brush away the conventions and make him feel that to seek to be alone was the natural thing for two old friends who had so much to say to each other. . . .

# ——24——

THEY LUNCHED slowly and meditatively, with mute intervals between rushes of talk; for, the spell once broken, they had much to say, and yet moments when saying became the mere accompaniment to long duologues of silence. Archer kept the talk from his own affairs, not with conscious intention but because he did not want to miss a word of her history; and leaning on the table, her chin resting on her clasped hands, she talked to him of the year and a half since they had met.

She had grown tired of what people called "society"; New York was kind, it was almost oppressively hospitable; she should never forget the way in which it had welcomed her back; but after the first flush of novelty she had found herself, as she phrased it, too "different" to care for the things it cared about—and so she had decided to try Washington, where one was supposed to meet more varieties of people and of opinion. And on the whole she should probably settle down in Washington, and make a home there for poor Medora, who had worn out the patience of all her other relations just at the time when she most needed looking after and protecting from matrimonial perils.

"But Dr. Carver—aren't you afraid of Dr. Carver? I hear he's been staying with you at the Blenkers'."

She smiled. "Oh, the Carver danger is over. Dr. Carver is a very clever man. He wants a rich wife to finance his plans, and Medora is simply a good advertisement as a convert."

"A convert to what?"

"To all sorts of new and crazy social schemes. But, do you know, they interest me more than the blind conformity to tradition—somebody else's tradition—that I see among our own friends. It seems stupid to have discovered America only to make it into a copy of another country." She smiled across the table. "Do you suppose Christopher Columbus would have taken all that trouble just to go to the opera with the Selfridge Merrys?"

Archer changed color. "And Beaufort—do you say these things to Beaufort?" he asked abruptly.

"I haven't seen him for a long time. But I used to, and he understands."

"Ah, it's what I've always told you; you don't like us. And you like Beaufort because he's so unlike us." He looked about the bare room and out at the bare beach and the row of stark white village houses strung along the shore. "We're damnably dull. We've no character, no color, no variety. I wonder," he broke out, "why you don't go back?"

Her eyes darkened, and he expected an indignant rejoinder. But she sat silent, as if thinking over what he had said, and he grew frightened lest she should answer that she wondered too.

At length she said: "I believe it's because of you."

It was impossible to make the confession more dispassionately, or in a tone less encouraging to the vanity of the person addressed. Archer reddened to the temples, but dared not move or speak: it was as if her words had been some rare butterfly that the least motion might drive off on startled wings, but that might gather a flock about it if it were left undisturbed.

"At least," she continued, "it was you who made me understand that under the dullness there are things so fine and sensitive and delicate that even those I most cared for in my other life look cheap in comparison. I don't know how to explain myself"— she drew together her troubled brows—"but it seems as if I'd never before understood with how much that is hard and shabby and base the most exquisite pleasures may be paid."

"Exquisite pleasures—it's something to have had them!" he felt like retorting, but the appeal in her eyes kept him silent.

"I want," she went on, "to be perfectly honest with you—and with myself. For a long time I've hoped this chance would come: that I might tell you how you've helped me, what you've made of me—"

Archer sat staring beneath frowning brows. He interrupted her with a laugh. "And what do you make out that you've made of me?"

She paled a little. "Of you?"

"Yes, for I'm of your making much more than you ever were of mine. I'm the man who married one woman because another one told him to."

Her paleness turned to a fugitive flush. "I thought—you promised—you were not to say such things today."

"Ah—how like a woman! None of you will ever see a bad business through!"

She lowered her voice. "*Is* it a bad business—for May?"

He stood in the window, drumming against the raised sash, and feeling in every fiber the wistful tenderness with which she had spoken her cousin's name.

"For that's the thing we've always got to think of—haven't we—by your own showing?" she insisted.

"My own showing?" he echoed, his blank eyes still on the sea.

"Or if not," she continued, pursuing her own thought with a painful application, "if it's not worthwhile to have given up, to have missed things, so that others may be saved from disillusionment and misery—then everything I came home for, everything that made my other life seem by contrast so bare and so poor because no one there took account of them—all these things are a sham or a dream—"

He turned around without moving from his place. "And in that case there's no reason on earth why you shouldn't go back?" he concluded for her.

Her eyes were clinging to him desperately. "Oh, *is* there no reason?"

"Not if you staked your all on the success of my marriage. My marriage," he said savagely, "isn't going to be a sight to keep you here." She made no answer, and he went on, "What's the use? You gave me my first glimpse of a real life, and at the same moment you asked me to go on with a sham one. It's beyond human enduring—that's all."

"Oh, don't say that, when I'm enduring it!" she burst out, her eyes filling.

Her arms had dropped along the table, and she sat with her face abandoned to his gaze as if in the recklessness of a desperate peril. The face exposed her as much as if it had been her whole person, with the soul behind it: Archer stood dumb, overwhelmed by what it suddenly told him.

"You too—oh, all this time, you too?"

For answer, she let the tears on her lids overflow and run slowly downward.

Half the width of the room was still between them, and neither made any show of moving. Archer was conscious of a curious indifference to her bodily presence: he would hardly have been aware of it if one of the hands she had flung out on the table had not drawn his gaze as on the occasion when, in the little Twenty-third Street house, he had kept his eye on it in order not to look at her face. Now his imagination spun about the hand as about the edge of a vortex, but still he made no effort to draw nearer. He had known the love that is fed on caresses and feeds them, but this passion that was closer than his bones was not to be superficially satisfied. His one terror was to do anything which might efface the sound and impression of her words; his one thought, that he should never again feel quite alone.

But after a moment the sense of waste and ruin overcame him. There they were, close together and safe and shut in, yet so chained to their separate destinies that they might as well have been half the world apart.

"What's the use—when you will go back?" he broke out, a great hopeless *How on earth can I keep you?* crying out to her beneath his words.

She sat motionless, with lowered lids. "Oh—I shan't go yet!"

"Not yet? Sometime, then? Sometime that you already foresee?"

At that she raised her clearest eyes. "I promise you: not as long as you hold out. Not as long as we can look straight at each other like this."

He dropped into his chair. What her answer really said was: "If you lift a finger you'll drive me back: back to all the abominations you know of, and all the temptations you half guess." He understood it as clearly as if she had uttered the words, and the thought kept him anchored to his side of the table in a kind of moved and sacred submission.

"What a life for you!—" he groaned.

"Oh—as long as it's a part of yours."

"And mine a part of yours?"

She nodded.

"And that's to be all—for either of us?"

"Well; it *is* all, isn't it?"

At that he sprang up, forgetting everything but the sweetness of her face. She rose too, not as if to meet him or to flee from him, but quietly, as though the worst of the task were done and she had only to wait, so quietly that, as he came close, her out-stretched hands acted not as a check but as a guide to him. They fell into his, while her arms, extended but not rigid, kept him far enough off to let her surrendered face say the rest.

They may have stood in that way for a long time, or only for a few moments, but it was long enough for her silence to communi-cate all she had to say, and for him to feel that only one thing mattered. He must do nothing to make this meeting their last; he must leave their future in her care, asking only that she should keep fast hold of it.

"Don't—don't be unhappy," she said, with a break in her voice as she drew her hands away, and he answered: "You won't go back—you won't go back?" as if it were the one possibility he could not bear.

"I won't go back," she said, and turning away she opened the door and led the way into the public dining room.

The strident schoolteachers were gathering up their posses-sions preparatory to a straggling flight to the wharf; across the beach lay the white steamboat at the pier; and over the sunlit waters Boston loomed in a line of haze.

# ─── 25 ───

ONCE MORE on the boat, and in the presence of others, Archer felt a tranquility of spirit that surprised as much as it sustained him.

The day, according to any current valuation, had been a rather ridiculous failure; he had not so much as touched Madame Olenska's hand with his lips, or extracted one word from her that gave promise of farther opportunities. Nevertheless, for a man sick with unsatisfied love, and parting for an indefinite period from the object of his passion, he felt himself almost humiliatingly calm and comforted. It was the perfect balance she had held between their loyalty to others and their honesty to themselves that had so stirred and yet tranquillized him; a balance not artfully calculated, as her tears and her falterings showed, but resulting naturally from her unabashed sincerity. It filled him with a tender awe, now the danger was over, and made him thank the fates that no personal vanity, no sense of playing a part before sophisticated witnesses, had tempted him to tempt her. Even after they had clasped hands for good-bye at the Fall River station, and he had turned away alone, the conviction remained with him of having saved out of their meeting much more than he had sacrificed.

He wandered back to the club, and went and sat alone in the deserted library, turning and turning over in his thoughts every separate second of their hours together. It was clear to him, and it grew more clear under closer scrutiny, that if she should finally decide on returning to Europe—returning to her husband—it would not be because her old life tempted her, even on the new terms offered. No, she would go only if she felt herself becoming a temptation to Archer, a temptation to fall away from the standard they had both set up. Her choice would be to stay near him as long as he did not ask her to come nearer, and it depended on himself to keep her just there, safe but secluded.

In the train these thoughts were still with him. They enclosed

197

him in a kind of golden haze, through which the faces about him looked remote and indistinct; he had a feeling that if he spoke to his fellow travelers they would not understand what he was saying. In this state of abstraction he found himself, the following morning, waking to the reality of a stifling September day in New York. The heat-withered faces in the long train streamed past him, and he continued to stare at them through the same golden blur; but suddenly, as he left the station, one of the faces detached itself, came closer and forced itself upon his consciousness. It was, as he instantly recalled, the face of the young man he had seen, the day before, passing out of the Parker House, and had noted as not conforming to type, as not having an American hotel face.

The same thing struck him now, and again he became aware of a dim stir of former associations. The young man stood looking about him with the dazed air of the foreigner flung upon the harsh mercies of American travel; then he advanced toward Archer, lifted his hat, and said in English "Surely, Monsieur, we met in London?"

"Ah, to be sure: in London!" Archer grasped his hand with curiosity and sympathy. "So you *did* get here, after all?" he exclaimed, casting a wondering eye on the astute and haggard little countenance of young Carfry's French tutor.

"Oh, I got here—yes," M. Rivière smiled with drawn lips. "But not for long; I return the day after tomorrow." He stood grasping his light valise in one neatly gloved hand, and gazing anxiously, perplexedly, almost appealingly, into Archer's face.

"I wonder, Monsieur, since I've had the good luck to run across you, if I might—"

"I was just going to suggest it: come to luncheon, won't you? Downtown, I mean: if you'll look me up in my office I'll take you to a very decent restaurant in that quarter."

M. Rivière was visibly touched and surprised. "You're too kind. But I was only going to ask if you would tell me how to reach some sort of conveyance. There are no porters, and no one here seems to listen—"

"I know: our American stations must surprise you. When you ask for a porter they give you chewing gum. But if you'll come along I'll extricate you; and you must really lunch with me, you know."

The young man, after a just perceptible hesitation, replied, with profuse thanks, and in a tone that did not carry complete conviction, that he was already engaged; but when they had reached the comparative reassurance of the street he asked if he might call that afternoon.

Archer, at ease in the midsummer leisure of the office, fixed an hour and scribbled his address, which the Frenchman pocketed with reiterated thanks and a wide flourish of his hat. A horse car received him, and Archer walked away.

Punctually at the hour M. Rivière appeared, shaved, smoothed out, but still unmistakably drawn and serious. Archer was alone in his office, and the young man, before accepting the seat he proffered, began abruptly: "I believe I saw you, sir, yesterday in Boston."

The statement was insignificant enough, and Archer was about to frame an assent when his words were checked by something mysterious yet illuminating in his visitor's insistent gaze.

"It is extraordinary, very extraordinary," M. Rivière continued, "that we should have met in the circumstances in which I find myself."

"What circumstances?" Archer asked, wondering a little crudely if he needed money.

M. Rivière continued to study him with tentative eyes. "I have come, not to look for employment, as I spoke of doing when we last met, but on a special mission—"

"Ah—!" Archer exclaimed. In a flash the two meetings had connected themselves in his mind. He paused to take in the situation thus suddenly lighted up for him, and M. Rivière also remained silent, as if aware that what he had said was enough.

"A special mission," Archer at length repeated.

The young Frenchman, opening his palms, raised them slightly, and the two men continued to look at each other across the office desk till Archer roused himself to say: "Do sit down"; whereupon M. Rivière bowed, took a distant chair, and again waited.

"It was about this mission that you wanted to consult me?" Archer finally asked.

M. Rivière bent his head. "Not in my own behalf: on that score

I—I have fully dealt with myself. I should like—if I may—to speak to you about the Countess Olenska."

Archer had known for the last few minutes that the words were coming; but when they came they sent the blood rushing to his temples as if he had been caught by a bent-back branch in a thicket.

"And on whose behalf," he said, "do you wish to do this?"

M. Rivière met the question sturdily. "Well—I might say *hers,* if it did not sound like a liberty. Shall I say instead, on behalf of abstract justice?"

Archer considered him ironically. "In other words, you are Count Olenski's messenger?"

He saw his blush more darkly reflected in M. Rivière's sallow countenance. "Not to *you,* Monsieur. If I come to you, it is on quite other grounds."

"What right have you, in the circumstances, to *be* on any other ground?" Archer retorted. "If you're an emissary you're an emissary."

The young man considered. "My mission is over: as far as the Countess Olenska goes, it has failed."

"I can't help that," Archer rejoined on the same note of irony.

"No: but you can help—" M. Rivière paused, turned his hat about in his still carefully gloved hands, looked into its lining and then back at Archer's face. "You can help, Monsieur, I am convinced, to make it equally a failure with her family."

Archer pushed back his chair and stood up. "Well—and by God I will!" he exclaimed. He stood with his hands in his pockets, staring down wrathfully at the little Frenchman, whose face, though he too had risen, was still an inch or two below the line of Archer's eyes.

M. Rivière paled to his normal hue: paler than that his complexion could hardly turn.

"Why the devil," Archer explosively continued, "should you have thought—since I suppose you're appealing to me on the ground of my relationship to Madame Olenska—that I should take a view contrary to the rest of her family?"

The change of expression in M. Rivière's face was for a time his only answer. His look passed from timidity to absolute distress: for a young man of his usually resourceful mien it would have been difficult to appear more disarmed and defenseless. "Oh, Monsieur—"

"I can't imagine," Archer continued, "why you should have come to me when there are others so much nearer to the countess; still less why you thought I should be more accessible to the arguments I suppose you were sent over with."

M. Rivière took this onslaught with a disconcerting humility. "The arguments I want to present to you, Monsieur, are my own and not those I was sent over with."

"Then I see still less reason for listening to them."

M. Rivière again looked into his hat, as if considering whether these last words were not a sufficiently broad hint to put it on and be gone. Then he spoke with sudden decision. "Monsieur—will you tell me one thing? Is it my right to be here that you question? Or do you perhaps believe the whole matter to be already closed?"

His quiet insistence made Archer feel the clumsiness of his own bluster. M. Rivière had succeeded in imposing himself: Archer, reddening slightly, dropped into his chair again, and signed to the young man to be seated.

"I beg your pardon: but why isn't the matter closed?"

M. Rivière gazed back at him with anguish. "You do, then, agree with the rest of the family that, in face of the new proposals I have brought, it is hardly possible for Madame Olenska not to return to her husband?"

"Good God!" Archer exclaimed, and his visitor gave out a low murmur of confirmation.

"Before seeing her, I saw—at Count Olenski's request—Mr. Lovell Mingott, with whom I had several talks before going to Boston. I understand that he represents his mother's view, and that Mrs. Manson Mingott's influence is great throughout her family."

Archer sat silent, with the sense of clinging to the edge of a sliding precipice. The discovery that he had been excluded from a share in these negotiations, and even from the knowledge that they were on foot, caused him a surprise hardly dulled by the acuter wonder of what he was learning. He saw in a flash that if the family had ceased to consult him it was because some deep tribal instinct warned them that he was no longer on their side;

and he recalled, with a start of comprehension, a remark of May's during their drive home from Mrs. Manson Mingott's on the day of the Archery Meeting: "Perhaps, after all, Ellen would be happier with her husband."

Even in the tumult of new discoveries Archer remembered his indignant exclamation, and the fact that since then his wife had never named Madame Olenska to him. Her careless allusion had no doubt been the straw held up to see which way the wind blew; the result had been reported to the family, and thereafter Archer had been tacitly omitted from their counsels. He admired the tribal discipline which made May bow to this decision. She would not have done so, he knew, had her conscience protested; but she probably shared the family view that Madame Olenska would be better off as an unhappy wife than as a separated one, and that there was no use in discussing the case with Newland, who had an awkward way of suddenly not seeming to take the most fundamental things for granted.

Archer looked up and met his visitor's anxious gaze. "Don't you know, Monsieur—is it possible you don't know—that the family begin to doubt if they have the right to advise the countess to refuse her husband's last proposals?"

"The proposals you brought?"

"The proposals I brought."

It was on Archer's lips to exclaim that whatever he knew or did not know was no concern of M. Rivière's; but something in the humble and yet courageous tenacity of M. Rivière's gaze made him reject this conclusion, and he met the young man's question with another. "What is your object in speaking to me of this?"

He had not to wait a moment for the answer. "To beg you, Monsieur—to beg you with all the force I'm capable of—not to let her go back.—Oh, don't let her!" M. Rivière exclaimed.

Archer looked at him with increasing astonishment. There was no mistaking the sincerity of his distress or the strength of his determination: he had evidently resolved to let everything go by the board but the supreme need of thus putting himself on record. Archer considered.

"May I ask," he said at length, "if this is the line you took with the Countess Olenska?"

M. Rivière reddened, but his eyes did not falter. "No, Monsieur, I accepted my mission in good faith. I really believed—for reasons I need not trouble you with—that it would be better for Madame Olenska to recover her situation, her fortune, the social consideration that her husband's standing gives her."

"So I supposed: you could hardly have accepted such a mission otherwise."

"I should not have accepted it."

"Well, then—?" Archer paused again, and their eyes met in another protracted scrutiny.

"Ah, Monsieur, after I had seen her, after I had listened to her, I knew she was better off here."

"You knew—?"

"Monsieur, I discharged my mission faithfully: I put the count's arguments, I stated his offers, without adding any comment of my own. The countess was good enough to listen patiently; she carried her goodness so far as to see me twice; she considered impartially all I had come to say. And it was in the course of these two talks that I changed my mind, that I came to see things differently."

"May I ask what led to this change?"

"Simply seeing the change in *her*," M. Rivière replied.

"The change in her? Then you knew her before?"

The young man's color again rose. "I used to see her in her husband's house. I have known Count Olenski for many years. You can imagine that he would not have sent a stranger on such a mission."

Archer's gaze, wandering away to the blank walls of the office, rested on a hanging calendar surmounted by the rugged features of the President of the United States. That such a conversation should be going on anywhere within the millions of square miles subject to his rule seemed as strange as anything that the imagination could invent.

"The change—what sort of a change?"

"Ah, Monsieur, if I could tell you!" M. Rivière paused. "*Tenez*— the discovery, I suppose, of what I'd never thought of before: that she's an American. And that if you're an American of *her* kind—of your kind—things that are accepted in certain other societies, or at least put up with as part of a general convenient give-and-take—become unthinkable, simply unthinkable. If Madame Olen-

ska's relations understood what these things were, their opposition to her returning would no doubt be as unconditional as her
own, but they seem to regard her husband's wish to have her back
as·proof of an irresistible longing for domestic life." M. Rivière
paused, and then added: "Whereas it's far from being as simple
as that."

Archer looked back to the President of the United States, and
then down at his desk and at the papers scattered on it. For a
second or two he could not trust himself to speak. During this
interval he heard M. Rivière's chair pushed back, and was aware
that the young man had risen. When he glanced up again he saw
that his visitor was as moved as himself.

"Thank you," Archer said simply.

"There's nothing to thank me for, Monsieur, it is I, rather—"
M. Rivière broke off, as if speech for him too were difficult. "I
should like though," he continued in a firmer voice, "to add one
thing. You asked me if I was in Count Olenski's employ. I am at
this moment: I returned to him, a few months ago, for reasons of
private necessity such as may happen to anyone who has persons,
ill and older persons, dependent on him. But from the moment
that I have taken the step of coming here to say these things to
you I consider myself discharged, and I shall tell him so on my
return, and give him the reasons. That's all, Monsieur."

M. Rivière bowed and drew back a step.

"Thank you," Archer said again, as their hands met.

# —— 26 ——

Every year on the fifteenth of October Fifth Avenue opened its shutters, unrolled its carpets and hung up its triple layer of window curtains.

By the first of November this household ritual was over, and society had begun to look about and take stock of itself. By the fifteenth the season was in full blast, opera and theaters were putting forth their new attractions, dinner engagements were accumulating, and dates for dances being fixed. And punctually at about this time Mrs. Archer always said that New York was very much changed.

Observing it from the lofty standpoint of a nonparticipant, she was able, with the help of Mr. Sillerton Jackson and Miss Sophy, to trace each new crack in its surface, and all the strange weeds pushing up between the ordered rows of social vegetables. It had been one of the amusements of Archer's youth to wait for this annual pronouncement of his mother's, and to hear her enumerate the minute signs of disintegration that his careless gaze had overlooked. For New York, to Mrs. Archer's mind, never changed without changing for the worse, and in this view Miss Sophy Jackson heartily concurred.

Mr. Sillerton Jackson, as became a man of the world, suspended his judgment and listened with an amused impartiality to the lamentations of the ladies. But even he never denied that New York had changed; and Newland Archer, in the winter of the second year of his marriage, was himself obliged to admit that if it had not actually changed it was certainly changing.

These points had been raised, as usual, at Mrs. Archer's Thanksgiving dinner. At the date when she was officially enjoined to give thanks for the blessings of the year it was her habit to take a mournful though not embittered stock of her world, and wonder what there was to be thankful for. At any rate, not the state of society; society, if it could be said to exist, was rather a spectacle on which to call down Biblical imprecations—and in fact, every-one knew what the Reverend Dr. Ashmore meant when he chose a text from Jeremiah (chap. ii., verse 25) for his Thanksgiving sermon. Dr. Ashmore, the new Rector of St. Matthew's, had been chosen because he was very "advanced": his sermons were considered bold in thought and novel in language. When he fulminated against fashionable society he always spoke of its "trend," and to Mrs. Archer it was terrifying and yet fascinating to feel herself part of a community that was trending.

"There's no doubt that Dr. Ashmore is right: there *is* a marked trend," she said, as if it were something visible and measurable, like a crack in a house.

"It was odd, though, to preach about it on Thanksgiving," Miss Jackson opined; and her hostess drily rejoined: "Oh, he means us to give thanks for what's left."

Archer had been wont to smile at these annual vaticinations of his mother's, but this year even he was obliged to acknowledge, as he listened to an enumeration of the changes, that the "trend" was visible.

"The extravagance in dress—" Miss Jackson began. "Sillerton took me to the first night of the opera, and I can only tell you that Jane Merry's dress was the only one I recognized from last year; and even that had had the front panel changed. Yet I know she got it out from Worth only two years ago, because my seamstress always goes in to make over her Paris dresses before she wears them."

"Ah, Jane Merry is one of *us*," said Mrs. Archer sighing, as if it were not such an enviable thing to be in an age when ladies were beginning to flaunt abroad their Paris dresses as soon as they were out of the Custom House, instead of letting them mellow under lock and key, in the manner of Mrs. Archer's contemporaries.

"Yes, she's one of the few. In my youth," Miss Jackson rejoined, "it was considered vulgar to dress in the newest fashions; and Amy Sillerton has always told me that in Boston the rule was to put away one's Paris dresses for two years. Old Mrs. Baxter Pennilow, who did everything handsomely, used to import twelve a year, two velvet, two satin, two silk, and the other six of poplin and the finest cashmere. It was a standing order, and as she was ill for two years before she died they found forty-eight Worth dresses that had never been taken out of tissue paper; and when the girls left off their mourning they were able to wear the first lot at the Symphony concerts without looking in advance of the fashion."

"Ah, well, Boston is more conservative than New York, but I always think it's a safe rule for a lady to lay aside her French dresses for one season," Mrs. Archer conceded.

"It was Beaufort who started the new fashion by making his wife clap her new clothes on her back as soon as they arrived: I must say at times it takes all Regina's distinction not to look like . . . like . . ." Miss Jackson glanced around the table, caught Janey's bulging gaze, and took refuge in an unintelligible murmur.

"Like her rivals," said Mr. Sillerton Jackson, with the air of producing an epigram.

"Oh," the ladies murmured, and Mrs. Archer added, partly to distract her daughter's attention from forbidden topics: "Poor Regina! Her Thanksgiving hasn't been a very cheerful one, I'm afraid. Have you heard the rumors about Beaufort's speculations, Sillerton?"

Mr. Jackson nodded carelessly. Everyone had heard the rumors in question, and he scorned to confirm a tale that was already common property.

A gloomy silence fell upon the party. No one really liked Beaufort, and it was not wholly unpleasant to think the worst of his private life, but the idea of his having brought financial dishonor on his wife's family was too shocking to be enjoyed even by his enemies. Archer's New York tolerated hypocrisy in private relations, but in business matters it exacted a limpid and impeccable honesty. It was a long time since any well-known banker had failed discreditably, but everyone remembered the social extinction visited on the heads of the firm when the last event of the kind had happened. It would be the same with the Beauforts, in spite of his power and her popularity; not all the leagued strength of the Dallas connection would save poor Regina if there were any truth in the reports of her husband's unlawful speculations.

The talk took refuge in less ominous topics, but everything

they touched on seemed to confirm Mrs. Archer's sense of an accelerated trend.

"Of course, Newland, I know you let dear May go to Mrs. Struthers's Sunday evenings—" she began, and May interposed gaily: "Oh, you know, everybody goes to Mrs. Struthers's now, and she was invited to Granny's last reception."

It was thus, Archer reflected, that New York managed its transitions: conspiring to ignore them till they were well over, and then, in all good faith, imagining that they had taken place in a preceding age. There was always a traitor in the citadel, and after he (or generally she) had surrendered the keys, what was the use of pretending that it was impregnable? Once people had tasted of Mrs. Struthers's easy Sunday hospitality they were not likely to sit at home remembering that her champagne was transmuted Shoe Polish.

"I know, dear, I know," Mrs. Archer sighed. "Such things have to be, I suppose, as long as *amusement* is what people go out for, but I've never quite forgiven your cousin Madame Olenska for being the first person to countenance Mrs. Struthers."

A sudden blush rose to young Mrs. Archer's face; it surprised her husband as much as the other guests about the table. "Oh, *Ellen*—" she murmured, much in the same accusing and yet deprecating tone in which her parents might have said: "Oh, *the Blenkers*—."

It was the note which the family had taken to sounding on the mention of the Countess Olenska's name, since she had surprised and inconvenienced them by remaining obdurate to her husband's advances; but on May's lips it gave food for thought, and Archer looked at her with the sense of strangeness that sometimes came over him when she was most in the tone of her environment.

His mother, with less than her usual sensitiveness to atmosphere, still insisted: "I've always thought that people like the Countess Olenska, who have lived in aristocratic societies, ought to help us to keep up our social distinctions, instead of ignoring them."

May's blush remained permanently vivid: it seemed to have a significance beyond that implied by the recognition of Madame Olenska's social bad faith.

"I've no doubt we all seem alike to foreigners," said Miss Jackson tartly.

"I don't think Ellen cares for society, but nobody knows exactly what she does care for," May continued, as if she had been groping for something noncommittal.

"Ah, well—" Mrs. Archer sighed again.

Everybody knew that the Countess Olenska was no longer in the good graces of her family. Even her devoted champion, old Mrs. Manson Mingott, had been unable to defend her refusal to return to her husband. The Mingotts had not proclaimed their disapproval aloud: their sense of solidarity was too strong. They had simply, as Mrs. Welland said, "let poor Ellen find her own level"—and that, mortifyingly and incomprehensibly, was in the dim depths where the Blenkers prevailed, and "people who wrote" celebrated their untidy rites. It was incredible, but it was a fact, that Ellen, in spite of all her opportunities and her privileges, had become simply "Bohemian." The fact enforced the contention that she had made a fatal mistake in not returning to Count Olenski. After all, a young woman's place was under her husband's roof, especially when she had left it in circumstances that . . . well . . . if one had cared to look into them . . .

"Madame Olenska is a great favorite with the gentlemen," said Miss Sophy, with her air of wishing to put forth something conciliatory when she knew that she was planting a dart.

"Ah, that's the danger that a young woman like Madame Olenska is always exposed to," Mrs. Archer mournfully agreed; and the ladies, on this conclusion, gathered up their trains to seek the carcel globes of the drawing room, while Archer and Mr. Sillerton Jackson withdrew to the Gothic library.

Once established before the grate, and consoling himself for the inadequacy of the dinner by the perfection of his cigar, Mr. Jackson became portentous and communicable.

"If the Beaufort smash comes," he announced, "there are going to be disclosures."

Archer raised his head quickly: he could never hear the name without the sharp vision of Beaufort's heavy figure, opulently furred and shod, advancing through the snow at Skuytercliff.

"There's bound to be," Mr. Jackson continued, "the nastiest kind of a cleaning up. He hasn't spent all his money on Regina."

"Oh, well—that's discounted, isn't it? My belief is he'll pull out yet," said the young man, wanting to change the subject.

"Perhaps—perhaps. I know he was to see some of the influential people today. Of course," Mr. Jackson reluctantly conceded, "it's to be hoped they can tide him over—this time anyhow. I shouldn't like to think of poor Regina's spending the rest of her life in some shabby foreign watering place for bankrupts."

Archer said nothing. It seemed to him so natural—however tragic—that money ill-gotten should be cruelly expiated, that his mind, hardly lingering over Mrs. Beaufort's doom, wandered back to closer questions. What was the meaning of May's blush when the Countess Olenska had been mentioned?

Four months had passed since the midsummer day that he and Madame Olenska had spent together, and since then he had not seen her. He knew that she had returned to Washington, to the little house which she and Medora Manson had taken there: he had written to her once—a few words, asking when they were to meet again—and she had even more briefly replied: "Not yet."

Since then there had been no farther communication between them, and he had built up within himself a kind of sanctuary in which she throned among his secret thoughts and longings. Little by little it became the scene of his real life, of his only rational activities; thither he brought the books he read, the ideas and feelings which nourished him, his judgments and his visions. Outside it, in the scene of his actual life, he moved with a growing sense of unreality and insufficiency, blundering against familiar prejudices and traditional points of view as an absent-minded man goes on bumping into the furniture of his own room. Absent—that was what he was: so absent from everything most densely real and near to those about him that it sometimes startled him to find they still imagined he was there.

He became aware that Mr. Jackson was clearing his throat preparatory to farther revelations.

"I don't know, of course, how far your wife's family are aware of what people say about—well, about Madame Olenska's refusal to accept her husband's latest offer."

Archer was silent, and Mr. Jackson obliquely continued: "It's a pity—it's certainly a pity—that she refused it."

"A pity? In God's name, why?"

Mr. Jackson looked down his leg to the unwrinkled sock that joined it to a glossy pump.

"Well—to put it on the lowest ground—what's she going to live on now?"

"Now—?"

"If Beaufort—"

Archer sprang up, his fist banging down on the black walnut edge of the writing table. The wells of the brass double inkstand danced in their sockets.

"What the devil do you mean, sir?"

Mr. Jackson, shifting himself slightly in his chair, turned a tranquil gaze on the young man's burning face.

"Well—I have it on pretty good authority—in fact, on old Catherine's herself—that the family reduced Countess Olenska's allowance considerably when she definitely refused to go back to her husband; and as, by this refusal, she also forfeits the money settled on her when she married—which Olenski was ready to make over to her if she returned—why, what the devil do *you* mean, my dear boy, by asking me what *I* mean?" Mr. Jackson good-humoredly retorted.

Archer moved toward the mantelpiece and bent over to knock his ashes into the grate.

"I don't know anything of Madame Olenska's private affairs; but I don't need to, to be certain that what you insinuate—"

"Oh, *I* don't: it's Lefferts, for one," Mr. Jackson interposed.

"Lefferts—who made love to her and got snubbed for it!" Archer broke out contemptuously.

"Ah—*did* he?" snapped the other, as if this were exactly the fact he had been laying a trap for. He still sat sideways from the fire, so that his hard old gaze held Archer's face as if in a spring of steel.

"Well, well: it's a pity she didn't go back before Beaufort's cropper," he repeated. "If she goes *now,* and if he fails, it will only confirm the general impression: which isn't by any means peculiar to Lefferts, by the way."

"Oh, she won't go back now: less than ever!" Archer had no sooner said it than he had once more the feeling that it was exactly what Mr. Jackson had been waiting for.

The old gentleman considered him attentively. "That's your

opinion, eh? Well, no doubt you know. But everybody will tell you that the few pennies Medora Manson has left are all in Beaufort's hands; and how the two women are to keep their heads above water unless he does, I can't imagine. Of course, Madame Olenska may still soften old Catherine, who's been the most inexorably opposed to her staying, and old Catherine could make her any allowance she chooses. But we all know that she hates parting with good money; and the rest of the family have no particular interest in keeping Madame Olenska here."

Archer was burning with unavailing wrath: he was exactly in the state when a man is sure to do something stupid, knowing all the while that he is doing it.

He saw that Mr. Jackson had been instantly struck by the fact that Madame Olenska's differences with her grandmother and her other relations were not known to him, and that the old gentleman had drawn his own conclusions as to the reasons for Archer's exclusion from the family councils. This fact warned Archer to go warily, but the insinuations about Beaufort made him reckless. He was mindful, however, if not of his own danger, at least of the fact that Mr. Jackson was under his mother's roof, and consequently his guest. Old New York scrupulously observed the etiquette of hospitality, and no discussion with a guest was ever allowed to degenerate into a disagreement.

"Shall we go up and join my mother?" he suggested curtly, as Mr. Jackson's last cone of ashes dropped into the brass ashtray at his elbow.

On the drive homeward May remained oddly silent; through the darkness, he still felt her enveloped in her menacing blush. What its menace meant he could not guess, but he was sufficiently warned by the fact that Madame Olenska's name had evoked it.

They went upstairs, and he turned into the library. She usually followed him, but he heard her passing down the passage to her bedroom.

"May!" he called out impatiently, and she came back, with a slight glance of surprise at his tone.

"This lamp is smoking again. I should think the servants might see that it's kept properly trimmed," he grumbled nervously.

"I'm so sorry: it shan't happen again," she answered in the firm bright tone she had learned from her mother, and it exasperated Archer to feel that she was already beginning to humor him like a younger Mr. Welland. She bent over to lower the wick, and as the light struck up on her white shoulders and the clear curves of her face he thought: "How young she is! For what endless years this life will have to go on!"

He felt, with a kind of horror, his own strong youth and the bounding blood in his veins. "Look here," he said suddenly, "I may have to go to Washington for a few days—soon; next week perhaps."

Her hand remained on the key of the lamp as she turned to him slowly. The heat from its flame had brought back a glow to her face, but it paled as she looked up.

"On business?" she asked, in a tone which implied that there could be no other conceivable reason, and that she had put the question automatically, as if merely to finish his own sentence.

"On business, naturally. There's a patent case coming up before the Supreme Court—" He gave the name of the inventor, and went on furnishing details with all Lawrence Leffert's practiced glibness, while she listened attentively, saying at intervals: "Yes, I see."

"The change will do you good," she said simply, when he had finished; "and you must be sure to go and see Ellen," she added, looking him straight in the eyes with her cloudless smile, and speaking in the tone she might have employed in urging him not to neglect some irksome family duty.

It was the only word that passed between them on the subject, but in the code in which they had both been trained it meant: "Of course you understand that I know all that people have been saying about Ellen, and heartily sympathize with my family in their effort to get her to return to her husband. I also know that, for some reason you have not chosen to tell me, you have advised her against this course, which all the older men of the family, as well as our grandmother, agree in approving; and that it is owing to your encouragement that Ellen defies us all, and exposes herself to the kind of criticism of which Mr. Sillerton Jackson probably gave you, this evening, the hint that has made you so irritable. . . . Hints have indeed not been wanting, but since you appear unwilling to take them from others, I offer you this one myself, in the only form in which well-bred people of our kind can communicate unpleasant things to each other: by letting you understand that I know you mean to see Ellen when you are in Washington, and are perhaps going there expressly for that purpose; and that, since you are sure to see her, I wish you to do so with my full and explicit approval—and to take the opportunity of letting her know what the course of conduct you have encouraged her in is likely to lead to."

Her hand was still on the key of the lamp when the last word of this mute message reached him. She turned the wick down, lifted off the globe, and breathed on the sulky flame.

"They smell less if one blows them out," she explained, with her bright housekeeping air. On the threshold she turned and paused for his kiss.

# —— 27 ——

WALL STREET, the next day, had more reassuring reports of Beaufort's situation. They were not definite, but they were hopeful. It was generally understood that he could call on powerful influences in case of emergency, and that he had done so with success; and that evening, when Mrs. Beaufort appeared at the opera wearing her old smile and a new emerald necklace, society drew a breath of relief.

New York was inexorable in its condemnation of business irregularities. So far there had been no exception to its tacit rule that those who broke the law of probity must pay, and everyone was aware that even Beaufort and Beaufort's wife would be offered up unflinchingly to this principle. But to be obliged to offer them up would be not only painful but inconvenient. The disappearance of the Beauforts would leave a considerable void in their compact little circle; and those who were too ignorant or too careless to shudder at the moral catastrophe bewailed in advance the loss of the best ballroom in New York.

Archer had definitely made up his mind to go to Washington. He was waiting only for the opening of the lawsuit of which he had spoken to May, so that its date might coincide with that of his visit; but on the following Tuesday he learned from Mr. Letterblair that the case might be postponed for several weeks. Nevertheless, he went home that afternoon determined in any event to leave the next evening. The chances were that May, who knew nothing of his professional life, and had never shown any interest in it, would not learn of the postponement, should it take place, nor remember the names of the litigants if they were mentioned before her; and at any rate he could no longer put off seeing Madame Olenska. There were too many things that he must say to her.

On the Wednesday morning, when he reached his office, Mr. Letterblair met him with a troubled face. Beaufort, after all, had not managed to "tide over"; but by setting afloat the rumor that he had done so he had reassured his depositors, and heavy payments had poured into the bank till the previous evening, when disturbing reports again began to predominate. In consequence, a run on the bank had begun, and its doors were likely to close before the day was over. The ugliest things were being said of Beaufort's dastardly maneuver, and his failure promised to be one of the most discreditable in the history of Wall Street.

The extent of the calamity left Mr. Letterblair white and incapacitated. "I've seen bad things in my time, but nothing as bad as this. Everybody we know will be hit, one way or another. And what will be done about Mrs. Beaufort? What *can* be done about her? I pity Mrs. Manson Mingott as much as anybody: coming at her age, there's no knowing what effect this affair may have on her. She always believed in Beaufort—she made a friend of him! And there's the whole Dallas connection: poor Mrs. Beaufort is related to every one of you. Her only chance would be to leave her husband—yet how can anyone tell her so? Her duty is at his side, and luckily she seems always to have been blind to his private weaknesses."

There was a knock, and Mr. Letterblair turned his head sharply. "What is it? I can't be disturbed."

A clerk brought in a letter for Archer and withdrew. Recognizing his wife's hand, the young man opened the envelope and read: "Won't you please come uptown as early as you can? Granny had a slight stroke last night. In some mysterious way she found out before anyone else this awful news about the bank. Uncle Lovell is away shooting, and the idea of the disgrace has made poor Papa so nervous that he has a temperature and can't leave his room. Mamma needs you dreadfully, and I do hope you can get away at once and go straight to Granny's."

Archer handed the note to his senior partner, and a few minutes later was crawling northward in a crowded horse car, which he exchanged at Fourteenth Street for one of the high staggering omnibuses of the Fifth Avenue line. It was after twelve o'clock when this laborious vehicle dropped him at old Catherine's. The sitting-room window on the ground floor, where she usually throned, was tenanted by the inadequate figure of her daughter, Mrs. Welland, who signed a haggard welcome as she caught sight

of Archer, and at the door he was met by May. The hall wore the
unnatural appearance peculiar to well-kept houses suddenly invaded by illness: wraps and furs lay in heaps on the chairs, a
doctor's bag and overcoat were on the table, and beside them
letters and cards had already piled up unheeded.

May looked pale but smiling: Dr. Bencomb, who had just come
for the second time, took a more hopeful view, and Mrs.
Mingott's dauntless determination to live and get well was already
having an effect on her family. May led Archer into the old lady's
sitting room, where the sliding doors opening into the bedroom
had been drawn shut, and the heavy yellow damask portières
dropped over them; and here Mrs. Welland communicated to
him in horrified undertones the details of the catastrophe. It appeared that the evening before something dreadful and mysterious had happened. At about eight o'clock, just after Mrs. Mingott
had finished the game of solitaire that she always played after
dinner, the doorbell had rung, and a lady so thickly veiled that
the servants did not immediately recognize her had asked to be
received.

The butler, hearing a familiar voice, had thrown open the sitting-room door, announcing: "Mrs. Julius Beaufort"—and had
then closed it again on the two ladies. They must have been together, he thought, about an hour. When Mrs. Mingott's bell
rang Mrs. Beaufort had already slipped away unseen, and the old
lady, white and vast and terrible, sat alone in her great chair, and
signed to the butler to help her into her room. She seemed, at
that time, though obviously distressed, in complete control of her
body and brain. The mulatto maid put her to bed, brought her a
cup of tea as usual, laid everything straight in the room, and went
away; but at three in the morning the bell rang again, and the two
servants, hastening in at this unwonted summons (for old Catherine usually slept like a baby), had found their mistress sitting up
against her pillows with a crooked smile on her face and one little
hand hanging limp from its huge arm.

The stroke had clearly been a slight one, for she was able to
articulate and to make her wishes known, and soon after the doctor's first visit she had begun to regain control of her facial muscles. But the alarm had been great, and proportionately great was
the indignation when it was gathered from Mrs. Mingott's frag-

mentary phrases that Regina Beaufort had come to ask her—
incredible effrontery!—to back up her husband, see them
through—not to "desert" them, as she called it—in fact to induce
the whole family to cover and condone their monstrous dishonor.

"I said to her: 'Honor's always been honor, and honesty honesty, in Manson Mingott's house, and will be till I'm carried out of
it feet first,' " the old woman had stammered into her daughter's
ear, in the thick voice of the partly paralyzed. "And when she
said: 'But my name, Auntie—my name's Regina Dallas,' I said: 'It
was Beaufort when he covered you with jewels, and it's got to stay
Beaufort now that he's covered you with shame.' "

So much, with tears and gasps of horror, Mrs. Welland imparted, blanched and demolished by the unwonted obligation of
having at last to fix her eyes on the unpleasant and the discreditable. "If only I could keep it from your father-in-law: he always
says: 'Augusta, for pity's sake, don't destroy my last illusions'—
and how am I to prevent his knowing these horrors?" the poor
lady wailed.

"After all, Mamma, he won't have *seen* them," her daughter
suggested, and Mrs. Welland sighed: "Ah, no; thank heaven he's
safe in bed. And Dr. Bencomb has promised to keep him there till
poor Mamma is better, and Regina has been got away somewhere."

Archer had seated himself near the window and was gazing out
blankly at the deserted thoroughfare. It was evident that he had
been summoned rather for the moral support of the stricken ladies than because of any specific aid that he could render. Mr.
Lovell Mingott had been telegraphed for, and messages were being despatched by hand to the members of the family living in
New York; and meanwhile there was nothing to do but to discuss
in hushed tones the consequences of Beaufort's dishonor and of
his wife's unjustifiable action.

Mrs. Lovell Mingott, who had been in another room writing
notes, presently reappeared, and added her voice to the discussion. In *their* day, the elder ladies agreed, the wife of a man who
had done anything disgraceful in business had only one idea: to
efface herself, to disappear with him. "There was the case of poor
Grandmamma Spicer; your great-grandmother, May. Of course,"
Mrs. Welland hastened to add, "your great-grandfather's money

difficulties were private—losses at cards, or signing a note for somebody—I never quite knew, because Mamma would never speak of it. But she was brought up in the country because her mother had to leave New York after the disgrace, whatever it was: they lived up the Hudson alone, winter and summer, till Mamma was sixteen. It would never have occured to Grandmamma Spicer to ask the family to 'countenance' her, as I understand Regina calls it, though a private disgrace is nothing compared to the scandal of ruining hundreds of innocent people."

"Yes, it would be more becoming in Regina to hide her own countenance than to talk about other people's," Mrs. Lovell Mingott agreed. "I understand that the emerald necklace she wore at the opera last Friday had been sent on approval from Ball and Black's in the afternoon. I wonder if they'll ever get it back?"

Archer listened unmoved to the relentless chorus. The idea of absolute financial probity as the first law of a gentleman's code was too deeply ingrained in him for sentimental considerations to weaken it. An adventurer like Lemuel Struthers might build up the millions of his Shoe Polish on any number of shady dealings; but unblemished honesty was the *noblesse oblige* of old financial New York. Nor did Mrs. Beaufort's fate greatly move Archer. He felt, no doubt, more sorry for her than her indignant relatives, but it seemed to him that the tie between husband and wife, even if breakable in prosperity, should be indissoluble in misfortune. As Mr. Letterblair had said, a wife's place was at her husband's side when he was in trouble; but society's place was not at his side, and Mrs. Beaufort's cool assumption that it was seemed almost to make her his accomplice. The mere idea of a woman's appealing to her family to screen her husband's business dishonor was inadmissible, since it was the one thing that the Family, as an institution, could not do.

The mulatto maid called Mrs. Lovell Mingott into the hall, and the latter came back in a moment with a frowning brow.

"She wants me to telegraph for Ellen Olenska. I had written to Ellen, of course, and to Medora, but now it seems that's not enough. I'm to telegraph to her immediately, and to tell her that she's to come alone."

The announcement was received in silence. Mrs. Welland

sighed resignedly, and May rose from her seat and went to gather up some newspapers that had been scattered on the floor.

"I suppose it must be done," Mrs. Lovell Mingott continued, as if hoping to be contradicted, and May turned back toward the middle of the room.

"Of course it must be done," she said. "Granny knows what she wants, and we must carry out all her wishes. Shall I write the telegram for you, Auntie? If it goes at once Ellen can probably catch tomorrow morning's train." She pronounced the syllables of the name with a peculiar clearness, as if she had tapped on two silver bells.

"Well, it can't go at once. Jasper and the pantry boy are both out with notes and telegrams."

May turned to her husband with a smile. "But here's Newland, ready to do anything. Will you take the telegram, Newland? There'll be just time before luncheon."

Archer rose with a murmur of readiness, and she seated herself at old Catherine's rosewood "Bonheur du Jour," and wrote out the message in her large immature hand. When it was written she blotted it neatly and handed it to Archer.

"What a pity," she said, "that you and Ellen will cross each other on the way!—Newland," she added, turning to her mother and aunt, "is obliged to go to Washington about a patent lawsuit that is coming up before the Supreme Court. I suppose Uncle Lovell will be back by tomorrow night, and with Granny improving so much it doesn't seem right to ask Newland to give up an important engagement for the firm—does it?"

She paused, as if for an answer, and Mrs. Welland hastily declared: "Oh, of course not, darling. Your Granny would be the last person to wish it." As Archer left the room with the telegram, he heard his mother-in-law add, presumably to Mrs. Lovell Mingott: "But why on earth she should make you telegraph for Ellen Olenska—" and May's clear voice rejoin: "Perhaps it's to urge on her again that after all her duty is with her husband."

The outer door closed on Archer and he walked hastily away toward the telegraph office.

# 28

 OL—OL—HOWJER spell it, anyhow?" asked the tart young lady to whom Archer had pushed his wife's telegram across the brass ledge of the Western Union office.

"Olenska—O-len-ska," he repeated, drawing back the message in order to print out the foreign syllables above May's rambling script.

"It's an unlikely name for a New York telegraph office, at least in this quarter," an unexpected voice observed; and turning around Archer saw Lawrence Lefferts at his elbow, pulling an imperturbable mustache and affecting not to glance at the message.

"Hallo, Newland: thought I'd catch you here. I've just heard of old Mrs. Mingott's stroke; and as I was on my way to the house I saw you turning down this street and nipped after you. I suppose you've come from there?"

Archer nodded, and pushed his telegram under the lattice.

"Very bad, eh?" Lefferts continued. "Wiring to the family, I suppose. I gather it *is* bad, if you're including Countess Olenska."

Archer's lips stiffened; he felt a savage impulse to dash his fist into the long vain handsome face at his side.

"Why?" he questioned.

Lefferts, who was known to shrink from discussion, raised his eyebrows with an ironic grimace that warned the other of the watching damsel behind the lattice. Nothing could be worse "form," the look reminded Archer, than any display of temper in a public place.

Archer had never been more indifferent to the requirements of form, but his impulse to do Lawrence Lefferts a physical injury was only momentary. The idea of bandying Ellen Olenska's name with him at such a time, and on whatsoever provocation, was unthinkable. He paid for his telegram, and the two young men went out together into the street. There Archer, having regained

221

his self-control, went on: "Mrs. Mingott is much better: the doctor feels no anxiety whatever"; and Lefferts, with profuse expressions of relief, asked him if he had heard that there were beastly bad rumors again about Beaufort. . . .

That afternoon the announcement of the Beaufort failure was in all the papers. It overshadowed the report of Mrs. Manson Mingott's stroke, and only the few who had heard of the mysterious connection between the two events thought of ascribing old Catherine's illness to anything but the accumulation of flesh and years.

The whole of New York was darkened by the tale of Beaufort's dishonor. There had never, as Mr. Letterblair said, been a worse case in his memory, nor, for that matter, in the memory of the far-off Letterblair who had given his name to the firm. The bank had continued to take in money for a whole day after its failure was inevitable; and as many of its clients belonged to one or another of the ruling clans, Beaufort's duplicity seemed doubly cynical. If Mrs. Beaufort had not taken the tone that such misfortunes (the word was her own) were "the test of friendship," compassion for her might have tempered the general indignation against her husband. As it was—and especially after the object of her nocturnal visit to Mrs. Manson Mingott had become known— her cynicism was held to exceed his; and she had not the excuse— nor her detractors the satisfaction—of pleading that she was "a foreigner." It was some comfort (to those whose securities were not in jeopardy) to be able to remind themselves that Beaufort *was;* but, after all, if a Dallas of South Carolina took his view of the case, and glibly talked of his soon being "on his feet again," the argument lost its edge, and there was nothing to do but to accept this awful evidence of the indissolubility of marriage. Society must manage to get on without the Beauforts, and there was an end of it—except indeed for such hapless victims of the disaster as Medora Manson, the poor old Miss Lannings, and certain other misguided ladies of good family who, if only they had listened to Mr. Henry van der Luyden . . .

"The best thing the Beauforts can do," said Mrs. Archer, summing it up as if she were pronouncing a diagnosis and prescribing a course of treatment, "is to go and live at Regina's little place in

North Carolina. Beaufort has always kept a racing stable, and he had better breed trotting horses. I should say he had all the qualities of a successful horse dealer." Everyone agreed with her, but no one condescended to inquire what the Beauforts really meant to do.

The next day Mrs. Manson Mingott was much better: she recovered her voice sufficiently to give orders that no one should mention the Beauforts to her again, and asked—when Dr. Bencomb appeared—what in the world her family meant by making such a fuss about her health.

"If people of my age *will* eat chicken salad in the evening, what are they to expect?" she inquired; and, the doctor having opportunely modified her dietary, the stroke was transformed into an attack of indigestion. But in spite of her firm tone old Catherine did not wholly recover her former attitude toward life. The growing remoteness of old age, though it had not diminished her curiosity about her neighbors, had blunted her never very lively compassion for their troubles; and she seemed to have no difficulty in putting the Beaufort disaster out of her mind. But for the first time she became absorbed in her own symptoms, and began to take a sentimental interest in certain members of her family to whom she had hitherto been contemptuously indifferent.

Mr. Welland, in particular, had the privilege of attracting her notice. Of her sons-in-law he was the one she had most consistently ignored; and all his wife's efforts to represent him as a man of forceful character and marked intellectual ability (if he had only "chosen") had been met with a derisive chuckle. But his eminence as a valetudinarian now made him an object of engrossing interest, and Mrs. Mingott issued an imperial summons to him to come and compare diets as soon as his temperature permitted; for old Catherine was now the first to recognize that one could not be too careful about temperatures.

Twenty-four hours after Madame Olenska's summons a telegram announced that she would arrive from Washington on the evening of the following day. At the Wellands', where the Newland Archers chanced to be lunching, the question as to who should meet her at Jersey City was immediately raised; and the material difficulties amid which the Welland household struggled as if it

had been a frontier outpost, lent animation to the debate. It was
agreed that Mrs. Welland could not possibly go to Jersey City
because she was to accompany her husband to old Catherine's
that afternoon, and the brougham could not be spared, since, if
Mr. Welland were "upset" by seeing his mother-in-law for the
first time after her attack, he might have to be taken home at a
moment's notice. The Welland sons would of course be "downtown," Mr. Lovell Mingott would be just hurrying back from his
shooting, and the Mingott carriage engaged in meeting him; and
one could not ask May, at the close of a winter afternoon, to go
alone across the ferry to Jersey City, even in her own carriage.
Nevertheless, it might appear inhospitable—and contrary to old
Catherine's express wishes—if Madame Olenska were allowed to
arrive without any of the family being at the station to receive her.
It was just like Ellen, Mrs. Welland's tired voice implied, to place
the family in such a dilemma. "It's always one thing after another," the poor lady grieved, in one of her rare revolts against
fate, "the only thing that makes me think Mamma must be less
well than Dr. Bencomb will admit is this morbid desire to have
Ellen come at once, however inconvenient it is to meet her."

The words had been thoughtless, as the utterances of impatience often are; and Mr. Welland was upon them with a pounce.

"Augusta," he said, turning pale and laying down his fork,
"have you any other reason for thinking that Bencomb is less to
be relied on than he was? Have you noticed that he has been less
conscientious than usual in following up my case or your
mother's?"

It was Mrs. Welland's turn to grow pale as the endless consequences of her blunder unrolled themselves before her; but she
managed to laugh, and take a second helping of scalloped oysters,
before she said, struggling back into her old armor of cheerfulness: "My dear, how could you imagine such a thing? I only
meant that, after the decided stand Mamma took about its being
Ellen's duty to go back to her husband, it seems strange that she
should be seized with this sudden whim to see her, when there
are half a dozen other grandchildren that she might have asked
for. But we must never forget that Mamma, in spite of her wonderful vitality, is a very old woman."

Mr. Welland's brow remained clouded, and it was evident that

his perturbed imagination had fastened at once on this last remark. "Yes, your mother's a very old woman, and for all we know
Bencomb may not be as successful with very old people. As you
say, my dear, it's always one thing after another, and in another
ten or fifteen years I suppose I shall have the pleasing duty of
looking about for a new doctor. It's always better to make such a
change before it's absolutely necessary." And having arrived at
this spartan decision Mr. Welland firmly took up his fork.

"But all the while," Mrs. Welland began again, as she rose from
the luncheon table and led the way into the wilderness of purple
satin and malachite known as the back drawing room, "I don't see
how Ellen's to be got here tomorrow evening; and I do like to
have things settled for at least twenty-four hours ahead."

Archer turned from the fascinated contemplation of a small
painting representing two cardinals carousing, in an octagonal
ebony frame set with medallions of onyx.

"Shall I fetch her?" he proposed. "I can easily get away from
the office in time to meet the brougham at the ferry, if May will
send it there." His heart was beating excitedly as he spoke.

Mrs. Welland heaved a sigh of gratitude, and May, who had
moved away to the window, turned to shed on him a beam of
approval. "So you see, Mamma, everything *will* be settled twenty-
four hours in advance," she said, stooping over to kiss her
mother's troubled forehead.

May's brougham awaited her at the door, and she was to drive
Archer to Union Square, where he could pick up a Broadway car
to carry him to the office. As she settled herself in her corner she
said: "I didn't want to worry Mamma by raising fresh obstacles,
but how can you meet Ellen tomorrow, and bring her back to
New York, when you're going to Washington?"

"Oh, I'm not going," Archer answered.

"Not going? Why, what's happened?" Her voice was as clear as
a bell, and full of wifely solicitude.

"The case is off—postponed."

"Postponed? How odd! I saw a note this morning from Mr.
Letterblair to Mamma saying that he was going to Washington
tomorrow for the big patent case that he was to argue before the
Supreme Court. You said it was a patent case, didn't you?"

"Well—that's it: the whole office can't go. Letterblair decided to go this morning."

"Then it's *not* postponed?" she continued, with an insistence so unlike her that he felt the blood rising to his face, as if he were blushing for her unwonted lapse from all the traditional delicacies.

"No, but my going is," he answered, cursing the unnecessary explanations that he had given when he had announced his intention of going to Washington, and wondering where he had read that clever liars give details, but that the cleverest do not. It did not hurt him half as much to tell May an untruth as to see her trying to pretend that she had not detected him.

"I'm not going till later on: luckily for the convenience of your family," he continued, taking base refuge in sarcasm. As he spoke he felt that she was looking at him, and he turned his eyes to hers in order not to appear to be avoiding them. Their glances met for a second, and perhaps let them into each other's meanings more deeply than either cared to go.

"Yes; it *is* awfully convenient," May brightly agreed, "that you should be able to meet Ellen after all; you saw how much Mamma appreciated your offering to do it."

"Oh, I'm delighted to do it." The carriage stopped, and as he jumped out she leaned to him and laid her hand on his. "Good-bye, dearest," she said, her eyes so blue that he wondered afterward if they had shone on him through tears.

He turned away and hurried across Union Square, repeating to himself, in a sort of inward chant: "It's all of two hours from Jersey City to old Catherine's. It's all of two hours—and it may be more."

# ——29——

His wife's dark blue brougham (with the wedding varnish still on it) met Archer at the ferry, and conveyed him luxuriously to the Pennsylvania terminus in Jersey City.

It was a somber snowy afternoon, and the gas lamps were lit in the big reverberating station. As he paced the platform, waiting for the Washington express, he remembered that there were people who thought there would one day be a tunnel under the Hudson through which the trains of the Pennsylvania railway would run straight into New York. They were of the brotherhood of visionaries who likewise predicted the building of ships that would cross the Atlantic in five days, the invention of a flying machine, lighting by electricity, telephonic communication without wires, and other Arabian Night marvels.

"I don't care which of their visions comes true," Archer mused, "as long as the tunnel isn't built yet." In his senseless schoolboy happiness he pictured Madame Olenska's descent from the train, his discovery of her a long way off, among the throngs of meaningless faces, her clinging to his arm as he guided her to the carriage, their slow approach to the wharf among slipping horses, laden carts, vociferating teamsters, and then the startling quiet of the ferryboat, where they would sit side by side under the snow, in the motionless carriage, while the earth seemed to glide away under them, rolling to the other side of the sun. It was incredible, the number of things he had to say to her, and in what eloquent order they were forming themselves on his lips . . .

The clanging and groaning of the train came nearer, and it staggered slowly into the station like a prey-laden monster into its lair. Archer pushed forward, elbowing through the crowd, and staring blindly into window after window of the high-hung carriages. And then, suddenly, he saw Madame Olenska's pale and surprised face close at hand, and had again the mortified sensation of having forgotten what she looked like.

They reached each other, their hands met, and he drew her arm through his. "This way—I have the carriage," he said.

After that it all happened as he had dreamed. He helped her into the brougham with her bags, and had afterward the vague recollection of having properly reassured her about her grandmother and given her a summary of the Beaufort situation (he was struck by the softness of her: "Poor Regina!"). Meanwhile the carriage had worked its way out of the coil about the station, and they were crawling down the slippery incline to the wharf, menaced by swaying coal carts, bewildered horses, disheveled express wagons, and an empty hearse—ah, that hearse! She shut her eyes as it passed, and clutched at Archer's hand.

"If only it doesn't mean—poor Granny!"

"Oh, no, no—she's much better—she's all right, really. There—we've passed it!" he exclaimed, as if that made all the difference. Her hand remained in his, and as the carriage lurched across the gangplank onto the ferry he bent over, unbuttoned her tight brown glove, and kissed her palm as if he had kissed a relic. She disengaged herself with a faint smile, and he said: "You didn't expect me today?"

"Oh, no."

"I meant to go to Washington to see you. I'd made all my arrangements—I very nearly crossed you in the train."

"Oh—" she exclaimed, as if terrified by the narrowness of their escape.

"Do you know—I hardly remembered you?"

"Hardly remembered me?"

"I mean: how shall I explain? I—it's always so. *Each time you happen to me all over again.*"

"Oh, yes. I know! I know!"

"Does it—do I too: to you?" he insisted.

She nodded, looking out of the window.

"Ellen—Ellen—Ellen!"

She made no answer, and he sat in silence, watching her profile grow indistinct against the snow-streaked dusk beyond the window. What had she been doing in all those four long months, he wondered? How little they knew of each other, after all! The precious moments were slipping away, but he had forgotten everything that he had meant to say to her and could only helplessly brood on the mystery of their remoteness and their proximity, which seemed to be symbolized by the fact of their sitting so close to each other, and yet being unable to see each other's faces.

"What a pretty carriage! Is it May's?" she asked, suddenly turning her face from the window.

"Yes."

"It was May who sent you to fetch me, then? How kind of her!"

He made no answer for a moment; then he said explosively: "Your husband's secretary came to see me the day after we met in Boston."

In his brief letter to her he had made no allusion to M. Rivière's visit, and his intention had been to bury the incident in his bosom. But her reminder that they were in his wife's carriage provoked him to an impulse of retaliation. He would see if she liked his reference to Rivière any better than he liked hers to May! As on certain other occasions when he had expected to shake her out of her usual composure, she betrayed no sign of surprise, and at once he concluded: "He writes to her, then."

"M. Rivière went to see you?"

"Yes, didn't you know?"

"No," she answered simply.

"And you're not surprised?"

She hesitated. "Why should I be? He told me in Boston that he knew you; that he'd met you in England I think."

"Ellen—I must ask you one thing."

"Yes."

"I wanted to ask it after I saw him, but I couldn't put it in a letter. It was Rivière who helped you to get away—when you left your husband?"

His heart was beating suffocatingly. Would she meet this question with the same composure?

"Yes, I owe him a great debt," she answered, without the least tremor in her quiet voice.

Her tone was so natural, so almost indifferent, that Archer's turmoil subsided. Once more she had managed, by her sheer simplicity, to make him feel stupidly conventional just when he thought he was flinging convention to the winds.

"I think you're the most honest woman I ever met!" he exclaimed.

"Oh, no—but probably one of the least fussy," she answered, a smile in her voice.

"Call it what you like: you look at things as they are."

"Ah—I've had to. I've had to look at the Gorgon."

"Well—it hasn't blinded you! You've seen that she's just an old bogey like all the others."

"She doesn't blind one; but she dries up one's tears."

The answer checked the pleading on Archer's lips: it seemed to come from depths of experience beyond his reach. The slow advance of the ferryboat had ceased, and her bows bumped against the piles of the slip with a violence that made the brougham stagger, and flung Archer and Madame Olenska against each other. The young man, trembling, felt the pressure of her shoulder, and passed his arm about her.

"If you're not blind, then, you must see that this can't last."

"What can't?"

"Our being together—and not together."

"No. You ought not to have come today," she said in an altered voice; and suddenly she turned, flung her arms about him and pressed her lips to his. At the same moment the carriage began to move, and a gas lamp at the head of the slip flashed its light into the window. She drew away, and they sat silent and motionless while the brougham struggled through the congestion of carriages about the ferry landing. As they gained the street Archer began to speak hurriedly.

"Don't be afraid of me: you needn't squeeze yourself back into your corner like that. A stolen kiss isn't what I want. Look, I'm not even trying to touch the sleeve of your jacket. Don't suppose that I don't understand your reasons for not wanting to let this feeling between us dwindle into an ordinary hole-and-corner love affair. I couldn't have spoken like this yesterday, because when we've been apart, and I'm looking forward to seeing you, every thought is burned up in a great flame. But then you come, and you're so much more than I remembered, and what I want of you is so much more than an hour or two every now and then, with wastes of thirsty waiting between, that I can sit perfectly still beside you, like this, with that other vision in my mind, just quietly trusting to it to come true."

For a moment she made no reply; then she asked, hardly above a whisper: "What do you mean by trusting to it to come true?"

"Why—you know it will, don't you?"

"Your vision of you and me together?" She burst into a sudden hard laugh. "You choose your place well to put it to me!"

"Do you mean because we're in my wife's brougham? Shall we get out and walk, then? I don't suppose you mind a little snow?"

She laughed again, more gently. "No, I shan't get out and walk, because my business is to get to Granny's as quickly as I can. And you'll sit beside me, and we'll look, not at visions, but at realities."

"I don't know what you mean by realities. The only reality to me is this."

She met the words with a long silence, during which the carriage rolled down an obscure side street and then turned into the searching illumination of Fifth Avenue.

"Is it your idea, then, that I should live with you as your mistress—since I can't be your wife?" she asked.

The crudeness of the question startled him: the word was one that women of his class fought shy of, even when their talk flitted closest about the topic. He noticed that Madame Olenska pronounced it as if it had a recognized place in her vocabulary, and he wondered if it had been used familiarly in her presence in the horrible life she had fled from. Her question pulled him up with a jerk, and he floundered.

"I want—I want somehow to get away with you into a world where words like that—categories like that—won't exist. Where we shall be simply two human beings who love each other, who are the whole of life to each other, and nothing else on earth will matter."

She drew a deep sigh that ended in another laugh. "Oh, my dear—where is that country? Have you ever been there?" she asked; and as he remained sullenly dumb she went on: "I know so many who've tried to find it; and, believe me, they all got out by mistake at wayside stations: at places like Boulogne, or Pisa, or Monte Carlo—and it wasn't at all different from the old world they'd left, but only rather smaller and dingier and more promiscuous."

He had never heard her speak in such a tone, and he remembered the phrase she had used a little while before.

"Yes, the Gorgon *has* dried your tears," he said.

"Well, she opened my eyes too; it's a delusion to say that she blinds people. What she does is just the contrary—she fastens their eyelids open, so that they're never again in the blessed darkness. Isn't there a Chinese torture like that? There ought to be. Ah, believe me, it's a miserable little country!"

The carriage had crossed Forty-second Street: May's sturdy brougham horse was carrying them northward as if he had been a Kentucky trotter. Archer choked with the sense of wasted minutes and vain words.

"Then what, exactly, is your plan for us?" he asked.

"For *us*? But there's no *us* in that sense! We're near each other only if we stay far from each other. Then we can be ourselves. Otherwise we're only Newland Archer, the husband of Ellen Olenska's cousin, and Ellen Olenska, the cousin of Newland Archer's wife, trying to be happy behind the backs of the people who trust them."

"Ah, I'm beyond that," he groaned.

"No, you're not! You've never been beyond. And *I* have," she said in a strange voice, "and I know what it looks like there."

He sat silent, dazed with inarticulate pain. Then he groped in the darkness of the carriage for the little bell that signaled orders to the coachman. He remembered that May rang twice when she wished to stop. He pressed the bell, and the carriage drew up beside the curbstone.

"Why are we stopping? This is not Granny's," Madame Olenska exclaimed.

"No, I shall get out here," he stammered, opening the door and jumping to the pavement. By the light of a streetlamp he saw her startled face, and the instinctive motion she made to detain him. He closed the door, and leaned for a moment in the window.

"You're right. I ought not to have come today," he said, lowering his voice so that the coachman should not hear. She bent forward, and seemed about to speak, but he had already called out the order to drive on, and the carriage rolled away while he stood on the corner. The snow was over, and a tingling wind had sprung up, that lashed his face as he stood gazing. Suddenly he felt something stiff and cold on his lashes, and perceived that he had been crying, and that the wind had frozen his tears.

He thrust his hands in his pockets, and walked at a sharp pace down Fifth Avenue to his own house.

# ─── 30 ───

🌿 THAT EVENING when Archer came down before dinner he found the drawing room empty.

He and May were dining alone, all the family engagements having been postponed since Mrs. Manson Mingott's illness, and as May was the more punctual of the two he was surprised that she had not preceded him. He knew that she was at home, for while he dressed he had heard her moving about in her room, and he wondered what had delayed her.

He had fallen into the way of dwelling on such conjectures as a means of tying his thoughts fast to reality. Sometimes he felt as if he had found the clue to his father-in-law's absorption in trifles; perhaps even Mr. Welland, long ago, had had escapes and visions, and had conjured up all the hosts of domesticity to defend himself against them.

When May appeared he thought she looked tired. She had put on the low-necked and tightly laced dinner dress which the Mingott ceremonial exacted on the most informal occasions, and had built her fair hair into its usual accumulated coils; and her face, in contrast, was wan and almost faded. But she shone on him with her usual tenderness, and her eyes had kept the blue dazzle of the day before.

"What became of you, dear?" she asked. "I was waiting at Granny's, and Ellen came alone, and said she had dropped you on the way because you had to rush off on business. There's nothing wrong?"

"Only some letters I'd forgotten, and wanted to get off before dinner."

"Ah—" she said, and a moment afterward: "I'm sorry you didn't come to Granny's—unless the letters were urgent."

"They were," he rejoined, surprised at her insistence. "Besides, I don't see why I should have gone to your grandmother's. I didn't know you were there."

She turned and moved to the looking glass above the mantel-piece. As she stood there, lifting her long arm to fasten a puff that had slipped from its place in her intricate hair, Archer was struck by something languid and inelastic in her attitude, and wondered if the deadly monotony of their lives had laid its weight on her also. Then he remembered that, as he had left the house that morning, she had called over the stairs that she would meet him at her grandmother's so that they might drive home together. He had called back a cheery "Yes!" and then, absorbed in other visions, had forgotten his promise. Now he was smitten with compunction, yet irritated that so trifling an omission should be stored up against him after nearly two years of marriage. He was weary of living in a perpetual tepid honeymoon, without the temperature of passion yet with all its exactions. If May had spoken out her grievances (he suspected her of many) he might have laughed them away, but she was trained to conceal imaginary wounds under a spartan smile.

To disguise his own annoyance he asked how her grandmother was, and she answered that Mrs. Mingott was still improving, but had been rather disturbed by the last news about the Beauforts.

"What news?"

"It seems they're going to stay in New York. I believe he's going into an insurance business, or something. They're looking about for a small house."

The preposterousness of the case was beyond discussion, and they went in to dinner. During dinner their talk moved in its usual limited circle, but Archer noticed that his wife made no allusion to Madame Olenska, nor to old Catherine's reception of her. He was thankful for the fact, yet felt it to be vaguely ominous.

They went up to the library for coffee, and Archer lit a cigar and took down a volume of Michelet. He had taken to history in the evenings since May had shown a tendency to ask him to read aloud whenever she saw him with a volume of poetry: not that he disliked the sound of his own voice, but because he could always foresee her comments on what he read. In the days of their engagement she had simply (as he now perceived) echoed what he told her, but since he had ceased to provide her with opinions she had begun to hazard her own, with results destructive to his enjoyment of the works commented on.

Seeing that he had chosen history she fetched her workbasket, drew up an armchair to the green-shaded student lamp, and uncovered a cushion she was embroidering for his sofa. She was not a clever needle-woman; her large capable hands were made for riding, rowing, and open-air activities; but since other wives embroidered cushions for their husbands she did not wish to omit this last link in her devotion.

She was so placed that Archer, by merely raising his eyes, could see her bent above her work frame, her ruffled elbow sleeves slipping back from her firm round arms, the betrothal sapphire shining on her left hand above her broad gold wedding ring, and the right hand slowly and laboriously stabbing the canvas. As she sat thus, the lamplight full on her clear brow, he said to himself with a secret dismay that he would always know the thoughts behind it, that never, in all the years to come, would she surprise him by an unexpected mood, by a new idea, a weakness, a cruelty, or an emotion. She had spent her poetry and romance on their short courting: the function was exhausted because the need was past. Now she was simply ripening into a copy of her mother, and mysteriously, by the very process, trying to turn him into a Mr. Welland. He laid down his book and stood up impatiently, and at once she raised her head.

"What's the matter?"

"The room is stifling. I want a little air."

He had insisted that the library curtains should draw backward and forward on a rod, so that they might be closed in the evening, instead of remaining nailed to a gilt cornice, and immovably looped up over layers of lace, as in the drawing room; and he pulled them back and pushed up the sash, leaning out into the icy night. The mere fact of not looking at May, seated beside his table, under his lamp, the fact of seeing other houses, roofs, chimneys, of getting the sense of other lives outside his own, other cities beyond New York, and a whole world beyond his world, cleared his brain and made it easier to breathe.

After he had leaned out into the darkness for a few minutes he heard her say: "Newland! Do shut the window. You'll catch your death."

He pulled the sash down and turned back. "Catch my death!"

he echoed, and he felt like adding: "But I've caught it already. I *am* dead—I've been dead for months and months."

And suddenly the play of the word flashed up a wild suggestion. What if it were *she* who was dead! If she were going to die—to die soon—and leave him free! The sensation of standing there, in that warm familiar room, and looking at her, and wishing her dead, was so strange, so fascinating and overmastering, that its enormity did not immediately strike him. He simply felt that chance had given him a new possibility to which his sick soul might cling. Yes, May might die—people did: young people, healthy people like herself: she might die, and set him suddenly free.

She glanced up, and he saw by her widening eyes that there must be something strange in his own.

"Newland! Are you ill?"

He shook his head and turned toward his armchair. She bent over her work frame, and as he passed he laid his hand on her hair. "Poor May!" he said.

"Poor? Why poor?" she echoed with a strained laugh.

"Because I shall never be able to open a window without worrying you," he rejoined, laughing also.

For a moment she was silent; then she said very low, her head bowed over her work: "I shall never worry if you're happy."

"Ah, my dear, and I shall never be happy unless I can open the windows!"

"In *this* weather?" she remonstrated, and with a sigh he buried his head in his book.

Six or seven days passed. Archer heard nothing from Madame Olenska, and became aware that her name would not be mentioned in his presence by any member of the family. He did not try to see her; to do so while she was at old Catherine's guarded bedside would have been almost impossible. In the uncertainty of the situation he let himself drift, conscious, somewhere below the surface of his thoughts, of a resolve which had come to him when he had leaned out from his library window into the icy night. The strength of that resolve made it easy to wait and make no sign.

Then one day May told him that Mrs. Manson Mingott had asked to see him. There was nothing surprising in the request, for

the old lady was steadily recovering, and she had always openly
declared that she preferred Archer to any of her other grand-
sons-in-law. May gave the message with evident pleasure: she was
proud of old Catherine's appreciation of her husband.

There was a moment's pause, and then Archer felt it incum-
bent on him to say: "All right. Shall we go together this afternoon?"

His wife's face brightened, but she instantly answered: "Oh,
you'd much better go alone. It bores Granny to see the same
people too often."

Archer's heart was beating violently when he rang old Mrs.
Mingott's bell. He had wanted above all things to go alone, for he
felt sure the visit would give him the chance of saying a word in
private to the Countess Olenska. He had determined to wait till
the chance presented itself naturally; and here it was, and here he
was on the doorstep. Behind the door, behind the curtains of the
yellow damask room next to the hall, she was surely awaiting him;
in another moment he should see her, and be able to speak to her
before she led him to the sick room.

He wanted only to put one question: after that his course
would be clear. What he wished to ask was simply the date of her
return to Washington; and that question she could hardly refuse
to answer.

But in the yellow sitting room it was the mulatto maid who
waited. Her white teeth shining like a keyboard, she pushed back
the sliding doors and ushered him into old Catherine's presence.

The old woman sat in a vast thronelike armchair near her bed.
Beside her was a mahogany stand bearing a cast bronze lamp with
an engraved globe, over which a green paper shade had been
balanced. There was not a book or a newspaper in reach, nor any
evidence of feminine employment: conversation had always been
Mrs. Mingott's sole pursuit, and she would have scorned to feign
an interest in fancywork.

Archer saw no trace of the slight distortion left by her stroke.
She merely looked paler, with darker shadows in the folds and
recesses of her obesity; and, in the fluted mob cap tied by a
starched bow between her first two chins, and the muslin kerchief
crossed over her billowing purple dressing gown, she seemed like

some shrewd and kindly ancestress of her own who might have yielded too freely to the pleasures of the table.

She held out one of the little hands that nestled in a hollow of her huge lap like pet animals, and called to the maid: "Don't let in anyone else. If my daughters call, say I'm asleep."

The maid disappeared, and the old lady turned to her grandson.

"My dear, am I perfectly hideous?" she asked gaily, launching out one hand in search of the folds of muslin on her inaccessible bosom. "My daughters tell me it doesn't matter at my age—as if hideousness didn't matter all the more the harder it gets to conceal!"

"My dear, you're handsomer than ever!" Archer rejoined in the same tone; and she threw back her head and laughed.

"Ah, but not as handsome as Ellen!" she jerked out, twinkling at him maliciously, and before he could answer she added: "Was she so awfully handsome the day you drove her up from the ferry?"

He laughed, and she continued: "Was it because you told her so that she had to put you out on the way? In my youth young men didn't desert pretty women unless they were made to!" She gave another chuckle, and interrupted it to say almost querulously: "It's a pity she didn't marry you. I always told her so. It would have spared me all this worry. But who ever thought of sparing their grandmother worry?"

Archer wondered if her illness had blurred her faculties, but suddenly she broke out: "Well, it's settled, anyhow: she's going to stay with me, whatever the rest of the family say! She hadn't been here five minutes before I'd have gone down on my knees to keep her—if only, for the last twenty years, I'd been able to see where the floor was!"

Archer listened in silence, and she went on: "They'd talked me over, as no doubt you know: persuaded me, Lovell, and Letterblair, and Augusta Welland, and all the rest of them, that I must hold out and cut off her allowance, till she was made to see that it was her duty to go back to Olenski. They thought they'd convinced me when the secretary, or whatever he was, came out with the last proposals: handsome proposals I confess they were. After all, marriage is marriage, and money's money—both useful

things in their way . . . and I didn't know what to answer—"
She broke off and drew a long breath, as if speaking had become
an effort. "But the minute I laid eyes on her, I said: 'You sweet
bird, you! Shut you up in that cage again? Never!' And now it's
settled that she's to stay here and nurse her Granny as long as
there's a Granny to nurse. It's not a gay prospect, but she doesn't
mind, and of course I've told Letterblair that she's to be given her
proper allowance."

The young man heard her with veins aglow, but in his confusion of mind he hardly knew whether her news brought joy or
pain. He had so definitely decided on the course he meant to
pursue that for the moment he could not readjust his thoughts.
But gradually there stole over him the delicious sense of difficulties deferred and opportunities miraculously provided. If Ellen
had consented to come and live with her grandmother it must
surely be because she had recognized the impossibility of giving
him up. This was her answer to his final appeal of the other day:
if she would not take the extreme step he had urged, she had at
last yielded to half-measures. He sank back into the thought with
the involuntary relief of a man who has been ready to risk everything, and suddenly tastes the dangerous sweetness of security.

"She couldn't have gone back—it was impossible!" he exclaimed.

"Ah, my dear, I always knew you were on her side; and that's
why I sent for you today, and why I said to your pretty wife, when
she proposed to come with you: 'No, my dear, I'm pining to see
Newland, and I don't want anybody to share our transports.' For
you see, my dear—" she drew her head back as far as its tethering
chins permitted, and looked him full in the eyes—"you see, we
shall have a fight yet. The family don't want her here, and they'll
say it's because I've been ill, because I'm a weak old woman, that
she's persuaded me. I'm not well enough yet to fight them one by
one, and you've got to do it for me."

"I?" he stammered.

"You. Why not?" she jerked back at him, her round eyes suddenly as sharp as penknives. Her hand fluttered from its chair
arm and lit on his with a clutch of little pale nails like bird claws.
"Why not?" she searchingly repeated.

Archer, under the exposure of her gaze, had recovered his self-possession.

"Oh, I don't count—I'm too insignificant."

"Well, you're Letterblair's partner, ain't you? You've got to get at them through Letterblair. Unless you've got a reason," she insisted.

"Oh, my dear, I back you to hold your own against them all without my help, but you shall have it if you need it," he reassured her.

"Then we're safe!" she sighed, and smiling on him with all her ancient cunning she added, as she settled her head among the cushions: "I always knew you'd back us up, because they never quote you when they talk about its being her duty to go home."

He winced a little at her terrifying perspicacity, and longed to ask: "And May—do they quote her?" But he judged it safer to turn the question.

"And Madame Olenska? When am I to see her?" he said.

The old lady chuckled, crumpled her lids, and went through the pantomime of archness. "Not today. One at a time, please. Madame Olenska's gone out."

He flushed with disappointment, and she went on: "She's gone out, my child: gone in my carriage to see Regina Beaufort."

She paused for this announcement to produce its effect. "That's what she's reduced me to already. The day after she got here she put on her best bonnet, and told me, as cool as a cucumber, that she was going to call on Regina Beaufort. 'I don't know her; who is she?' says I. 'She's your grandniece, and a most unhappy woman,' she says. 'She's the wife of a scoundrel,' I answered. 'Well,' she says, 'and so am I, and yet all my family want me to go back to him.' Well, that floored me, and I let her go; and finally one day she said it was raining too hard to go out on foot, and she wanted me to lend her my carriage. 'What for?' I asked her, and she said: 'To go and see cousin Regina'—*cousin!* Now, my dear, I looked out of the window, and saw it wasn't raining a drop, but I understood her, and I let her have the carriage. . . . After all, Regina's a brave woman, and so is she; and I've always liked courage above everything."

Archer bent down and pressed his lips on the little hand that still lay on his.

"Eh—eh—eh! Whose hand did you think you were kissing, young man—your wife's, I hope?" the old lady snapped out with her mocking cackle, and as he rose to go she called out after him: "Give her her Granny's love; but you'd better not say anything about our talk."

# —31—

ARCHER HAD been stunned by old Catherine's news. It was only natural that Madame Olenska should have hastened from Washington in response to her grandmother's summons; but that she should have decided to remain under her roof—especially now that Mrs. Mingott had almost regained her health—was less easy to explain.

Archer was sure that Madame Olenska's decision had not been influenced by the change in her financial situation. He knew the exact figure of the small income which her husband had allowed her at their separation. Without the addition of her grandmother's allowance it was hardly enough to live on, in any sense known to the Mingott vocabulary; and now that Medora Manson, who shared her life, had been ruined, such a pittance would barely keep the two women clothed and fed. Yet Archer was convinced that Madame Olenska had not accepted her grandmother's offer from interested motives.

She had the heedless generosity and the spasmodic extravagance of persons used to large fortunes, and indifferent to money; but she could go without many things which her relations considered indispensable, and Mrs. Lovell Mingott and Mrs. Welland had often been heard to deplore that anyone who had enjoyed the cosmopolitan luxuries of Count Olenski's establishments should care so little about "how things were done." Moreover, as Archer knew, several months had passed since her allowance had been cut off; yet in the interval she had made no effort to regain her grandmother's favor. Therefore if she had changed her course it must be for a different reason.

He did not have far to seek for that reason. On the way from the ferry she had told him that he and she must remain apart, but she had said it with her head on his breast. He knew that there was no calculated coquetry in her words; she was fighting her fate as he had fought his, and clinging desperately to her resolve that they should not break faith with the people who trusted them. But during the ten days which had elapsed since her return to New York she had perhaps guessed from his silence, and from the fact of his making no attempt to see her, that he was meditating a decisive step, a step from which there was no turning back. At the thought, a sudden fear of her own weakness might have seized her, and she might have felt that, after all, it was better to accept the compromise usual in such cases, and follow the line of least resistance.

An hour earlier, when he had rung Mrs. Mingott's bell, Archer had fancied that his path was clear before him. He had meant to have a word alone with Madame Olenska, and failing that, to learn from her grandmother on what day, and by which train, she was returning to Washington. In that train he intended to join her, and travel with her to Washington, or as much farther as she was willing to go. His own fancy inclined to Japan. At any rate she would understand at once that, wherever she went, he was going. He meant to leave a note for May that should cut off any other alternative.

He had fancied himself not only nerved for this plunge but eager to take it; yet his first feeling on hearing that the course of events was changed had been one of relief. Now, however, as he walked home from Mrs. Mingott's, he was conscious of a growing distaste for what lay before him. There was nothing unknown or unfamiliar in the path he was presumably to tread; but when he had trodden it before it was as a free man, who was accountable to no one for his actions, and could lend himself with an amused detachment to the game of precautions and prevarications, concealments and compliances, that the part required. This procedure was called "protecting a woman's honor"; and the best fiction, combined with the after-dinner talk of his elders, had long since initiated him into every detail of its code.

Now he saw the matter in a new light, and his part in it seemed singularly diminished. It was, in fact, that which, with a secret fatuity, he had watched Mrs. Thorley Rushworth play toward a fond and unperceiving husband: a smiling, bantering, humoring, watchful, and incessant lie. A lie by day, a lie by night, a lie in every touch and every look; a lie in every caress and every quarrel; a lie in every word and in every silence.

It was easier, and less dastardly on the whole, for a wife to play such a part toward her husband. A woman's standard of truthfulness was tacitly held to be lower: she was the subject creature, and versed in the arts of the enslaved. Then she could always plead moods and nerves, and the right not to be held too strictly to account; and even in the most strait-laced societies the laugh was always against the husband.

But in Archer's little world no one laughed at a wife deceived, and a certain measure of contempt was attached to men who continued their philandering after marriage. In the rotation of crops there was a recognized season for wild oats, but they were not to be sown more than once.

Archer had always shared this view: in his heart he thought Lefferts despicable. But to love Ellen Olenska was not to become a man like Lefferts: for the first time Archer found himself face to face with the dread argument of the individual case. Ellen Olenska was like no other woman, he was like no other man: their situation, therefore, resembled no one else's, and they were answerable to no tribunal but that of their own judgment.

Yes, but in ten minutes more he would be mounting his own doorstep; and there were May, and habit, and honor, and all the old decencies that he and his people had always believed in . . .

At his corner he hesitated, and then walked on down Fifth Avenue.

Ahead of him, in the winter night, loomed a big unlit house. As he drew near he thought how often he had seen it blazing with lights, its steps awninged and carpeted, and carriages waiting in double line to draw up at the curbstone. It was in the conservatory that stretched its dead-black bulk down the side street that he had taken his first kiss from May; it was under the myriad candles of the ballroom that he had seen her appear, tall and silver-shining as a young Diana.

Now the house was as dark as the grave, except for a faint flare of gas in the basement, and a light in one upstairs room where the blind had not been lowered. As Archer reached the corner he saw that the carriage standing at the door was Mrs. Manson Mingott's. What an opportunity for Sillerton Jackson, if he should chance to pass! Archer had been greatly moved by old Catherine's account of Madame Olenska's attitude toward Mrs. Beaufort; it made the righteous reprobation of New York seem like a passing by on the other side. But he knew well enough what construction the clubs and drawing rooms would put on Ellen Olenska's visits to her cousin.

He paused and looked up at the lighted window. No doubt the two women were sitting together in that room: Beaufort had probably sought consolation elsewhere. There were even rumors that he had left New York with Fanny Ring; but Mrs. Beaufort's attitude made the report seem improbable.

Archer had the nocturnal perspective of Fifth Avenue almost to himself. At that hour most people were indoors, dressing for dinner; and he was secretly glad that Ellen's exit was likely to be unobserved. As the thought passed through his mind the door opened, and she came out. Behind her was a faint light, such as might have been carried down the stairs to show her the way. She turned to say a word to someone; then the door closed, and she came down the steps.

"Ellen," he said in a low voice, as she reached the pavement.

She stopped with a slight start, and just then he saw two young men of fashionable cut approaching. There was a familiar air about their overcoats and the way their smart silk mufflers were folded over their white ties; and he wondered how youths of their quality happened to be dining out so early. Then he remembered that the Reggie Chiverses, whose house was a few doors above, were taking a large party that evening to see Adelaide Neilson in *Romeo and Juliet,* and guessed that the two were of the number. They passed under a lamp, and he recognized Lawrence Lefferts and a young Chivers.

A mean desire not to have Madame Olenska seen at the Beauforts' door vanished as he felt the penetrating warmth of her hand.

"I shall see you now—we shall be together," he broke out, hardly knowing what he said.

"Ah," she answered. "Granny has told you?"

While he watched her he was aware that Lefferts and Chivers, on reaching the farther side of the street corner, had discreetly struck away across Fifth Avenue. It was the kind of masculine solidarity that he himself often practiced; now he sickened at their connivance. Did she really imagine that he and she could live like this? And if not, what else did she imagine?

"Tomorrow I must see you—somewhere where we can be alone," he said, in a voice that sounded almost angry to his own ears.

She wavered, and moved toward the carriage.

"But I shall be at Granny's—for the present that is," she added, as if conscious that her change of plans required some explanation.

"Somewhere where we can be alone," he insisted.

She gave a faint laugh that grated on him.

"In New York? But there are no churches . . . no monuments."

"There's the art museum—in the park," he explained, as she looked puzzled. "At half-past two. I shall be at the door . . ."

She turned away without answering and got quickly into the carriage. As it drove off she leaned forward, and he thought she waved her hand in the obscurity. He stared after her in a turmoil of contradictory feelings. It seemed to him that he had been speaking not to the woman he loved but to another, a woman he was indebted to for pleasures already wearied of: it was hateful to find himself the prisoner of this hackneyed vocabulary.

"She'll come!" he said to himself, almost contemptuously.

Avoiding the popular "Wolfe collection," whose anecdotic canvases filled one of the main galleries of the queer wilderness of cast-iron and encaustic tiles known as the Metropolitan Museum, they had wandered down a passage to the room where the "Cesnola antiquities" moldered in unvisited loneliness.

They had this melancholy retreat to themselves, and seated on the divan enclosing the central steam radiator, they were staring silently at the glass cabinets mounted in ebonized wood which contained the recovered fragments of Ilium.

"It's odd," Madame Olenska said, "I never came here before."

"Ah, well—. Someday, I suppose, it will be a great museum."

"Yes," she assented absently.

She stood up and wandered across the room. Archer, remaining seated, watched the light movements of her figure, so girlish even under its heavy furs, the cleverly planted heron wing in her fur cap, and the way a dark curl lay like a flattened vine spiral on each cheek above the ear. His mind, as always when they first met, was wholly absorbed in the delicious details that made her herself and no other. Presently he rose and approached the case before which she stood. Its glass shelves were crowded with small broken objects—hardly recognizable domestic utensils, ornaments and personal trifles—made of glass, of clay, of discolored bronze, and other time-blurred substances.

"It seems cruel," she said, "that after a while nothing matters . . . any more than these little things, that used to be necessary and important to forgotten people, and now have to be guessed at under a magnifying glass and labeled: 'Use unknown.' "

"Yes, but meanwhile—"

"Ah, meanwhile—"

As she stood there, in her long sealskin coat, her hands thrust in a small round muff, her veil drawn down like a transparent mask to the tip of her nose, and the bunch of violets he had brought her stirring with her quickly taken breath, it seemed incredible that this pure harmony of line and color should ever suffer the stupid law of change.

"Meanwhile everything matters—that concerns you," he said.

She looked at him thoughtfully, and turned back to the divan. He sat down beside her and waited, but suddenly he heard a step echoing far off down the empty rooms, and felt the pressure of the minutes.

"What is it you wanted to tell me?" she asked, as if she had received the same warning.

"What I wanted to tell you?" he rejoined. "Why, that I believe you came to New York because you were afraid."

"Afraid?"

"Of my coming to Washington."

She looked down at her muff, and he saw her hands stir in it uneasily.

"Well—?"

"Well—yes," she said.

"You *were* afraid? You knew—?"

"Yes, I knew . . ."

"Well, then?" he insisted.

"Well, then: this is better, isn't it?" she returned with a long questioning sigh.

"Better—?"

"We shall hurt others less. Isn't it, after all, what you always wanted?"

"To have you here, you mean—in reach and yet out of reach? To meet you in this way, on the sly? It's the very reverse of what I want. I told you the other day what I wanted."

She hesitated. "And you still think this—worse?"

"A thousand times!" He paused. "It would be easy to lie to you, but the truth is I think it detestable."

"Oh, so do I!" she cried with a deep breath of relief.

He sprang up impatiently. "Well, then—it's my turn to ask: what is it, in God's name, that you think better?"

She hung her head and continued to clasp and unclasp her hands in her muff. The step drew nearer, and a guardian in a braided cap walked listlessly through the room like a ghost stalking through a necropolis. They fixed their eyes simultaneously on the case opposite them, and when the official figure had vanished down a vista of mummies and sarcophagi Archer spoke again.

"What do you think better?"

Instead of answering she murmured: "I promised Granny to stay with her because it seemed to me that here I should be safer."

"From me?"

She bent her head slightly, without looking at him.

"Safer from loving me?"

Her profile did not stir, but he saw a tear overflow on her lashes and hang in a mesh of her veil.

"Safer from doing irreparable harm. Don't let us be like all the others!" she protested.

"What others? I don't profess to be different from my kind. I'm consumed by the same wants and the same longings."

She glanced at him with a kind of terror, and he saw a faint color steal into her cheeks.

"Shall I—once come to you, and then go home?" she suddenly hazarded in a low clear voice.

The blood rushed to the young man's forehead. "Dearest!" he said, without moving. It seemed as if he held his heart in his hands, like a full cup that the least motion might overbrim.

Then her last phrase struck his ear and his face clouded. "Go home? What do you mean by going home?"

"Home to my husband."

"And you expect me to say yes to that?"

She raised her troubled eyes to his. "What else is there? I can't stay here and lie to the people who've been good to me."

"But that's the very reason why I ask you to come away!"

"And destroy their lives, when they've helped me to remake mine?"

Archer sprang to his feet and stood looking down on her in inarticulate despair. It would have been easy to say, "Yes, come, come once." He knew the power she would put in his hands if she consented; there would be no difficulty then in persuading her not to go back to her husband.

But something silenced the word on his lips. A sort of passionate honesty in her made it inconceivable that he should try to draw her into that familiar trap. "If I were to let her come," he said to himself, "I should have to let her go again." And that was not to be imagined.

But he saw the shadow of the lashes on her wet cheek, and wavered.

"After all," he began again, "we have lives of our own. . . . There's no use attempting the impossible. You're so unprejudiced about some things, so used, as you say, to looking at the Gorgon, that I don't know why you're afraid to face our case, and see it as it really is—unless you think the sacrifice is not worth making."

She stood up also, her lips tightening under a rapid frown.

"Call it that, then—I must go," she said, drawing her little watch from her bosom.

She turned away, and he followed and caught her by the wrist. "Well, then: come to me once," he said, his head turning suddenly at the thought of losing her, and for a second or two they looked at each other almost like enemies.

"When?" he insisted. "Tomorrow?"

She hesitated. "The day after."

"Dearest—!" he said again.

She had disengaged her wrist, but for a moment they continued to hold each other's eyes, and he saw that her face, which had grown very pale, was flooded with a deep inner radiance. His heart beat with awe: he felt that he had never before beheld love visible.

"Oh, I shall be late—good-bye. No, don't come any farther than this," she cried, walking hurriedly away down the long room, as if the reflected radiance in his eyes had frightened her. When she reached the door she turned for a moment to wave a quick farewell.

Archer walked home alone. Darkness was falling when he let himself into his house, and he looked about at the familiar objects in the hall as if he viewed them from the other side of the grave.

The parlormaid, hearing his step, ran up the stairs to light the gas on the upper landing.

"Is Mrs. Archer in?"

"No, sir. Mrs. Archer went out in the carriage after luncheon, and hasn't come back."

With a sense of relief he entered the library and flung himself down in his armchair. The parlormaid followed, bringing the student lamp and shaking some coals onto the dying fire. When she left he continued to sit motionless, his elbows on his knees, his chin on his clasped hands, his eyes fixed on the red grate.

He sat there without conscious thoughts, without sense of the lapse of time, in a deep and grave amazement that seemed to suspend life rather than quicken it. "This was what had to be, then . . . this was what had to be," he kept repeating to himself, as if he hung in the clutch of doom. What he had dreamed of had been so different that there was a mortal chill in his rapture.

The door opened and May came in.

"I'm dreadfully late—you weren't worried, were you?" she asked, laying her hand on his shoulder with one of her rare caresses.

He looked up astonished. "Is it late?"

"After seven. I believe you've been asleep!" She laughed, and drawing out her hat pins tossed her velvet hat on the sofa. She looked paler than usual, but sparkling with an unwonted animation.

"I went to see Granny, and just as I was going away Ellen came in from a walk; so I stayed and had a long talk with her. It was ages since we'd had a real talk. . . ." She had dropped into her

usual armchair, facing his, and was running her fingers through
her rumpled hair. He fancied she expected him to speak.

"A really good talk," she went on, smiling with what seemed to
Archer an unnatural vividness. "She was so dear—just like the old
Ellen. I'm afraid I haven't been fair to her lately. I've sometimes
thought—"

Archer stood up and leaned against the mantelpiece, out of the
radius of the lamp.

"Yes, you've thought—?" he echoed as she paused.

"Well, perhaps I haven't judged her fairly. She's so different—
at least on the surface. She takes up such odd people—she seems
to like to make herself conspicuous. I suppose it's the life she's led
in that fast European society; no doubt we seem dreadfully dull to
her. But I don't want to judge her unfairly."

She paused again, a little breathless with the unwonted length
of her speech, and sat with her lips slightly parted and a deep
blush on her cheeks.

Archer, as he looked at her, was reminded of the glow which
had suffused her face in the Mission Garden at St. Augustine. He
became aware of the same obscure effort in her, the same reaching out toward something beyond the usual range of her vision.

"She hates Ellen," he thought, "and she's trying to overcome
the feeling, and to get me to help her to overcome it."

The thought moved him, and for a moment he was on the
point of breaking the silence between them, and throwing himself
on her mercy.

"You understand, don't you," she went on, "why the family
have sometimes been annoyed? We all did what we could for her
at first, but she never seemed to understand. And now this idea of
going to see Mrs. Beaufort, of going there in Granny's carriage!
I'm afraid she's quite alienated the van der Luydens . . ."

"Ah," said Archer with an impatient laugh. The open door had
closed between them again.

"It's time to dress; we're dining out, aren't we?" he asked,
moving from the fire.

She rose also, but lingered near the hearth. As he walked past
her she moved forward impulsively, as though to detain him:
their eyes met, and he saw that hers were of the same swimming
blue as when he had left her to drive to Jersey City.

She flung her arms about his neck and pressed her cheek to his.

"You haven't kissed me today," she said in a whisper, and he felt her tremble in his arms.

AT THE COURT of the Tuileries," said Mr. Sillerton Jackson with his reminiscent smile, "such things were pretty openly tolerated."

The scene was the van der Luydens' black walnut dining room in Madison Avenue, and the time the evening after Newland Archer's visit to the museum of art. Mr. and Mrs. van der Luyden had come to town for a few days from Skuytercliff, whither they had precipitately fled at the announcement of Beaufort's failure. It had been represented to them that the disarray into which society had been thrown by this deplorable affair made their presence in town more necessary than ever. It was one of the occasions when, as Mrs. Archer put it, they "owed it to society" to show themselves at the opera, and even to open their own doors.

"It will never do, my dear Louisa, to let people like Mrs. Lemuel Struthers think they can step into Regina's shoes. It is just at such times that new people push in and get a footing. It was owing to the epidemic of chicken pox in New York the winter Mrs. Struthers first appeared that the married men slipped away to her house while their wives were in the nursery. You and dear Henry, Louisa, must stand in the breach as you always have."

Mr. and Mrs. van der Luyden could not remain deaf to such a call, and reluctantly but heroically they had come to town, unmuffled the house, and sent out invitations for two dinners and an evening reception.

On this particular evening they had invited Sillerton Jackson, Mrs. Archer, and Newland and his wife to go with them to the opera, where Faust was being sung for the first time that winter. Nothing was done without ceremony under the van der Luyden roof, and though there were but four guests the repast had begun at seven punctually, so that the proper sequence of courses might be served without haste before the gentlemen settled down to their cigars.

Archer had not seen his wife since the evening before. He had left early for the office, where he had plunged into an accumulation of unimportant business. In the afternoon one of the senior partners had made an unexpected call on his time, and he had reached home so late that May had preceded him to the van der Luydens', and sent back the carriage.

Now, across the Skuytercliff carnations and the massive plate, she struck him as pale and languid; but her eyes shone, and she talked with exaggerated animation.

The subject which had called forth Mr. Sillerton Jackson's favorite allusion had been brought up (Archer fancied not without intention) by their hostess. The Beaufort failure, or rather the Beaufort attitude since the failure, was still a fruitful theme for the drawing-room moralist; and after it had been thoroughly examined and condemned Mrs. van der Luyden had turned her scrupulous eyes on May Archer.

"Is it possible, dear, that what I hear is true? I was told your grandmother Mingott's carriage was seen standing at Mrs. Beaufort's door." It was noticeable that she no longer called the offending lady by her Christian name.

May's color rose, and Mrs. Archer put in hastily: "If it was, I'm convinced it was there without Mrs. Mingott's knowledge."

"Ah, you think—?" Mrs. van der Luyden paused, sighed, and glanced at her husband.

"I'm afraid," Mr. van der Luyden said, "that Madame Olenska's kind heart may have led her into the imprudence of calling on Mrs. Beaufort."

"Or her taste for peculiar people," put in Mrs. Archer in a dry tone, while her eyes dwelt innocently on her son's.

"I'm sorry to think it of Madame Olenska," said Mrs. van der Luyden, and Mrs. Archer murmured: "Ah, my dear—and after you'd had her twice at Skuytercliff!"

It was at this point that Mr. Jackson seized the chance to place his favorite allusion.

"At the Tuileries," he repeated, seeing the eyes of the company expectantly turned on him, "the standard was excessively lax in some respects; and if you'd asked where Morny's money came from—! Or who paid the debts of some of the Court beauties . . ."

"I hope, dear Sillerton," said Mrs. Archer, "you are not suggesting that we should adopt such standards?"

"I never suggest," returned Mr. Jackson imperturbably. "But Madame Olenska's foreign bringing-up may make her less particular—"

"Ah," the two elder ladies sighed.

"Still, to have kept her grandmother's carriage at a defaulter's door!" Mr. van der Luyden protested; and Archer guessed that he was remembering, and resenting, the hampers of carnations he had sent to the little house in Twenty-third Street.

"Of course I've always said that she looks at things quite differently," Mrs. Archer summed up.

A flush rose to May's forehead. She looked across the table at her husband, and said precipitately: "I'm sure Ellen meant it kindly."

"Imprudent people are often kind," said Mrs. Archer, as if the fact were scarcely an extenuation, and Mrs. van der Luyden murmured: "If only she had consulted someone—"

"Ah, that she never did!" Mrs. Archer rejoined.

At this point Mr. van der Luyden glanced at his wife, who bent her head slightly in the direction of Mrs. Archer, and the glimmering trains of the three ladies swept out of the door while the gentlemen settled down to their cigars. Mr. van der Luyden supplied short ones on opera nights, but they were so good that they made his guests deplore his inexorable punctuality.

Archer, after the first act, had detached himself from the party and made his way to the back of the club box. From there he watched, over various Chivers, Mingott, and Rushworth shoulders, the same scene that he had looked at, two years previously, on the night of his first meeting with Ellen Olenska. He had half-expected her to appear again in old Mrs. Mingott's box, but it remained empty; and he sat motionless, his eyes fastened on it, till suddenly Madame Nilsson's pure soprano broke out into *"M'ama, non m'ama . . ."*

Archer turned to the stage, where, in the familiar setting of giant roses and pen-wiper pansies, the same large blond victim was succumbing to the same small brown seducer.

From the stage his eyes wandered to the point of the horseshoe where May sat between two older ladies, just as, on that former evening, she had sat between Mrs. Lovell Mingott and her newly arrived "foreign" counsin. As on that evening, she was all in white; and Archer, who had not noticed what she wore, recognized the blue-white satin and old lace of her wedding dress.

It was the custom, in old New York, for brides to appear in this costly garment during the first year or two of marriage: his mother, he knew, kept hers in tissue paper in the hope that Janey might someday wear it, though poor Janey was reaching the age when pearl gray poplin and no bridesmaids would be thought more "appropriate."

It struck Archer that May, since their return from Europe, had seldom worn her bridal satin, and the surprise of seeing her in it made him compare her appearance with that of the young girl he had watched with such blissful anticipations two years earlier.

Though May's outline was slightly heavier, as her goddesslike build had foretold, her athletic erectness of carriage, and the girlish transparency of her expression, remained unchanged: but for the slight languor that Archer had lately noticed in her she would have been the exact image of the girl playing with the bouquet of lilies-of-the-valley on her betrothal evening. The fact seemed an additional appeal to his pity: such innocence was as moving as the trustful clasp of a child. Then he remembered the passionate generosity latent under that incurious calm. He recalled her glance of understanding when he had urged that their engagement should be announced at the Beaufort ball; he heard the voice in which she had said, in the Mission garden: "I couldn't have my happiness made out of a wrong—a wrong to someone else;" and an uncontrollable longing seized him to tell her the truth, to throw himself on her generosity, and ask for the freedom he had once refused.

Newland Archer was a quiet and self-controlled young man. Conformity to the discipline of a small society had become almost his second nature. It was deeply distasteful to him to do anything melodramatic and conspicuous, anything Mr. van der Luyden would have deprecated and the club box condemned as bad form. But he had become suddenly unconscious of the club box, of Mr. van der Luyden, of all that had so long enclosed him in the warm shelter of habit. He walked along the semicircular passage at the back of the house, and opened the door of Mrs. van der Luyden's box as if it had been a gate into the unknown.

*"M'ama!"* thrilled out the triumphant Marguerite, and the occupants of the box looked up in surprise at Archer's entrance. He had already broken one of the rules of his world, which forbade the entering of a box during a solo.

Slipping between Mr. van der Luyden and Sillerton Jackson, he leaned over his wife.

"I've got a beastly headache; don't tell anyone, but come home, won't you?" he whispered.

May gave him a glance of comprehension, and he saw her whisper to his mother, who nodded sympathetically; then she murmured an excuse to Mrs. van der Luyden, and rose from her seat just as Marguerite fell into Faust's arms. Archer, while he helped her on with her opera cloak, noticed the exchange of a significant smile between the older ladies.

As they drove away May laid her hand shyly on his. "I'm so sorry you don't feel well. I'm afraid they've been overworking you again at the office."

"No—it's not that: do you mind if I open the window?" he returned confusedly, letting down the pane on his side. He sat staring out into the street, feeling his wife beside him as a silent watchful interrogation, and keeping his eyes steadily fixed on the passing houses. At their door she caught her skirt in the step of the carriage, and fell against him.

"Did you hurt yourself?" he asked, steadying her with his arm.

"No, but my poor dress—see how I've torn it!" she exclaimed. She bent to gather up a mud-stained breadth, and followed him up the steps into the hall. The servants had not expected them so early, and there was only a glimmer of gas on the upper landing.

Archer mounted the stairs, turned up the light, and put a match to the brackets on each side of the library mantelpiece. The curtains were drawn, and the warm friendly aspect of the room smote him like that of a familiar face met during an unavowable errand.

He noticed that his wife was very pale, and asked if he should get her some brandy.

"Oh, no," she exclaimed with a momentary flush, as she took off her cloak. "But hadn't you better go to bed at once?" she added, as he opened a silver box on the table and took out a cigarette.

Archer threw down the cigarette and walked to his usual place by the fire.

"No, my head is not as bad as that." He paused. "And there's something I want to say; something important—that I must tell you at once."

She had dropped into an armchair, and raised her head as he spoke. "Yes, dear?" she rejoined, so gently that he wondered at the lack of wonder with which she received this preamble.

"May—" he began, standing a few feet from her chair, and looking over at her as if the slight distance between them were an unbridgeable abyss. The sound of his voice echoed uncannily through the homelike hush, and he repeated: "There is something I've got to tell you . . . about myself . . ."

She sat silent, without a movement or a tremor of her lashes. She was still extremely pale, but her face had a curious tranquillity of expression that seemed drawn from some secret inner source.

Archer checked the conventional phrases of self-accusal that were crowding to his lips. He was determined to put the case baldly, without vain recrimination or excuse.

"Madame Olenska—" he said, but at the name his wife raised her hand as if to silence him. As she did so the gaslight struck on the gold of her wedding ring.

"Oh, why should we talk about Ellen tonight?" she asked, with a slight pout of impatience.

"Because I ought to have spoken before."

Her face remained calm. "Is it really worthwhile, dear? I know I've been unfair to her at times—perhaps we all have. You've understood her, no doubt, better than we did: you've always been kind to her. But what does it matter, now it's all over?"

Archer looked at her blankly. Could it be possible that the sense of unreality in which he felt himself imprisoned had communicated itself to his wife?

"All over—what do you mean?" he asked in an indistinct stammer.

May still looked at him with transparent eyes. "Why—since she's going back to Europe so soon; since Granny approves and understands, and has arranged to make her independent of her husband—"

She broke off, and Archer, grasping the corner of the mantel-piece in one convulsed hand, and steadying himself against it, made a vain effort to extend the same control to his reeling thoughts.

"I supposed," he heard his wife's even voice go on, "that you had been kept at the office this evening about the business arrangements. It was settled this morning, I believe." She lowered her eyes under his unseeing stare, and another fugitive flush passed over her face.

He understood that his own eyes must be unbearable, and turning away, rested his elbows on the mantel shelf and covered his face. Something drummed and clanged furiously in his ears; he could not tell if it were the blood in his veins, or the tick of the clock on the mantel.

May sat without moving or speaking while the clock slowly measured out five minutes. A lump of coal fell forward in the grate, and hearing her rise to push it back, Archer at length turned and faced her.

"It's impossible," he exclaimed.

"Impossible—?"

"How do you know—what you've just told me?"

"I saw Ellen yesterday—I told you I'd seen her at Granny's."

"It wasn't then that she told you?"

"No, I had a note from her this afternoon. Do you want to see it?"

He could not find his voice, and she went out of the room, and came back almost immediately.

"I thought you knew," she said simply.

She laid a sheet of paper on the table, and Archer put out his hand and took it up. The letter contained only a few lines.

"May dear, I have at last made Granny understand that my visit to her could be no more than a visit, and she has been as kind and generous as ever. She sees now that if I return to Europe I must live by myself, or rather with poor Aunt Medora, who is coming with me. I am hurrying back to Washington to pack up, and we sail next week. You must be very good to Granny when I'm gone—as good as you've always been to me. Ellen.

"If any of my friends wish to urge me to change my mind, please tell them it would be utterly useless."

Archer read the letter over two or three times, then he flung it down and burst out laughing.

The sound of his laugh startled him. It recalled Janey's midnight fright when she had caught him rocking with incomprehensible mirth over May's telegram announcing that the date of their marriage had been advanced.

"Why did she write this?" he asked, checking his laugh with a supreme effort.

May met the question with her unshaken candor. "I suppose because we talked things over yesterday—"

"What things?"

"I told her I was afraid I hadn't been fair to her—hadn't always understood how hard it must have been for her here, alone among so many people who were relations and yet strangers; who felt the right to criticize, and yet didn't always know the circumstances." She paused. "I knew you'd been the one friend she could always count on; and I wanted her to know that you and I were the same—in all our feelings."

She hesitated, as if waiting for him to speak, and then added slowly: "She understood my wishing to tell her this. I think she understands everything."

She went up to Archer, and taking one of his cold hands pressed it quickly against her cheek.

"My head aches too; good night, dear," she said, and turned to the door, her torn and muddy wedding dress dragging after her across the room.

# —— 33 ——

It was, as Mrs. Archer smilingly said to Mrs. Welland, a great event for a young couple to give their first big dinner.

The Newland Archers, since they had set up their household, had received a good deal of company in an informal way. Archer was fond of having three or four friends to dine, and May welcomed them with the beaming readiness of which her mother had set her the example in conjugal affairs. Her husband questioned whether, if left to herself, she would ever have asked anyone to the house; but he had long given up trying to disengage her real self from the shape into which tradition and training had molded her. It was expected that well-off young couples in New York should do a good deal of informal entertaining, and a Welland married to an Archer was doubly pledged to the tradition.

But a big dinner, with a hired chef and two borrowed footmen, with Roman punch, roses from Henderson's, and menus on gilt-edged cards, was a different affair, and not to be lightly undertaken. As Mrs. Archer remarked, the Roman punch made all the difference; not in itself but by its manifold implications—since it signified either canvasbacks or terrapin, two soups, a hot and a cold sweet, full *décolletage* with short sleeves, and guests of a proportionate importance.

It was always an interesting occasion when a young pair launched their first invitations in the third person, and their summons was seldom refused even by the seasoned and sought-after. Still, it was admittedly a triumph that the van der Luydens, at May's request, should have stayed over in order to be present at her farewell dinner for the Countess Olenska.

The two mothers-in-law sat in May's drawing room on the afternoon of the great day, Mrs. Archer writing out the menus on Tiffany's thickest gilt-edged bristol, while Mrs. Welland superintended the placing of the palms and standard lamps.

Archer, arriving late from his office, found them still there.

Mrs. Archer had turned her attention to the name cards for the table, and Mrs. Welland was considering the effect of bringing forward the large gilt sofa, so that another "corner" might be created between the piano and the window.

May, they told him, was in the dining room inspecting the mound of Jacqueminot roses and maidenhair in the center of the long table, and the placing of the Maillard bonbons in openwork silver baskets between the candelabra. On the piano stood a large basket of orchids which Mr. van der Luyden had had sent from Skuytercliff. Everything was, in short, as it should be on the approach of so considerable an event.

Mrs. Archer ran thoughtfully over the list, checking off each name with her sharp gold pen.

"Henry van der Luyden—Louisa—the Lovell Mingotts—the Reggie Chiverses—Lawrence Lefferts and Gertrude—(yes, I suppose May was right to have them)—the Selfridge Merrys, Sillerton Jackson, Van Newland and his wife. (How time passes! It seems only yesterday that he was your best man, Newland)—and Countess Olenska—yes, I think that's all. . . ."

Mrs. Welland surveyed her son-in-law affectionately. "No one can say, Newland, that you and May are not giving Ellen a handsome sendoff."

"Ah, well," said Mrs. Archer, "I understand May's wanting her cousin to tell people abroad that we're not quite barbarians."

"I'm sure Ellen will appreciate it. She was to arrive this morning, I believe. It will make a most charming last impression. The evening before sailing is usually so dreary," Mrs. Welland cheerfully continued.

Archer turned toward the door, and his mother-in-law called to him: "Do go in and have a peep at the table. And don't let May tire herself too much." But he affected not to hear, and sprang up the stairs to his library. The room looked at him like an alien countenance composed into a polite grimace; and he perceived that it had been ruthlessly "tidied," and prepared, by a judicious distribution of ashtrays and cedarwood boxes, for the gentlemen to smoke in.

"Ah, well," he thought, "it's not for long—" and he went on to his dressing room.

\* \* \*

Ten days had passed since Madame Olenska's departure from New York. During those ten days Archer had had no sign from her but that conveyed by the return of a key wrapped in tissue paper, and sent to his office in a sealed envelope addressed in her hand. This retort to his last appeal might have been interpreted as a classic move in a familiar game, but the young man chose to give it a different meaning. She was still fighting against her fate; but she was going to Europe, and she was not returning to her husband. Nothing, therefore, was to prevent his following her; and once he had taken the irrevocable step, and had proved to her that it was irrevocable, he believed she would not send him away.

This confidence in the future had steadied him to play his part in the present. It had kept him from writing to her, or betraying, by any sign or act, his misery and mortification. It seemed to him that in the deadly silent game between them the trumps were still in his hands, and he waited.

There had been, nevertheless, moments sufficiently difficult to pass; as when Mr. Letterblair, the day after Madame Olenska's departure, had sent for him to go over the details of the trust which Mrs. Manson Mingott wished to create for her grand-daughter. For a couple of hours Archer had examined the terms of the deed with his senior, all the while obscurely feeling that if he had been consulted it was for some reason other than the obvious one of his cousinship; and that the close of the conference would reveal it.

"Well, the lady can't deny that it's a handsome arrangement," Mr. Letterblair had summed up, after mumbling over a summary of the settlement. "In fact I'm bound to say she's been treated pretty handsomely all round."

"All round?" Archer echoed with a touch of derision. "Do you refer to her husband's proposal to give her back her own money?"

Mr. Letterblair's bushy eyebrows went up a fraction of an inch. "My dear sir, the law's the law; and your wife's cousin was married under the French law. It's to be presumed she knew what that meant."

"Even if she did, what happened subsequently—." But Archer paused. Mr. Letterblair had laid his pen handle against his big corrugated nose, and was looking down it with the expression assumed by virtuous elderly gentlemen when they wish their youngers to understand that virtue is not synonymous with ignorance.

"My dear sir, I've no wish to extenuate the count's transgressions; but—but on the other side . . . I wouldn't put my hand in the fire . . . well, that there hadn't been tit for tat . . . with the young champion. . . ." Mr. Letterblair unlocked a drawer and pushed a folded paper toward Archer. "This report, the result of discreet inquiries . . ." And then, as Archer made no effort to glance at the paper or to repudiate the suggestion, the lawyer somewhat flatly continued: "I don't say it's conclusive, you observe; far from it. But straws show . . . and on the whole it's eminently satisfactory for all parties that this dignified solution has been reached."

"Oh, eminently," Archer assented, pushing back the paper.

A day or two later, on responding to a summons from Mrs. Manson Mingott, his soul had been more deeply tried.

He had found the old lady depressed and querulous.

"You know she's deserted me?" she began at once, and without waiting for his reply: "Oh, don't ask me why! She gave so many reasons that I've forgotten them all. My private belief is that she couldn't face the boredom. At any rate that's what Augusta and my daughters-in-law think. And I don't know that I altogether blame her. Olenski's a finished scoundrel, but life with him must have been a good deal gayer than it is in Fifth Avenue. Not that the family would admit that: they think Fifth Avenue is Heaven with the rue de la Paix thrown in. And poor Ellen, of course, has no idea of going back to her husband. She held out as firmly as ever against that. So she's to settle down in Paris with that fool Medora. . . . Well, Paris is Paris, and you can keep a carriage there on next to nothing. But she was as gay as a bird, and I shall miss her." Two tears, the parched tears of the old, rolled down her puffy cheeks and vanished in the abysses of her bosom.

"All I ask is," she concluded, "that they shouldn't bother me anymore. I must really be allowed to digest my gruel. . . ." And she twinkled a little wistfully at Archer.

It was that evening, on his return home, that May announced her intention of giving a farewell dinner to her cousin. Madame

Olenska's name had not been pronounced between them since the night of her flight to Washington; and Archer looked at his wife with surprise.

"A dinner—why?" he interrogated.

Her color rose. "But you like Ellen—I thought you'd be pleased."

"It's awfully nice—your putting it in that way. But I really don't see—"

"I mean to do it, Newland," she said, quietly rising and going to her desk. "Here are the invitations all written. Mother helped me—she agrees that we ought to." She paused, embarrassed and yet smiling, and Archer suddenly saw before him the embodied image of the Family.

"Oh, all right," he said, staring with unseeing eyes at the list of guests that she had put in his hand.

When he entered the drawing room before dinner May was stooping over the fire and trying to coax the logs to burn in their unaccustomed setting of immaculate tiles.

The tall lamps were all lit, and Mr. van der Luyden's orchids had been conspicuously disposed in various receptacles of modern porcelain and knobby silver. Mrs. Newland Archer's drawing room was generally thought a great success. A gilt bamboo *jardinière,* in which the primulas and cinerarias were punctually renewed, blocked the access to the bay window (where the old-fashioned would have preferred a bronze reduction of the *Venus of Milo);* the sofas and armchairs of pale brocade were cleverly grouped about little plush tables densely covered with silver toys, porcelain animals, and efflorescent photograph frames; and tall rosy-shaded lamps shot up like tropical flowers among the palms.

"I don't think Ellen has ever seen this room lighted up," said May, rising flushed from her struggle, and sending about her a glance of pardonable pride. The brass tongs which she had propped against the side of the chimney fell with a crash that drowned her husband's answer; and before he could restore them Mr. and Mrs. van der Luyden were announced.

The other guests quickly followed, for it was known that the van der Luydens liked to dine punctually. The room was nearly full, and Archer was engaged in showing to Mrs. Selfridge Merry a small highly varnished Verbeckhoven *Study of Sheep,* which Mr. Welland had given May for Christmas, when he found Madame Olenska at his side.

She was excessively pale, and her pallor made her dark hair seem denser and heavier than ever. Perhaps that, or the fact that she had wound several rows of amber beads about her neck, reminded him suddenly of the little Ellen Mingott he had danced with at children's parties, when Medora Manson had first brought her to New York.

The amber beads were trying to her complexion, or her dress was perhaps unbecoming: her face looked lusterless and almost ugly, and he had never loved it as he did at that minute. Their hands met, and he thought he heard her say: "Yes, we're sailing tomorrow in the *Russia*—"; then there was an unmeaning noise of opening doors, and after an interval May's voice: "Newland! Dinner's been announced. Won't you please take Ellen in?"

Madame Olenska put her hand on his arm, and he noticed that the hand was ungloved, and remembered how he had kept his eyes fixed on it the evening that he had sat with her in the little Twenty-third Street drawing room. All the beauty that had forsaken her face seemed to have taken refuge in the long pale fingers and faintly dimpled knuckles on his sleeve, and he said to himself: "If it were only to see her hand again I should have to follow her—."

It was only at an entertainment ostensibly offered to a "foreign visitor" that Mrs. van der Luyden could suffer the diminution of being placed on her host's left. The fact of Madame Olenska's "foreignness" could hardly have been more adroitly emphasized than by this farewell tribute; and Mrs. van der Luyden accepted her displacement with an affability which left no doubt as to her approval. There were certain things that had to be done, and if done at all, done handsomely and thoroughly; and one of these, in the old New York code, was the tribal rally around a kinswoman about to be eliminated from the tribe. There was nothing on earth that the Wellands and Mingotts would not have done to proclaim their unalterable affection for the Countess Olenska now that her passage for Europe was engaged; and Archer, at the head of his table, sat marveling at the silent untiring activity with which her popularity had been retrieved, grievances against her silenced, her past countenanced, and her present irradiated by the family approval. Mrs. van der Luyden shone on her with the dim benevolence which was her nearest approach to cordiality, and Mr. van der Luyden, from his seat at May's right, cast down the table glances plainly intended to justify all the carnations he had sent from Skuytercliff.

Archer, who seemed to be assisting at the scene in a state of odd imponderability, as if he floated somewhere between chandelier and ceiling, wondered at nothing so much as his own share in the proceedings. As his glance traveled from one placid well-fed face to another he saw all the harmless-looking people engaged upon May's canvasbacks as a band of dumb conspirators, and himself and the pale woman on his right as the center of their conspiracy. And then it came over him, in a vast flash made up of many broken gleams, that to all of them he and Madame Olenska were lovers, lovers in the extreme sense peculiar to "foreign" vocabularies. He guessed himself to have been, for months, the center of countless silently observing eyes and patiently listening ears, he understood that, by means as yet unknown to him, the separation between himself and the partner of his guilt had been achieved, and that now the whole tribe had rallied about his wife on the tacit assumption that nobody knew anything, or had ever imagined anything, and that the occasion of the entertainment was simply May Archer's natural desire to take an affectionate leave of her friend and cousin.

It was the old New York way of taking life "without effusion of blood": the way of people who dreaded scandal more than disease, who placed decency above courage, and who considered that nothing was more ill-bred than "scenes," except the behavior of those who gave rise to them.

As these thoughts succeeded each other in his mind Archer felt like a prisoner in the center of an armed camp. He looked about the table, and guessed at the inexorableness of his captors from the tone in which, over the asparagus from Florida, they were dealing with Beaufort and his wife. "It's to show me," he thought, "what would happen to *me*—" and a deathly sense of the superiority of implication and analogy over direct action, and of silence over rash words, closed in on him like the doors of the family vault.

He laughed, and met Mrs. van der Luyden's startled eyes.

"You think it laughable?" she said with a pinched smile. "Of course poor Regina's idea of remaining in New York has its ridiculous side, I suppose," and Archer muttered: "Of course."

At this point, he became conscious that Madame Olenska's other neighbor had been engaged for some time with the lady on his right. At the same moment he saw that May, serenely enthroned between Mr. van der Luyden and Mr. Selfridge Merry, had cast a quick glance down the table. It was evident that the host and the lady on his right could not sit through the whole meal in silence. He turned to Madame Olenska, and her pale smile met him. "Oh, do let's see it through," it seemed to say.

"Did you find the journey tiring?" he asked in a voice that surprised him by it naturalness; and she answered that, on the contrary, she had seldom traveled with fewer discomforts.

"Except, you know, the dreadful heat in the train," she added, and he remarked that she would not suffer from that particular hardship in the country she was going to.

"I never," he declared with intensity, "was more nearly frozen than once, in April, in the train between Calais and Paris."

She said she did not wonder, but remarked that, after all, one could always carry an extra rug, and that every form of travel had its hardships; to which he abruptly returned that he thought them all of no account compared with the blessedness of getting away. She changed color, and he added, his voice suddenly rising in pitch: "I mean to do a lot of traveling myself before long." A tremor crossed her face, and leaning over to Reggie Chivers, he cried out: "I say, Reggie, what do you say to a trip around the world: now, next month, I mean? I'm game if you are—" at which Mrs. Reggie piped up that she could not think of letting Reggie go till after the Martha Washington ball she was getting up for the Blind Asylum in Easter week; and her husband placidly observed that by that time he would have to be practicing for the International Polo match.

But Mr. Selfridge Merry had caught the phrase "round the world," and having once circled the globe in his steam yacht, he seized the opportunity to send down the table several striking items concerning the shallowness of the Mediterranean ports. Though, after all, he added, it didn't matter, for when you'd seen

Athens and Smyrna and Constantinople, what else was there? And Mrs. Merry said she could never be too grateful to Dr. Bencomb for having made them promise not to go to Naples on account of the fever.

"But you must have three weeks to do India properly," her husband conceded, anxious to have it understood that he was no frivolous globetrotter.

And at this point the ladies went up to the drawing room.

In the library, in spite of weightier presences, Lawrence Lefferts predominated.

The talk, as usual, had veered around to the Beauforts, and even Mr. van der Luyden and Mr. Selfridge Merry, installed in the honorary armchairs tacitly reserved for them, paused to listen to the younger man's philippic.

Never had Lefferts so abounded in the sentiments that adorn Christian manhood and exalt the sanctity of the home. Indignation lent him a scathing eloquence, and it was clear that if others had followed his example, and acted as he talked, society would never have been weak enough to receive a foreign upstart like Beaufort—no, sir, not even if he'd married a van der Luyden or a Lanning instead of a Dallas. And what chance would there have been, Lefferts wrathfully questioned, of his marrying into such a family as the Dallases, if he had not already wormed his way into certain houses, as people like Mrs. Lemuel Struthers had managed to worm theirs in his wake? If society chose to open its doors to vulgar women the harm was not great, though the gain was doubtful; but once it got in the way of tolerating men of obscure origin and tainted wealth the end was total disintegration—and at no distant date.

"If things go on at this pace," Lefferts thundered, looking like a young prophet dressed by Poole, and who had not yet been stoned, "we shall see our children fighting for invitations to swindlers' houses, and marrying Beaufort's bastards."

"Oh, I say—draw it mild!" Reggie Chivers and young Newland protested, while Mr. Selfridge Merry looked genuinely alarmed, and an expression of pain and disgust settled on Mr. van der Luyden's sensitive face.

"Has he got any?" cried Mr. Sillerton Jackson, pricking up his ears; and while Lefferts tried to turn the question with a laugh, the old gentleman twittered into Archer's ear: "Queer, those fellows who are always wanting to set things right. The people who have the worst cooks are always telling you they're poisoned when they dine out. But I hear there are pressing reasons for our friend Lawrence's diatribe—typewriter this time, I understand. . . ."

The talk swept past Archer like some senseless river running and running because it did not know enough to stop. He saw, on the faces about him, expressions of interest, amusement, and even mirth. He listened to the younger men's laughter, and to the praise of the Archer Madeira, which Mr. van der Luyden and Mr. Merry were thoughtfully celebrating. Through it all he was dimly aware of a general attitude of friendliness toward himself, as if the guard of the prisoner he felt himself to be were trying to soften his captivity; and the perception increased his passionate determination to be free.

In the drawing room, where they presently joined the ladies, he met May's triumphant eyes, and read in them the conviction that everything had "gone off" beautifully. She rose from Madame Olenska's side, and immediately Mrs. van der Luyden beckoned the latter to a seat on the gilt sofa where she throned. Mrs. Selfridge Merry bore across the room to join them, and it became clear to Archer that here also a conspiracy of rehabilitation and obliteration was going on. The silent organization which held his little world together was determined to put itself on record as never for a moment having questioned the propriety of Madame Olenska's conduct, or the completeness of Archer's domestic felicity. All these amiable and inexorable persons were resolutely engaged in pretending to each other that they had never heard of, suspected, or even conceived possible, the least hint to the contrary; and from this tissue of elaborate mutual dissimulation Archer once more disengaged the fact that New York believed him to be Madame Olenska's lover. He caught the glitter of victory in his wife's eyes, and for the first time understood that she shared the belief. The discovery roused a laughter of inner devils that reverberated through all his efforts to discuss the Martha Washington ball with Mrs. Reggie Chivers and little Mrs. Newland; and so the evening swept on, running and running like a senseless river that did not know how to stop.

At length he saw that Madame Olenska had risen and was saying good-bye. He understood that in a moment she would be gone, and tried to remember what he had said to her at dinner; but he could not recall a single word they had exchanged.

She went up to May, the rest of the company making a circle about her as she advanced. The two young women clasped hands; then May bent forward and kissed her cousin.

"Certainly our hostess is much the handsomer of the two," Archer heard Reggie Chivers say in an undertone to young Mrs. Newland; and he remembered Beaufort's coarse sneer at May's ineffectual beauty.

A moment later he was in the hall, putting Madame Olenska's cloak about her shoulders.

Through all his confusion of mind he had held fast to the resolve to say nothing that might startle or disturb her. Convinced that no power could now turn him from his purpose he had found strength to let events shape themselves as they would. But as he followed Madame Olenska into the hall he thought with a sudden hunger of being for a moment alone with her at the door of her carriage.

"Is your carriage here?" he asked, and at that moment Mrs. van der Luyden, who was being majestically inserted into her sables, said gently: "We are driving dear Ellen home."

Archer's heart gave a jerk, and Madame Olenska, clasping her cloak and fan with one hand, held out the other to him. "Good-bye," she said.

"Good-bye—but I shall see you soon in Paris," he answered aloud—it seemed to him that he had shouted it.

"Oh," she murmured, "if you and May could come—!"

Mr. van der Luyden advanced to give her his arm, and Archer turned to Mrs. van der Luyden. For a moment, in the billowy darkness inside the big landau, he caught the dim oval of a face, eyes shining steadily—and she was gone.

As he went up the steps he crossed Lawrence Lefferts coming down with his wife. Lefferts caught his host by the sleeve, drawing back to let Gertrude pass.

"I say, old chap: do you mind just letting it be understood that

I'm dining with you at the club tomorrow night? Thanks so much, you old brick! Good night."

"It *did* go off beautifully, didn't it?" May questioned from the threshold of the library.

Archer roused himself with a start. As soon as the last carriage had driven away, he had come up to the library and shut himself in, with the hope that his wife, who still lingered below, would go straight to her room. But there she stood, pale and drawn, yet radiating the factitious energy of one who has passed beyond fatigue.

"May I come and talk it over?" she asked.

"Of course, if you like. But you must be awfully sleepy—"

"No, I'm not sleepy. I should like to sit with you a little."

"Very well," he said, pushing her chair near the fire.

She sat down and he resumed his seat, but neither spoke for a long time. At length Archer began abruptly: "Since you're not tired, and want to talk, there's something I must tell you. I tried to the other night—."

She looked at him quickly. "Yes, dear. Something about yourself?"

"About myself. You say you're not tired: well, I am. Horribly tired . . ."

In an instant she was all tender anxiety. "Oh, I've seen it coming on, Newland! You've been so wickedly overworked—"

"Perhaps it's that. Anyhow, I want to make a break—"

"A break? To give up the law?"

"To go away, at any rate—at once. On a long trip, ever so far off—away from everything—"

He paused, conscious that he had failed in his attempt to speak with the indifference of a man who longs for a change, and is yet too weary to welcome it. Do what he would, the chord of eagerness vibrated. "Away from everything—" he repeated.

"Ever so far? Where, for instance?" she asked.

"Oh, I don't know. India—or Japan."

She stood up, and as he sat with bent head, his chin propped on his hands, he felt her warmly and fragrantly hovering over him.

"As far as that? But I'm afraid you can't, dear . . ." she said in an unsteady voice. "Not unless you'll take me with you." And then, as he was silent, she went on, in tones so clear and evenly pitched that each separate syllable tapped like a little hammer on his brain: "That is, if the doctors will let me go . . . but I'm afraid they won't. For you see, Newland, I've been sure since this morning of something I've been so longing and hoping for—"

He looked up at her with a sick stare, and she sank down, all dew and roses, and hid her face against his knee.

"Oh, my dear," he said, holding her to him while his cold hand stroked her hair.

There was a long pause, which the inner devils filled with strident laughter, then May freed herself from his arms and stood up.

"You didn't guess—?"

"Yes—I; no. That is, of course I hoped—"

They looked at each other for an instant and again fell silent; then, turning his eyes from hers, he asked abruptly: "Have you told anyone else?"

"Only Mamma and your mother." She paused, and then added hurriedly, the blood flushing up to her forehead: "That is—and Ellen. You know I told you we'd had a long talk one afternoon—and how dear she was to me."

"Ah—" said Archer, his heart stopping.

He felt that his wife was watching him intently. "Did you *mind* my telling her first, Newland?"

"Mind? Why should I?" He made a last effort to collect himself. "But that was a fortnight ago, wasn't it? I thought you said you weren't sure till today."

Her color burned deeper, but she held his gaze. "No, I wasn't sure then—but I told her I was. And you see I was right!" she exclaimed, her blue eyes wet with victory.

# ——34——

NEWLAND ARCHER sat at the writing table in his library in East Thirty-ninth Street.

He had just got back from a big official reception for the inauguration of the new galleries at the Metropolitan Museum, and the spectacle of those great spaces crowded with the spoils of the ages, where the throng of fashion circulated through a series of scientifically catalogued treasures, had suddenly pressed on a rusted spring of memory.

"Why, this used to be one of the old Cesnola rooms," he heard someone say; and instantly everything about him vanished, and he was sitting alone on a hard leather divan against a radiator, while a slight figure in a long sealskin cloak moved away down the meagrely fitted vista of the old museum.

The vision had roused a host of other associations, and he sat looking with new eyes at the library which, for over thirty years, had been the scene of his solitary musings and of all the family confabulations.

It was the room in which most of the real things of his life had happened. There his wife, nearly twenty-six years ago, had broken to him, with a blushing circumlocution that would have caused the young women of the new generation to smile, the news that she was to have a child; and there their eldest boy, Dallas, too delicate to be taken to church in midwinter, had been christened by their old friend the Bishop of New York, the ample magnificent irreplaceable bishop, so long the pride and ornament of his diocese. There Dallas had first staggered across the floor shouting "Dad," while May and the nurse laughed behind the door; there their second child, Mary (who was so like her mother), had announced her engagement to the dullest and most reliable of Reggie Chivers's many sons; and there Archer had kissed her through her wedding veil before they went down to the motor which was to carry them to Grace Church—for in a world where all else had reeled on its foundations the "Grace Church wedding" remained an unchanged institution.

It was in the library that he and May had always discussed the future of the children: the studies of Dallas and his young brother Bill, Mary's incurable indifference to "accomplishments," and passion for sport and philanthropy, and the vague leanings toward "art" which had finally landed the restless and curious Dallas in the office of a rising New York architect.

The young men nowadays were emancipating themselves from the law and business and taking up all sorts of new things. If they were not absorbed in state politics or municipal reform, the chances were that they were going in for Central American archeology, for architecture or landscape engineering; taking a keen and learned interest in the prerevolutionary buildings of their own country, studying and adapting Georgian types, and protesting at the meaningless use of the word "Colonial." Nobody nowadays had "Colonial" houses except the millionaire grocers of the suburbs.

But above all—sometimes Archer put it above all—it was in that library that the Governor of New York, coming down from Albany one evening to dine and spend the night, had turned to his host, and said, banging his clenched fist on the table and gnashing his eyeglasses: "Hang the professional politician! You're the kind of man the country wants, Archer. If the stable's ever to be cleaned out, men like you have got to lend a hand in the cleaning."

"Men like you—" how Archer had glowed at the phrase! How eagerly he had risen up at the call! It was an echo of Ned Winsett's old appeal to roll his sleeves up and get down into the muck; but spoken by a man who set the example of the gesture, and whose summons to follow him was irresistible.

Archer, as he looked back, was not sure that men like himself *were* what his country needed, at least in the active service to which Theodore Roosevelt had pointed; in fact, there was reason to think it did not, for after a year in the State Assembly he had not been reelected, and had dropped back thankfully into obscure if useful municipal work, and from that again to the writing of occasional articles in one of the reforming weeklies that were trying to shake the country out of its apathy. It was little enough to look back on; but when he remembered to what the young men of his generation and his set had looked forward—the narrow groove of moneymaking, sport, and society to which their vision had been limited—even his small contribution to the new state of things seemed to count, as each brick counts in a well-built wall. He had done little in public life; he would always be by nature a contemplative and a dilettante; but he had had high things to contemplate, great things to delight in; and one great man's friendship to be his strength and pride.

He had been, in short, what people were beginning to call "a good citizen." In New York, for many years past, every new movement, philanthropic, municipal, or artistic, had taken account of his opinion and wanted his name. People said: "Ask Archer" when there was a question of starting the first school for crippled children, reorganizing the Museum of Art, founding the Grolier Club, inaugurating the new library, or getting up a new society of chamber music. His days were full, and they were filled decently. He supposed it was all a man ought to ask.

Something he knew he had missed: the flower of life. But he thought of it now as a thing so unattainable and improbable that to have repined would have been like despairing because one had not drawn the first prize in a lottery. There were a hundred million tickets in *his* lottery, and there was only one prize; the chances had been too decidedly against him. When he thought of Ellen Olenska it was abstractly, serenely, as one might think of some imaginary beloved in a book or a picture: she had become the composite vision of all that he had missed. That vision, faint and tenuous as it was, had kept him from thinking of other women. He had been what was called a faithful husband; and when May had suddenly died—carried off by the infectious pneumonia through which she had nursed their youngest child—he had honestly mourned her. Their long years together had shown him that it did not so much matter if marriage was a dull duty, as long as it kept the dignity of a duty: lapsing from that, it became a mere battle of ugly appetites. Looking about him, he honored his own past, and mourned for it. After all, there was good in the old ways.

His eyes, making the round of the room—done over by Dallas with English mezzotints, Chippendale cabinets, bits of chosen blue-and-white and pleasantly shaded electric lamps—came back to the old Eastlake writing table that he had never been willing to banish, and to his first photograph of May, which still kept its place beside his inkstand.

There she was, tall, round-bosomed and willowy, in her starched muslin and flapping Leghorn, as he had seen her under the orange trees in the Mission garden. And as he had seen her that day, so she had remained; never quite at the same height, yet never far below it: generous, faithful, unwearied; but so lacking in imagination, so incapable of growth, that the world of her youth had fallen into pieces and rebuilt itself without her ever being conscious of the change. This hard bright blindness had kept her immediate horizon apparently unaltered. Her incapacity to recognize change made her children conceal their views from her as Archer concealed his; there had been, from the first, a joint pretense of sameness, a kind of innocent family hypocrisy, in which father and children had unconsciously collaborated. And she had died thinking the world a good place, full of loving and harmonious households like her own, and resigned to leave it because she was convinced that, whatever happened, Newland would continue to inculcate in Dallas the same principles and prejudices which had shaped his parents' lives, and that Dallas in turn (when Newland followed her) would transmit the sacred trust to little Bill. And of Mary she was sure as of her own self. So, having snatched little Bill from the grave, and given her life in the effort, she went contentedly to her place in the Archer vault in St. Mark's, where Mrs. Archer already lay safe from the terrifying "trend" which her daughter-in-law had never even become aware of.

Opposite May's portrait stood one of her daughter. Mary Chivers was as tall and fair as her mother, but large-waisted, flat-chested, and slightly slouching, as the altered fashion required. Mary Chivers's mighty feats of athleticism could not have been performed with the twenty-inch waist that May Archer's azure sash so easily spanned. And the difference seemed symbolic; the mother's life had been as closely girt as her figure. Mary, who was no less conventional, and no more intelligent, yet led a larger life and held more tolerant views. There was good in the new order too.

The telephone clicked, and Archer, turning from the photographs, unhooked the transmitter at his elbow. How far they were from the days when the legs of the brass-buttoned messenger boy had been New York's only means of quick communication!

"Chicago wants you."

Ah—it must be a long-distance from Dallas, who had been sent to Chicago by his firm to talk over the plan of the lakeside palace they were to build for a young millionaire with ideas. The firm always sent Dallas on such errands.

"Hallo, Dad—Yes: Dallas. I say—how do you feel about sailing on Wednesday? *Mauretania*: Yes, next Wednesday as ever is. Our client wants me to look at some Italian gardens before we settle anything, and has asked me to nip over on the next boat. I've got to be back on the first of June—" the voice broke into a joyful conscious laugh—"so we must look alive. I say, Dad, I want your help: do come."

Dallas seemed to be speaking in the room: the voice was as nearby and natural as if he had been lounging in his favorite armchair by the fire. The fact would not ordinarily have surprised Archer, for long-distance telephoning had become as much a matter of course as electric lighting and five-day Atlantic voyages. But the laugh did startle him; it still seemed wonderful that across all those miles and miles of country—forest, river, mountain, prairie, roaring cities, and busy indifferent millions—Dallas's laugh should be able to say: "Of course, whatever happens, I must get back on the first, because Fanny Beaufort and I are to be married on the fifth."

The voice began again: "Think it over? No, sir: not a minute. You've got to say yes now. Why not, I'd like to know? If you can allege a single reason—No, I knew it. Then it's a go, eh? Because I count on you to ring up the Cunard office first thing tomorrow, and you'd better book a return on a boat from Marseilles. I say, Dad; it'll be our last time together, in this kind of way—. Oh, good! I knew you would."

Chicago rang off, and Archer rose and began to pace up and down the room.

It would be their last time together in this kind of way: the boy was right. They would have lots of other "times" after Dallas's marriage, his father was sure; for the two were born comrades, and Fanny Beaufort, whatever one might think of her, did not seem likely to interfere with their intimacy. On the contrary, from what he had seen of her, he thought she would be naturally included in it. Still, change was change, and differences were differences, and much as he felt himself drawn toward his future daughter-in-law, it was tempting to seize this last chance of being alone with his boy.

There was no reason why he should not seize it, except the profound one that he had lost the habit of travel. May had disliked to move except for valid reasons, such as taking the children to the sea or in the mountains: she could imagine no other motive for leaving the house in Thirty-ninth Street or their comfortable quarters at the Wellands' in Newport. After Dallas had taken his degree she had thought it her duty to travel for six months; and the whole family had made the old-fashioned tour through England, Switzerland, and Italy. Their time being limited (no one knew why) they had omitted France. Archer remembered Dallas's wrath at being asked to contemplate Mont Blanc instead of Rheims and Chartres. But Mary and Bill wanted mountain climbing, and had already yawned their way in Dallas's wake through the English cathedrals; and May, always fair to her children, had insisted on holding the balance evenly between their athletic and artistic proclivities. She had indeed proposed that her husband should go to Paris for a fortnight, and join them on the Italian lakes after they had "done" Switzerland, but Archer had declined. "We'll stick together," he said, and May's face had brightened at his setting such a good example to Dallas.

Since her death, nearly two years before, there had been no reason for his continuing in the same routine. His children had urged him to travel: Mary Chivers had felt sure it would do him good to go abroad and "see the galleries." The very mysteriousness of such a cure made her the more confident of its efficacy. But Archer had found himself held fast by habit, by memories, by a sudden startled shrinking from new things.

Now, as he reviewed his past, he saw into what a deep rut he had sunk. The worst of doing one's duty was that it apparently unfitted one for doing anything else. At least that was the view that the men of his generation had taken. The trenchant divisions between right and wrong, honest and dishonest, respectable and the reverse, had left so little scope for the unforeseen. There are moments when a man's imagination, so easily subdued to what it lives in, suddenly rises above its daily level, and surveys the long windings of destiny. Archer hung there and wondered. . . .

What was left of the little world he had grown up in, and whose standards had bent and bound him? He remembered a sneering prophecy of poor Lawrence Lefferts's, uttered years ago in that very room: "If things go on at this rate, our children will be marrying Beaufort's bastards."

It was just what Archer's eldest son, the pride of his life, was doing; and nobody wondered or reproved. Even the boy's Aunt Janey, who still looked so exactly as she used to in her elderly youth, had taken her mother's emeralds and seed pearls out of their pink cotton wool, and carried them with her own twitching hands to the future bride; and Fanny Beaufort, instead of looking disappointed at not receiving a "set" from a Paris jeweler, had exclaimed at their old-fashioned beauty, and declared that when she wore them she should feel like an Isabey miniature.

Fanny Beaufort, who had appeared in New York at eighteen, after the death of her parents, had won its heart much as Madame Olenska had won it thirty years earlier; only instead of being distrustful and afraid of her, society took her joyfully for granted. She was pretty, amusing, and accomplished: what more did anyone want? Nobody was narrow-minded enough to rake up against her the half-forgotten facts of her father's past and her own origin. Only the older people remembered so obscure an incident in the business life of New York as Beaufort's failure, or the fact that after his wife's death he had been quietly married to the notorious Fanny Ring, and had left the country with his new wife, and a little girl who inherited her beauty. He was subsequently heard of in Constantinople, then in Russia; and a dozen years later American travelers were handsomely entertained by him in Buenos Ayres, where he represented a large insurance agency. He and his wife died there in the odor of prosperity; and one day their orphaned daughter had appeared in New York in charge of May Archer's sister-in-law, Mrs. Jack Welland, whose husband had been appointed the girl's guardian. The fact threw her into almost cousinly relationship with Newland Archer's children, and nobody was surprised when Dallas's engagement was announced.

Nothing could more clearly give the measure of the distance that the world had traveled. People nowadays were too busy— busy with reforms and "movements," with fads and fetishes and frivolities—to bother much about their neighbors. And of what account was anybody's past, in the huge kaleidoscope where all the social atoms spun around on the same plane?

Newland Archer, looking out of his hotel window at the stately gaiety of the Paris streets, felt his heart beating with the confusion and eagerness of youth.

It was long since it had thus plunged and reared under his widening waistcoat, leaving him, the next minute, with an empty breast and hot temples. He wondered if it was thus that his son's conducted itself in the presence of Miss Fanny Beaufort—and decided that it was not. "It functions as actively, no doubt, but the rhythm is different," he reflected, recalling the cool composure with which the young man had announced his engagement, and taken for granted that his family would approve.

"The difference is that these young people take it for granted that they're going to get whatever they want, and that we almost always took it for granted that we shouldn't. Only, I wonder—the thing one's so certain of in advance: can it ever make one's heart beat as wildly?"

It was the day after their arrival in Paris, and the spring sun- shine held Archer in his open window, above the wide silvery prospect of the Place Vendôme. One of the things he had stipu- lated—almost the only one—when he had agreed to come abroad with Dallas, was that, in Paris, he shouldn't be made to go to one of the newfangled "places."

"Oh, all right—of course," Dallas good-naturedly agreed. "I'll take you to some jolly old-fashioned place—the Bristol say—" leaving his father speechless at hearing that the century-long home of kings and emperors was now spoken of as an old-fash- ioned inn, where one went for its quaint inconveniences and lin- gering local color.

Archer had pictured often enough, in the first impatient years, the scene of his return to Paris; then the personal vision had

faded, and he had simply tried to see the city as the setting of
Madame Olenska's life. Sitting alone at night in his library, after
the household had gone to bed, he had evoked the radiant outbreak of spring down the avenues of horse chestnuts, the flowers
and statues in the public gardens, the whiff of lilacs from the
flower carts, the majestic roll of the river under the great bridges,
and the life of art and study and pleasure that filled each mighty
artery to bursting. Now the spectacle was before him in its glory,
and as he looked out on it he felt shy, old-fashioned, inadequate:
a mere gray speck of a man compared with the ruthless magnificent fellow he had dreamed of being. . . .

Dallas's hand came down cheerily on his shoulder. "Hullo, Father: this is something like, isn't it?" They stood for a while looking out in silence, and then the young man continued: "By the
way, I've got a message for you: the Countess Olenska expects us
both at half-past five."

He said it lightly, carelessly, as he might have imparted any
casual item of information, such as the hour at which their train
was to leave for Florence the next evening. Archer looked at him,
and thought he saw in his gay young eyes a gleam of his great-
grandmother Mingott's malice.

"Oh, didn't I tell you?" Dallas pursued. "Fanny made me
swear to do three things while I was in Paris: get her the score of
the last Debussy songs, go to the Grand-Guignol, and see Madame Olenska. You know she was awfully good to Fanny when
Mr. Beaufort sent her over from Buenos Ayres to the Assomption.
Fanny hadn't any friends in Paris, and Madame Olenska used to
be kind to her and trot her about on holidays. I believe she was a
great friend of the first Mrs. Beaufort's. And she's our cousin, of
course. So I rang her up this morning, before I went out, and told
her you and I were here for two days and wanted to see her."

Archer continued to stare at him. "You told her I was here?"

"Of course—why not?" Dallas's eye brows went up whimsically.
Then, getting no answer, he slipped his arm through his father's
with a confidential pressure.

"I say, Father: what was she like?"

Archer felt his color rise under his son's unabashed gaze.
"Come, own up: you and she were great pals, weren't you? Wasn't
she most awfully lovely?"

"Lovely? I don't know. She was different."

"Ah—there you have it! That's what it always comes to, doesn't it? When she comes, *she's different*—and one doesn't know why. It's exactly what I feel about Fanny."

His father drew back a step, releasing his arm. "About Fanny? But, my dear fellow—I should hope so! Only I don't see—"

"Dash it, Dad, don't be prehistoric! Wasn't she—once—your Fanny?"

Dallas belonged body and soul to the new generation. He was the firstborn of Newland and May Archer, yet it had never been possible to inculcate in him even the rudiments of reserve. "What's the use of making mysteries? It only makes people want to nose 'em out," he always objected when enjoined to discretion. But Archer, meeting his eyes, saw the filial light under their banter.

"My Fanny—?"

"Well, the woman you'd have chucked everything for: only you didn't," continued his surprising son.

"I didn't," echoed Archer with a kind of solemnity.

"No: you date, you see, dear old boy. But Mother said—"

"Your mother?"

"Yes, the day before she died. It was when she sent for me alone—you remember? She said she knew we were safe with you, and always would be, because once, when she asked you to, you'd given up the thing you most wanted."

Archer received this strange communication in silence. His eyes remained unseeingly fixed on the thronged sunlit square below the window. At length he said in a low voice: "She never asked me."

"No. I forgot. You never did ask each other anything, did you? And you never told each other anything. You just sat and watched each other, and guessed at what was going on underneath. A deaf-and-dumb asylum, in fact! Well, I back your generation for knowing more about each other's private thoughts than we ever have time to find out about our own. I say, Dad," Dallas broke off, "you're not angry with me? If you are, let's make it up and go and lunch at Henri's. I've got to rush out to Versailles afterward."

\*   \*   \*

Archer did not accompany his son to Versailles. He preferred to spend the afternoon in solitary roamings through Paris. He had to deal all at once with the packed regrets and stifled memories of an inarticulate lifetime.

After a little while he did not regret Dallas's indiscretion. It seemed to take an iron band from his heart to know that, after all, someone had guessed and pitied. . . . And that it should have been his wife moved him indescribably. Dallas, for all his affectionate insight, would not have understood that. To the boy, no doubt, the episode was only a pathetic instance of vain frustration, of wasted forces. But was it really no more? For a long time Archer sat on a bench in the Champs Elysées and wondered, while the stream of life rolled by. . . .

A few streets away, a few hours away, Ellen Olenska waited. She had never gone back to her husband, and when he had died, some years before, she had made no change in her way of living. There was nothing now to keep her and Archer apart—and that afternoon he was to see her.

He got up and walked across the Place de la Concorde and the Tuileries gardens to the Louvre. She had once told him that she often went there, and he had a fancy to spend the intervening time in a place where he could think of her as perhaps having lately been. For an hour or more he wandered from gallery to gallery through the dazzle of afternoon light, and one by one the pictures burst on him in their half-forgotten splendor, filling his soul with the long echoes of beauty. After all, his life had been too starved. . . .

Suddenly, before an effulgent Titian, he found himself saying: "But I'm only fifty-seven—" and then he turned away. For such summer dreams it was too late, but surely not for a quiet harvest of friendship, of comradeship, in the blessed hush of her nearness.

He went back to the hotel, where he and Dallas were to meet; and together they walked again across the Place de la Concorde and over the bridge that leads to the Chamber of Deputies.

Dallas, unconscious of what was going on in his father's mind, was talking excitedly and abundantly of Versailles. He had had but one previous glimpse of it, during a holiday trip in which he had tried to pack all the sights he had been deprived of when he had had to go with the family to Switzerland; and tumultuous enthusiasm and cocksure criticism tripped each other up on his lips.

As Archer listened, his sense of inadequacy and inexpressiveness increased. The boy was not insensitive, he knew, but he had the facility and self-confidence that came of looking at fate not as a master but as an equal. "That's it: they feel equal to things— they know their way about," he mused, thinking of his son as the spokesman of the new generation which had swept away all the old landmarks, and with them the signposts and the danger signal.

Suddenly Dallas stopped short, grasping his father's arm. "Oh, by Jove," he exclaimed.

They had come out into the great tree-planted space before the Invalides. The dome of Mansart floated ethereally above the budding trees and the long gray front of the building: drawing up into itself all the rays of afternoon light, it hung there like the visible symbol of the race's glory.

Archer knew that Madame Olenska lived in a square near one of the avenues radiating from the Invalides; and he had pictured the quarter as quiet and almost obscure, forgetting the central splendor that lit it up. Now, by some queer process of association, that golden light became for him the pervading illumination in which she lived. For nearly thirty years, her life—of which he knew so strangely little—had been spent in this rich atmosphere that he already felt to be too dense and yet too stimulating for his lungs. He thought of the theaters she must have been to, the pictures she must have looked at, the sober and splendid old houses she must have frequented, the people she must have talked with, the incessant stir of ideas, curiosities, images, and associations thrown out by an intensely social race in a setting of immemorial manners; and suddenly he remembered the young Frenchman who had once said to him: "Ah, good conversation— there is nothing like it, is there?"

Archer had not seen M. Rivière, or heard of him, for nearly thirty years; and that fact gave the measure of his ignorance of Madame Olenska's existence. More than half a lifetime divided them, and she had spent the long interval among people he did not know, in a society he but faintly guessed at, in conditions he would never wholly understand. During that time he had been living with his youthful memory of her; but she had doubtless had other and more tangible companionship. Perhaps she too had kept her memory of him as something apart; but if she had, it must have been like a relic in a small dim chapel, where there was not time to pray every day. . . .

They had crossed the Place des Invalides, and were walking down one of the thoroughfares flanking the building. It was a quiet quarter, after all, in spite of its splendor and its history; and the fact gave one an idea of the riches Paris had to draw on, since such scenes as this were left to the few and the indifferent.

The day was fading into a soft sun-shot haze, pricked here and there by a yellow electric light, and passers were rare in the little square into which they had turned. Dallas stopped again, and looked up.

"It must be here," he said, slipping his arm through his father's with a movement from which Archer's shyness did not shrink; and they stood together looking up at the house.

It was a modern building, without distinctive character, but many windowed, and pleasantly balconied up its wide cream-colored front. On one of the upper balconies, which hung well above the rounded tops of the horse chestnuts in the square, the awnings were still lowered, as though the sun had just left it.

"I wonder which floor—?" Dallas conjectured, and moving toward the *porte-cochère* he put his head into the porter's lodge, and came back to say: "The fifth. It must be the one with the awnings."

Archer remained motionless, gazing at the upper windows as if the end of their pilgrimage had been attained.

"I say, you know, it's nearly six," his son at length reminded him.

The father glanced away at an empty bench under the trees.

"I believe I'll sit there a moment," he said.

"Why—aren't you well?" his son exclaimed.

"Oh, perfectly. But I should like you, please, to go up without me."

Dallas paused before him, visibly bewildered. "But, I say, Dad: do you mean you won't come up at all?"

"I don't know," said Archer slowly.

"If you don't she won't understand."

"Go, my boy; perhaps I shall follow you."

Dallas gave him a long look through the twilight.

"But what on earth shall I say?"

"My dear fellow, don't you always know what to say?" his father rejoined with a smile.

"Very well. I shall say you're old-fashioned, and prefer walking up the five flights because you don't like lifts."

His father smiled again. "Say I'm old-fashioned: that's enough."

Dallas looked at him again, and then, with an incredulous gesture, passed out of sight under the vaulted doorway.

Archer sat down on the bench and continued to gaze at the awninged balcony. He calculated the time it would take his son to be carried up in the lift to the fifth floor, to ring the bell, and be admitted to the hall, and then ushered into the drawing room. He pictured Dallas entering that room with his quick assured step and his delightful smile, and wondered if the people were right who said that his boy "took after him."

Then he tried to see the persons already in the room—for probably at that sociable hour there would be more than one— and among them a dark lady, pale and dark, who would look up quickly, half rise, and hold out a long thin hand with three rings on it. . . . He thought she would be sitting in a sofa corner near the fire, with azaleas banked behind her on a table.

"It's more real to me here than if I went up," he suddenly heard himself say; and the fear lest that last shadow of reality should lose its edge kept him rooted to his seat as the minutes succeeded each other.

He sat for a long time on the bench in the thickening dusk, his eyes never turning from the balcony. At length a light shone through the windows, and a moment later a manservant came out on the balcony, drew up the awnings, and closed the shutters.

At that, as if it had been the signal he waited for, Newland Archer got up slowly and walked back alone to his hotel.

# SUMMER

# ——— 1 ———

A GIRL came out of lawyer Royall's house, at the end of the one street of North Dormer, and stood on the doorstep.

It was the beginning of a June afternoon. The springlike transparent sky shed a rain of silver sunshine on the roofs of the village, and on the pastures and larchwoods surrounding it. A little wind moved among the round white clouds on the shoulders of the hills, driving their shadows across the fields and down the grassy road that takes the name of street when it passes through North Dormer. The place lies high and in the open, and lacks the lavish shade of the more protected New England villages. The clump of weeping willows about the duck pond, and the Norway spruces in front of the Hatchard gate, cast almost the only roadside shadow between lawyer Royall's house and the point where, at the other end of the village, the road rises above the church and skirts the black hemlock wall enclosing the cemetery.

The little June wind, frisking down the street, shook the doleful fringes of the Hatchard spruces, caught the straw hat of a young man just passing under them, and spun it clean across the road into the duck pond.

As he ran to fish it out the girl on lawyer Royall's doorstep noticed that he was a stranger, that he wore city clothes, and that he was laughing with all his teeth, as the young and careless laugh at such mishaps.

Her heart contracted a little, and the shrinking that sometimes came over her when she saw people with holiday faces made her draw back into the house and pretend to look for the key that she knew she had already put into her pocket. A narrow greenish mirror with a gilt eagle over it hung on the passage wall, and she looked critically at her reflection, wished for the thousandth time that she had blue eyes like Annabel Balch, the girl who sometimes came from Springfield to spend a week with old Miss Hatchard, straightened the sunburned hat over her small swarthy face, and turned out again into the sunshine.

"How I hate everything!" she murmured.

The young man had passed through the Hatchard gate, and she had the street to herself. North Dormer is at all times an empty place, and at three o'clock on a June afternoon its few able-bodied men are off in the fields or woods, and the women in-doors, engaged in languid household drudgery.

The girl walked along, swinging her key on a finger, and look-ing about her with the heightened attention produced by the presence of a stranger in a familiar place: What, she wondered, did North Dormer look like to people from other parts of the world? She herself had lived there since the age of five, and had long supposed it to be a place of some importance. But about a year before, Mr. Miles, the new Episcopal clergyman at Hepburn, who drove over every other Sunday—when the roads were not plowed up by hauling—to hold a service in the North Dormer church, had proposed, in a fit of missionary zeal, to take the young people down to Nettleton to hear an illustrated lecture on the Holy Land; and the dozen girls and boys who represented the future of North Dormer had been piled into a farm wagon, driven over the hills to Hepburn, put into a way train and carried to Nettleton. In the course of that incredible day Charity Royall had, for the first and only time, experienced railway travel, looked into shops with plate-glass fronts, tasted coconut pie, sat in a theater, and listened to a gentleman saying unintelligible things before pictures that she would have enjoyed looking at if his ex-planations had not prevented her from understanding them. This initiation had shown her that North Dormer was a small place, and developed in her a thirst for information that her posi-tion as custodian of the village library had previously failed to excite. For a month or two she dipped feverishly and disconnect-edly into the dusty volumes of the Hatchard Memorial Library; then the impression of Nettleton began to fade, and she found it easier to take North Dormer as the norm of the universe than to go on reading.

The sight of the stranger once more revived memories of Net-tleton, and North Dormer shrank to its real size. As she looked up and down it, from lawyer Royall's faded red house at one end to the white church at the other, she pitilessly took its measure. There it lay, a weather-beaten sunburned village of the hills, abandoned of men, left apart by railway, trolley, telegraph, and all the forces that link life to life in modern communities. It had no shops, no theaters, no lectures, no "business block"; only a church that was opened every other Sunday if the state of the roads permitted, and a library for which no new books had been bought for twenty years, and where the old ones moldered undisturbed on the damp shelves. Yet Charity Royall had always been told that she ought to consider it a privilege that her lot had been cast in North Dormer. She knew that, compared to the place she had come from, North Dormer represented all the blessings of the most refined civilization. Everyone in the village had told her so ever since she had been brought there as a child. Even old Miss Hatchard had said to her, on a terrible occasion in her life: "My child, you must never cease to remember that it was Mr. Royall who brought you down from the Mountain."

She had been "brought down from the Mountain"; from the scarred cliff that lifted its sullen wall above the lesser slopes of Eagle Range, making a perpetual background of gloom to the lonely valley. The Mountain was a good fifteen miles away, but it rose so abruptly from the lower hills that it seemed almost to cast its shadow over North Dormer. And it was like a great magnet drawing the clouds and scattering them in storm across the valley. If ever, in the purest summer sky, there trailed a thread of vapor over North Dormer, it drifted to the Mountain as a ship drifts to a whirlpool, and was caught among the rocks, torn up and multiplied, to sweep back over the village in rain and darkness.

Charity was not very clear about the Mountain; but she knew it was a bad place, and a shame to have come from, and that, whatever befell her in North Dormer, she ought, as Miss Hatchard had once reminded her, to remember that she had been brought down from there, and hold her tongue and be thankful. She looked up at the Mountain, thinking of these things, and tried as usual to be thankful. But the sight of the young man turning in at Miss Hatchard's gate had brought back the vision of the glittering streets of Nettleton, and she felt ashamed of her old sunhat, and sick of North Dormer, and jealously aware of Annabel Balch of

Springfield, opening her blue eyes somewhere far off on glories greater than the glories of Nettleton.

"How I hate everything!" she said again.

Halfway down the street she stopped at a weak-hinged gate. Passing through it, she walked down a brick path to a queer little brick temple with white wooden columns supporting a pediment on which was inscribed in tarnished gold letters: "The Honorius Hatchard Memorial Library, 1832."

Honorius Hatchard had been old Miss Hatchard's great-uncle; though she would undoubtedly have reversed the phrase, and put forward, as her only claim to distinction, the fact that she was his great-niece. For Honorius Hatchard, in the early years of the nineteenth century, had enjoyed a modest celebrity. As the marble tablet in the interior of the library informed its infrequent visitors, he had possessed marked literary gifts, written a series of papers called "The Recluse of Eagle Range," enjoyed the acquaintance of Washington Irving and Fitz-Greene Halleck, and been cut off in his flower by a fever contracted in Italy. Such had been the sole link between North Dormer and literature, a link piously commemorated by the erection of the monument where Charity Royall, every Tuesday and Thursday afternoon, sat at her desk under a freckled steel engraving of the deceased author, and wondered if he felt any deader in his grave than she did in his library.

Entering her prison house with a listless step she took off her hat, hung it on a plaster bust of Minerva, opened the shutters, leaned out to see if there were any eggs in the swallow's nest above one of the windows, and finally, seating herself behind the desk, drew out a roll of cotton lace and a steel crochet hook. She was not an expert workwoman, and it had taken her many weeks to make the half-yard of narrow lace which she kept wound about the buckram back of a disintegrated copy of *The Lamplighter*. But there was no other way of getting any lace to trim her summer blouse, and since Ally Hawes, the poorest girl in the village, had shown herself in church with enviable transparencies about the shoulders, Charity's hook had traveled faster. She unrolled the lace, dug the hook into a loop, and bent to the task with furrowed brows.

Suddenly the door opened, and before she had raised her eyes she knew that the young man she had seen going in at the Hatchard gate had entered the library.

Without taking any notice of her he began to move slowly about the long vaultlike room, his hands behind his back, his shortsighted eyes peering up and down the rows of rusty bindings. At length he reached the desk and stood before her.

"Have you a card catalogue?" he asked in a pleasant abrupt voice, and the oddness of the question caused her to drop her work.

"A *what?*"

"Why, you know—" He broke off, and she became conscious that he was looking at her for the first time, having apparently, on his entrance, included her in his general shortsighted survey as part of the furniture of the library.

The fact that, in discovering her, he lost the thread of his remark, did not escape her attention, and she looked down and smiled. He smiled also.

"No, I don't suppose you *do* know," he corrected himself. "In fact, it would be almost a pity—"

She thought she detected a slight condescension in his tone, and asked sharply: "Why?"

"Because it's so much pleasanter, in a small library like this, to poke about by one's self—with the help of the librarian."

He added the last phrase so respectfully that she was mollified, and rejoined with a sigh: "I'm afraid I can't help you much."

"Why?" he questioned in his turn, and she replied that there weren't many books anyhow, and that she'd hardly read any of them. "The worms are getting at them," she added gloomily.

"Are they? That's a pity, for I see there are some good ones." He seemed to have lost interest in their conversation, and strolled away again, apparently forgetting her. His indifference nettled her, and she picked up her work, resolved not to offer him the least assistance. Apparently he did not need it, for he spent a long time with his back to her, lifting down, one after another, the tall cobwebby volumes from a distant shelf.

"Oh, I say!" he exclaimed, and looking up she saw that he had drawn out his handkerchief and was carefully wiping the edges of the book in his hand. The action struck her as an unwarranted criticism on her care of the books, and she said irritably: "It's not my fault if they're dirty."

He turned around and looked at her with reviving interest. "Ah—then you're not the librarian?"

"Of course I am, but I can't dust all these books. Besides, nobody ever looks at them, now Miss Hatchard's too lame to come round."

"No, I suppose not." He laid down the book he had been wiping, and stood considering her in silence. She wondered if Miss Hatchard had sent him round to pry into the way the library was looked after, and the suspicion increased her resentment. "I saw you going into her house just now, didn't I?" she asked, with the New England avoidance of the proper name. She was determined to find out why he was poking about among her books.

"Miss Hatchard's house? Yes—she's my cousin and I'm staying there," the young man answered; adding, as if to disarm a visible distrust: "My name is Harney—Lucius Harney. She may have spoken of me."

"No, she hasn't," said Charity, wishing she could have said: "Yes, she has."

"Oh, well—" said Miss Hatchard's cousin with a laugh and after another pause, during which it occurred to Charity that her answer had not been encouraging, he remarked: "You don't seem strong on architecture."

Her bewilderment was complete: the more she wished to appear to understand him the more unintelligible his remarks became. He reminded her of the gentleman who had "explained" the pictures at Nettleton, and the weight of her ignorance settled down on her again like a pall.

"I mean, I can't see that you have any books on the old houses about here. I suppose, for that matter, this part of the country hasn't been much explored. They all go on doing Plymouth and Salem. So stupid. My cousin's house, now, is remarkable. This place must have had a past—it must have been more of a place once." He stopped short, with the blush of a shy man who overhears himself, and fears he has been voluble. "I'm an architect, you see, and I'm hunting up old houses in these parts."

She stared. "Old houses? Everything's old in North Dormer, isn't it? The folks are, anyhow."

He laughed, and wandered away again.

"Haven't you any kind of a history of the place? I think there was one written about 1840: a book or pamphlet about its first settlement," he presently said from the farther end of the room.

She pressed her crochet hook against her lip and pondered. There was such a work, she knew: "North Dormer and the Early Townships of Eagle County." She had a special grudge against it because it was a limp weakly book that was always either falling off the shelf or slipping back and disappearing if one squeezed it in between sustaining volumes. She remembered, the last time she had picked it up, wondering how anyone could have taken the trouble to write a book about North Dormer and its neighbors: Dormer, Hamblin, Creston and Creston River. She knew them all, mere lost clusters of houses in the folds of the desolate ridges: Dormer, where North Dormer went for its apples; Creston River, where there used to be a papermill, and its gray walls stood decaying by the stream; and Hamblin, where the first snow always fell. Such were their titles to fame.

She got up and began to move about vaguely before the shelves. But she had no idea where she had last put the book, and something told her that it was going to play her its usual trick and remain invisible. It was not one of her lucky days.

"I guess it's somewhere," she said, to prove her zeal, but she spoke without conviction, and felt that her words conveyed none.

"Oh, well—" he said again. She knew he was going, and wished more than ever to find the book.

"It will be for next time," he added; and picking up the volume he had laid on the desk he handed it to her. "By the way, a little air and sun would do this good; it's rather valuable."

He gave her a nod and smile, and passed out.

# —— 2 ——

❧ THE HOURS of the Hatchard Memorial librarian were from three to five; and Charity Royall's sense of duty usually kept her at her desk until nearly half-past four.

But she had never perceived that any practical advantage thereby accrued either to North Dormer or to herself; and she had no scruple in decreeing, when it suited her, that the library should close an hour earlier. A few minutes after Mr. Harney's departure she formed this decision, put away her lace, fastened the shutters, and turned the key in the door of the temple of knowledge.

The street upon which she emerged was still empty: and after glancing up and down it she began to walk toward her house. But instead of entering she passed on, turned into a field path and mounted to a pasture on the hillside. She let down the bars of the gate, followed a trail along the crumbling wall of the pasture, and walked on till she reached a knoll where a clump of larches shook out their fresh tassels to the wind. There she lay down on the slope, tossed off her hat and hid her face in the grass.

She was blind and insensible to many things, and dimly knew it; but to all that was light and air, perfume and color, every drop of blood in her responded. She loved the roughness of the dry mountain grass under her palms, the smell of the thyme into which she crushed her face, the fingering of the wind in her hair and through her cotton blouse, and the creak of the larches as they swayed to it.

She often climbed up the hill and lay there alone for the mere pleasure of feeling the wind and of rubbing her cheeks in the grass. Generally at such times she did not think of anything, but lay immersed in an inarticulate well-being. Today the sense of well-being was intensified by her joy at escaping from the library. She liked well enough to have a friend drop in and talk to her when she was on duty, but she hated to be bothered about books.

How could she remember where they were, when they were so seldom asked for? Orma Fry occasionally took out a novel, and her brother Ben was fond of what he called "jography," and of books relating to trade and bookkeeping; but no one else asked for anything except, at intervals, *Uncle Tom's Cabin,* or *Opening a Chestnut Burr,* or Longfellow. She had these under her hand, and could have found them in the dark; but unexpected demands came so rarely that they exasperated her like an injustice. . . .

She had liked the young man's looks, and his shortsighted eyes, and his odd way of speaking, that was abrupt yet soft, just as his hands were sunburned and sinewy, yet with smooth nails like a woman's. His hair was sunburned-looking too, or rather the color of bracken after frost; his eyes gray, with the appealing look of the shortsighted, his smile shy yet confident, as if he knew lots of things she had never dreamed of, and yet wouldn't for the world have had her feel his superiority. But she did feel it, and liked the feeling; for it was new to her. Poor and ignorant as she was, and knew herself to be—humblest of the humble even in North Dormer, where to come from the Mountain was the worst disgrace—yet in her narrow world she had always ruled. It was partly, of course, owing to the fact that lawyer Royall was "the biggest man in North Dormer"; so much too big for it, in fact, that outsiders, who didn't know, always wondered how it held him. In spite of everything—and in spite even of Miss Hatchard—lawyer Royall ruled in North Dormer; and Charity ruled in lawyer Royall's house. She had never put it to herself in those terms; but she knew her power, knew what it was made of, and hated it. Confusedly, the young man in the library had made her feel for the first time what might be the sweetness of dependence.

She sat up, brushed the bits of grass from her hair, and looked down on the house where she held sway. It stood just below her, cheerless and untended, its faded red front divided from the road by a "yard" with a path bordered by gooseberry bushes, a stone well overgrown with traveler's joy, and a sickly Crimson Rambler tied to a fan-shaped support, which Mr. Royall had once brought up from Hepburn to please her. Behind the house a bit of uneven ground with clotheslines strung across it stretched up to a dry wall, and beyond the wall a patch of corn and a few rows of potatoes strayed vaguely into the adjoining wilderness of rock and fern.

Charity could not recall her first sight of the house. She had been told that she was ill of a fever when she was brought down from the Mountain; and she could only remember waking one day in a cot at the foot of Mrs. Royall's bed, and opening her eyes on the cold neatness of the room that was afterward to be hers.

Mrs. Royall died seven or eight years later, and by that time Charity had taken the measure of most things about her. She knew that Mrs. Royall was sad and timid and weak; she knew that lawyer Royall was harsh and violent, and still weaker. She knew that she had been christened Charity (in the white church at the other end of the village) to commemorate Mr. Royall's disinterestedness in "bringing her down," and to keep alive in her a becoming sense of her dependence; she knew that Mr. Royall was her guardian, but that he had not legally adopted her, though everybody spoke of her as Charity Royall; and she knew why he had come back to live at North Dormer, instead of practicing at Nettleton, where he had begun his legal career.

After Mrs. Royall's death there was some talk of sending her to a boarding school. Miss Hatchard suggested it, and had a long conference with Mr. Royall, who, in pursuance of her plan, departed one day for Starkfield to visit the institution she recommended. He came back the next night with a black face; worse, Charity observed, than she had ever seen him; and by that time she had had some experience.

When she asked him how soon she was to start he answered shortly, "You ain't going," and shut himself up in the room he called his office; and the next day the lady who kept the school at Starkfield wrote that "under the circumstances" she was afraid she could not make room just then for another pupil.

Charity was disappointed; but she understood. It wasn't the temptations of Starkfield that had been Mr. Royall's undoing; it was the thought of losing her. He was a dreadfully "lonesome" man; she had made that out because she was so "lonesome" herself. He and she, face to face in that sad house, had sounded the depths of isolation; and though she felt no particular affection for him, and not the slightest gratitude, she pitied him because she was conscious that he was superior to the people about him, and that she was the only being between him and solitude. Therefore, when Miss Hatchard sent for her a day or two later, to talk of a school at Nettleton, and to say that this time a friend of hers would "make the necessary arrangements," Charity cut her short with the announcement that she had decided not to leave North Dormer.

Miss Hatchard reasoned with her kindly, but to no purpose; she simply repeated: "I guess Mr. Royall's too lonesome."

Miss Hatchard blinked perplexedly behind her eyeglasses. Her long frail face was full of puzzled wrinkles, and she leaned forward, resting her hands on the arms of her mahogany armchair, with the evident desire to say something that ought to be said.

"The feeling does you credit, my dear."

She looked about the pale walls of her sitting room, seeking counsel of ancestral daguerreotypes and didactic samplers; but they seemed to make utterance more difficult.

"The fact is, it's not only—not only because of the advantages. There are other reasons. You're too young to understand—"

"Oh, no, I ain't," said Charity harshly, and Miss Hatchard blushed to the roots of her blond cap. But she must have felt a vague relief at having her explanation cut short, for she concluded, again invoking the daguerreotypes: "Of course I shall always do what I can for you; and in case . . . in case . . . you know you can always come to me. . . ."

Lawyer Royall was waiting for Charity in the porch when she returned from this visit. He had shaved, and brushed his black coat, and looked a magnificent monument of a man; at such moments she really admired him.

"Well," he said, "is it settled?"

"Yes, it's settled. I ain't going."

"Not to the Nettleton school?"

"Not anywhere."

He cleared his throat and asked sternly: "Why?"

"I'd rather not," she said, swinging past him on her way to her room. It was the following week that he brought her up the Crimson Rambler and its fan from Hepburn. He had never given her anything before.

The next outstanding incident of her life had happened two years later, when she was seventeen. Lawyer Royall, who hated to go to Nettleton, had been called there in connection with a case. He still exercised his profession, though litigation languished in North Dormer and its outlying hamlets; and for once he had had an opportunity that he could not afford to refuse. He spent three days in Nettleton, won his case, and came back in high good humor. It was a rare mood with him, and manifested itself on this occasion by his talking impressively at the supper table of the "rousing welcome" his old friends had given him. He wound up confidentially: "I was a damn fool ever to leave Nettleton. It was Mrs. Royall that made me do it."

Charity immediately perceived that something bitter had happened to him, and that he was trying to talk down the recollection. She went up to bed early, leaving him seated in moody thought, his elbows propped on the worn oilcloth of the supper table. On the way up she had extracted from his overcoat pocket the key of the cupboard where the bottle of whiskey was kept.

She was awakened by a rattling at her door and jumped out of bed. She heard Mr. Royall's voice, low and peremptory, and opened the door, fearing an accident. No other thought had occurred to her; but when she saw him in the doorway, a ray from the autumn moon falling on his discomposed face, she understood.

For a moment they looked at each other in silence; then, as he put his foot across the threshold, she stretched out her arm and stopped him.

"You go right back from here," she said, in a shrill voice that startled her; "you ain't going to have that key tonight."

"Charity, let me in. I don't want the key. I'm a lonesome man," he began, in the deep voice that sometimes moved her.

Her heart gave a startled plunge, but she continued to hold him back contemptuously. "Well, I guess you made a mistake, then. This ain't your wife's room any longer."

She was not frightened, she simply felt a deep disgust; and perhaps he divined it or read it in her face, for after staring at her a moment he drew back and turned slowly away from the door. With her ear to her keyhole she heard him feel his way down the dark stairs, and toward the kitchen; and she listened for the crash of the cupboard panel. But instead she heard him, after an interval, unlock the door of the house, and his heavy steps came to her through the silence as he walked down the path. She crept to the window and saw his bent figure striding up the road in the moonlight. Then a belated sense of fear came to her with the consciousness of victory, and she slipped into bed, cold to the bone.

A day or two later poor Eudora Skeff, who for twenty years had been the custodian of the Hatchard library, died suddenly of pneumonia; and the day after the funeral Charity went to see Miss Hatchard, and asked to be appointed librarian. The request seemed to surprise Miss Hatchard: she evidently questioned the new candidate's qualifications.

"Why, I don't know, my dear. Aren't you rather too young?" she hesitated.

"I want to earn some money," Charity merely answered.

"Doesn't Mr. Royall give you all you require? No one is rich in North Dormer."

"I want to earn money enough to get away."

"To get away?" Miss Hatchard's puzzled wrinkles deepened, and there was a distressful pause. "You want to leave Mr. Royall?"

"Yes, or I want another woman in the house with me," said Charity resolutely.

Miss Hatchard clasped her nervous hands about the arms of her chair. Her eyes invoked the faded countenances on the wall, and after a faint cough of indecision she brought out: "The . . . the housework's too hard for you, I suppose?"

Charity's heart grew cold. She understood that Miss Hatchard had no help to give her and that she would have to fight her way out of her difficulty alone. A deeper sense of isolation overcame her; she felt incalculably old. "She's got to be talked to like a baby," she thought, with a feeling of compassion for Miss Hatchard's long immaturity. "Yes, that's it," she said aloud. "The housework's too hard for me: I've been coughing a good deal this fall."

She noted the immediate effect of this suggestion. Miss Hatchard paled at the memory of poor Eudora's taking-off, and promised to do what she could. But of course there were people she must consult: the clergyman, the selectmen of North Dormer, and a distant Hatchard relative at Springfield. "If you'd only gone to school!" she sighed. She followed Charity to the door, and there, in the security of the threshold, said with a glance of evasive appeal: "I know Mr. Royall is . . . trying at times; but his wife bore with him; and you must always remember, Charity, that it was Mr. Royall who brought you down from the Mountain."

Charity went home and opened the door of Mr. Royall's "office." He was sitting there by the stove reading Daniel Webster's speeches. They had met at meals during the five days that had elapsed since he had come to her door, and she had walked at his side at Eudora's funeral; but they had not spoken a word to each other.

He glanced up in surprise as she entered, and she noticed that he was unshaved, and that he looked unusually old; but as she had always thought of him as an old man the change in his appearance did not move her. She told him she had been to see Miss Hatchard, and with what object. She saw that he was astonished, but he made no comment.

"I told her the housework was too hard for me, and I wanted to earn the money to pay for a hired girl. But I ain't going to pay for her: you've got to. I want to have some money of my own."

Mr. Royall's bushy black eyebrows were drawn together in a frown, and he sat drumming with ink-stained nails on the edge of his desk.

"What do you want to earn money for?" he asked.

"So's to get away when I want to."

"Why do you want to get away?"

Her contempt flashed out. "Do you suppose anybody'd stay at North Dormer if they could help it? You wouldn't, folks say!"

With lowered head he asked: "Where'd you go to?"

"Anywhere where I can earn my living. I'll try here first, and if I can't do it here I'll go somewhere else. I'll go up the Mountain if I have to." She paused on this threat, and saw that it had taken effect. "I want you should get Miss Hatchard and the selectmen to take me at the library: and I want a woman here in the house with me," she repeated.

Mr. Royall had grown exceedingly pale. When she ended he stood up ponderously, leaning against the desk, and for a second or two they looked at each other.

"See here," he said at length, as though utterance were difficult, "there's something I've been wanting to say to you; I'd ought to have said it before. I want you to marry me."

The girl still stared at him without moving. "I want you to marry me," he repeated, clearing his throat. "The minister'll be up here next Sunday and we can fix it up then. Or I'll drive you down to Hepburn to the Justice, and get it done there. I'll do whatever you say." His eyes fell under the merciless stare she continued to fix on him, and he shifted his weight uneasily from one foot to the other. As he stood there before her, unwieldy, shabby, disordered, the purple veins distorting the hands he pressed against the desk, and his long orator's jaw trembling with the effort of his avowal, he seemed like a hideous parody of the fatherly old man she had always known.

"Marry you? Me?" she burst out with a scornful laugh. "Was that what you came to ask me the other night? What's come over you, I wonder? How long is it since you've looked at yourself in the glass?" She straightened herself, insolently conscious of her youth and strength. "I suppose you think it would be cheaper to marry me than to keep a hired girl. Everybody knows you're the closest man in Eagle County; but I guess you're not going to get your mending done for you that way twice."

Mr. Royall did not move while she spoke. His face was ash-colored and his black eyebrows quivered as though the blaze of her scorn had blinded him. When she ceased he held up his hand.

"That'll do—that'll about do," he said. He turned to the door and took his hat from the hat peg. On the threshold he paused. "People ain't been fair to me—from the first they ain't been fair to me," he said. Then he went out.

A few days later North Dormer learned with surprise that Charity had been appointed librarian of the Hatchard Memorial at a salary of eight dollars a month, and that old Verena Marsh, from the Creston Almshouse, was coming to live at lawyer Royall's and do the cooking.

# 3

IT WAS NOT in the room known at the red house as Mr. Royall's "office" that he received his infrequent clients. Professional dignity and masculine independence made it necessary that he should have a real office, under a different roof; and his standing as the only lawyer of North Dormer required that the roof should be the same as that which sheltered the Town Hall and the post office.

It was his habit to walk to his office twice a day, morning and afternoon. It was on the ground floor of the building, with a separate entrance, and a weathered nameplate on the door. Before going in he stepped into the post office for his mail—usually an empty ceremony—said a word or two to the town clerk, who sat across the passage in idle state, and then went over to the store on the opposite corner, where Carrick Fry, the storekeeper, always kept a chair for him, and where he was sure to find one or two selectmen leaning on the long counter, in an atmosphere of rope, leather, tar, and coffee beans. Mr. Royall, though monosyllabic at home, was not averse, in certain moods, to imparting his views to his fellow townsmen; perhaps, also, he was unwilling that his rare clients should surprise him sitting, clerkless and unoccupied, in his dusty office. At any rate, his hours there were not much longer or more regular than Charity's at the library; the rest of the time he spent either at the store or in driving about the country on business connected with the insurance companies that he represented, or in sitting at home reading Bancroft's *History of the United States* and the speeches of Daniel Webster.

Since the day when Charity had told him that she wished to succeed to Eudora Skeff's post their relations had undefinably but definitely changed. Lawyer Royall had kept his word. He had obtained the place for her at the cost of considerable maneuvering, as she guessed from the number of rival candidates, and from the acerbity with which two of them, Orma Fry and the eldest Targatt girl, treated her for nearly a year afterward. And he had engaged Verena Marsh to come up from Creston and do the cooking. Verena was a poor old widow, doddering and shiftless: Charity suspected that she came for her keep. Mr. Royall was too close a man to give a dollar a day to a smart girl when he could get a deaf pauper for nothing. But at any rate, Verena was there, in the attic just over Charity, and the fact that she was deaf did not greatly trouble the young girl.

Charity knew that what had happened on that hateful night would not happen again. She understood that, profoundly as she had despised Mr. Royall ever since, he despised himself still more profoundly. If she had asked for a woman in the house it was far less for her own defense than for his humiliation. She needed no one to defend her: his humbled pride was her surest protection. He had never spoken a word of excuse or extenuation; the incident was as if it had never been. Yet its consequences were latent in every word that he and she exchanged, in every glance they instinctively turned from each other. Nothing now would ever shake her rule in the red house.

On the night of her meeting with Miss Hatchard's cousin Charity lay in bed, her bare arms clasped under her rough head, and continued to think of him. She supposed that he meant to spend some time in North Dormer. He had said he was looking up the old houses in the neighborhood; and though she was not very clear as to his purpose, or as to why anyone should look for old houses, when they lay in wait for one on every roadside, she understood that he needed the help of books, and resolved to hunt up the next day the volume she had failed to find, and any others that seemed related to the subject.

Never had her ignorance of life and literature so weighed on her as in reliving the short scene of her discomfiture. "It's no use trying to be anything in this place," she muttered to her pillow; and she shriveled at the vision of vague metropolises, shining super-Nettletons, where girls in better clothes than Belle Balch's talked fluently of architecture to young men with hands like Lucius Harney's. Then she remembered his sudden pause when he had come close to the desk and had his first look at her. The sight had made him forget what he was going to say; she recalled the change in his face, and jumping up she ran over the bare boards

to her washstand, found the matches, lit a candle, and lifted it to
the square of looking glass on the whitewashed wall. Her small
face, usually so darkly pale, glowed like a rose in the faint orb of
light, and under her rumpled hair her eyes seemed deeper and
larger than by day. Perhaps after all it was a mistake to wish they
were blue. A clumsy band and button fastened her unbleached
nightgown about the throat. She undid it, freed her thin shoulders, and saw herself a bride in low-necked satin, walking down
an aisle with Lucius Harney. He would kiss her as they left the
church. . . . She put down the candle and covered her face with
her hands as if to imprison the kiss. At that moment she heard
Mr. Royall's step as he came up the stairs to bed, and a fierce
revulsion of feeling swept over her. Until then she had merely
despised him; now deep hatred of him filled her heart. He became to her a horrible old man. . . .

The next day, when Mr. Royall came back to dinner, they faced
each other in silence as usual. Verena's presence at the table was
an excuse for their not talking, though her deafness would have
permitted the freest interchange of confidences. But when the
meal was over, and Mr. Royall rose from the table, he looked back
at Charity, who had stayed to help the old woman clear away the
dishes.

"I want to speak to you a minute," he said, and she followed
him across the passage, wondering.

He seated himself in his black horsehair armchair, and she
leaned against the window, indifferently. She was impatient to be
gone to the library, to hunt for the book on North Dormer.

"See here," he said, "why ain't you at the library the days
you're supposed to be there?"

The question, breaking in on her mood of blissful abstraction,
deprived her of speech, and she stared at him for a moment
without answering.

"Who says I ain't?"

"There's been some complaints made, it appears. Miss Hatchard sent for me this morning—"

Charity's smoldering resentment broke into a blaze. "I know!
Orma Fry, and that toad of a Targatt girl—and Ben Fry, like as
not. He's going round with her. The low-down sneaks—I always

knew they'd try to have me out! As if anybody ever came to the library, anyhow!"

"Somebody did yesterday, and you weren't there."

"Yesterday?" she laughed at her happy recollection. "At what time wasn't I there yesterday, I'd like to know?"

"Round about four o'clock."

Charity was silent. She had been so steeped in the dreamy remembrance of young Harney's visit that she had forgotten having deserted her post as soon as he had left the library.

"Who came at four o'clock?"

"Miss Hatchard did."

"Miss Hatchard? Why, she ain't ever been near the place since she's been lame. She couldn't get up the steps if she tried."

"She can be helped up, I guess. She was yesterday, anyhow, by the young fellow that's staying with her. He found you there, I understand, earlier in the afternoon; and he went back and told Miss Hatchard the books were in bad shape and needed attending to. She got excited, and had herself wheeled straight round, and when she got there the place was locked. So she sent for me, and told me about that, and about the other complaints. She claims you've neglected things, and that she's going to get a trained librarian."

Charity had not moved while he spoke. She stood with her head thrown back against the window frame, her arms hanging against her sides, and her hand so tightly clenched that she felt, without knowing what hurt her, the sharp edge of her nails against her palms.

Of all Mr. Royall had said she had retained only the phrase: "He told Miss Hatchard the books were in bad shape." What did she care for the other charges against her? Malice or truth, she despised them as she despised her detractors. But that the stranger to whom she had felt herself so mysteriously drawn should have betrayed her! That at the very moment when she had fled up the hillside to think of him more deliciously he should have been hastening home to denounce her shortcomings! She remembered how, in the darkness of her room, she had covered her face to press his imagined kiss closer; and her heart raged against him for the liberty he had not taken.

"Well, I'll go," she said suddenly. "I'll go right off."

"Go where?" She heard the startled note in Mr. Royall's voice.

"Why, out of their old library: straight out, and never set foot in it again. They needn't think I'm going to wait round and let them say they've discharged me!"

"Charity—Charity Royall, you listen—" he began, getting heavily out of his chair; but she waved him aside, and walked out of the room.

Upstairs she took the library key from the place where she always hid it under her pincushion—who said she wasn't careful?—put on her hat, and swept down again and out into the street. If Mr. Royall heard her go he made no motion to detain her: his sudden rages probably made him understand the uselessness of reasoning with hers.

She reached the brick temple, unlocked the door, and entered into the glacial twilight. "I'm glad I'll never have to sit in this old vault again when other folks are out in the sun!" she said aloud as the familiar chill took her. She looked with abhorrence at the long dingy rows of books, the sheep-nosed Minerva on her black pedestal, and the mild-faced young man in a high stock whose effigy pined above her desk. She meant to take out of the drawer her roll of lace and the library register, and go straight to Miss Hatchard to announce her resignation. But suddenly a great desolation overcame her, and she sat down and laid her face against the desk. Her heart was ravaged by life's cruelest discovery: the first creature who had come toward her out of the wilderness had brought her anguish instead of joy. She did not cry; tears came hard to her, and the storms of her heart spent themselves inwardly. But as she sat there in her dumb woe she felt her life to be too desolate, too ugly and intolerable.

"What have I ever done to it, that it should hurt me so?" she groaned, and pressed her fists against her lids, which were beginning to swell with weeping.

"I won't—I won't go there looking like a horror!" she muttered, springing up and pushing back her hair as if it stifled her. She opened the drawer, dragged out the register, and turned toward the door. As she did so it opened, and the young man from Miss Hatchard's came in whistling.

# 4

He stopped and lifted his hat with a shy smile. "I beg your pardon," he said, "I thought there was no one here."

Charity stood before him, barring his way. "You can't come in. The library ain't open to the public Wednesdays."

"I know it's not, but my cousin gave me her key."

"Miss Hatchard's got no right to give her key to other folks, any more'n I have. I'm the librarian and I know the bylaws. This is my library."

The young man looked profoundly surprised.

"Why, I know it is; I'm so sorry if you mind my coming."

"I suppose you came to see what more you could say to set her against me? But you needn't trouble: it's my library today, but it won't be this time tomorrow. I'm on the way now to take her back the key and the register."

Young Harney's face grew grave, but without betraying the consciousness of guilt she had looked for.

"I don't understand," he said. "There must be some mistake. Why should I say things against you to Miss Hatchard—or to anyone?"

The apparent evasiveness of the reply caused Charity's indignation to overflow. "I don't know why you should. I could understand Orma Fry's doing it, because she's always wanted to get me out of here ever since the first day. I can't see why, when she's got her own home, and her father to work for her; nor Ida Targatt, neither, when she got a legacy from her stepbrother on'y last year. But anyway we all live in the same place, and when it's a place like North Dormer it's enough to make people hate each other just to have to walk down the same street every day. But you don't live here, and you don't know anything about any of us, so what did you have to meddle for? Do you suppose the other girls'd have kept the books any better'n I did? Why, Orma Fry don't hardly know a book from a flatiron! And what if I don't

311

always sit round here doing nothing till it strikes five up at the church? Who cares if the library's open or shut? Do you suppose anybody ever comes here for books? What they'd like to come for is to meet the fellows they're going with—if I'd let 'em. But I wouldn't let Bill Sollas from over the hill hang round here waiting for the youngest Targatt girl, because I know him . . . that's all . . . even if I don't know about books all I ought to. . . ."

She stopped with a choking in her throat. Tremors of rage were running through her, and she steadied herself against the edge of the desk lest he should see her weakness.

What he saw seemed to affect him deeply, for he grew red under his sunburn, and stammered out: "But, Miss Royall, I assure you . . . I assure you . . ."

His distress inflamed her anger, and she regained her voice to fling back: "If I was you I'd have the nerve to stick to what I said!"

The taunt seemed to restore his presence of mind. "I hope I should if I knew; but I don't. Apparently something disagreeable has happened, for which you think I'm to blame. But I don't know what it is, because I've been up on Eagle Ridge ever since the early morning."

"I don't know where you've been this morning, but I know you were here in this library yesterday; and it was you that went home and told your cousin the books were in bad shape, and brought her round to see how I'd neglected them."

Young Harney looked sincerely concerned. "Was that what you were told? I don't wonder you're angry. The books *are* in bad shape, and as some are interesting it's a pity. I told Miss Hatchard they were suffering from dampness and lack of air; and I brought her here to show her how easily the place could be ventilated. I also told her you ought to have someone to help you do the dusting and airing. If you were given a wrong version of what I said I'm sorry; but I'm so fond of old books that I'd rather see them made into a bonfire than left to molder away like these."

Charity felt her sobs rising and tried to stifle them in words. "I don't care what you say you told her. All I know is she thinks it's all my fault, and I'm going to lose my job, and I wanted it more'n anyone in the village, because I haven't got anybody belonging to me, the way other folks have. All I wanted was to put aside money enough to get away from here sometime. D'you suppose if it hadn't been for that I'd have kept on sitting day after day in this old vault?"

Of this appeal her hearer took up only the last question. "It *is* an old vault; but need it be? That's the point. And it's my putting the question to my cousin that seems to have been the cause of the trouble." His glance explored the melancholy penumbra of the long narrow room, resting on the blotched walls, the discolored rows of books, and the stern rosewood desk surmounted by the portrait of the young Honorius. "Of course it's a bad job to do anything with a building jammed against a hill like this ridiculous mausoleum: you couldn't get a good draft through it without blowing a hole in the mountain. But it can be ventilated after a fashion, and the sun can be let in: I'll show you how if you like. . . ." The architect's passion for improvement had already made him lose sight of her grievance, and he lifted his stick instructively toward the cornice. But her silence seemed to tell him that she took no interest in the ventilation of the library, and turning back to her abruptly he held out both hands. "Look here—you don't mean what you said? You don't really think I'd do anything to hurt you?"

A new note in his voice disarmed her: no one had ever spoken to her in that tone.

"Oh, what *did* you do it for then?" she wailed. He had her hands in his, and she was feeling the smooth touch that she had imagined the day before on the hillside.

He pressed her hands lightly and let them go. "Why, to make things pleasanter for you here, and better for the books. I'm sorry if my cousin twisted around what I said. She's excitable, and she lives on trifles: I ought to have remembered that. Don't punish me by letting her think you take her seriously."

It was wonderful to hear him speak of Miss Hatchard as if she were a querulous baby: in spite of his shyness he had the air of power that the experience of cities probably gave. It was the fact of having lived in Nettleton that made lawyer Royall, in spite of his infirmities, the strongest man in North Dormer; and Charity was sure that this young man had lived in bigger places than Nettleton.

She felt that if she kept up her denunciatory tone he would

secretly class her with Miss Hatchard; and the thought made her suddenly simple.

"It don't matter to Miss Hatchard how I take her. Mr. Royall says she's going to get a trained librarian; and I'd sooner resign than have the village say she sent me away."

"Naturally you would. But I'm sure she doesn't mean to send you away. At any rate, won't you give me the chance to find out first and let you know? It will be time enough to resign if I'm mistaken."

Her pride flamed into her cheeks at the suggestion of his intervening. "I don't want anybody should coax her to keep me if I don't suit."

He colored too. "I give you my word I won't do that. Only wait till tomorrow, will you?" He looked straight into her eyes with his shy gray glance. "You can trust me, you know—you really can."

All the old frozen woes seemed to melt in her, and she murmured awkwardly, looking away from him: "Oh, I'll wait."

# — 5 —

❧ THERE HAD never been such a June in Eagle County. Usually it was a month of moods, with abrupt alternations of belated frost and midsummer heat; this year, day followed day in a sequence of temperate beauty. Every morning a breeze blew steadily from the hills. Toward noon it built up great canopies of white cloud that threw a cool shadow over fields and woods; then before sunset the clouds dissolved again, and the western light rained its unobstructed brightness on the valley.

On such an afternoon Charity Royall lay on a ridge above a sunlit hollow, her face pressed to the earth and the warm currents of the grass running through her. Directly in her line of vision a blackberry branch laid its frail white flowers and blue-green leaves against the sky. Just beyond, a tuft of sweet-fern uncurled between the beaded shoots of the grass, and a small yellow butterfly vibrated over them like a fleck of sunshine. This was all she saw; but she felt, above her and about her, the strong growth of the beeches clothing the ridge, the rounding of pale green cones on countless spruce branches, the push of myriads of sweet-fern fronds in the cracks of the stony slope below the wood, and the crowding shoots of meadowsweet and yellow flags in the pasture beyond. All this bubbling of sap and slipping of sheaths and bursting of calyxes was carried to her on mingled currents of fragrance. Every leaf and bud and blade seemed to contribute its exhalation to the pervading sweetness in which the pungency of pine sap prevailed over the spice of thyme and the subtle perfume of fern, and all were merged in a moist earth smell that was like the breath of some huge sun-warmed animal.

Charity had lain there a long time, passive and sun-warmed as the slope on which she lay, when there came between her eyes and the dancing butterfly the sight of a man's foot in a large worn boot covered with red mud.

"Oh, don't!" she exclaimed, raising herself on her elbow and stretching out a warning hand.

"Don't what?" a hoarse voice asked above her head.

"Don't stamp on those bramble flowers, you dolt!" she retorted, springing to her knees. The foot paused and then descended clumsily on the frail branch, and raising her eyes she saw above her the bewildered face of a slouching man with a thin sunburned beard, and white arms showing through his ragged shirt.

"Don't you ever *see* anything, Liff Hyatt?" she assailed him, as he stood before her with the look of a man who has stirred up a wasp's nest.

He grinned. "I seen you! That's what I come down for."

"Down from where?" she questioned, stooping to gather up the petals his foot had scattered.

He jerked his thumb toward the heights. "Been cutting down trees for Dan Targatt."

Charity sank back on her heels and looked at him musingly. She was not in the least afraid of poor Liff Hyatt, though he "came from the Mountain," and some of the girls ran when they saw him. Among the more reasonable he passed for a harmless creature, a sort of link between the mountain and civilized folk, who occasionally came down and did a little wood-cutting for a farmer when hands were short. Besides, she knew the Mountain people would never hurt her: Liff himself had told her so once when she was a little girl, and had met him one day at the edge of lawyer Royall's pasture. "They won't any of 'em touch you up there, f'ever you was to come up. . . . But I don't s'pose you will," he had added philosophically, looking at her new shoes, and at the red ribbon that Mrs. Royall had tied in her hair.

Charity had, in truth, never felt any desire to visit her birthplace. She did not care to have it known that she was of the Mountain, and was shy of being seen in talk with Liff Hyatt. But today she was not sorry to have him appear. A great many things had happened to her since the day when young Lucius Harney had entered the doors of the Hatchard Memorial, but none, perhaps, so unforeseen as the fact of her suddenly finding it a convenience to be on good terms with Liff Hyatt. She continued to look up curiously at his freckled weather-beaten face, with feverish hollows below the cheekbones and the pale yellow eyes of a harmless animal. "I wonder if he's related to me?" she thought, with a shiver of disdain.

"Is there any folks living in the brown house by the swamp, up under Porcupine?" she presently asked in an indifferent tone.

Liff Hyatt, for a while, considered her with surprise; then he scratched his head and shifted his weight from one tattered sole to the other.

"There's always the same folks in the brown house," he said with his vague grin.

"They're from up your way, ain't they?"

"Their name's the same as mine," he rejoined uncertainly.

Charity still held him with resolute eyes. "See here, I want to go there someday and take a gentleman with me that's boarding with us. He's up in these parts drawing pictures."

She did not offer to explain this statement. It was too far beyond Liff Hyatt's limitations for the attempt to be worth making. "He wants to see the brown house, and go all over it," she pursued.

Liff was still running his fingers perplexedly through his shock of straw-colored hair. "Is it a fellow from the city?" he asked.

"Yes. He draws pictures of things. He's down there now drawing the Bonner house." She pointed to a chimney just visible over the dip of the pasture below the wood.

"The Bonner house?" Liff echoed incredulously.

"Yes. You won't understand—and it don't matter. All I say is: he's going to the Hyatts' in a day or two."

Liff looked more and more perplexed. "Bash is ugly sometimes in the afternoons."

"I know. But I guess he won't trouble me." She threw her head back, her eyes full on Hyatt's. "I'm coming too: you tell him."

"They won't none of them trouble you, the Hyatts won't. What d'you want a take a stranger with you, though?"

"I've told you, haven't I? You've got to tell Bash Hyatt."

He looked away at the blue mountains on the horizon; then his gaze dropped to the chimney top below the pasture.

"He's down there now?"

"Yes."

He shifted his weight again, crossed his arms, and continued to survey the distant landscape. "Well, so long," he said at last, in-conclusively; and turning away he shambled up the hillside. From the ledge above her, he paused to call down: "I wouldn't go there a Sunday," then he clambered on till the trees closed in on him. Presently, from high overhead, Charity heard the ring of his ax.

She lay on the warm ridge, thinking of many things that the woodsman's appearance had stirred up in her. She knew nothing of her early life, and had never felt any curiosity about it: only a sullen reluctance to explore the corner of her memory where certain blurred images lingered. But all that had happened to her within the last few weeks had stirred her to the sleeping depths. She had become absorbingly interesting to herself, and every-thing that had to do with her past was illuminated by this sudden curiosity.

She hated more than ever the fact of coming from the Moun-tain; but it was no longer indifferent to her. Everything that in any way affected her was alive and vivid: even the hateful things had grown interesting because they were a part of herself.

"I wonder if Liff Hyatt knows who my mother was?" she mused; and it filled her with a tremor of surprise to think that some woman who was once young and slight, with quick motions of the blood like hers, had carried her in her breast, and watched her sleeping. She had always thought of her mother as so long dead as to be no more than a nameless pinch of earth; but now it occurred to her that the once-young woman might be alive, and wrinkled and elf-locked like the woman she had sometimes seen in the door of the brown house that Lucius Harney wanted to draw.

The thought brought her back to the central point in her mind, and she strayed away from the conjectures roused by Liff Hyatt's presence. Speculations concerning the past could not hold her long when the present was so rich, the future so rosy, and when Lucius Harney, a stone's throw away, was bending over his sketchbook, frowning, calculating, measuring, and then throwing his head back with the sudden smile that had shed its brightness over everything.

She scrambled to her feet, but as she did so she saw him com-ing up the pasture and dropped down on the grass to wait. When he was drawing and measuring one of "his houses," as she called them, she often strayed away by herself into the woods or up the hillside. It was partly from shyness that she did so: from a sense of inadequacy that came to her most painfully when her companion, absorbed in his job, forgot her ignorance and her inability to follow his least allusion, and plunged into a monologue on art and life. To avoid the awkwardness of listening with a blank face, and also to escape the surprised stare of the inhabitants of the houses before which he would abruptly pull up their horse and open his sketchbook, she slipped away to some spot from which, without being seen, she could watch him at work, or at least look down on the house he was drawing. She had not been displeased, at first, to have it known to North Dormer and the neighborhood that she was driving Miss Hatchard's cousin about the country in the buggy he had hired of lawyer Royall. She had always kept to herself, contemptuously aloof from village lovemaking, without exactly knowing whether her fierce pride was due to the sense of her tainted origin, or whether she was reserving herself for a more brilliant fate. Sometimes she envied the other girls their sentimental preoccupations, their long hours of inarticulate philandering with one of the few youths who still lingered in the village; but when she pictured herself curling her hair or putting a new ribbon on her hat for Ben Fry or one of the Sollas boys the fever dropped and she relapsed into indifference.

Now she knew the meaning of her disdains and reluctances. She had learned what she was worth when Lucius Harney, looking at her for the first time, had lost the thread of his speech, and leaned reddening on the edge of her desk. But another kind of shyness had been born in her: a terror of exposing to vulgar perils the sacred treasure of her happiness. She was not sorry to have the neighbors suspect her of "going with" a young man from the city, but she did not want it known to all the countryside how many hours of the long June days she spent with him. What she most feared was that the inevitable comments should reach Mr. Royall. Charity was instinctively aware that few things concerning her escaped the eyes of the silent man under whose roof she lived; and in spite of the latitude which North Dormer accorded to courting couples she had always felt that, on the day when she showed too open a preference, Mr. Royall might, as she phrased it, make her "pay for it." How, she did not know, and her fear was the greater because it was undefinable. If she had been accepting the attentions of one of the village youths she would have been less apprehensive: Mr. Royall could not prevent her marrying when she chose to. But everybody knew that "going with a city fellow" was a different and less straightforward affair: almost every village could show a victim of the perilous venture. And her dread of Mr. Royall's intervention gave a sharpened joy to the hours she spent with young Harney, and made her, at the same time, shy of being too generally seen with him.

As he approached she rose to her knees, stretching her arms above her head with the indolent gesture that was her way of expressing a profound well-being.

"I'm going to take you to that house up under Porcupine," she announced.

"What house? Oh, yes; that ramshackle place near the swamp, with the gypsy-looking people hanging about. It's curious that a house with traces of real architecture should have been built in such a place. But the people were a sulky-looking lot—do you suppose they'll let us in?"

"They'll do whatever I tell them," she said with assurance.

He threw himself down beside her. "Will they?" he rejoined with a smile. "Well, I should like to see what's left inside the house. And I should like to have a talk with the people. Who was it who was telling me the other day that they had come down from the Mountain?"

Charity shot a sideward look at him. It was the first time he had spoken of the Mountain except as a feature of the landscape. What else did he know about it, and about her relation to it? Her heart began to beat with the fierce impulse of resistance which she instinctively opposed to every imagined slight.

"The Mountain? I ain't afraid of the Mountain!"

Her tone of defiance seemed to escape him. He lay breast-down on the grass, breaking off sprigs of thyme and pressing them against his lips. Far off, above the folds of the nearer hills, the Mountain thrust itself up menacingly against a yellow sunset.

"I must go up there someday: I want to see it," he continued.

Her heartbeats slackened and she turned again to examine his profile. It was innocent of all unfriendly intention.

"What'd you want to go up the Mountain for?"

"Why, it must be rather a curious place. There's a queer colony up there, you know: sort of outlaws, a little independent kingdom. Of course you've heard them spoken of; but I'm told they have nothing to do with the people in the valleys—rather look down on them, in fact. I suppose they're rough customers; but they must have a good deal of character."

She did not quite know what he meant by having a good deal of character; but his tone was expressive of admiration, and deepened her dawning curiosity. It struck her now as strange that she knew so little about the Mountain. She had never asked, and no one had ever offered to enlighten her. North Dormer took the Mountain for granted, and implied its disparagement by an intonation rather than by explicit criticism.

"It's queer, you know," he continued, "that, just over there, on top of that hill, there should be a handful of people who don't give a damn for anybody."

The words thrilled her. They seemed the clue to her own revolts and defiances, and she longed to have him tell her more.

"I don't know much about them. Have they always been there?"

"Nobody seems to know exactly how long. Down at Creston they told me that the first colonists are supposed to have been men who worked on the railway that was built forty or fifty years ago between Springfield and Nettleton. Some of them took to drink, or got into trouble with the police, and went off—disappeared into the woods. A year or two later there was a report that they were living up on the Mountain. Then I suppose others joined them—and children were born. Now they say there are over a hundred people up there. They seem to be quite outside the jurisdiction of the valleys. No school, no church—and no sheriff ever goes up to see what they're about. But don't people ever talk of them at North Dormer?"

"I don't know. They say they're bad."

He laughed. "Do they? We'll go and see, shall we?"

She flushed at the suggestion, and turned her face to his. "You never heard, I suppose—I come from there. They brought me down when I was little."

"You?" He raised himself on his elbow, looking at her with

sudden interest. "You're from the Mountain? How curious! I suppose that's why you're so different. . . ."

Her happy blood bathed her to the forehead. He was praising her—and praising her because she came from the Mountain!

"Am I . . . different?" she triumphed, with affected wonder.

"Oh, awfully!" He picked up her hand and laid a kiss on the sunburned knuckles.

"Come," he said, "let's be off." He stood up and shook the grass from his loose gray clothes. "What a good day! Where are you going to take me tomorrow?"

# 6

THAT EVENING after supper Charity sat alone in the kitchen and listened to Mr. Royall and young Harney talking in the porch.

She had remained indoors after the table had been cleared and old Verena had hobbled up to bed. The kitchen window was open, and Charity seated herself near it, her idle hands on her knee. The evening was cool and still. Beyond the black hills an amber west passed into pale green, and then to a deep blue in which a great star hung. The soft hoot of a little owl came through the dusk, and between its calls the men's voices rose and fell.

Mr. Royall's was full of a sonorous satisfaction. It was a long time since he had had anyone of Lucius Harney's quality to talk to: Charity divined that the young man symbolized all his ruined and unforgotten past. When Miss Hatchard had been called to Springfield by the illness of a widowed sister, and young Harney, by that time seriously embarked on his task of drawing and measuring all the old houses between Nettleton and the New Hampshire border, had suggested the possibility of boarding at the red house in his cousin's absence, Charity had trembled lest Mr. Royall should refuse. There had been no question of lodging the young man: there was no room for him. But it appeared that he could still live at Miss Hatchard's if Mr. Royall would let him take his meals at the red house, and after a day's deliberation Mr. Royall consented.

Charity suspected him of being glad of the chance to make a little money. He had the reputation of being an avaricious man, but she was beginning to think he was probably poorer than people knew. His practice had become little more than a vague legend, revived only at lengthening intervals by a summons to Hepburn or Nettleton; and he appeared to depend for his living mainly on the scant produce of his farm, and on the commissions received from the few insurance agencies that he represented in the neighborhood. At any rate, he had been prompt in accepting Harney's offer to hire the buggy at a dollar and a half a day; and his satisfaction with the bargain had manifested itself, unexpectedly enough, at the end of the first week, by his tossing a ten-dollar bill into Charity's lap as she sat one day retrimming her old hat.

"Here—go get yourself a Sunday bonnet that'll make all the other girls mad," he said, looking at her with a sheepish twinkle in his deep-set eyes; and she immediately guessed that the unwonted present—the only gift of money she had ever received from him—represented Harney's first payment.

But the young man's coming had brought Mr. Royall other than pecuniary benefit. It gave him, for the first time in years, a man's companionship. Charity had only a dim understanding of her guardian's needs; but she knew he felt himself above the people among whom he lived, and she saw that Lucius Harney thought him so. She was surprised to find how well he seemed to talk now that he had a listener who understood him; and she was equally struck by young Harney's friendly deference.

Their conversation was mostly about politics, and beyond her range; but tonight it had a peculiar interest for her, for they had begun to speak of the Mountain. She drew back a little, lest they should see she was in hearing.

"The Mountain? The Mountain?" she heard Mr. Royall say. "Why, the Mountain's a blot—that's what it is, sir, a blot. That scum up there ought to have been run in long ago—and would have, if the people down here hadn't been clean scared of them. The Mountain belongs to this township, and it's North Dormer's fault if there's a gang of thieves and outlaws living over there, in sight of us, defying the laws of their country. Why, there ain't a sheriff or a tax collector or a coroner'd durst go up there. When they hear of trouble on the Mountain the selectmen look the other way, and pass an appropriation to beautify the town pump. The only man that ever goes up is the minister, and he goes because they send down and get him whenever there's any of them dies. They think a lot of Christian burial on the Mountain—but I never heard of their having the minister up to marry them.

And they never trouble the Justice of the Peace either. They just herd together like the heathen."

He went on, explaining in somewhat technical language how the little colony of squatters had contrived to keep the law at bay, and Charity, with burning eagerness, awaited young Harney's comment; but the young man seemed more concerned to hear Mr. Royall's views than to express his own.

"I suppose you've never been up there yourself?" he presently asked.

"Yes, I have," said Mr. Royall with a contemptuous laugh. "The wiseacres down here told me I'd be done for before I got back, but nobody lifted a finger to hurt me. And I'd just had one of their gang sent up for seven years too."

"You went up after that?"

"Yes, sir: right after it. The fellow came down to Nettleton and ran amuck, the way they sometimes do. After they've done a wood-cutting job they come down and blow the money in; and this man ended up with manslaughter. I got him convicted, though they were scared of the Mountain even at Nettleton; and then a queer thing happened. The fellow sent for me to go and see him in jail. I went, and this is what he says: 'The fool that defended me is a chicken-livered son of a——and all the rest of it,' he says. 'I've got a job to be done for me up on the Mountain, and you're the only man I seen in court that looks as if he'd do it.' He told me he had a child up there—or thought he had—a little girl; and he wanted her brought down and reared like a Christian. I was sorry for the fellow, so I went up and got the child." He paused, and Charity listened with a throbbing heart. "That's the only time I ever went up the Mountain," he concluded.

There was a moment's silence; then Harney spoke. "And the child—had she no mother?"

"Oh, yes; there was a mother. But she was glad enough to have her go. She'd have given her to anybody. They ain't half human up there. I guess the mother's dead by now, with the life she was leading. Anyhow, I've never heard of her from that day to this."

"My God, how ghastly," Harney murmured; and Charity, choking with humiliation, sprang to her feet and ran upstairs. She knew at last: knew that she was the child of a drunken convict and of a mother who wasn't "half human," and was glad to have her go; and she had heard this history of her origin related to the one being in whose eyes she longed to appear superior to the people about her! She had noticed that Mr. Royall had not named her, had even avoided any allusion that might identify her with the child he had brought down from the Mountain; and she knew it was out of regard for her that he had kept silent. But of what use was his discretion, since only that afternoon, misled by Harney's interest in the outlaw colony, she had boasted to him of coming from the Mountain? Now every word that had been spoken showed her how such an origin must widen the distance between them.

During his ten days' sojourn at North Dormer Lucius Harney had not spoken a word of love to her. He had intervened in her behalf with his cousin, and had convinced Miss Hatchard of her merits as a librarian; but that was a simple act of justice, since it was by his own fault that those merits had been questioned. He had asked her to drive him about the country when he hired lawyer Royall's buggy to go on his sketching expeditions; but that too was natural enough, since he was unfamiliar with the region. Lastly, when his cousin was called to Springfield, he had begged Mr. Royall to receive him as a boarder; but where else in North Dormer could he have boarded? Not with Carrick Fry, whose wife was paralyzed, and whose large family crowded his table to over-flowing; not with the Targatts, who lived a mile up the road, nor with poor old Mrs. Hawes, who, since her eldest daughter had deserted her, barely had the strength to cook her own meals while Ally picked up her living as a seamstress. Mr. Royall's was the only house where the young man could have been offered a decent hospitality. There had been nothing, therefore, in the out-ward course of events to raise in Charity's breast the hopes with which it trembled. But beneath the visible incidents resulting from Lucius Harney's arrival there ran an undercurrent as mys-terious and potent as the influence that makes the forest break into leaf before the ice is off the pools.

The business on which Harney had come was authentic; Char-ity had seen the letter from a New York publisher commissioning him to make a study of the eighteenth-century houses in the less familiar districts of New England. But incomprehensible as the whole affair was to her, and hard as she found it to understand why he paused enchanted before certain neglected and paintless houses, while others, refurbished and "improved" by the local builder, did not arrest a glance, she could not but suspect that Eagle County was less rich in architecture than he averred, and that the duration of his stay (which he had fixed at a month) was not unconnected with the look in his eyes when he had first paused before her in the library. Everything that had followed seemed to have grown out of that look: his way of speaking to her, his quickness in catching her meaning, his evident eagerness to prolong their excursions and to seize on every chance of being with her.

The signs of his liking were manifest enough; but it was hard to guess how much they meant, because his manner was so different from anything North Dormer had ever shown her. He was at once simpler and more deferential than anyone she had known; and sometimes it was just when he was simplest that she most felt the distance between them. Education and opportunity had divided them by a width that no effort of hers could bridge, and even when his youth and his admiration brought him nearest, some chance word, some unconscious allusion, seemed to thrust her back across the gulf.

Never had it yawned so wide as when she fled up to her room carrying with her the echo of Mr. Royall's tale. Her first confused thought was the prayer that she might never see young Harney again. It was too bitter to picture him as the detached impartial listner to such a story. "I wish he'd go away: I wish he'd go tomorrow, and never come back!" she moaned to her pillow; and far into the night she lay there, in the disordered dress she had forgotten to take off, her whole soul a tossing misery on which her hopes and dreams spun about like drowning straws.

Of all this tumult only a vague heart-soreness was left when she opened her eyes the next morning. Her first thought was of the weather, for Harney had asked her to take him to the brown house under Porcupine, and then around by Hamblin; and as the trip was a long one they were to start at nine. The sun rose without a cloud, and earlier than usual she was in the kitchen, making cheese sandwiches, decanting buttermilk into a bottle, wrapping up slices of apple pie, and accusing Verena of having given away a basket she needed, which had always hung on a hook in the passage. When she came out into the porch, in her pink calico, which had run a little in the washing, but was still bright enough to set off her dark tints, she had such a triumphant sense of being a part of the sunlight and the morning that the last trace of her misery vanished. What did it matter where she came from, or whose child she was, when love was dancing in her veins, and down the road she saw young Harney coming toward her?

Mr. Royall was in the porch too. He had said nothing at breakfast, but when she came out in her pink dress, the basket in her hand, he looked at her with surprise. "Where you going to?" he asked.

"Why—Mr. Harney's starting earlier than usual today," she answered.

"Mr. Harney, Mr. Harney? Ain't Mr. Harney learned how to drive a horse yet?"

She made no answer, and he sat tilted back in his chair, drumming on the rail of the porch. It was the first time he had ever spoken of the young man in that tone, and Charity felt a faint chill of apprehension. After a moment he stood up and walked away toward the bit of ground behind the house, where the hired man was hoeing.

The air was cool and clear, with the autumnal sparkle that a north wind brings to the hills in early summer, and the night had been so still that the dew hung on everything, not as a lingering moisture, but in separate beads that glittered like diamonds on the ferns and grasses. It was a long drive to the foot of Porcupine: first across the valley, with blue hills bounding the open slopes; then down into the beech woods, following the course of the Creston, a brown brook leaping over velvet ledges; then out again onto the farmlands about Creston Lake, and gradually up the ridges of the Eagle Range. At last they reached the yoke of the hills, and before them opened another valley, green and wild, and beyond it more blue heights eddying away to the sky like the waves of a receding tide.

Harney tied the horse to a tree stump, and they unpacked their basket under an aged walnut with a riven trunk out of which bumblebees darted. The sun had grown hot, and behind them was the noonday murmur of the forest. Summer insects danced on the air, and a flock of white butterflies fanned the mobile tips of the crimson fireweed. In the valley below not a house was visible; it seemed as if Charity Royall and young Harney were the only living beings in the great hollow of earth and sky.

Charity's spirits flagged and disquieting thoughts stole back on her. Young Harney had grown silent, and as he lay beside her, his arms under his head, his eyes on the network of leaves above him, she wondered if he were musing on what Mr. Royall had told him, and if it had really debased her in his thoughts. She wished he had not asked her to take him that day to the brown house; she did not want him to see the people she came from while the story of her birth was fresh in his mind. More than once she had been on the point of suggesting that they should follow the ridge and drive straight to Hamblin, where there was a little deserted house he wanted to see, but shyness and pride held her back. "He'd better know what kind of folks I belong to," she said to herself, with a somewhat forced defiance; for in reality it was shame that kept her silent.

Suddenly she lifted her hand and pointed to the sky. "There's a storm coming up."

He followed her glance and smiled. "Is it that scrap of cloud among the pines that frightens you?"

"It's over the Mountain; and a cloud over the Mountain always means trouble."

"Oh, I don't believe half the bad things you all say of the Mountain! But anyhow, we'll get down to the brown house before the rain comes."

He was not far wrong, for only a few isolated drops had fallen when they turned into the road under the shaggy flank of Porcupine, and came upon the brown house. It stood alone beside a swamp bordered with alder thickets and tall bulrushes. Not another dwelling was in sight, and it was hard to guess what motive could have actuated the early settler who had made his home in so unfriendly a spot.

Charity had picked up enough of her companion's erudition to understand what had attracted him to the house. She noticed the fan-shaped tracery of the broken light above the door, the flutings of the paintless pilasters at the corners, and the round window set in the gable; and she knew that, for reasons that still escaped her, these were things to be admired and recorded. Still, they had seen other houses far more "typical" (the word was Harney's); and as he threw the reins on the horse's neck he said with a slight shiver of repugnance: "We won't stay long."

Against the restless alders turning their white lining to the storm the house looked singularly desolate. The paint was almost gone from the clapboards, the windowpanes were broken and patched with rags, and the garden was a poisonous tangle of nettles, burdocks, and tall swamp weeds over which big bluebottles hummed.

At the sound of wheels a child with towhead and pale eyes like Liff Hyatt's peered over the fence and then slipped away behind an outhouse. Harney jumped down and helped Charity out; and as he did so the rain broke on them. It came slantwise, on a furious gale, laying shrubs and young trees flat, tearing off their leaves like an autumn storm, turning the road into a river, and making hissing pools of every hollow. Thunder rolled incessantly through the roar of the rain, and a strange glitter of light ran along the ground under the increasing blackness.

"Lucky we're here after all," Harney laughed. He fastened the horse under a half-roofless shed, and wrapping Charity in his coat ran with her to the house. The boy had not reappeared, and as there was no response to their knocks Harney turned the door handle and they went in.

There were three people in the kitchen to which the door admitted them. An old woman with a handkerchief over her head was sitting by the window. She held a sickly-looking kitten on her knees, and whenever it jumped down and tried to limp away she stooped and lifted it back without any change of her aged, unnoticing face. Another woman, the unkempt creature that Charity had once noticed in driving by, stood leaning against the window frame and stared at them; and near the stove an unshaved man in a tattered shirt sat on a barrel asleep.

The place was bare and miserable and the air heavy with the smell of dirt and stale tobacco. Charity's heart sank. Old derided tales of the Mountain people came back to her, and the woman's stare was so disconcerting, and the face of the sleeping man so sodden and bestial, that her disgust was tinged with a vague dread. She was not afraid for herself; she knew the Hyatts would not be likely to trouble her; but she was not sure how they would treat a "city fellow."

Lucius Harney would certainly have laughed at her fears. He glanced about the room, uttered a general "How are you?" to which no one responded, and then asked the younger woman if they might take shelter till the storm was over.

She turned her eyes away from him and looked at Charity. "You're the girl from Royall's, ain't you?"

The color rose in Charity's face. "I'm Charity Royall," she said, as if asserting her right to the name in the very place where it might have been most open to question.

The woman did not seem to notice. "You kin stay," she merely said; then she turned away and stooped over a dish in which she was stirring something.

Harney and Charity sat down on a bench made of a board resting on two starch boxes. They faced a door hanging on a broken hinge, and through the crack they saw the eyes of the towheaded boy and of a pale little girl with a scar across her cheek. Charity smiled, and signed to the children to come in; but as soon as they saw they were discovered they slipped away on bare feet. It occurred to her that they were afraid of rousing the sleeping man; and probably the woman shared their fear, for she moved about as noiselessly and avoided going near the stove.

The rain continued to beat against the house, and in one or two places it sent a stream through the patched panes and ran into pools on the floor. Every now and then the kitten mewed and struggled down, and the old woman stooped and caught it, holding it tight in her bony hands; and once or twice the man on the barrel half woke, changed his position and dozed again, his head falling forward on his hairy breast. As the minutes passed, and the rain still streamed against the windows, a loathing of the place and the people came over Charity. The sight of the weak-minded old woman, of the cowed children, and the ragged man sleeping off his liquor, made the setting of her own life seem a vision of peace and plenty. She thought of the kitchen at Mr. Royall's, with its scrubbed floor and dresser full of china, and the peculiar smell of yeast and coffee and soft soap that she had always hated, but that now seemed the very symbol of household order. She saw Mr. Royall's room, with the high-backed horsehair chair, the faded rag carpet, the row of books on a shelf, the engraving of *The Surrender of Burgoyne* over the stove, and the mat with a brown and white spaniel in a moss-green border. And then her mind traveled to Miss Hatchard's house, where all was freshness, purity, and fragrance, and compared to which the red house had always seemed so poor and plain.

"This is where I belong—this is where I belong," she kept repeating to herself, but the words had no meaning for her. Every instinct and habit made her a stranger among these poor swamp people living like vermin in their lair. With all her soul she wished she had not yielded to Harney's curiosity, and brought him there.

The rain had drenched her, and she began to shiver under the thin folds of her dress. The younger woman must have noticed it, for she went out of the room and came back with a broken teacup which she offered to Charity. It was half full of whiskey, and Charity shook her head; but Harney took the cup and put his lips to it. When he had set it down Charity saw him feel in his pocket and draw out a dollar; he hesitated a moment, and then put it back, and she guessed that he did not wish her to see him offering money to people she had spoken of as being her kin.

The sleeping man stirred, lifted his head and opened his eyes. They rested vacantly for a moment on Charity and Harney, and then closed again, and his head drooped; but a look of anxiety came into the woman's face. She glanced out of the window and then came up to Harney. "I guess you better go along now," she said. The young man understood and got to his feet. "Thank you," he said, holding out his hand. She seemed not to notice the gesture, and turned away as they opened the door.

The rain was still coming down, but they hardly noticed it: the pure air was like balm in their faces. The clouds were rising and breaking, and between their edges the light streamed down from remote blue hollows. Harney untied the horse, and they drove off through the diminishing rain, which was already beaded with sunlight.

For a while Charity was silent, and her companion did not speak. She looked timidly at his profile: it was graver than usual, as though he too were oppressed by what they had seen. Then she broke out abruptly: "Those people back there are the kind of folks I come from. They may be my relations, for all I know." She did not want him to think that she regretted having told him her story.

"Poor creatures," he rejoined. "I wonder why they came down to that feverhole."

She laughed ironically. "To better themselves! It's worse up on the Mountain. Bash Hyatt married the daughter of the farmer that used to own the brown house. That was him by the stove, I suppose."

Harney seemed to find nothing to say and she went on: "I saw you take out a dollar to give to that poor woman. Why did you put it back?"

He reddened, and leaned forward to flick a swamp fly from the horse's neck. "I wasn't sure—"

"Was it because you knew they were my folks, and thought I'd be ashamed to see you give them money?"

He turned to her with eyes full of reproach. "Oh, Charity—" It was the first time he had ever called her by her name. Her misery welled over.

"I ain't—I ain't ashamed. They're my people, and I ain't ashamed of them," she sobbed.

"My dear . . ." he murmured, putting his arm about her, and she leaned against him and wept out her pain.

It was too late to go around to Hamblin, and all the stars were out in a clear sky when they reached the North Dormer valley and drove up to the red house.

# 7

**S**INCE HER reinstatement in Miss Hatchard's favor Charity had not dared to curtail by a moment her hours of attendance at the library. She even made a point of arriving before the time, and showed a laudable indignation when the youngest Targatt girl, who had been engaged to help in the cleaning and re-arranging of the books, came trailing in late and neglected her task to peer through the window at the Sollas boy. Nevertheless, "library days" seemed more than ever irksome to Charity after her vivid hours of liberty; and she would have found it hard to set a good example to her subordinate if Lucius Harney had not been commissioned, before Miss Hatchard's departure, to ex-amine with the local carpenter the best means of ventilating the "Memorial."

He was careful to prosecute this inquiry on the days when the library was open to the public, and Charity was therefore sure of spending part of the afternoon in his company. The Targatt girl's presence, and the risk of being interrupted by some passerby suddenly smitten with a thirst for letters, restricted their inter-course to the exchange of commonplaces; but there was a fascina-tion to Charity in the contrast between these public civilities and their secret intimacy.

The day after their drive to the brown house was "library day," and she sat at her desk working at the revised catalogue, while the Targatt girl, one eye on the window, chanted out the titles of a pile of books. Charity's thoughts were far away, in the dismal house by the swamp, and under the twilight sky during the long drive home, when Lucius Harney had consoled her with endear-ing words. That day, for the first time since he had been boarding with them, he had failed to appear as usual at the midday meal. No message had come to explain his absence, and Mr. Royall, who was more than usually taciturn, had betrayed no surprise, and made no comment. In itself this indifference was not particularly significant, for Mr. Royall, in common with most of his fellow citizens, had a way of accepting events passively, as if he had long since come to the conclusion that no one who lived in North Dormer could hope to modify them. But to Charity, in the reaction from her mood of passionate exaltation, there was something disquieting in his silence. It was almost as if Lucius Harney had never had a part in their lives: Mr. Royall's imperturbable indifference seemed to relegate him to the domain of unreality.

As she sat at work, she tried to shake off her disappointment at Harney's nonappearing. Some trifling incident had probably kept him from joining them at midday; but she was sure he must be eager to see her again, and that he would not want to wait till they met at supper, between Mr. Royall and Verena. She was wondering what his first words would be, and trying to devise a way of getting rid of the Targatt girl before he came, when she heard steps outside, and he walked up the path with Mr. Miles.

The clergyman from Hepburn seldom came to North Dormer except when he drove over to officiate at the old white church which, by an unusual chance, happened to belong to the Episcopal communion. He was a brisk affable man, eager to make the most of the fact that a little nucleus of church-people had survived in the sectarian wilderness, and resolved to undermine the influence of the gingerbread-colored Baptist chapel at the other end of the village; but he was kept busy by parochial work at Hepburn, where there were papermills and saloons, and it was not often that he could spare time for North Dormer.

Charity, who went to the white church (like all the best people in North Dormer), admired Mr. Miles, and had even, during the memorable trip to Nettleton, imagined herself married to a man who had such a straight nose and such a beautiful way of speaking, and who lived in a brownstone rectory covered with Virginia creeper. It had been a shock to discover that the privilege was already enjoyed by a lady with crimped hair and a large baby; but the arrival of Lucius Harney had long since banished Mr. Miles from Charity's dreams, and as he walked up the path at Harney's side she saw him as he really was: a fat middle-aged man with a baldness showing under his clerical hat, and spectacles on his Grecian nose. She wondered what had called him to North Dor-

mer on a weekday, and felt a little hurt that Harney should have
brought him to the library.

It presently appeared that his presence there was due to Miss
Hatchard. He had been spending a few days at Springfield, to fill
a friend's pulpit, and had been consulted by Miss Hatchard as to
young Harney's plan for ventilating the "Memorial." To lay
hands on the Hatchard ark was a grave matter, and Miss Hatchard, always full of scruples, and of scruples about her scruples (it
was Harney's phrase), wished to have Mr. Miles's opinion before
deciding.

"I couldn't," Mr. Miles explained, "quite make out from your
cousin what changes you wanted to make, and as the other trust-
ees did not understand either I thought I had better drive over
and take a look—though I'm sure," he added, turning his
friendly spectacles on the young man, "that no one could be more
competent—but of course this spot has its peculiar sanctity!"

"I hope a little fresh air won't desecrate it," Harney laughingly
rejoined, and they walked to the other end of the library while he
set forth his idea to the Rector.

Mr. Miles had greeted the two girls with his usual friendliness,
but Charity saw that he was occupied with other things, and she
presently became aware, by the scraps of conversation drifting
over to her, that he was still under the charm of his visit to
Springfield, which appeared to have been full of agreeable incidents.

"Ah, the Coopersons . . . yes, you know them, of course," she
heard. "That's a fine old house! And Ned Cooperson has collected some really remarkable impressionist pictures. . . ." The
names he cited were unknown to Charity. "Yes, yes, the Schaefer
quartette played at Lyric Hall on Saturday evening; and on Monday I had the privilege of hearing them again at the Towers.
Beautifully done . . . Bach and Beethoven . . . a lawn party
first . . . I saw Miss Balch several times, by the way . . . looking
extremely handsome. . . ."

Charity dropped her pencil and forgot to listen to the Targatt
girl's singsong. Why had Mr. Miles suddenly brought up Annabel
Balch's name?

"Oh, really?" she heard Harney rejoin; and, raising his stick,
he pursued: "You see, my plan is to move these shelves away, and

open a round window in this wall, on the axis of the one under the pediment."

"I suppose she'll be coming up here later to stay with Miss Hatchard?" Mr. Miles went on, following on his train of thought; then, spinning about and tilting his head back: "Yes, yes, I see—I understand: that will give a draft without materially altering the look of things. I can see no objection."

The discussion went on for some minutes, and gradually the two men moved back toward the desk. Mr. Miles stopped again and looked thoughtfully at Charity. "Aren't you a little pale, my dear? Not overworking? Mr. Harney tells me you and Mamie are giving the library a thorough overhauling." He was always careful to remember his parishioners' Christian names, and at the right moment he bent his benignant spectacles on the Targatt girl.

Then he turned to Charity. "Don't take things hard, my dear; don't take things hard. Come down and see Mrs. Miles and me some day at Hepburn," he said, pressing her hand and waving a farewell to Mamie Targatt. He went out of the library, and Harney followed him.

Charity thought she detected a look of constraint in Harney's eyes. She fancied he did not want to be alone with her; and with a sudden pang she wondered if he repented the tender things he had said to her the night before. His words had been more fraternal than loverlike; but she had lost their exact sense in the caressing warmth of his voice. He had made her feel that the fact of her being a waif from the Mountain was only another reason for holding her close and soothing her with consolatory murmurs; and when the drive was over, and she got out of the buggy, tired, cold, and aching with emotion, she stepped as if the ground were a sunlit wave and she the spray on its crest.

Why, then, had his manner suddenly changed, and why did he leave the library with Mr. Miles? Her restless imagination fastened on the name of Annabel Balch: from the moment it had been mentioned she fancied that Harney's expression had altered. Annabel Balch at a garden party at Springfield, looking "extremely handsome" . . . perhaps Mr. Miles had seen her there at the very moment when Charity and Harney were sitting in the Hyatts' hovel, between a drunkard and a half-witted old woman! Charity did not know exactly what a garden party was, but her glimpse of the flower-edged lawns of Nettleton helped her to visualize the scene, and envious recollections of the "old things" which Miss Balch avowedly "wore out" when she came to North Dormer made it only too easy to picture her in her splendor. Charity understood what associations the name must have called up, and felt the uselessness of struggling against the unseen influences in Harney's life.

When she came down from her room for supper he was not there; and while she waited in the porch she recalled the tone in which Mr. Royall had commented the day before on their early start. Mr. Royall sat at her side, his chair tilted back, his broad black boots with side elastics resting against the lower bar of the railings. His rumpled gray hair stood up above his forehead like the crest of an angry bird, and the leather-brown of his veined cheeks was blotched with red. Charity knew that those red spots were the signs of a coming explosion.

Suddenly he said: "Where's supper? Has Verena Marsh slipped up again on her soda biscuits?"

Charity threw a startled glance at him. "I presume she's waiting for Mr. Harney."

"Mr. Harney, is she? She'd better dish up, then. He ain't coming." He stood up, walked to the door, and called out, in the pitch necessary to penetrate the old woman's tympanum: "Get along with the supper, Verena."

Charity was trembling with apprehension. Something had happened—she was sure of it now—and Mr. Royall knew what it was. But not for the world would she have gratified him by showing her anxiety. She took her usual place, and he seated himself opposite, and poured out a strong cup of tea before passing her the teapot. Verena brought some scrambled eggs, and he piled his plate with them. "Ain't you going to take any?" he asked. Charity roused herself and began to eat.

The tone with which Mr. Royall had said "He's not coming" seemed to her full of an ominous satisfaction. She saw that he had suddenly begun to hate Lucius Harney, and guessed herself to be the cause of this change of feeling. But she had no means of finding out whether some act of hostility on his part had made the young man stay away, or whether he simply wished to avoid seeing her again after their drive back from the brown house. She ate her supper with a studied show of indifference, but she knew that Mr. Royall was watching her and that her agitation did not escape him.

After supper she went up to her room. She heard Mr. Royall cross the passage, and presently the sounds below her window showed that he had returned to the porch. She seated herself on her bed and began to struggle against the desire to go down and ask him what had happened. "I'd rather die than do it," she muttered to herself. With a word he could have relieved her uncertainty; but never would she gratify him by saying it.

She rose and leaned out of the window. The twilight had deepened into night, and she watched the frail curve of the young moon dropping to the edge of the hills. Through the darkness she saw one or two figures moving down the road; but the evening was too cold for loitering, and presently the strollers disappeared. Lamps were beginning to show here and there in the windows. A bar of light brought out the whiteness of a clump of lilies in the Hawes's yard: and farther down the street Carrick Fry's Rochester lamp cast its bold illumination on the rustic flower tub in the middle of his grass plot.

For a long time she continued to lean in the window. But a fever of unrest consumed her, and finally she went downstairs, took her hat from its hook, and swung out of the house. Mr. Royall sat in the porch, Verena beside him, her old hands crossed on her patched skirt. As Charity went down the steps Mr. Royall called after her: "Where you going?" She could easily have answered: "To Orma's," or "Down to the Targatts'," and either answer might have been true, for she had no purpose. But she swept on in silence, determined not to recognize his right to question her.

At the gate she paused and looked up and down the road. The darkness drew her, and she thought of climbing the hill and plunging into the depths of the larch wood above the pasture. Then she glanced irresolutely along the street, and as she did so a gleam appeared through the spruces at Miss Hatchard's gate. Lucius Harney was there, then—he had not gone down to Hepburn with Mr. Miles, as she had at first imagined. But where had he taken his evening meal, and what had caused him to stay away from Mr. Royall's? The light was positive proof of his presence,

for Miss Hatchard's servants were away on a holiday, and her
farmer's wife came only in the mornings, to make the young
man's bed and prepare his coffee. Beside that lamp he was doubtless sitting at this moment. To know the truth Charity had only to
walk half the length of the village, and knock at the lighted window. She hesitated a minute or two longer, and then turned
toward Miss Hatchard's.

She walked quickly, straining her eyes to detect anyone who
might be coming along the street; and before reaching the Frys'
she crossed over to avoid the light from their window. Whenever
she was unhappy she felt herself at bay against a pitiless world,
and a kind of animal secretiveness possessed her. But the street
was empty, and she passed unnoticed through the gate and up
the path to the house. Its white front glimmered indistinctly
through the trees, showing only one oblong of light on the lower
floor. She had supposed that the lamp was in Miss Hatchard's
sitting room; but she now saw that it shone through a window at
the farther corner of the house. She did not know the room to
which this window belonged, and she paused under the trees,
checked by a sense of strangeness. Then she moved on, treading
softly on the short grass, and keeping so close to the house that
whoever was in the room, even if roused by her approach, would
not be able to see her.

The window opened on a narrow verandah with a trellised
arch. She leaned close to the trellis, and parting the sprays of
clematis that covered it looked into a corner of the room. She saw
the foot of a mahogany bed, an engraving on the wall, a washstand on which a towel had been tossed, and one end of the
green-covered table which held the lamp. Half of the lampshade
projected into her field of vision, and just under it two smooth
sunburned hands, one holding a pencil and the other a ruler,
were moving to and fro over a drawing board.

Her heart jumped and then stood still. He was there, a few feet
away; and while her soul was tossing on seas of woe he had been
quietly sitting at his drawing board. The sight of those two hands,
moving with their usual skill and precision, woke her out of her
dream. Her eyes were opened to the disproportion between what
she had felt and the cause of her agitation; and she was turning

away from the window when one hand abruptly pushed aside the drawing board and the other flung down the pencil.

Charity had often noticed Harney's loving care of his drawings, and the neatness and method with which he carried on and concluded each task. The impatient sweeping aside of the drawing board seemed to reveal a new mood. The gesture suggested sudden discouragement, or distaste for his work, and she wondered if he too were agitated by secret perplexities. Her impulse of flight was checked; she stepped up on the verandah and looked into the room.

Harney had put his elbows on the table and was resting his chin on his locked hands. He had taken off his coat and waistcoat, and unbuttoned the low collar of his flannel shirt; she saw the vigorous lines of his young throat, and the root of the muscles where they joined the chest. He sat staring straight ahead of him, a look of weariness and self-disgust on his face: it was almost as if he had been gazing at a distorted reflection of his own features. For a moment Charity looked at him with a kind of terror, as if he had been a stranger under familiar lineaments; then she glanced past him and saw on the floor an open portmanteau half full of clothes. She understood that he was preparing to leave, and that he had probably decided to go without seeing her. She saw that the decision, from whatever cause it was taken, had disturbed him deeply; and she immediately concluded that his change of plan was due to some surreptitious interference of Mr. Royall's. All her old resentments and rebellions flamed up, confusedly mingled with the yearning roused by Harney's nearness. Only a few hours earlier she had felt secure in his comprehending pity; now she was flung back on herself, doubly alone after that moment of communion.

Harney was still unaware of her presence. He sat without moving, moodily staring before him at the same spot in the wallpaper. He had not even had the energy to finish his packing, and his clothes and papers lay on the floor about the portmanteau. Presently he unlocked his clasped hands and stood up; and Charity, drawing back hastily, sank down on the step of the verandah. The night was so dark that there was not much chance of his seeing her unless he opened the window, and before that she would have time to slip away and be lost in the shadow of the trees. He stood for a minute or two looking around the room with the same expression of self-disgust, as if he hated himself and everything about him; then he sat down again at the table, drew a few more strokes, and threw his pencil aside. Finally he walked across the floor, kicking the portmanteau out of his way, and lay down on the bed, folding his arms under his head, and staring up morosely at the ceiling. Just so, Charity had seen him at her side, on the grass or the pine needles, his eyes fixed on the sky, and pleasure flashing over his face like the flickers of sun the branches shed on it. But now the face was so changed that she hardly knew it; and grief at his grief gathered in her throat, rose to her eyes and ran over.

She continued to crouch on the steps, holding her breath and stiffening herself into complete immobility. One motion of her hand, one tap on the pane, and she could picture the sudden change in his face. In every pulse of her rigid body she was aware of the welcome his eyes and lips would give her; but something kept her from moving. It was not the fear of any sanction, human or heavenly; she had never in her life been afraid. It was simply that she had suddenly understood what would happen if she went in. It was the thing that *did* happen between young men and girls, and that North Dormer ignored in public and snickered over on the sly. It was what Miss Hatchard was still ignorant of, but every girl of Charity's class knew about before she left school. It was what had happened to Ally Hawes's sister Julia, and had ended in her going to Nettleton, and in people's never mentioning her name.

It did not, of course, always end so sensationally; nor, perhaps, on the whole, so untragically. Charity had always suspected that the shunned Julia's fate might have its compensations. There were other worse endings that the village knew of, mean, miserable, unconfessed; other lives that went on drearily, without visible change, in the same cramped setting of hypocrisy. But these were not the reasons that held her back. Since the day before, she had known exactly what she would feel if Harney should take her in his arms: the melting of palm into palm and mouth on mouth, and the long flame burning her from head to foot. But mixed with this feeling was another: the wondering pride in his liking for her, the startled softness that his sympathy had put into her heart. Sometimes, when her youth flushed up in her, she had imagined yielding like other girls to furtive caresses in the twilight; but she could not so cheapen herself to Harney. She did not know why he was going; but since he was going she felt she must do nothing to deface the image of her that he carried away. If he wanted her he must seek her: he must not be surprised into taking her as girls like Julia Hawes were taken. . . .

No sound came from the sleeping village, and in the deep darkness of the garden she heard now and then a secret rustle of branches, as though some night bird brushed them. Once a footfall passed the gate, and she shrank back into her corner, but the steps died away and left a profounder quiet. Her eyes were still on Harney's tormented face: she felt she could not move till he moved. But she was beginning to grow numb from her constrained position, and at times her thoughts were so indistinct that she seemed to be held there only by a vague weight of weariness.

A long time passed in this strange vigil. Harney still lay on the bed, motionless and with fixed eyes, as though following his vision to its bitter end. At last he stirred and changed his attitude slightly, and Charity's heart began to tremble. But he only flung out his arms and sank back into his former position. With a deep sigh he tossed the hair from his forehead; then his whole body relaxed, his head turned sideways on the pillow, and she saw that he had fallen asleep. The sweet expression came back to his lips, and the haggardness faded from his face, leaving it as fresh as a boy's.

She rose and crept away.

# 8

She had lost the sense of time, and did not know how late it was till she came out into the street and saw that all the windows were dark between Miss Hatchard's and the Royall house.

As she passed from under the black pall of the Norway spruces she fancied she saw two figures in the shade about the duckpond. She drew back and watched; but nothing moved, and she had stared so long into the lamplit room that the darkness confused her, and she thought she must have been mistaken.

She walked on, wondering whether Mr. Royall was still in the porch. In her exalted mood she did not greatly care whether he was waiting for her or not: she seemed to be floating high over life, on a great cloud of misery beneath which everyday realities had dwindled to mere specks in space. But the porch was empty, Mr. Royall's hat hung on its peg in the passage, and the kitchen lamp had been left to light her to bed. She took it and went up.

The morning hours of the next day dragged by without incident. Charity had imagined that, in some way or other, she would learn whether Harney had already left; but Verena's deafness prevented her being a source of news, and no one came to the house who could bring enlightenment.

Mr. Royall went out early, and did not return till Verena had set the table for the midday meal. When he came in he went straight to the kitchen and shouted to the old woman: "Ready for dinner—" then he turned into the dining room, where Charity was already seated. Harney's plate was in its usual place, but Mr. Royall offered no explanation of his absence, and Charity asked none. The feverish exaltation of the night before had dropped, and she said to herself that he had gone away, indifferently, almost callously, and that now her life would lapse again into the narrow rut out of which he had lifted it. For a moment she was inclined to sneer at herself for not having used the arts that might have kept him.

She sat at table till the meal was over, lest Mr. Royall should
remark on her leaving, but when he stood up she rose also, without waiting to help Verena. She had her foot on the stairs when
he called to her to come back.

"I've got a headache. I'm going up to lie down."

"I want you should come in here first; I've got something to
say to you."

She was sure from his tone that in a moment she would learn
what every nerve in her ached to know, but as she turned back
she made a last effort of indifference.

Mr. Royall stood in the middle of the office, his thick eyebrows
beetling, his lower jaw trembling a little. At first she thought he
had been drinking; then she saw that he was sober, but stirred by
a deep and stern emotion totally unlike his usual transient angers.
And suddenly she understood that, until then, she had never
really noticed him or thought about him. Except on the occasion
of his one offense he had been to her merely the person who is
always there, the unquestioned central fact of life, as inevitable
but as uninteresting as North Dormer itself, or any of the other
conditions fate had laid on her. Even then she had regarded him
only in relation to herself, and had never speculated as to his own
feelings, beyond instinctively concluding that he would not trouble her again in the same way. But now she began to wonder what
he was really like.

He had grasped the back of his chair with both hands, and
stood looking hard at her. At length he said: "Charity, for once
let's you and me talk together like friends."

Instantly she felt that something had happened, and that he
held her in his hand.

"Where is Mr. Harney? Why hasn't he come back? Have you
sent him away?" she broke out, without knowing what she was
saying.

The change in Mr. Royall frightened her. All the blood seemed
to leave his veins and against his swarthy pallor the deep lines in
his face looked black.

"Didn't he have time to answer some of those questions last
night? You was with him long enough!" he said.

Charity stood speechless. The taunt was so unrelated to what had been happening in her soul that she hardly understood it. But the instinct of self-defense awoke in her.

"Who says I was with him last night?"

"The whole place is saying it by now."

"Then it was you that put the lie into their mouths. Oh, how I've always hated you!" she cried.

She had expected a retort in kind, and it startled her to hear her exclamation sounding on through silence.

"Yes, I know," Mr. Royall said slowly. "But that ain't going to help us much now."

"It helps me not to care a straw what lies you tell about me!"

"If they're lies, they're not my lies: my Bible oath on that, Charity. I didn't know where you were: I wasn't out of this house last night."

She made no answer and he went on: "Is it a lie that you were seen coming out of Miss Hatchard's nigh onto midnight?"

She straightened herself with a laugh, all her reckless insolence recovered. "I didn't look to see what time it was."

"You lost girl . . . you . . . you . . . Oh, my God, why did you tell me?" he broke out, dropping into his chair, his head bowed down like an old man's.

Charity's self-possession had returned with the sense of her danger. "Do you suppose I'd take the trouble to lie to *you*? Who are you, anyhow, to ask me where I go to when I go out at night?"

Mr. Royall lifted his head and looked at her. His face had grown quiet and almost gentle, as she remembered seeing it sometimes when she was a little girl, before Mrs. Royall died.

"Don't let's go on like this, Charity. It can't do any good to either of us. You were seen going into that fellow's house . . . you were seen coming out of it. . . . I've watched this thing coming, and I've tried to stop it. As God sees me, I have. . . ."

"Ah, it *was* you, then? I knew it was you that sent him away!"

He looked at her in surprise. "Didn't he tell you so? I thought he understood." He spoke slowly, with difficult pauses. "I didn't name you to him: I'd have cut my hand off sooner. I just told him I couldn't spare the horse any longer; and that the cooking was getting too heavy for Verena. I guess he's the kind that's heard the same thing before. Anyhow, he took it quietly enough. He said his job here was about done, anyhow; and there didn't another word pass between us. . . . If he told you otherwise he told you an untruth."

Charity listened in a cold trance of anger. It was nothing to her what the village said . . . but all this fingering of her dreams!

"I've told you he didn't tell me anything. I didn't speak with him last night."

"You didn't speak with him?"

"No. . . . It's not that I care what any of you say . . . but you may as well know. Things ain't between us the way you think . . . and the other people in this place. He was kind to me; he was my friend; and all of a sudden he stopped coming, and I knew it was you that done it—*you!*" All her unreconciled memory of the past flamed out at him. "So I went there last night to find out what you'd said to him: that's all."

Mr. Royall drew a heavy breath. "But, then—if he wasn't there, what were you doing there all that time?—Charity, for pity's sake, tell me. I've got to know, to stop their talking."

This pathetic abdication of all authority over her did not move her: she could feel only the outrage of his interference.

"Can't you see that I don't care what anybody says? It's true I went there to see him; and he was in his room, and I stood outside for ever so long and watched him; but I dursn't go in for fear he'd think I'd come after him. . . ." She felt her voice breaking, and gathered it up in a last defiance. "As long as I live I'll never forgive you!" she cried.

Mr. Royall made no answer. He sat and pondered with sunken head, his veined hands clasped about the arms of his chair. Age seemed to have come down on him as winter comes on the hills after a storm. At length he looked up.

"Charity, you say you don't care; but you're the proudest girl I know, and the last to want people to talk against you. You know there's always eyes watching you: you're handsomer and smarter than the rest, and that's enough. But till lately you've never given them a chance. Now they've got it, and they're going to use it. I believe what you say, but they won't. . . . It was Mrs. Tom Fry seen you going in . . . and two or three of them watched for you to come out again. . . . You've been with the fellow all day long every day since he come here . . . and I'm a lawyer, and I know how hard slander dies." He paused, but she stood motionless, without giving him any sign of acquiescence or even of attention. "He's a pleasant fellow to talk to—I liked having him here myself. The young men up here ain't had his chances. But there's one thing as old as the hills and as plain as daylight: if he'd wanted you the right way he'd have said so."

Charity did not speak. It seemed to her that nothing could exceed the bitterness of hearing such words from such lips.

Mr. Royall rose from his seat. "See here, Charity Royall: I had a shameful thought once, and you've made me pay for it. Isn't that score pretty near wiped out? . . . There's a streak in me I ain't always master of; but I've always acted straight to you but that once. And you've known I would—you've trusted me. For all your sneers and your mockery you've always known I loved you the way a man loves a decent woman. I'm a good many years older than you, but I'm head and shoulders above this place and everybody in it, and you know that too. I slipped up once, but that's no reason for not starting again. If you'll come with me I'll do it. If you'll marry me we'll leave here and settle in some big town, where there's men, and business, and things doing. It's not too late for me to find an opening. . . . I can see it by the way folks treat me when I go down to Hepburn or Nettleton. . . ."

Charity made no movement. Nothing in his appeal reached her heart, and she thought only of words to wound and wither. But a growing lassitude restrained her. What did anything matter that he was saying? She saw the old life closing in on her, and hardly heeded his fanciful picture of renewal.

"Charity—Charity—say you'll do it," she heard him urge, all his lost years and wasted passion in his voice.

"Oh, what's the use of all this? When I leave here it won't be with you."

She moved toward the door as she spoke, and he stood up and placed himself between her and the threshold. He seemed suddenly tall and strong, as though the extremity of his humiliation had given him new vigor.

"That's all, is it? It's not much." He leaned against the door, so towering and powerful that he seemed to fill the narrow room. "Well, then—look here. . . . You're right: I've no claim on you— why should you look at a broken man like me? You want the other fellow . . . and I don't blame you. You picked out the best when you seen it . . . well, that was always my way." He fixed his stern eyes on her, and she had the sense that the struggle within him was at its highest. "Do you want him to marry you?" he asked.

They stood and looked at each other for a long moment, eye to eye, with the terrible equality of courage that sometimes made her feel as if she had his blood in her veins.

"Do you want him to—say? I'll have him here in an hour if you do. I ain't been in the law thirty years for nothing. He's hired Carrick Fry's team to take him to Hepburn, but he ain't going to start for another hour. And I can put things to him so he won't be long deciding. . . . He's soft: I could see that. I don't say you won't be sorry afterward—but, by God, I'll give you the chance to be, if you say so."

She heard him out in silence, too remote from all he was feeling and saying for any sally of scorn to relieve her. As she listened, there flitted through her mind the vision of Liff Hyatt's muddy boot coming down on the white bramble flowers. The same thing had happened now; something transient and exquisite had flowered in her, and she had stood by and seen it trampled to earth. While the thought passed through her she was aware of Mr. Royall, still leaning against the door, but crestfallen, diminished, as though her silence were the answer he most dreaded.

"I don't want any chance you can give me: I'm glad he's going away," she said.

He kept his place a moment longer, his hand on the doorknob. "Charity!" he pleaded. She made no answer, and he turned the knob and went out. She heard him fumble with the latch of the front door, and saw him walk down the steps. He passed out of the gate, and his figure, stooping and heavy, receded slowly up the street.

For a while she remained where he had left her. She was still trembling with the humiliation of his last words, which rang so loud in her ears that it seemed as though they must echo through the village, proclaiming her a creature to lend herself to such vile suggestions. Her shame weighed on her like a physical oppression: the roof and walls seemed to be closing in on her, and she was seized by the impulse to get away, under the open sky, where there would be room to breathe. She went to the front door, and as she did so Lucius Harney opened it.

He looked graver and less confident than usual, and for a moment or two neither of them spoke. Then he held out his hand. "Are you going out?" he asked. "May I come in?"

Her heart was beating so violently that she was afraid to speak, and stood looking at him with tear-dilated eyes; then she became aware of what her silence must betray, and said quickly: "Yes, come in."

She led the way into the dining room, and they sat down on opposite sides of the table, the cruet stand and japanned bread basket between them. Harney had laid his straw hat on the table, and as he sat there, in his easy-looking summer clothes, a brown tie knotted under his flannel collar, and his smooth brown hair brushed back from his forehead, she pictured him as she had seen him the night before, lying on his bed, with the tossed locks falling into his eyes, and his bare throat rising out of his unbuttoned shirt. He had never seemed so remote as at the moment when that vision flashed through her mind.

"I'm so sorry it's good-bye: I suppose you know I'm leaving," he began, abruptly and awkwardly; she guessed that he was wondering how much she knew of his reasons for going.

"I presume you found your work was over quicker than what you expected," she said.

"Well, yes—that is, no: there are plenty of things I should have liked to do. But my holiday's limited; and now that Mr. Royall needs the horse for himself it's rather difficult to find means of getting about."

"There ain't any too many teams for hire around here," she acquiesced, and there was another silence.

"These days here have been—awfully pleasant: I wanted to thank you for making them so," he continued, his color rising.

She could not think of any reply, and he went on: "You've been wonderfully kind to me, and I wanted to tell you. . . . I wish I could think of you as happier, less lonely. . . . Things are sure to change for you by and by. . . ."

"Things don't change at North Dormer: people just get used to them."

The answer seemed to break up the order of his prearranged consolations, and he sat looking at her uncertainly. Then he said, with his sweet smile: "That's not true of you. It can't be."

The smile was like a knife thrust through her heart: everything in her began to tremble and break loose. She felt her tears run over, and stood up.

"Well, good-bye," she said.

She was aware of his taking her hand, and of feeling that his touch was lifeless.

"Good-bye." He turned away, and stopped on the threshold. "You'll say good-bye for me to Verena?"

She heard the closing of the outer door and the sound of his quick tread along the path. The latch of the gate clicked after him.

The next morning when she arose in the cold dawn and opened her shutters she saw a freckled boy standing on the other side of the road and looking up at her. He was a boy from a farm three or four miles down the Creston road, and she wondered what he was doing there at that hour, and why he looked so hard at her window. When he saw her he crossed over and leaned against the gate unconcernedly. There was no one stirring in the house, and she threw a shawl over her nightgown and ran down and let herself out. By the time she reached the gate the boy was sauntering down the road, whistling carelessly; but she saw that a letter had been thrust between the slats and the crossbar of the gate. She took it out and hastened back to her room.

The envelope bore her name, and inside was a leaf torn from a pocket diary.

DEAR CHARITY:

I can't go away like this. I am staying for a few days at Creston River. Will you come down and meet me at Creston pool? I will wait for you till evening.

# 9

CHARITY sat before the mirror trying on a hat which Ally Hawes, with much secrecy, had trimmed for her. It was of white straw, with a drooping brim and a cherry-colored lining that made her face glow like the inside of the shell on the parlor mantelpiece.

She propped the square of looking glass against Mr. Royall's black leather Bible, steadying it in front with a white stone on which a view of the Brooklyn Bridge was painted; and she sat before her reflection, bending the brim this way and that, while Ally Hawes's pale face looked over her shoulder like the ghost of wasted opportunities.

"I look awful, don't I?" she said at last with a happy sigh.

Ally smiled and took back the hat. "I'll stitch the roses on right here, so's you can put it away at once."

Charity laughed, and ran her fingers through her rough dark hair. She knew that Harney liked to see its reddish edges ruffled about her forehead and breaking into little rings at the nape. She sat down on her bed and watched Ally stoop over the hat with a careful frown.

"Don't you ever feel like going down to Nettleton for a day?" she asked.

Ally shook her head without looking up. "No, I always remember that awful time I went down with Julia—to that doctor's."

"Oh, Ally—"

"I can't help it. The house is on the corner of Wing Street and Lake Avenue. The trolley from the station goes right by it, and the day the minister took us down to see those pictures I recognized it right off, and couldn't seem to see anything else. There's a big black sign with gold letters all across the front—'Private Consultations.' She came as near as anything to dying. . . ."

"Poor Julia!" Charity sighed from the height of her purity and her security. She had a friend whom she trusted and who re-

spected her. She was going with him to spend the next day—the
Fourth of July—at Nettleton. Whose business was it but hers, and
what was the harm? The pity of it was that girls like Julia did not
know how to choose, and to keep bad fellows at a distance. . . .
Charity slipped down from the bed, and stretched out her hands.

"Is it sewed? Let me try it on again." She put the hat on, and
smiled at her image. The though of Julia had vanished. . . .

The next morning she was up before dawn, and saw the yellow
sunrise broaden behind the hills, and the silvery luster preceding
a hot day tremble across the sleeping fields.

Her plans had been made with great care. She had announced
that she was going down to the Band of Hope picnic at Hepburn,
and as no one else from North Dormer intended to venture so far
it was not likely that her absence from the festivity would be reported. Besides, if it were she would not greatly care. She was
determined to assert her independence, and if she stooped to fib
about the Hepburn picnic it was chiefly from the secretive instinct
that made her dread the profanation of her happiness. Whenever
she was with Lucius Harney she would have liked some impenetrable mountain mist to hide her.

It was arranged that she should walk to a point of the Creston
road where Harney was to pick her up and drive her across the
hills to Hepburn in time for the nine-thirty train to Nettleton.
Harney at first had been rather lukewarm about the trip. He
declared himself ready to take her to Nettleton, but urged her not
to go on the Fourth of July, on account of the crowds, the probable lateness of the trains, the difficulty of her getting back before
night; but her evident disappointment caused him to give way,
and even to affect a faint enthusiasm for the adventure. She understood why he was not more eager: he must have seen sights
beside which even a Fourth of July at Nettleton would seem tame.
But she had never seen anything; and a great longing possessed
her to walk the streets of a big town on a holiday, clinging to his
arm and jostled by idle crowds in their best clothes. The only
cloud on the prospect was the fact that the shops would be closed;
but she hoped he would take her back another day, when they
were open.

She started out unnoticed in the early sunlight, slipping

through the kitchen while Verena bent above the stove. To avoid attracting notice, she carried her new hat carefully wrapped up, and had thrown a long gray veil of Mrs. Royall's over the new white muslin dress which Ally's clever fingers had made for her. All of the ten dollars Mr. Royall had given her, and a part of her own savings as well, had been spent on renewing her wardrobe; and when Harney jumped out of the buggy to meet her she read her reward in his eyes.

The freckled boy who had brought her the note two weeks earlier was to wait with the buggy at Hepburn till their return. He perched at Charity's feet, his legs dangling between the wheels, and they could not say much because of his presence. But it did not greatly matter, for their past was now rich enough to have given them a private language; and with the long day stretching before them like the blue distance beyond the hills there was a delicate pleasure in postponement.

When Charity, in response to Harney's message, had gone to meet him at the Creston pool her heart had been so full of mortification and anger that his first words might easily have estranged her. But it happened that he had found the right word, which was one of simple friendship. His tone had instantly justified her, and put her guardian in the wrong. He had made no allusion to what had passed between Mr. Royall and himself, but had simply let it appear that he had left because means of conveyance were hard to find at North Dormer, and because Creston River was a more convenient center. He told her that he had hired by the week the buggy of the freckled boy's father, who served as livery-stable keeper to one or two melancholy summer boardinghouses on Creston Lake, and had discovered, within driving distance, a number of houses worthy of his pencil; and he said that he could not, while he was in the neighborhood, give up the pleasure of seeing her as often as posible.

When they took leave of each other she promised to continue to be his guide; and during the fortnight which followed they roamed the hills in happy comradeship. In most of the village friendships between youths and maidens lack of conversation was made up for by tentative fondling; but Harney, except when he had tried to comfort her in her trouble on their way back from the Hyatts', had never put his arm about her, or sought to betray her into any sudden caress. It seemed to be enough for him to breathe her nearness like a flower's; and since his pleasure at being with her, and his sense of her youth and her grace, perpetually shone in his eyes and softened the inflections of his voice, his reserve did not suggest coldness, but the deference due to a girl of his own class.

The buggy was drawn by an old trotter who whirled them along so briskly that the pace created a little breeze; but when they reached Hepburn the full heat of the airless morning descended on them. At the railway station the platform was packed with a sweltering throng, and they took refuge in the waiting room, where there was another throng, already dejected by the heat and the long waiting for retarded trains. Pale mothers were struggling with fretful babies, or trying to keep their older offspring from the fascination of the track; girls and their "fellows" were giggling and shoving, and passing about candy in sticky bags, and older men, collarless and perspiring, were shifting heavy children from one arm to the other, and keeping a haggard eye on the scattered members of their families.

At last the train rumbled in, and engulfed the waiting multitude. Harney swept Charity up onto the first car and they captured a bench for two, and sat in happy isolation while the train swayed and roared along through rich fields and languid tree clumps. The haze of the morning had become a sort of clear tremor over everything, like the colorless vibration about a flame; and the opulent landscape seemed to droop under it. But to Charity the heat was a stimulant: it enveloped the whole world in the same glow that burned at her heart. Now and then a lurch of the train flung her against Harney, and through her thin muslin she felt the touch of his sleeve. She steadied herself, their eyes met, and the flaming breath of the day seemed to enclose them.

The train roared into the Nettleton station, the descending mob caught them on its tide, and they were swept out into a vague dusty square thronged with seedy "hacks," and long curtained omnibuses drawn by horses with tasseled fly nets over their withers, who stood swinging their depressed heads drearily from side to side.

A mob of 'bus and hack drivers were shouting "To the Eagle House," "To the Washington House," "This way to the Lake,"

"Just starting for Greytop;" and through their yells came the popping of firecrackers, the explosion of torpedoes, the banging of toy guns, and the crash of a fireman's band trying to play the *Merry Widow* while they were being packed into a waggonette streaming with bunting.

The ramshackle wooden hotels about the square were all hung with flags and paper lanterns, and as Harney and Charity turned into the main street, with its brick and granite business blocks crowding out the old low-storied shops, and its towering poles strung with innumerable wires that seemed to tremble and buzz in the heat, they saw the double line of flags and lanterns tapering away gaily to the park at the other end of the perspective. The noise and color of this holiday vision seemed to transform Nettleton into a metropolis. Charity could not believe that Springfield or even Boston had anything grander to show, and she wondered if, at this very moment, Annabel Balch, on the arm of as brilliant a young man, were threading her way through scenes as resplendent.

"Where shall we go first?" Harney asked; but as she turned her happy eyes on him he guessed the answer and said: "We'll take a look round, shall we?"

The street swarmed with their fellow travelers, with other excursionists arriving from other directions, with Nettleton's own population, and with the millhands trooping in from the factories on the Creston. The shops were closed, but one would scarcely have noticed it, so numerous were the glass doors swinging open on saloons, on restaurants, on drugstores gushing from every sodawater tap, on fruit and confectionery shops stacked with strawberry cake, coconut drops, trays of glistening molasses candy, boxes of carmels and chewing gum, baskets of sodden strawberries, and dangling branches of bananas. Outside of some of the doors were trestles with banked-up oranges and apples, spotted pears and dusty raspberries; and the air reeked with the smell of fruit and stale coffee, beer and sarsaparilla and fried potatoes.

Even the shops that were closed offered, through wide expanses of plate glass, hints of hidden riches. In some, waves of silk and ribbon broke over shores of imitation moss from which ravishing hats rose like tropical orchids. In others, the pink throats of gramophones opened their giant convolutions in a soundless chorus; or bicycles shining in neat ranks seemed to await the signal of an invisible starter; or tiers of fancy goods in leatherette and paste and celluloid dangled their insidious graces; and, in one vast bay that seemed to project them into exciting contact with the public, wax ladies in daring dresses chatted elegantly, or, with gestures intimate yet blameless, pointed to their pink corsets and transparent hosiery.

Presently Harney found that his watch had stopped, and turned in at a small jeweler's shop which chanced to be still open. While the watch was being examined Charity leaned over the glass counter where, on a background of dark blue velvet, pins, rings, and brooches glittered like the moon and stars. She had never seen jewelery so near by, and she longed to lift the glass lid and plunge her hand among the shining treasures. But already Harney's watch was repaired, and he laid his hand on her arm and drew her from her dream.

"Which do you like best?" he asked, leaning over the counter at her side.

"I don't know. . . ." She pointed to a gold lily-of-the-valley with white flowers.

"Don't you think the blue pin's better?" he suggested, and immediately she saw that the lily of the valley was mere trumpery compared to the small round stone, blue as a mountain lake, with little sparks of light all round it. She colored at her want of discrimination.

"It's so lovely I guess I was afraid to look at it," she said.

He laughed, and they went out of the shop; but a few steps away he exclaimed: "Oh, by Jove, I forgot something," and turned back and left her in the crowd. She stood staring down a row of pink gramophone throats till he rejoined her and slipped his arm through hers.

"You mustn't be afraid of looking at the blue pin any longer, because it belongs to you," he said, and she felt a little box being pressed into her hand. Her heart gave a leap of joy, but it reached her lips only in a shy stammer. She remembered other girls whom she had heard planning to extract presents from their fellows, and was seized with a sudden dread lest Harney should have imagined that she had leaned over the pretty things in the glass case in the hope of having one given to her. . . .

A little farther down the street they turned in at a glass doorway opening on a shining hall with a mahogany staircase, and brass cages in its corners. "We must have something to eat," Harney said; and the next moment Charity found herself in a dressing room all looking glass and lustrous surfaces, where a party of showy-looking girls were dabbing on powder and straightening immense plumed hats. When they had gone she took courage to bathe her hot face in one of the marble basins, and to straighten her own hat brim, which the parasols of the crowd had indented. The dresses in the shops had so impressed her that she scarcely dared look at her reflection; but when she did so, the glow of her face under her cherry-colored hat, and the curve of her young shoulders through the transparent muslin, restored her courage; and when she had taken the blue brooch from its box and pinned it on her bosom she walked toward the restaurant with her head high, as if she had always strolled through tessellated halls beside young men in flannels.

Her spirit sank a little at the sight of the slim-waisted waitresses in black, with bewitching mobcaps on their haughty heads, who were moving disdainfully between the tables. "No f'r another hour," one of them dropped to Harney in passing, and he stood doubtfully glancing about him.

"Oh, well, we can't stay sweltering here," he decided; "let's try somewhere else—" and with a sense of relief Charity followed him from that scene of inhospitable splendor.

The "somewhere else" turned out—after more hot tramping, and several failures—to be, of all things, a little open-air place in a back street that called itself a French restaurant, and consisted in two or three rickety tables under a scarlet-runner, between a patch of zinnias and petunias and a big elm bending over from the next yard. Here they lunched on queerly flavored things, while Harney, leaning back in a crippled rocking chair, smoked cigarettes between the courses and poured into Charity's glass a pale yellow wine which he said was the very same one drank in just such jolly places in France.

Charity did not think the wine as good as sarsaparilla, but she sipped a mouthful for the pleasure of doing what he did, and of fancying herself alone with him in foreign countries. The illusion was increased by their being served by a deep-bosomed woman with smooth hair and a pleasant laugh, who talked to Harney in unintelligible words, and seemed amazed and overjoyed at his answering her in kind. At the other tables other people sat, mill-hands probably, homely but pleasant looking, who spoke the same shrill jargon, and looked at Harney and Charity with friendly eyes; and between the table legs a poodle with bald patches and pink eyes nosed about for scraps, and sat up on his hind legs absurdly.

Harney showed no inclination to move, for hot as their corner was, it was at least shaded and quiet; and, from the main thoroughfares came the clanging of trolleys, the incessant popping of torpedoes, the jingle of street organs, the bawling of megaphone men and the loud murmur of increasing crowds. He leaned back, smoking his cigar, patting the dog, and stirring the coffee that steamed in their chipped cups. "It's the real thing, you know," he explained; and Charity hastily revised her previous conception of the beverage.

They had made no plans for the rest of the day, and when Harney asked her what she wanted to do next she was too bewildered by rich possibilties to find an answer. Finally she confessed that she longed to go to the Lake, where she had not been taken on her former visit, and when he answered, "Oh, there's time for that—it will be pleasanter later," she suggested seeing some pictures like the ones Mr. Miles had taken her to. She thought Harney looked a little disconcerted; but he passed his fine handkerchief over his warm brow, said gaily, "Come along, then," and rose with a last pat for the pink-eyed dog.

Mr. Miles's pictures had been shown in an austere YMCA hall, with white walls and an organ; but Harney led Charity to a glittering place—everything she saw seemed to glitter—where they passed, between immense pictures of yellow-haired beauties stabbing villains in evening dress, into a velvet-curtained auditorium packed with spectators to the last limit of compression. After that, for a while, everything was merged in her brain in swimming circles of heat and blinding alternations of light and darkness. All the world has to show seemed to pass before her in a chaos of palms and minarets, charging cavalry regiments, roaring lions, comic policemen and scowling murderers; and the crowd around her, the hundreds of hot sallow candy-munching faces, young, old, middle-aged, but all kindled with the same contagious excitement, became part of the spectacle, and danced on the screen with the rest.

Presently the thought of the cool trolley run to the Lake grew irresistible, and they struggled out of the theater. As they stood on the pavement, Harney pale with the heat, and even Charity a little confused by it, a young man drove by in an electric runabout with a calico band bearing the words: "Ten dollars to take you round the Lake." Before Charity knew what was happening, Harney had waved a hand, and they were climbing in. "Say, for twenny-five I'll run·you out first to see the ball game and back," the driver proposed with an insinuating grin; but Charity said quickly: "Oh, I'd rather go rowing on the Lake." The street was so thronged that progress was slow; but the glory of sitting in the little carriage while it wriggled its way between laden omnibuses and trolleys made the moments seem too short. "Next turn is Lake Avenue," the young man called out over his shoulder; and as they paused in the wake of a big omnibus groaning with Knights of Pythias in cocked hats and swords, Charity looked up and saw on the corner a brick house with a conspicuous black and gold sign across its front. "Dr. Merkle; Private Consultations at all hours. Lady Attendants," she read; and suddenly she remembered Ally Hawes's words: "The house was at the corner of Wing Street and Lake Avenue . . . there's a big black sign across the front. . . ." Through all the heat and the rapture a shiver of cold ran over her.

# ——10——

THE LAKE at last—a sheet of shining metal brooded over by drooping trees. Charity and Harney had secured a boat and, getting away from the wharves and the refreshment booths, they drifted idly along, hugging the shadow of the shore. Where the sun struck the water its shafts flamed back blindingly at the heat-veiled sky; and the least shade was black by contrast. The Lake was so smooth that the reflection of the trees on its edge seemed enameled on a solid surface; but gradually, as the sun declined, the water grew transparent, and Charity, leaning over, plunged her fascinated gaze into depths so clear that she saw the inverted treetops interwoven with the green growths of the bottom.

They rounded a point at the farther end of the Lake, and entering an inlet pushed their bow against a protruding tree trunk. A green veil of willows overhung them. Beyond the trees, wheat fields sparkled in the sun; and all along the horizon the clear hills throbbed with light. Charity leaned back in the stern, and Harney unshipped the oars and lay in the bottom of the boat without speaking.

Ever since their meeting at the Creston pool he had been subject to these brooding silences, which were as different as possible from the pauses when they ceased to speak because words were needless. At such times his face wore the expression she had seen on it when she had looked in at him from the darkness, and again there came over her a sense of the mysterious distance between them; but usually his fits of abstraction were followed by bursts of gaiety that chased away the shadow before it chilled her.

She was still thinking of the ten dollars he had handed to the driver of the runabout. It had given them twenty minutes of pleasure, and it seemed unimaginable that anyone should be able to buy amusement at that rate. With ten dollars he might have bought her an engagement ring; she knew that Mrs. Tom Fry's, which came from Springfield, and had a diamond in it, had cost only eight seventy-five. But she did not know why the thought had occurred to her. Harney would never buy her an engagement ring: they were friends and comrades, but no more. He had been perfectly fair to her: he had never said a word to mislead her. She wondered what the girl was like whose hand was waiting for his ring. . . .

Boats were beginning to thicken on the Lake and the clang of incessantly arriving trolleys announced the return of the crowds from the ball field. The shadows lengthened across the pearl-gray water and two white clouds near the sun were turning golden. On the opposite shore men were hammering hastily at a wooden scaffolding in a field. Charity asked what it was for.

"Why, the fireworks. I suppose there'll be a big show." Harney looked at her and a smile crept into his moody eyes. "Have you never seen any good fireworks?"

"Miss Hatchard always send up lovely rockets on the Fourth," she answered doubtfully.

"Oh—" his contempt was unbounded. "I mean a big performance like this: illuminated boats, and all the rest."

She flushed at the picture. "Do they send them up from the Lake, too?"

"Rather. Didn't you notice that big raft we passed? It's wonderful to see the rockets completing their orbits down under one's feet." She said nothing, and he put the oars into the rowlocks. "If we stay we'd better go and pick up something to eat."

"But how can we get back afterward?" she ventured, feeling it would break her heart if she missed it.

He consulted a timetable, found a ten o'clock train, and reassured her. "The moon rises so late that it will be dark by eight, and we'll have over an hour of it."

Twilight fell, and lights began to show along the shore. The trolleys roaring out from Nettleton became great luminous serpents coiling in and out among the trees. The wooden eating houses at the Lake's edge danced with lanterns, and the dusk echoed with laughter and shouts and the clumsy splashing of oars.

Harney and Charity had found a table in the corner of a balcony built over the Lake, and were patiently awaiting an unattainable chowder. Close under them the water lapped the piles, agitated by the evolutions of a little white steamboat trellised with colored globes which was to run passengers up and down the Lake. It was already black with them as it sheered off on its first trip.

Suddenly Charity heard a woman's laugh behind her. The sound was familiar, and she turned to look. A band of showily dressed girls and dapper young men wearing badges of secret societies, with new straw hats tilted far back on their square-clipped hair, had invaded the balcony and were loudly clamoring for a table. The girl in the lead was the one who had laughed. She wore a large hat with a long white feather, and from under its brim her painted eyes looked at Charity with amused recognition.

"Say! If this ain't like Old Home Week," she remarked to the girl at her elbow; and giggles and glances passed between them. Charity knew at once that the girl with the white feather was Julia Hawes. She had lost her freshness, and the paint under her eyes made her face seem thinner; but her lips had the same lovely curve, and the same cold mocking smile, as if there were some secret absurdity in the person she was looking at, and she had instantly detected it.

Charity flushed to the forehead and looked away. She felt herself humiliated by Julia's sneer, and vexed that the mockery of such a creature should affect her. She trembled lest Harney should notice that the noisy troop had recognized her; but they found no table free, and passed on tumultuously.

Presently there was a soft rush through the air and a shower of silver fell from the blue evening sky. In another direction, pale Roman candles shot up singly through the trees, and a fire-haired rocket swept the horizon like a portent. Between these intermittent flashes the velvet curtains of the darkness were descending, and in the intervals of eclipse the voices of the crowds seemed to sink to smothered murmurs.

Charity and Harney, dispossessed by newcomers, were at length obliged to give up their table and struggle through the throng about the boat landings. For a while there seemed no escape from the tide of late arrivals; but finally Harney secured the last two places on the stand from which the more privileged were to see the fireworks. The seats were at the end of a row, one above the other. Charity had taken off her hat to have an uninterrupted view; and whenever she leaned back to follow the curve of some disheveled rocket she could feel Harney's knees against her head.

After a while the scattered fireworks ceased. A longer interval of darkness followed, and then the whole night broke into flower. From every point of the horizon, gold and silver arches sprang up and crossed each other, sky orchards broke into blossom, shed their flaming petals and hung their branches with golden fruit; and all the while the air was filled with a soft supernatural hum, as though great birds were building their nests in those invisible treetops.

Now and then there came a lull, and a wave of moonlight swept the Lake. In a flash it revealed hundreds of boats, steel-dark against lustrous ripples; then it withdrew as if with a furling of vast translucent wings. Charity's heart throbbed with delight. It was as if all the latent beauty of things had been unveiled to her. She could not imagine that the world held anything more won-derful; but near her she heard someone say, "You wait till you see the set piece," and instantly her hopes took a fresh flight. At last, just as it was beginning to seem as though the whole arch of the sky were one great lid pressed against her dazzled eyeballs, and striking out of them continuous jets of jeweled light, the velvet darkness settled down again, and a murmur of expectation ran through the crowd.

"Now—now!" the same voice said excitedly; and Charity, grasping the hat on her knee, crushed it tight in the effort to restrain her rapture.

For a moment the night seemed to grow more impenetrably black; then a great picture stood out against it like a constellation. It was surmounted by a golden scroll bearing the inscription, "Washington crossing the Delaware," and across a flood of mo-tionless golden ripples the National Hero passed, erect, solemn and gigantic, standing with folded arms in the stern of a slowly moving golden boat.

A long "Oh-h-h" burst from the spectators: the stand creaked and shook with their blissful trepidations. "Oh-h-h," Charity gasped: she had forgotten where she was, had at last forgotten even Harney's nearness. She seemed to have been caught up into the star. . . .

The picture vanished and darkness came down. In the obscurity she felt her head clasped by two hands: her face was drawn backward, and Harney's lips were pressed on hers. With sudden vehemence he wound his arms about her, holding her head against his breast while she gave him back his kisses. An unknown Harney had revealed himself, a Harney who dominated her and yet over whom she felt herself possessed of a new mysterious power.

But the crowd was beginning to move, and he had to release her. "Come," he said in a confused voice. He scrambled over the side of the stand, and holding up his arm caught her as she sprang to the ground. He passed his arm about her waist, steadying her against the descending rush of people; and she clung to him, speechless, exultant, as if all the crowding and confusion about them were a mere vain stirring of the air.

"Come," he repeated, "we must try to make the trolley." He drew her along, and she followed, still in her dream. They walked as if they were one, so isolated in ecstasy that the people jostling them on every side seemed impalpable. But when they reached the terminus the illuminated trolley was already clanging on its way, its platforms black with passengers. The cars waiting behind it were as thickly packed; and the throng about the terminus was so dense that it seemed hopeless to struggle for a place.

"Last trip up the Lake," a megaphone bellowed from the wharf; and the lights of the little steamboat came dancing out of the darkness.

"No use waiting here; shall we run up the Lake?" Harney suggested.

They pushed their way back to the edge of the water just as the gangplank was lowered from the white side of the boat. The electric light at the end of the wharf flashed full on the descending passengers, and among them Charity caught sight of Julia Hawes, her white feather askew, and the face under it flushed with coarse laughter. As she stepped from the gangplank she stopped short, her dark-ringed eyes darting malice.

"Hullo, Charity Royall!" she called out; and then, looking back over her shoulder: "Didn't I tell you it was a family party? Here's Grandpa's little darling come to take him home!"

A snigger ran through the group; and then, towering above

them, and steadying himself by the handrail in a desperate effort
at erectness, Mr. Royall stepped stiffly ashore. Like the young
men of the party, he wore a secret society emblem in the buttonhole of his black frock coat. His head was covered by a new Pan-
ama hat, and his narrow black tie, half undone, dangled down on
his rumpled shirtfront. His face, a livid brown, with red blotches
of anger and lips sunken in like an old man's, was a lamentable
ruin in the searching glare.

He was just behind Julia Hawes, and had one hand on her
arm; but as he left the gangplank he freed himself, and moved a
step or two away from his companions. He had seen Charity at
once, and his glance passed slowly from her to Harney, whose
arm was still about her. He stood staring at them, and trying to
master the senile quiver of his lips; then he drew himself up with
the tremulous majesty of drunkenness, and stretched out his arm.

"You whore—you damn—bare-headed whore, you!" he enun-
ciated slowly.

There was a scream of tipsy laughter from the party, and Charity involuntarily put her hands to her head. She remembered that
her hat had fallen from her lap when she jumped up to leave the
stand; and suddenly she had a vision of herself, hatless, disheveled, with a man's arm about her, confronting that drunken crew,
headed by her guardian's pitiable figure. The picture filled her
with shame. She had known since childhood about Mr. Royall's
"habits": had seen him, as she went up to bed, sitting morosely in
his office, a bottle at his elbow; or coming home, heavy and quar-
relsome, from his business expeditions to Hepburn or Springfield; but the idea of his associating himself publicly with a band of
disreputable girls and barroom loafers was new and dreadful to
her.

"Oh—" she said in a gasp of misery; and releasing herself from
Harney's arm she went straight up to Mr. Royall.

"You come home with me—you come right home with me,"
she said in a low stern voice, as if she had not heard his apostro-
phe; and one of the girls called out: "Say, how many fellers does
she want?"

There was another laugh, followed by a pause of curiosity,
during which Mr. Royall continued to glare at Charity. At length

his twitching lips parted. "I said, 'You—damn—whore!' " he repeated with precision, steadying himself on Julia's shoulder.

Laughs and jeers were beginning to spring up from the circle of people beyond their group; and a voice called out from the gangway: "Now, then, step lively there—all *aboard!*" The pressure of approaching and departing passengers forced the actors in the rapid scene apart, and pushed them back into the throng. Charity found herself clinging to Harney's arm and sobbing desperately. Mr. Royall had disappeared, and in the distance she heard the receding sound of Julia's laugh.

The boat, laden to the taffrail, was puffing away on her last trip.

# 11

AT TWO o'clock in the morning the freckled boy from Creston stopped his sleepy horse at the door of the red house, and Charity got out. Harney had taken leave of her at Creston River, charging the boy to drive her home. Her mind was still in a fog of misery, and she did not remember very clearly what had happened, or what they had said to each other, during the interminable interval since their departure from Nettleton; but the secretive instinct of the animal in pain was so strong in her that she had a sense of relief when Harney got out and she drove on alone.

The full moon hung over North Dormer, whitening the mist that filled the hollows between the hills and floated transparently above the fields. Charity stood a moment at the gate, looking out into the waning night. She watched the boy drive off, his horse's head wagging heavily to and fro; then she went around to the kitchen door and felt under the mat for the key. She found it, unlocked the door and went in. The kitchen was dark, but she discovered a box of matches, lit a candle, and went upstairs. Mr. Royall's door, opposite hers, stood open on his unlit room; evidently he had not come back. She went into her room, bolted her door and began slowly to untie the ribbon about her waist, and to take off her dress. Under the bed she saw the paper bag in which she had hidden her new hat from inquisitive eyes. . . .

She lay for a long time sleepless on her bed, staring up at the moonlight on the low ceiling; dawn was in the sky when she fell asleep, and when she woke the sun was on her face.

She dressed and went down to the kitchen. Verena was there alone: she glanced at Charity tranquilly, with her old deaf-looking eyes. There was no sign of Mr. Royall about the house and the hours passed without his reappearing. Charity had gone up to her room, and sat there listlessly, her hands on her lap. Puffs of sultry air fanned her dimity window curtains and flies buzzed stiflingly against the bluish panes.

At one o'clock Verena hobbled up to see if she were not coming down to dinner; but she shook her head, and the old woman went away, saying: "I'll cover up, then."

The sun turned and left her room, and Charity seated herself in the window, gazing down the village street through the half-opened shutters. Not a thought was in her mind; it was just a dark whirlpool of crowding images; and she watched the people passing along the street, Dan Targatt's team hauling a load of pine trunks down to Hepburn, the sexton's old white horse grazing on the bank across the way, as if she looked at these familiar sights from the other side of the grave.

She was roused from her apathy by seeing Ally Hawes come out of the Frys' gate and walk slowly toward the red house with her uneven limping step. At the sight Charity recovered her severed contact with reality. She divined that Ally was coming to hear about her day: no one else was in the secret of the trip to Nettleton, and it had flattered Ally profoundly to be allowed to know of it.

At the thought of having to see her, of having to meet her eyes and answer or evade her questions, the whole horror of the previous night's adventure rushed back upon Charity. What had been a feverish nightmare became a cold and unescapable fact. Poor Ally, at that moment, represented North Dormer, with all its mean curiosities, its furtive malice, its sham unconsciousness of evil. Charity knew that, although all relations with Julia were supposed to be severed, the tenderhearted Ally still secretly communicated with her; and no doubt Julia would exult in the chance of retailing the scandal of the wharf. The story, exaggerated and distorted, was probably already on its way to North Dormer.

Ally's dragging pace had not carried her far from the Frys' gate when she was stopped by old Mrs. Sollas, who was a great talker, and spoke very slowly because she had never been able to get used to her new teeth from Hepburn. Still, even this respite would not last long; in another ten minutes Ally would be at the door, and Charity would hear her greeting Verena in the kitchen, and then calling up from the foot of the stairs.

Suddenly it became clear that flight, and instant flight, was the only thing conceivable. The longing to escape, to get away from familiar faces, from places where she was known, had always been strong in her in moments of distress. She had a childish belief in the miraculous power of strange scenes and new faces to transform her life and wipe out bitter memories. But such impulses were mere fleeting whims compared to the cold resolve which now possessed her. She felt she could not remain an hour longer under the roof of the man who had publicly dishonored her, and face to face with the people who would presently be gloating over all the details of her humiliation.

Her passing pity for Mr. Royall had been swallowed up in loathing: everything in her recoiled from the disgraceful spectacle of the drunken old man apostrophizing her in the presence of a band of loafers and streetwalkers. Suddenly, vividly, she relived again the horrible moment when he had tried to force himself into her room, and what she had before supposed to be a mad aberration now appeared to her as a vulgar incident in a debauched and degraded life.

While these thoughts were hurrying through her she had dragged out her old canvas schoolbag, and was thrusting into it a few articles of clothing and the little packet of letters she had received from Harney. From under her pincushion she took the library key, and laid it in full view; then she felt at the back of a drawer for the blue brooch that Harney had given her. She would not have dared to wear it openly at North Dormer, but now she fastened it on her bosom as if it were a talisman to protect her in her flight. These preparations had taken but a few minutes, and when they were finished Ally Hawes was still at the Frys' corner talking to old Mrs. Sollas. . . .

She had said to herself, as she always said in moments of revolt: "I'll go to the Mountain—I'll go back to my own folks." She had never really meant it before; but now, as she considered her case, no other course seemed open. She had never learned any trade that would have given her independence in a strange place, and she knew no one in the big towns of the valley, where she might have hoped to find employment. Miss Hatchard was still away; but even had she been at North Dormer she was the last person to whom Charity would have turned, since one of the motives urging her to flight was the wish not to see Lucius Harney. Traveling back from Nettleton, in the crowded brightly lit train, all exchange of confidence between them had been impossible; but during their drive from Hepburn to Creston River she had gathered from Harney's snatches of consolatory talk—again hampered by the freckled boy's presence—that he intended to see her the next day. At the moment she had found a vague comfort in the assurance; but in the desolate lucidity of the hours that followed she had come to see the impossibility of meeting him again. Her dream of comradeship was over; and the scene on the wharf—vile and disgraceful as it had been—had after all shed the light of truth on her minute of madness. It was as if her guardian's words had stripped her bare in the face of the grinning crowd and proclaimed to the world the secret admonitions of her conscience.

She did not think these things out clearly; she simply followed the blind propulsion of her wretchedness. She did not want, ever again, to see anyone she had known; above all, she did not want to see Harney. . . .

She climbed the hill path behind the house and struck through the woods by a shortcut leading to the Creston road. A lead-colored sky hung heavily over the fields, and in the forest the motionless air was stifling; but she pushed on, impatient to reach the road which was the shortest way to the Mountain.

To do so, she had to follow the Creston road for a mile or two, and go within half a mile of the village; and she walked quickly, fearing to meet Harney. But there was no sign of him, and she had almost reached the branch road when she saw the flanks of a large white tent projecting through the trees by the roadside. She supposed that it sheltered a traveling circus which had come there for the Fourth; but as she drew nearer she saw, over the folded-back flap, a large sign bearing the inscription "Gospel Tent." The interior seemed to be empty; but a young man in a black alpaca coat, his lank hair parted over a round white face, stepped from under the flap and advanced toward her with a smile.

"Sister, your Savior knows everything. Won't you come in and lay your guilt before Him?" he asked insinuatingly, putting his hand on her arm.

Charity started back and flushed. For a moment she thought the evangelist must have heard a report of the scene at Nettleton; then she saw the absurdity of the supposition.

"I on'y wish't I had any to lay!" she retorted, with one of her fierce flashes of self-derision; and the young man murmured, aghast: "Oh, Sister, don't speak blasphemy. . . ."

But she had jerked her arm out of his hold, and was running up the branch road, trembling with the fear of meeting a familiar face. Presently she was out of sight of the village and climbing into the heart of the forest. She could not hope to do the fifteen miles to the Mountain that afternoon; but she knew of a place halfway to Hamblin where she could sleep, and where no one would think of looking for her. It was a little deserted house on a slope in one of the lonely rifts of the hills. She had seen it once, years before, when she had gone on a nutting expedition to the grove of walnuts below it. The party had taken refuge in the house from a sudden mountain storm, and she remembered that Ben Sollas, who liked frightening girls, had told them that it was said to be haunted.

She was growing faint and tired, for she had eaten nothing since morning, and was not used to walking so far. Her head felt light and she sat down for a moment by the roadside. As she sat there she heard the click of a bicycle bell, and started up to plunge back into the forest; but before she could move the bicycle had swept around the curve of the road, and Harney, jumping off, was approaching her with outstretched arms.

"Charity! What on earth are you doing here?"

She stared as if he were a vision, so startled by the unexpectedness of his being there that no words came to her.

"Where were you going? Had you forgotten that I was coming?" he continued, trying to draw her to him, but she shrank from his embrace.

"I was going away—I don't want to see you—I want you should leave me alone," she broke out wildly.

He looked at her and his face grew grave, as though the shadow of a premonition brushed it.

"Going away—from me, Charity?"

"From everybody. I want you should leave me."

He stood glancing doubtfully up and down the lonely forest road that stretched away into sun-flecked distances.

"Where were you going?"

"Home."

"Home—this way?"

She threw her head back defiantly. "To my home—up yonder: to the Mountain."

As she spoke she became aware of a change in his face. He was no longer listening to her, he was only looking at her, with the passionate absorbed expression she had seen in his eyes after they had kissed on the stand at Nettleton. He was the new Harney again, the Harney abruptly revealed in that embrace, who seemed so penetrated with the joy of her presence that he was utterly careless of what she was thinking or feeling.

He caught her hands with a laugh. "How do you suppose I found you?" he said gaily. He drew out the little packet of his letters and flourished them before her bewildered eyes.

"You dropped them, you imprudent young person—dropped them in the middle of the road, not far from here; and the young man who is running the Gospel tent picked them up just as I was riding by." He drew back, holding her at arm's length, and scrutinizing her troubled face with the minute searching gaze of his shortsighted eyes.

"Did you really think you could run away from me? You see you weren't meant to," he said; and before she could answer he had kissed her again, not vehemently, but tenderly, almost fraternally, as if he had guessed her confused pain, and wanted her to know he understood it. He wound his fingers through hers.

"Come—let's walk a little. I want to talk to you. There's so much to say."

He spoke with a boy's gaiety, carelessly and confidently, as if nothing had happened that could shame or embarrass them; and for a moment, in the sudden relief of her release from lonely pain, she felt herself yielding to his mood. But he had turned, and was drawing her back along the road by which she had come. She stiffened herself and stopped short.

"I won't go back," she said.

They looked at each other a moment in silence; then he answered gently: "Very well: let's go the other way, then."

She remained motionless, gazing silently at the ground, and he went on: "Isn't there a house up here somewhere—a little abandoned house—you meant to show me someday?" Still she made no answer, and he continued, in the same tone of tender reassurance: "Let us go there now and sit down and talk quietly." He took one of the hands that hung by her side and pressed his lips to the palm. "Do you suppose I'm going to let you send me away? Do you suppose I don't understand?"

The little old house—its wooden walls sun-bleached to a ghostly gray—stood in an orchard above the road. The garden palings had fallen, but the broken gate dangled between its posts, and the path to the house was marked by rose bushes run wild and hanging their small pale blossoms above the crowding grasses. Slender pilasters and an intricate fanlight framed the opening where the door had hung; and the door itself lay rotting in the grass, with an old apple tree fallen across it.

Inside, also, wind and weather had blanched everything to the same wan silvery tint: the house was as dry and pure as the interior of a long-empty shell. But it must have been exceptionally well built, for the little rooms had kept something of their human aspect: the wooden mantels with their neat classic ornaments were in place, and the corners of one ceiling retained a light film of plaster tracery.

Harney had found an old bench at the back door and dragged it into the house. Charity sat on it, leaning her head against the wall in a state of drowsy lassitude. He had guessed that she was hungry and thirsty, and had brought her some tablets of chocolate from his bicycle bag, and filled his drinking cup from a spring in the orchard; and now he sat at her feet, smoking a cigarette, and looking up at her without speaking. Outside, the afternoon shadows were lengthening across the grass, and through the empty window frame that faced her she saw the Mountain thrusting its dark mass against a sultry sunset. It was time to go.

She stood up, and he sprang to his feet also, and passed his arm through hers with an air of authority. "Now, Charity, you're coming back with me."

She looked at him and shook her head. "I ain't ever going back. You don't know."

"What don't I know?" She was silent, and he continued: "What happened on the wharf was horrible—it's natural you should feel as you do. But it doesn't make any real difference: you can't be hurt by such things. You must try to forget. And you must try to understand that men . . . men sometimes . . ."

"I know about men. That's why."

He colored a little at the retort, as though it had touched him in a way she did not suspect.

"Well, then . . . you must know one has to make allowances. . . . He'd been drinking. . . ."

"I know all that, too. I've seen him so before. But he wouldn't have dared speak to me that way if he hadn't . . ."

"Hadn't what? What do you mean?"

"Hadn't wanted me to be like those other girls. . . ." She lowered her voice and looked away from him. "So's 't he wouldn't have to go out. . . ."

Harney stared at her. For a moment he did not seem to seize her meaning; then his face grew dark. "The damned hound! The villainous low hound!" His wrath blazed up, crimsoning him to the temples. "I never dreamed—good God, it's too vile," he broke off, as if his thoughts recoiled from the discovery.

"I won't never go back there," she repeated doggedly.

"No—" he assented.

There was a long interval of silence, during which she imagined that he was searching her face for more light on what she had revealed to him; and a flush of shame swept over her.

"I know the way you must feel about me," she broke out, ". . . telling you such things. . . ."

But once more, as she spoke, she became aware that he was no longer listening. He came close and caught her to him as if he were snatching her from some imminent peril: his impetuous eyes were in hers, and she could feel the hard beat of his heart as he held her against it.

"Kiss me again—like last night," he said, pushing her hair back as if to draw her whole face up into his kiss.

# ——12——

ONE AFTERNOON toward the end of August a group of girls sat in a room at Miss Hatchard's in a gay confusion of flags, Turkey red, blue, and white paper muslin, harvest sheaves, and illuminated scrolls.

North Dormer was preparing for its Old Home Week. That form of sentimental decentralization was still in its early stages, and, precedents being few, and the desire to set an example contagious, the matter had become a subject of prolonged and passionate discussion under Miss Hatchard's roof. The incentive to the celebration had come rather from those who had left North Dormer than from those who had been obliged to stay there, and there was some difficulty in rousing the village to the proper state of enthusiasm. But Miss Hatchard's pale prim drawing room was the center of constant comings and goings from Hepburn, Nettleton, Springfield, and even more distant cities; and whenever a visitor arrived he was led across the hall and treated to a glimpse of the group of girls deep in their pretty preparations.

"All the old names . . . all the old names. . . ." Miss Hatchard would be heard, tapping across the hall on her crutches. "Targatt . . . Sollas . . . Fry: this is Miss Orma Fry sewing the stars on the drapery for the organ loft. Don't move, girls . . . and this is Miss Ally Hawes, our cleverest needle-woman . . . and Miss Charity Royall making our garlands of evergreen. . . . I like the idea of its all being homemade, don't you? We haven't had to call in any foreign talent: my young cousin Lucius Harney, the architect—you know he's up here preparing a book on Colonial houses—he's taken the whole thing in hand so cleverly; but you must come and see his sketch for the stage we're going to put up in the Town Hall."

One of the first results of the Old Home Week agitation had, in fact, been the reappearance of Lucius Harney in the village street. He had been vaguely spoken of as being not far off, but for some weeks past no one had seen him at North Dormer, and there was a recent report of his having left Creston River, where he was said to have been staying, and gone away from the neighborhood for good. Soon after Miss Hatchard's return, however, he came back to his old quarters in her house, and began to take a leading part in the planning of the festivities. He threw himself into the idea with extraordinary good humor, and was so prodigal of sketches, and so inexhaustible in devices, that he gave an immediate impetus to the rather languid movement, and infected the whole village with his enthusiasm.

"Lucius has such a feeling for the past that he has roused us all to a sense of our privileges," Miss Hatchard would say, lingering on the last word, which was a favorite one. And before leading her visitor back to the drawing room she would repeat, for the hundredth time, that she supposed he thought it very bold of little North Dormer to start up and have a Home Week of its own, when so many bigger places hadn't thought of it yet; but that, after all, Associations counted more than the size of the population, didn't they? And of course North Dormer was so full of Associations . . . historic, literary (here a filial sigh for Honorius), and ecclesiastical . . . he knew about the old pewter communion service imported from England in 1769, she supposed? And it was so important, in a wealthy materialistic age, to set the example of reverting to the old ideals, the family and the homestead, and so on. This peroration usually carried her halfway back across the hall, leaving the girls to return to their interrupted activities.

The day on which Charity Royall was weaving hemlock garlands for the procession was the last before the celebration. When Miss Hatchard called upon the North Dormer maidenhood to collaborate in the festal preparations Charity had at first held aloof; but it had been made clear to her that her nonappearance might excite conjecture, and reluctantly, she had joined the other workers. The girls, at first shy and embarrassed, and puzzled as to the exact nature of the projected commemoration, had soon become interested in the amusing details of their task and excited by the notice they received. They would not for the world have missed their afternoons at Miss Hatchard's, and, while they cut out and sewed and draped and pasted, their tongues kept up

such an accompaniment to the sewing machine that Charity's silence sheltered itself unperceived under their chatter.

In spirit she was still almost unconscious of the pleasant stir
about her. Since her return to the red house, on the evening of
the day when Harney had overtaken her on her way to the Mountain, she had lived at North Dormer as if she were suspended in
the void. She had come back there because Harney, after appearing to agree to the impossibility of her doing so, had ended by
persuading her that any other course would be madness. She had
nothing further to fear from Mr. Royall. Of this she had declared
herself sure, though she had failed to add, in his exoneration,
that he had twice offered to make her his wife. Her hatred of him
made it impossible, at the moment, for her to say anything that
might partly excuse him in Harney's eyes.

Harney, however, once satisfied of her security, had found
plenty of reasons for urging her to return. The first, and the most
unanswerable, was that she had nowhere else to go. But the one
on which he laid the greatest stress was that flight would be equiv-
alent to avowal. If—as was almost inevitable—rumors of the scandalous scene at Nettleton should reach North Dormer, how else
would her disappearnce be interpreted? Her guardian had publicly taken away her character, and she immediately vanished
from his house. Seekers after motives could hardly fail to draw an
unkind conclusion. But if she came back at once, and was seen
leading her usual life, the incident was reduced to its true propor-
tions, as the outbreak of a drunken old man furious at being
surprised in disreputable company. People would say that Mr.
Royall had insulted his ward to justify himself, and the sordid tale
would fall into its place in the chronicle of his obscure debauch-
eries.

Charity saw the force of the argument; but if she acquiesced it
was not so much because of that as because it was Harney's wish.
Since that evening in the deserted house she could imagine no
reason for doing or not doing anything except the fact that Harney wished or did not wish it. All her tossing contradictory impulses were merged in a fatalistic acceptance of his will. It was not
that she felt in him any ascendency of character—there were moments already when she knew she was the stronger—but that all
the rest of life had become a mere cloudy rim about the central

glory of their passion. Whenever she stopped thinking about that for a moment she felt as she sometimes did after lying on the grass and staring up too long at the sky; her eyes were so full of light that everything about her was a blur.

Each time that Miss Hatchard, in the course of her periodical incursions into the workroom, dropped an allusion to her young cousin, the architect, the effect was the same on Charity. The hemlock garland she was wearing fell to her knees and she sat in a kind of trance. It was so manifestly absurd that Miss Hatchard should talk of Harney in that familiar possessive way, as if she had any claim on him, or knew anything about him. She, Charity Royall, was the only being on earth who really knew him, knew him from the soles of his feet to the rumpled crest of his hair, knew the shifting lights in his eyes, and the inflexions of his voice, and the things he liked and disliked, and everything there was to know about him, as minutely and yet unconsciously as a child knows the walls of the room it wakes up in every morning. It was this fact, which nobody about her guessed, or would have understood, that made her life something apart and inviolable, as if nothing had any power to hurt or disturb her as long as her secret was safe.

The room in which the girls sat was the one which had been Harney's bedroom. He had been sent upstairs, to make room for the Home Week workers; but the furniture had not been moved, and as Charity sat there she had perpetually before her the vision she had looked in on from the midnight garden. The table at which Harney had sat was the one about which the girls were gathered; and her own seat was near the bed on which she had seen him lying. Sometimes, when the others were not looking, she bent over as if to pick up something, and laid her cheek for a moment against the pillow.

Toward sunset the girls disbanded. Their work was done, and the next morning at daylight the draperies and garlands were to be nailed up, and the illuminated scrolls put in place in the Town Hall. The first guests were to drive over from Hepburn in time for the midday banquet under a tent in Miss Hatchard's field; and after that the ceremonies were to begin. Miss Hatchard, pale with fatigue and excitement, thanked her young assistants, and stood in the porch, leaning on her crutches and waving a farewell as she watched them troop away down the street.

Charity had slipped off among the first; but at the gate she heard Ally Hawes calling after her, and reluctantly turned.

"Will you come over now and try on your dress?" Ally asked, looking at her with wistful admiration. "I want to be sure the sleeves don't ruck up the same as they did yesterday."

Charity gazed at her with dazzled eyes. "Oh, it's lovely," she said, and hastened away without listening to Ally's protest. She wanted her dress to be as pretty as the other girls—wanted it, in fact, to outshine the rest, since she was to take part in the "exercise"—but she had no time just then to fix her mind on such matters. . . .

She sped up the street to the library, of which she had the key about her neck. From the passage at the back she dragged forth a bicycle, and guided it to the edge of the street. She looked about to see if any of the girls were approaching; but they had drifted away together toward the Town Hall, and she sprang into the saddle and turned toward the Creston road. There was an almost continual descent to Creston, and with her feet against the pedals she floated through the still evening air like one of the hawks she had often watched slanting downward on motionless wings. Twenty minutes from the time when she had left Miss Hatchard's door she was turning up the wood road on which Harney had overtaken her on the day of her flight; and a few minutes afterward she had jumped from her bicycle at the gate of the deserted house.

In the gold-powdered sunset it looked more than ever like some frail shell dried and washed by many seasons; but at the back, whither Charity advanced, drawing her bicycle after her, there were signs of recent habitation. A rough door made of boards hung in the kitchen doorway, and pushing it open she entered a room furnished in primitive camping fashion. In the window was a table, also made of boards, with an earthenware jar holding a big bunch of wild asters. Two canvas chairs stood nearby, and in one corner was a mattress with a Mexican blanket over it.

The room was empty, and leaning her bicycle against the house Charity clambered up the slope and sat down on a rock under an old apple tree. The air was perfectly still, and from where she sat she would be able to hear the tinkle of a bicycle bell a long way down the road. . . .

She was always glad when she got to the little house before Harney. She like to have time to take in every detail of its secret sweetness—the shadows of the apple trees swaying on the grass, the old walnuts rounding their domes below the road, the meadows sloping westward in the afternoon light—before his first kiss blotted it all out. Everything unrelated to the hours spent in that tranquil place was as faint as the remembrance of a dream. The only reality was the wondrous unfolding of her new self, the reaching out to the light of all her contracted tendrils. She had lived all her life among people whose sensibilities seemed to have withered for lack of use; and more wonderful, at first, than Harney's endearments were the words that were a part of them. She had always thought of love as something confused and furtive, and he made it as bright and open as the summer air.

On the morrow of the day when she had shown him the way to the deserted house he had packed up and left Creston River for Boston; but at the first station he had jumped off the train with a handbag and scrambled up into the hills. For two golden rainless August weeks he had camped in the house, getting eggs and milk from the solitary farm in the valley, where no one knew him, and doing his cooking over a spirit lamp. He got up every day with the sun, took a plunge in a brown pool he knew of, and spent long hours lying in the scented hemlock woods above the house, or wandering along the yoke of the Eagle Ridge, far above the misty blue valleys that swept away east and west between the endless hills. And in the afternoon Charity came to him.

With part of what was left of her savings she had hired a bicycle for a month, and every day after dinner, as soon as her guardian started to his office, she hurried to the library, got out her bicycle, and flew down the Creston road. She knew that Mr. Royall, like everyone else in North Dormer, was perfectly aware of her acquisition: possibly he, as well as the rest of the village, knew what use she made of it. She did not care: she felt him to be so powerless that if he had questioned her she would probably have told him the truth. But they had never spoken to each other since the night on the wharf at Nettleton. He had returned to North Dormer only on the third day after that encounter, arriving just as Charity and Verena were sitting down to supper. He had drawn up his chair, taken his napkin from the sideboard drawer, pulled it out of its ring, and seated himself as unconcernedly as if he had come in from his usual afternoon session at Carrick Fry's; and the long habit of the household made it seem almost natural that Charity should not so much as raise her eyes when he entered. She had simply let him understand that her silence was not accidental by leaving the table while he was still eating, and going up without a word to shut herself into her room. After that he formed the habit of talking loudly and genially to Verena whenever Charity was in the room; but otherwise there was no apparent change in their relations.

She did not think connectedly of these things while she sat waiting for Harney, but they remained in her mind as a sullen background against which her short hours with him flamed out like forest fires. Nothing else mattered, neither the good nor the bad, or what might have seemed so before she knew him. He had caught her up and carried her away into a new world, from which, at stated hours, the ghost of her came back to perform certain customary acts, but all so thinly and insubstantially that she sometimes wondered that the people she went about among could see her. . . .

Behind the swarthy Mountain the sun had gone down in waveless gold. From a pasture up the slope a tinkle of cowbells sounded; a puff of smoke hung over the farm in the valley, trailed on the pure air and was gone. For a few minutes, in the clear light that is all shadow, fields and woods were outlined with an unreal precision; then the twilight blotted them out, and the little house turned gray and spectral under its wizened apple branches.

Charity's heart contracted. The first fall of night after a day of radiance often gave her a sense of hidden menace: it was like looking out over the world as it would be when love had gone from it. She wondered if someday she would sit in that same place and watch in vain for her lover. . . .

His bicycle bell sounded down the lane, and in a minute she was at the gate and his eyes were laughing in hers. They walked back through the long grass, and pushed open the door behind the house. The room at first seemed quite dark and they had to grope their way in hand in hand. Through the window frame the sky looked light by contrast, and above the black mass of asters in the earthern jar one white star glimmered like a moth.

"There was such a lot to do at the last minute," Harney was explaining, "and I had to drive down to Creston to meet someone who has come to stay with my cousin for the show."

He had his arms about her, and his kisses were in her hair and on her lips. Under his touch things deep down in her struggled to the light and sprang up like flowers in sunshine. She twisted her fingers into his, and they sat down side by side on the improvised couch. She hardly heard his excuses for being late: in his absence a thousand doubts tormented her, but as soon as he appeared she ceased to wonder where he had come from, what had delayed him, who had kept him from her. It seemed as if the places he had been in, and the people he had been with, must cease to exist when he left them, just as her own life was suspended in his absence.

He continued, now, to talk to her volubly and gaily, deploring his lateness, grumbling at the demands on his time, and good-humoredly mimicking Miss Hatchard's benevolent agitation. "She hurried off Miles to ask Mr. Royall to speak at the Town Hall tomorrow: I didn't know till it was done." Charity was silent, and he added: "After all, perhaps it's just as well. No one else could have done it."

Charity made no answer: she did not care what part her guardian played in the morrow's ceremonies. Like all the other figures peopling her meager world he had grown nonexistent to her. She had even put off hating him.

"Tomorrow I shall only see you from far off," Harney continued. "But in the evening there'll be the dance in the Town Hall. Do you want me to promise not to dance with any other girl?"

Any other girl? Were there any others? She had forgotten even that peril, so enclosed did he and she seem in their secret world. Her heart gave a frightened jerk.

"Yes, promise."

He laughed and took her in his arms. "You goose—not even if they're hideous?"

He pushed the hair from her forehead, bending her face back, as his way was, and leaning over so that his head loomed black

between her eyes and the paleness of the sky, in which the white
star floated . . .

Side by side they sped back along the dark wood road to the
village. A late moon was rising, full orbed and fiery, turning the
mountain ranges from fluid gray to a massive blackness, and
making the upper sky so light that the stars looked as faint as their
own reflections in water. At the edge of the wood, half a mile from
North Dormer, Harney jumped from his bicycle, took Charity in
his arms for a last kiss, and then waited while she went on alone.

They were later than usual, and instead of taking the bicycle to
the library she propped it against the back of the woodshed and
entered the kitchen of the red house. Verena sat there alone;
when Charity came in she looked at her with mild impenetrable
eyes and then took a plate and a glass of milk from the shelf and
set them silently on the table. Charity nodded her thanks, and
sitting down fell hungrily upon her piece of pie and emptied the
glass. Her face burned with her quick flight through the night,
and her eyes were dazzled by the twinkle of the kitchen lamp. She
felt like a night bird suddenly caught and caged.

"He ain't come back since supper," Verena said. "He's down to
the Hall."

Charity took no notice. Her soul was still winging through the
forest. She washed her plate and tumbler, and then felt her way
up the dark stairs. When she opened her door a wonder arrested
her. Before going out she had closed her shutters against the
afternoon heat, but they had swung partly open, and a bar of
moonlight, crossing the room, rested on her bed and showed a
dress of China silk laid out on it in virgin whiteness. Charity had
spent more than she could afford on the dress, which was to
surpass those of all the other girls; she had wanted to let North
Dormer see that she was worthy of Harney's admiration. Above
the dress, folded on the pillow, was the white veil which the
young women who took part in the exercises were to wear under
a wreath of asters; and beside the veil a pair of slim white satin
shoes that Ally had produced from an old trunk in which she
stored mysterious treasures.

Charity stood gazing at all the outspread whiteness. It recalled
a vision that had come to her in the night after her first meeting

with Harney. She no longer had such visions . . . warmer spendors had displace them . . . but it was stupid of Ally to have paraded all those white things on her bed, exactly as Hattie Targatt's wedding dress from Springfield had been spread out for the neighbors to see when she married Tom Fry. . . .

Charity took up the satin shoes and looked at them curiously. By day, no doubt, they would appear a little worn, but in the moonlight they seemed carved of ivory. She sat down on the floor to try them on, and they fitted her perfectly, though when she stood up she lurched a little on the high heels. She looked down at her feet, which the graceful mold of the slippers had marvelously arched and narrowed. She had never seen such shoes before, even in the shop windows at Nettleton . . . never, except . . . yes, once, she had noticed a pair of the same shape on Annabel Balch.

A blush of mortification swept over her. Ally sometimes sewed for Miss Balch when that brilliant being descended on North Dormer, and no doubt she picked up presents of cast-off clothing: the treasures in the mysterious trunk all came from the people she worked for. There could be no doubt that the white slippers were Annabel Balch's. . . .

As she stood there, staring down moodily at her feet, she heard the triple click-click-click of a bicycle bell under her window. It was Harney's secret signal as he passed on his way home. She stumbled to the window on her high heels, flung open the shutters and leaned out. He waved to her and sped by, his black shadow dancing merrily ahead of him down the empty moonlit road; and she leaned there watching him till he vanished under the Hatchard spruces.

# —— 13 ——

THE TOWN HALL was crowded and exceedingly hot. As Charity marched into it, third in the white muslin file headed by Orma Fry, she was conscious mainly of the brilliant effect of the wreathed columns framing the green-carpeted stage toward which she was moving and of the unfamiliar faces turning from the front rows to watch the advance of the procession.

But it was all a bewildering blur of eyes and colors till she found herself standing at the back of the stage, her great bunch of asters and goldenrod held well in front of her, and answering the nervous glance of Lambert Sollas, the organist from Mr. Miles's church, who had come up from Nettleton to play the harmonium, and sat behind it, running his conductor's eye over the fluttered girls.

A moment later Mr. Miles, pink and twinkling, emerged from the background, as if buoyed up on his broad white gown, and briskly dominated the bowed heads in the front rows. He prayed energetically and briefly and then retired, and a fierce nod from Lambert Sollas warned the girls that they were to follow at once with "Home, Sweet Home." It was a joy to Charity to sing: it seemed as though, for the first time, her secret rapture might burst from her and flash its defiance at the world. All the glow in her blood, the breath of the summer earth, the rustle of the forest, the fresh call of birds at sunrise, and the brooding midday languors, seemed to pass into her untrained voice, lifted and led by the sustaining chorus.

And then suddenly the song was over, and after an uncertain pause, during which Miss Hatchard's pearl-gray gloves started a furtive signaling down the hall, Mr. Royall, emerging in turn, ascended the steps of the stage and appeared behind the flower-wreathed desk. He passed close to Charity, and she noticed that his gravely set face wore the look of majesty that used to awe and fascinate her childhood. His frock coat had been carefully brushed and ironed, and the ends of his narrow black tie were so nearly even that the tying must have cost him a protracted struggle. His appearance struck her all the more because it was the first time she had looked him full in the face since the night at Nettleton, and nothing in his grave and impressive demeanor revealed a trace of the lamentable figure on the wharf.

He stood a moment behind the desk, resting his fingertips against it, and bending slightly toward his audience; then he straightened himself and began.

At first she paid no heed to what he was saying: only fragments of sentences, sonorous quotations, allusions to illustrious men, including the obligatory tribute to Honorius Hatchard, drifted past her inattentive ears. She was trying to discover Harney among the notable people in the front row; but he was nowhere near Miss Hatchard, who, crowned by a pearl-gray hat that matched her gloves, sat just below the desk, supported by Mrs. Miles and an important-looking unknown lady. Charity was near one end of the stage, and from where she sat the other end of the first row of seats was cut off by the screen of foliage masking the harmonium. The effort to see Harney around the corner of the screen, or through its interstices, made her unconscious of everything else; but the effort was unsuccessful, and gradually she found her attention arrested by her guardian's discourse.

She had never heard him speak in public before, but she was familiar with the rolling music of his voice when he read aloud, or held forth to the selectmen about the stove at Carrick Fry's. Today his inflections were richer and graver than she had ever known them: he spoke slowly, with pauses that seemed to invite his hearers to silent participation in his thought; and Charity perceived a light of response in their faces.

He was nearing the end of his address . . . "Most of you," he said, "most of you who have returned here today, to take contact with this little place for a brief hour, have come only on a pious pilgrimage, and will go back presently to busy cities and lives full of larger duties. But that is not the only way of coming back to North Dormer. Some of us, who went out from here in our youth . . . went out, like you, to busy cities and larger duties . . . have come back in another way—come back for good. I am one of those, as many of you know. . . ." He paused, and there was a sense of suspense in the listening hall. "My history is without interest, but it has its lesson: not so much for those of you who have already made your lives in other places, as for the young men who are perhaps planning even now to leave these quiet hills and go down into the struggle. Things they cannot foresee may send some of those young men back someday to the little township and the old homestead: they may come back for good. . . ." He looked about him, and repeated gravely: "For *good*. There's the point I want to make . . . North Dormer is a poor little place, almost lost in a mighty landscape: perhaps, by this time, it might have been a bigger place, and more in scale with the landscape, if those who had to come back had come with that feeling in their minds—that they wanted to come back for *good* . . . and not for bad . . . or just for indifference. . . .

"Gentlemen, let us look at things as they are. Some of us have come back to our native town because we'd failed to get on elsewhere. One way or other, things had gone wrong with us . . . what we'd dreamed of hadn't come true. But the fact that we had failed elsewhere is no reason why we should fail here. Our very experiments in larger places, even if they were unsuccessful, ought to have helped us to make North Dormer a larger place . . . and you young men who are preparing even now to follow the call of ambition, and turn your back on the old homes—well, let me say this to you, that if ever you do come back to them it's worthwhile to come back to them for their good. . . . And to do that, you must keep on loving them while you're away from them; and even if you come back against your will—and thinking it's all a bitter mistake of Fate or Providence—you must try to make the best of it, and to make the best of your old town; and after a while—well, ladies and gentlemen, I give you my recipe for what it's worth; after a while, I believe you'll be able to say, as I can say today: 'I'm glad I'm here.' Believe me, all of you, the best way to help the places we live in is to be glad we live there."

He stopped, and a murmur of emotion and surprise ran through the audience. It was not in the least what they had expected, but it moved them more than what they had expected would have moved them. "Hear, hear!" a voice cried out in the middle of the hall. An outburst of cheers caught up the cry, and as they subsided Charity heard Mr. Miles saying to someone near him: "That was a *man* talking——" He wiped his spectacles.

Mr. Royall had stepped back from the desk, and taken his seat in the row of chairs in front of the harmonium. A dapper white-haired gentleman—a distant Hatchard—succeeded him behind the goldenrod, and began to say beautiful things about the old oaken bucket, patient white-haired mothers, and where the boys used to go nutting . . . and Charity began again to search for Harney. . . .

Suddenly Mr. Royall pushed back his seat, and one of the maple branches in front of the harmonium collapsed with a crash. It uncovered the end of the first row and in one of the seats Charity saw Harney, and in the next a lady whose face was turned toward him, and almost hidden by the brim of her drooping hat. Charity did not need to see the face. She knew at a glance the slim figure, the fair hair heaped up under the hat brim, the long pale wrinkled gloves with bracelets slipping over them. At the fall of the branch Miss Balch turned her head toward the stage, and in her pretty thin-lipped smile there lingered the reflection of something her neighbor had been whispering to her. . . .

Someone came forward to replace the fallen branch, and Miss Balch and Harney were once more hidden. But to Charity the vision of their two faces had blotted out everything. In a flash they had shown her the bare reality of her situation. Behind the frail screen of her lover's caresses was the whole inscrutable mystery of his life: his relations with other people—with other women—his opinions, his prejudices, his principles, the net of influences and interests and ambitions in which every man's life is entangled. Of all these she knew nothing, except what he had told her of his architectural aspirations. She had always dimly guessed him to be in touch with important people, involved in complicated relations—but she felt it all to be so far beyond her understanding that the whole subject hung like a luminous mist on the farthest verge of her thoughts. In the foreground, hiding all else, there was the glow of his presence, the light and shadow of his face, the way his shortsighted eyes, at her approach, widened and deepened as if to draw her down into them; and, above all, the flush of youth and tenderness in which his words enclosed her.

Now she saw him detached from her, drawn back into the

unknown, and whispering to another girl things that provoked the same smile of mischievous complicity he had so often called to her own lips. The feeling possessing her was not one of jealousy; she was too sure of his love. It was rather a terror of the unknown, of all the mysterious attractions that must even now be dragging him away from her, and of her own powerlessness to contend with them.

She had given him all she had—but what was it compared to the other gifts life held for him? She understood now the case of girls like herself to whom this kind of thing happened. They gave all they had, but their all was not enough: it could not buy more than a few moments. . . .

The heat had grown suffocating—she felt it descend on her in smothering waves, and the faces in the crowded hall began to dance like the pictures flashed on the screen at Nettleton. For an instant Mr. Royall's countenance detached itself from the general blur. He had resumed his place in front of the harmonium, and sat close to her, his eyes on her face; and his look seemed to pierce to the very center of her confused sensations. . . . A feeling of physical sickness rushed over her—and then deadly apprehension. The light of the fiery hours in the little house swept back on her in a glare of fear. . . .

She forced herself to look away from her guardian, and became aware that the oratory of the Hatchard cousin had ceased, and that Mr. Miles was again flapping his wings. Fragments of his peroration floated through her bewildered brain. . . . "A rich harvest of hallowed memories. . . . A sanctified hour to which, in moments of trial, your thoughts will prayerfully return. . . . And now, O Lord, let us humbly and fervently give thanks for this blessed day of reunion, here in the old home to which we have come back from so far. Preserve it to us, O Lord, in times to come, in all its homely sweetness—in the kindliness and wisdom of its old people, in the courage and industry of its young men, in the piety and purity of this group of innocent girls—" He flapped a white wing in their direction, and at the same moment Lambert Sollas, with his fierce nod, struck the opening bars of "Auld Lang Syne." . . . Charity stared straight ahead of her and then, dropping her flowers, fell face downward at Mr. Royall's feet.

# —— 14 ——

NORTH DORMER'S celebration naturally included the villages attached to its township, and the festivities were to radiate over the whole group, from Dormer and the two Crestons to Hamblin, the lonely hamlet on the north slope of the Mountain where the first snow always fell. On the third day there were speeches and ceremonies at Creston and Creston River; on the fourth the principal performers were to be driven in buckboards to Dormer and Hamblin.

It was on the fourth day that Charity returned for the first time to the little house. She had not seen Harney alone since they had parted at the wood's edge the night before the celebrations began. In the interval she had passed through many moods, but for the moment the terror which had seized her in the Town Hall had faded to the edge of consciousness. She had fainted because the hall was stiflingly hot, and because the speakers had gone on and on. . . . Several other people had been affected by the heat, and had had to leave before the exercises were over. There had been thunder in the air all the afternoon, and everyone said afterward that something ought to have been done to ventilate the hall. . . .

At the dance that evening—where she had gone reluctantly, and only because she feared to stay away, she had sprung back into instant reassurance. As soon as she entered she had seen Harney waiting for her, and he had come up with kind gay eyes, and swept her off in a waltz. Her feet were full of music, and though her only training had been with the village youths she had no difficulty in tuning her steps to his. As they circled about the floor all her vain fears dropped from her, and she even forgot that she was probably dancing in Annabel Balch's slippers.

When the waltz was over Harney, with a last handclasp, left her to meet Miss Hatchard and Miss Balch, who were just entering. Charity had a moment of anguish as Miss Balch appeared; but it did not last. The triumphant fact of her own greater beauty, and of Harney's sense of it, swept her apprehensions aside. Miss Balch, in an unbecoming dress, looked sallow and pinched, and Charity fancied there was a worried expression in her pale-lashed eyes. She took a seat near Miss Hatchard and it was presently apparent that she did not mean to dance. Charity did not dance often either. Harney explained to her that Miss Hatchard had begged him to give each of the other girls a turn; but he went through the form of asking Charity's permission each time he led one out, and that gave her a sense of secret triumph even completer than when she was whirling about the room with him. . . .

She was thinking of all this as she waited for him in the deserted house. The late afternoon was sultry, and she had tossed aside her hat and stretched herself at full length on the Mexican blanket because it was cooler indoors than under the trees. She lay with her arms folded beneath her head, gazing out at the shaggy shoulder of the Mountain. The sky behind it was full of the splintered glories of the descending sun, and before long she expected to hear Harney's bicycle bell in the lane. He had bicycled to Hamblin, instead of driving there with his cousin and her friends, so that he might be able to make his escape earlier and stop on the way back at the deserted house, which was on the road to Hamblin. They had smiled together at the joke of hearing the crowded buckboards roll by on the return, while they lay close in their hiding above the road. Such childish triumphs still gave her a sense of reckless security.

Nevertheless she had not wholly forgotten the vision of fear that had opened before her in the Town Hall. The sense of lastingness was gone from her, and every moment with Harney would now be ringed with doubt.

The Mountain was turning purple against a fiery sunset from which it seemed to be divided by a knife-edge of quivering light; and above this wall of flame the whole sky was a pure pale green, like some cold mountain lake in shadow. Charity lay gazing up at it, and watching for the first white star. . . .

Her eyes were still fixed on the upper reaches of the sky when she became aware that a shadow had flitted across the glory-flooded room: it must have been Harney passing the window against the sunset. . . . She half raised herself, and then dropped back on her folded arms. The combs had slipped from her hair, and it trailed in a rough dark rope across her breast. She lay quite still, a sleepy smile on her lips, her indolent lids half shut. There was a fumbling at the padlock and she called out: "Have you slipped the chain?" The door opened, and Mr. Royall walked into the room.

She started up, sitting back against the cushions, and they looked at each other without speaking. Then Mr. Royall closed the door latch and advanced a few steps.

Charity jumped to her feet. "What have you come for?" she stammered.

The last glare of the sunset was on her guardian's face, which looked ash-colored in the yellow radiance.

"Because I knew you were here," he answered simply.

She had become conscious of the hair hanging loose across her breast, and it seemed as though she could not speak to him till she had set herself in order. She groped for her combs, and tried to fasten up the coil. Mr. Royall silently watched her.

"Charity," he said, "he'll be here in a minute. Let me talk to you first."

"You've got no right to talk to me. I can do what I please."

"Yes. What is it you mean to do?"

"I needn't answer that, or anything else."

He had glanced away, and stood looking curiously about the illuminated room. Purple asters and red maple leaves filled the jar on the table; on a shelf against the wall stood a lamp, the kettle, a little pile of cups and saucers. The canvas chairs were grouped about the table.

"So this is where you meet," he said.

His tone was quiet and controlled, and the fact disconcerted her. She had been ready to give him violence for violence, but this calm acceptance of things as they were left her without a weapon.

"See here, Charity—you're always telling me I've got no rights over you. There might be two ways of looking at that—but I ain't going to argue it. All I know is I raised you as good as I could, and meant fairly by you always—except once, for a bad half hour. There's no justice in weighing that half hour against the rest, and you know it. If you hadn't, you wouldn't have gone on living under my roof. Seems to me the fact of your doing that gives me some sort of right; the right to try and keep you out of trouble. I'm not asking you to consider any other."

She listened in silence, and then gave a slight laugh. "Better wait till I'm in trouble," she said.

He paused a moment, as if weighing her words. "Is that all your answer?"

"Yes, that's all."

"Well—I'll wait."

He turned away slowly, but as he did so the thing she had been waiting for happened; the door opened again and Harney entered.

He stopped short with a face of astonishment, and then, quickly controlling himself, went up to Mr. Royall with a frank look.

"Have you come to see me, sir?" he said coolly, throwing his cap on the table with an air of proprietorship.

Mr. Royall again looked slowly about the room; then his eyes turned to the young man.

"Is this your house?" he inquired.

Harney laughed: "Well—as much as it's anybody's. I come here to sketch occasionally."

"And to receive Miss.Royall's visits?"

"When she does me the honor—"

"Is this the home you propose to bring her to when you get married?"

There was an immense and oppressive silence. Charity, quivering with anger, started forward, and then stood silent, too humbled for speech. Harney's eyes had dropped under the old man's gaze; but he raised them presently, and looking steadily at Mr. Royall, said: "Miss Royall is not a child. Isn't it rather absurd to talk of her as if she were? I believe she considers herself free to come and go as she pleases, without any questions from anyone." He paused and added: "I'm ready to answer any she wishes to ask me."

Mr. Royall turned to her. "Ask him when he's going to marry you, then—" There was another silence, and he laughed in his turn—a broken laugh, with a scraping sound in it. "You darsn't!" he shouted out with sudden passion. He went close up to Charity, his right arm lifted, not in menace but in tragic exhortation.

"You darsn't, and you know it—and you know why!" He swung back again upon the young man. "And you know why you ain't asked her to marry you, and why you don't mean to. It's because you hadn't need to; nor any other man either. I'm the only one that was fool enough not to know that; and I guess nobody'll repeat my mistake—not in Eagle County, anyhow. They all know what she is, and what she came from. They all know her mother was a woman of the town from Nettleton, that followed one of those Mountain fellows up to his place and lived there with him like a heathen. I saw her there sixteen years ago, when I went to bring this child down. I went to save her from the kind of life her mother was leading—but I'd better have left her in the kennel she came from. . . ." He paused and stared darkly at the two young people, and out beyond them, at the menacing Mountain with its rim of fire; then he sat down beside the table on which they had so often spread their rustic supper, and covered his face with his hands. Harney leaned in the window, a frown on his face: he was twirling between his fingers a small package that dangled from a loop of string. . . . Charity heard Mr. Royall draw a hard breath or two, and his shoulders shook a little. Presently he stood up and walked across the room. He did not look again at the young people: they saw him feel his way to the door and fumble for the latch; and then he went out into the darkness.

After he had gone there was a long silence. Charity waited for Harney to speak; but he seemed at first not to find anything to say. At length he broke out irrelevantly: "I wonder how he found out?"

She made no answer and he tossed down the package he had been holding, and went up to her.

"I'm so sorry, dear . . . that this should have happened. . . ."

She threw her head back proudly. "I ain't ever been sorry—not a minute!"

"No."

She waited to be caught into his arms, but he turned away from her irresolutely. The last glow was gone from behind the Mountain. Everything in the room had turned gray and indistinct, and an autumnal dampness crept up from the hollow below the orchard, laying its cold touch on their flushed faces. Harney walked the length of the room, and then turned back and sat down at the table.

"Come," he said imperiously.

She sat down beside him, and he untied the string about the package and spread out a pile of sandwiches.

"I stole them from the love feast at Hamblin," he said with a laugh, pushing them over to her. She laughed too, and took one, and began to eat.

"Didn't you make the tea?"

"No," she said. "I forgot—"

"Oh, well—it's too late to boil the water now." He said nothing more, and sitting opposite to each other they went on silently eating the sandwiches. Darkness had descended in the little room, and Harney's face was a dim blur to Charity. Suddenly he leaned across the table and laid his hand on hers.

"I shall have to go off for a while—a month or two, perhaps— to arrange some things; and then I'll come back . . . and we'll get married."

His voice seemed like a stranger's: nothing was left in it of the vibrations she knew. Her hand lay inertly under his, and she left it there, and raised her head, trying to answer him. But the words died in her throat. They sat motionless, in their attitude of confident endearment, as if some strange death had surprised them. At length Harney sprang to his feet with a slight shiver. "God! it's damp—we couldn't have come here much longer." He went to the shelf, took down a tin candlestick and lit the candle; then he propped an unhinged shutter against the empty window frame and put the candle on the table. It threw up a queer shadow on his frowning forehead, and made the smile on his lips a grimace.

"But it's been good, though, hasn't it, Charity? . . . What's the matter—why do you stand there staring at me? Haven't the days here been good?" He went up to her and caught her to his breast. "And there'll be others—lots of others . . . jollier . . . even jollier . . . won't there, darling?"

He turned her head back, feeling for the curve of her throat below the ear, and kissing her there, and on the hair and eyes and lips. She clung to him desperately, and as he drew her to his knees on the couch she felt as if they were being sucked down together into some bottomless abyss.

# —— 15 ——

THAT NIGHT, as usual, they said good-bye at the wood's edge.

Harney was to leave the next morning early. He asked Charity to say nothing of their plans till his return, and, strangely even to herself, she was glad of the postponement. A leaden weight of shame hung on her, benumbing every other sensation, and she bade him good-bye with hardly a sign of emotion. His reiterated promises to return seemed almost wounding. She had no doubt that he intended to come back; her doubts were far deeper and less definable.

Since the fanciful vision of the future that had flitted through her imagination at their first meeting she had hardly ever thought of his marrying her. She had not had to put the thought from her mind; it had not been there. If ever she looked ahead she felt instinctively that the gulf between them was too deep, and that the bridge their passion had flung across it was as insubstantial as a rainbow. But she seldom looked ahead; each day was so rich that it absorbed her. . . . Now her first feeling was that everything would be different, and that she herself would be a different being to Harney. Instead of remaining separate and absolute, she would be compared with other people, and unknown things would be expected of her. She was too proud to be afraid, but the freedom of her spirit drooped. . . .

Harney had not fixed any date for his return; he had said he would have to look about first, and settle things. He had promised to write as soon as there was anything definite to say, and had left her his address, and asked her to write also. But the address frightened her. It was in New York, at a club with a long name in Fifth Avenue: it seemed to raise an insurmountable barrier between them. Once or twice, in the first days, she got out a sheet of paper, and sat looking at it, and trying to think what to say; but she had the feeling that her letter would never reach its destination. She had never written to anyone farther away than Hepburn.

Harney's first letter came after he had been gone about ten days. It was tender but grave, and bore no resemblance to the gay little notes he had sent her by the freckled boy from Creston River. He spoke positively of his intention of coming back, but named no date, and reminded Charity of their agreement that their plans should not be divulged till he had had time to "settle things." When that would be he could not yet foresee; but she could count on his returning as soon as the way was clear.

She read the letter with a strange sense of its coming from immeasurable distances and having lost most of its meaning on the way; and in reply she sent him a colored postcard of Creston Falls, on which she wrote: "With love from Charity." She felt the pitiful inadequacy of this, and understood, with a sense of despair, that in her inability to express herself she must give him an impression of coldness and reluctance; but she could not help it. She could not forget that he had never spoken to her of marriage till Mr. Royall had forced the word from his lips; though she had not had the strength to shake off the spell that bound her to him she had lost all spontaneity of feeling, and seemed to herself to be passively awaiting a fate she could not avert.

She had not seen Mr. Royall on her return to the red house. The morning after her parting from Harney, when she came down from her room, Verena told her that her guardian had gone off to Worcester and Portland. It was the time of year when he usually reported to the insurance agencies he represented, and there was nothing unusual in his departure except its suddenness. She thought little about him, except to be glad he was not there. . . .

She kept to herself for the first days, while North Dormer was recovering from its brief plunge into publicity, and the subsiding agitation left her unnoticed. But the faithful Ally could not be long avoided. For the first few days after the close of the Old Home Week festivities Charity escaped her by roaming the hills all day when she was not at her post in the library; but after that a period of rain set in, and one pouring afternoon Ally, sure that she would find her friend indoors, came around to the red house with her sewing.

The two girls sat upstairs in Charity's room. Charity, her idle hands in her lap, was sunk in a kind of leaden dream, through which she was only half-conscious of Ally, who sat opposite her in a low rush-bottomed chair, her work pinned to her knee, and her thin lips pursed up as she bent above it.

"It was my idea running a ribbon through the gauging," she said proudly, drawing back to contemplate the blouse she was trimming. "It's for Miss Balch: she was awfully pleased." She paused and then added, with a queer tremor in her piping voice: "I darsn't have told her I got the idea from one I saw on Julia."

Charity raised her eyes listlessly. "Do you still see Julia sometimes?"

Ally reddened, as if the allusion had escaped her unintentionally. "Oh, it was a long time ago I seen her with those gaugings. . . ."

Silence fell again, and Ally presently continued: "Miss Balch left me a whole lot of things to do over this time."

"Why—has she gone?" Charity inquired with an inner start of apprehension.

"Didn't you know? She went off the morning after they had the celebration at Hamblin. I seen her drive by early with Mr. Harney."

There was another silence, measured by the steady tick of the rain against the window, and, at intervals, by the snipping sound of Ally's scissors.

Ally gave a meditative laugh. "Do you know what she told me before she went away? She told me she was going to send for me to come over to Springfield and make some things for her wedding."

Charity again lifted her heavy lids and stared at Ally's pale pointed face, which moved to and fro above her moving fingers.

"Is she going to get married?"

Ally let the blouse sink to her knee, and sat gazing at it. Her lips seemed suddenly dry, and she moistened them a little with her tongue.

"Why, I presume so . . . from what she said. . . . Didn't you know?"

"Why should I know?"

Ally did not answer. She bent above the blouse, and began picking out a basting thread with the point of the scissors.

"Why should I know?" Charity repeated harshly.

"I didn't know but what . . . folks here say she's engaged to Mr. Harney."

Charity stood up with a laugh, and stretched her arms lazily above her head.

"If all the people got married that folks say are going to you'd have your time full making wedding dresses," she said ironically.

"Why—don't you believe it?" Ally ventured.

"It wouldn't make it true if I did—nor prevent it if I didn't."

"That's so. . . . I only know I seen her crying the night of the party because her dress didn't set right. That was why she wouldn't dance any. . . ."

Charity stood absently gazing down at the lacy garment on Ally's knee. Abruptly she stooped and snatched it up.

"Well, I guess she won't dance in this either," she said with sudden violence; and grasping the blouse in her strong young hands she tore it in two and flung the tattered bits to the floor.

"Oh, Charity—" Ally cried, springing up. For a long interval the two girls faced each other across the ruined garment. Ally burst into tears.

"Oh, what'll I say to her? What'll I do? It was real lace!" she wailed between her piping sobs.

Charity glared at her unrelentingly. "You'd oughtn't to have brought it here," she said, breathing quickly. "I hate other people's clothes—it's just as if they was there themselves." The two stared at each other again over this avowal, till Charity brought out, in a gasp of anguish: "Oh, go—go—go—or I'll hate you too. . . ."

When Ally left her, she fell sobbing across her bed.

The long storm was followed by a northwest gale, and when it was over the hills took on their first umber tints, the sky grew more densely blue, and the big white clouds lay against the hills like snowbanks. The first crisp maple leaves began to spin across Miss Hatchard's lawn, and the Virginia creeper on the Memorial splashed the white porch with scarlet. It was a golden triumphant September. Day by day the flame of the Virginia creeper spread to the hillsides in wider waves of carmine and crimson, the larches

glowed like the thin yellow halo about a fire, the maples blazed
and smoldered, and the black hemlocks turned to indigo against
the incandescence of the forest.

The nights were cold, with a dry glitter of stars so high up that
they seemed smaller and more vivid. Sometimes, as Charity lay
sleepless on her bed through the long hours, she felt as though
she were bound to those wheeling fires and swinging with them
around the great black vault. At night she planned many things
. . . it was then she wrote to Harney. But the letters were never
put on paper, for she did not know how to express what she
wanted to tell him. So she waited. Since her talk with Ally she had
felt sure that Harney was engaged to Annabel Balch, and that the
process of "settling things" would involve the breaking of this tie.
Her first rage of jealousy over, she felt no fear on this score. She
was still sure that Harney would come back, and she was equally
sure that, for the moment at least, it was she whom he loved and
not Miss Balch. Yet the girl, no less, remained a rival, since she
represented all the things that Charity felt herself most incapable
of understanding or achieving. Annabel Balch was, if not the girl
Harney ought to marry, at least the kind of girl it would be natural for him to marry. Charity had never been able to picture
herself as his wife; had never been able to arrest the vision and
follow it out in its daily consequences; but she could perfectly
imagine Annabel Balch in that relation to him.

The more she thought of these things the more the sense of
fatality weighed on her: she felt the uselessness of struggling
against the circumstances. She had never known how to adapt
herself; she could only break and tear and destroy. The scene
with Ally had left her stricken with shame at her own childish
savagery. What would Harney have thought if he had witnessed
it? But when she turned the incident over in her puzzled mind
she could not imagine what a civilized person would have done in
her place. She felt herself too unequally pitted against unknown
forces. . . .

At length this feeling moved her to sudden action. She took a
sheet of letter paper from Mr. Royall's office, and sitting by the
kitchen lamp, one night after Verena had gone to bed, began her
first letter to Harney. It was very short:

I want you should marry Annabel Balch if you promised to. I think maybe you were afraid I'd feel too bad about it. I feel I'd rather you acted right.

Your loving
CHARITY

She posted the letter early the next morning, and for a few days her heart felt strangely light. Then she began to wonder why she received no answer.

One day as she sat alone in the library pondering these things the walls of books began to spin around her, and the rosewood desk to rock under her elbows. The dizziness was followed by a wave of nausea like that she had felt on the day of the exercises in the Town Hall. But the Town Hall had been crowded and stiflingly hot, and the library was empty, and so chilly that she had kept on her jacket. Five minutes before she had felt perfectly well; and now it seemed as if she were going to die. The bit of lace at which she still languidly worked dropped from her fingers, and the steel crochet hook clattered to the floor. She pressed her temples hard between her damp hands, steadying herself against the desk while the wave of sickness swept over her. Little by little it subsided, and after a few minutes she stood up, shaken and terrified, groped for her hat, and stumbled out into the air. But the whole sunlit autumn world reeled and roared around her as she dragged herself along the interminable length of the road home.

As she approached the red house she saw a buggy standing at the door, and her heart gave a leap. But it was only Mr. Royall who got out, his traveling bag in hand. He saw her coming, and waited in the porch. She was conscious that he was looking at her intently, as if there was something strange in her appearance, and she threw back her head with a desperate effort at ease. Their eyes met, and she said: "You back?" as if nothing had happened, and he answered: "Yes, I'm back," and walked in ahead of her, pushing open the door of his office. She climbed to her room, every step of the stairs holding her fast as if her feet were lined with glue.

Two days later, she descended from the train at Nettleton, and walked out of the station into the dusty square. The brief interval of cold weather was over, and the day was as soft, and almost as hot, as when she and Harney had emerged on the same scene on the Fourth of July. In the square the same broken-down hacks and carryalls stood drawn up in a despondent line, and the lank horses with fly nets over their withers swayed their heads drearily to and fro. She recognized the staring signs over the eating houses and billiard saloons, and the long lines of wires on lofty poles tapering down the main street to the park at its other end. Taking the way the wires pointed, she went on hastily, with bent head, till she reached a wide transverse street with a brick building at the corner. She crossed this street and glanced furtively up at the front of the brick building; then she returned, and entered a door opening on a flight of steep brass-rimmed stairs. On the second landing she rang a bell, and a mulatto girl with a bushy head and a frilled apron let her into a hall where a stuffed fox on his hind legs proffered a brass card tray to visitors. At the back of the hall was a glazed door marked "Office." After waiting a few minutes in a handsomely furnished room, with plush sofas surmounted by large gold-framed photographs of showy young women, Charity was shown into the office. . . .

When she came out of the glazed door Dr. Merkle followed, and led her into another room, smaller, and still more crowded with plush and gold frames. Dr. Merkle was a plump woman with small bright eyes, an immense mass of black hair coming down low on her forehead, and unnaturally white and even teeth. She wore a rich black dress, with gold chains and charms hanging from her bosom. Her hands were large and smooth, and quick in all their movements; and she smelt of musk and carbolic acid.

She smiled on Charity with all her faultless teeth. "Sit down, my dear. Wouldn't you like a little drop of something to pick you up? . . . No. . . . Well, just lay back a minute then. . . . There's nothing to be done just yet; but in about a month, if you'll step round again . . . I could take you right into my own house for two or three days, and there wouldn't be a mite of trouble. Mercy me! The next time you'll know better'n to fret like this. . . ."

Charity gazed at her with widening eyes. This woman with the false hair, the false teeth, the false murderous smile—what was she offering her but immunity from some unthinkable crime?

Charity, till then, had been conscious only of a vague self-disgust and a frightening physical distress; now, of a sudden, there came to her the grave surprise of motherhood. She had come to this dreadful place because she knew of no other way of making sure that she was not mistaken about her state; and the woman had taken her for a miserable creature like Julia. : . . The thought was so horrible that she sprang up, white and shaking, one of her great rushes of anger sweeping over her.

Dr. Merkle, still smiling, also rose. "Why do you run off in such a hurry? You can stretch out right here on my sofa. . . ." She paused, and her smile grew more motherly "Afterwards—if there's been any talk at home, and you want to get away for a while . . . I have a lady friend in Boston who's looking for a companion . . . you're the very one to suit her, my dear. . . ."

Charity had reached the door. "I don't want to stay. I don't want to come back here," she stammered, her hand on the knob; but with a swift movement Dr. Merkle edged her from the threshold.

"Oh, very well. Five dollars, please."

Charity looked helplessly at the doctor's tight lips and rigid face. Her last savings had gone in repaying Ally for the cost of Miss Balch's ruined blouse, and she had had to borrow four dollars from her friend to pay for her railway ticket and cover the doctor's fee. It had never occurred to her that medical advice could cost more than two dollars.

"I didn't know . . . I haven't got that much . . ." she faltered, bursting into tears.

Dr. Merkle gave a short laugh which did not show her teeth, and inquired with concision if Charity supposed she ran the establishment for her own amusement? She leaned her firm shoulders against the door as she spoke, like a grim jailer making terms with her captive.

"You say you'll come round and settle later? I've heard that pretty often too. Give me your address, and if you can't pay me I'll send the bill to your folks. . . . What? I can't understand what you say. . . . That don't suit you either? My, you're pretty particular for a girl that ain't got enough to settle her own bills. . . ." She paused, and fixed her eyes on the brooch with a blue stone that Charity had pinned to her blouse.

"Ain't you ashamed to talk that way to a lady that's got to earn her living, when you go about with jewelry like that on you? . . . It ain't in my line, and I do it only as a favor . . . but if you're a mind to leave that brooch as a pledge, I don't say no. . . . Yes, of course, you can get it back when you bring me my money. . . ."

On the way home, she felt an immense and unexpected quietude. It had been horrible to have to leave Harney's gift in the woman's hands, but even at that price the news she brought away had not been too dearly bought. She sat with half-closed eyes as the train rushed through the familiar landscape; and now the memories of her former journey, instead of flying before her like dead leaves, seemed to be ripening in her blood like sleeping grain. She would never again know what it was to feel herself alone. Everything seemed to have grown suddenly clear and simple. She no longer had any difficulty in picturing herself as Harney's wife now that she was the mother of his child; and compared to her sovereign right Annabel Balch's claim seemed no more than a girl's sentimental fancy.

That evening, at the gate of the red house, she found Ally waiting in the dusk. "I was down at the post office just as they were closing up, and Will Targatt said there was a letter for you, so I brought it."

Ally held out the letter, looking at Charity with piercing sympathy. Since the scene of the torn blouse there had been a new and fearful admiration in the eyes she bent on her friend.

Charity snatched the letter with a laugh. "Oh, thank you—good night," she called out over her shoulder as she ran up the path. If she had lingered a moment she knew she would have had Ally at her heels.

She hurried upstairs and felt her way into her dark room. Her hands trembled as she groped for the matches and lit her candle, and the flap of the envelope was so closely stuck that she had to find her scissors and slit it open. At length she read:

DEAR CHARITY:
    I have your letter, and it touches me more than I can say. Won't you trust me, in return, to do my best? There are things it

is hard to explain, much less to justify; but your generosity makes everything easier. All I can do now is to thank you from my soul for understanding. Your telling me that you wanted me to do right has helped me beyond expression. If ever there is a hope of realizing what we dreamed of you will see me back on the instant; and I haven't yet lost that hope.

She read the letter with a rush; then she went over and over it, each time more slowly and painstakingly. It was so beautifully expressed that she found it almost as difficult to understand as the gentleman's explanation of the Bible pictures at Nettleton; but gradually she became aware that the gist of its meaning lay in the last few words. "If ever there is a hope of realizing what we dreamed of . . ."

But then he wasn't even sure of that? She understood now that every word and every reticence was an avowal of Annabel Balch's prior claim. It was true that he was engaged to her, and that he had not yet found a way of breaking his engagement.

As she read the letter over Charity understood what it must have cost him to write it. He was not trying to evade an importunate claim; he was honestly and contritely struggling between opposing duties. She did not even reproach him in her thoughts for having concealed from her that he was not free: she could not see anything more reprehensible in his conduct than in her own. From the first she had needed him more than he had wanted her, and the power that had swept them together had been as far beyond resistance as a great gale loosening the leaves of the forest. . . . Only, there stood between them, fixed and upright in the general upheaval, the indestructible figure of Annabel Balch. . . .

Face to face with his admission of the fact, she sat staring at the letter. A cold tremor ran over her, and the hard sobs struggled up into her throat and shook her from head to foot. For a while she was caught and tossed on great waves of anguish that left her hardly conscious of anything but the blind struggle against their assaults. Then, little by little, she began to relive, with a dreadful poignancy, each separate stage of her poor romance. Foolish things she had said came back to her, gay answers Harney had made, his first kiss in the darkness between the fireworks, their choosing the blue brooch together, the way he had teased her about the letters she had dropped in her flight from the evangelist. All these memories, and a thousand others, hummed through her brain till his nearness grew so vivid that she felt his fingers in her hair, and his warm breath on her cheek as he bent her head back like a flower. These things were hers; they had passed into her blood, and become a part of her, they were building the child in her womb; it was impossible to tear asunder strands of life so interwoven.

The conviction gradually strengthened her, and she began to form in her mind the first words of the letter she meant to write to Harney. She wanted to write it at once, and with feverish hands she began to rummage in her drawer for a sheet of letter paper. But there was none left; she must go downstairs to get it. She had a superstitious feeling that the letter must be written on the instant, that setting down her secret in words would bring her reassurance and safety; and taking up her candle she went down to Mr. Royall's office.

At that hour she was not likely to find him there: he had probably had his supper and walked over to Carrick Fry's. She pushed open the door of the unlit room, and the light of her lifted candle fell on his figure, seated in the darkness in his high-backed chair. His arms lay along the arms of the chair, and his head was bent a little; but he lifted it quickly as Charity entered. She started back as their eyes met, remembering that her own were red with weeping, and that her face was livid with the fatigue and emotion of her journey. But it was too late to escape, and she stood and looked at him in silence.

He had risen from his chair, and came toward her with outstretched hands. The gesture was so unexpected that she let him take her hands in his, and they stood thus, without speaking, till Mr. Royall said gravely: "Charity—was you looking for me?"

She freed herself abruptly and fell back. "Me? No—" She set down the candle on his desk. "I wanted some letter paper, that's all."

His face contracted, and the bushy brows jutted forward over his eyes. Without answering he opened the drawer of the desk, took out a sheet of paper and an envelope, and pushed them toward her. "Do you want a stamp too?" he asked.

She nodded, and he gave her the stamp. As he did so she felt that he was looking at her intently, and she knew that the candle-light flickering up on her white face must be distorting her swollen features and exaggerating the dark rings about her eyes. She snatched up the paper, her reassurance dissolving under his pitiless gaze, in which she seemed to read the grim perception of her state, and the ironic recollection of the day when, in that very room, he had offered to compel Harney to marry her. His look seemed to say that he knew she had taken the paper to write to her lover, who had left her as he had warned her she would be left. She remembered the scorn with which she had turned from him that day, and knew, if he guessed the truth, what a list of old scores it must settle. She turned and fled upstairs; but when she got back to her room all the words that had been waiting had vanished. . . .

If she could have gone to Harney it would have been different; she would only have had to show herself to let his memories speak for her. But she had no money left, and there was no one from whom she could have borrowed enough for such a journey. There was nothing to do but to write, and await his reply. For a long time she sat bent above the blank page; but she found nothing to say that really expressed what she was feeling. . . .

Harney had written that she had made it easier for him, and she was glad it was so; she did not want to make things hard. She knew she had it in her power to do that; she held his fate in her hands. All she had to do was to tell him the truth; but that was the very fact that held her back. . . . Her five minutes face to face with Mr. Royall had stripped her of her last illusion, and brought her back to North Dormer's point of view. Distinctly and pitilessly there rose before her the fate of the girl who was married "to make things right." She had seen too many village love stories end in that way. Poor Rose Coles's miserable marriage was of the number; and what good had come of it for her or for Halston Skeff? They had hated each other from the day the minister married them; and whenever old Mrs. Skeff had a fancy to humiliate her daughter-in-law she had only to say: "Who'd ever think the baby's only two? And for a seven months' child—ain't it a wonder what a size he is?" North Dormer had treasures of indulgence for brands in the burning, but only derision for those who succeeded in getting snatched from it; and Charity had always understood Julia Hawes's refusal to be snatched. . . .

Only—was there no alternative but Julia's? Her soul recoiled from the vision of the white-faced woman among the plush sofas and gilt frames. In the established order of things as she knew them she saw no place for her individual adventure. . . .

She sat in her chair without undressing till faint gray streaks began to divide the black slats of the shutters. Then she stood up and pushed them open, letting in the light. The coming of a new day brought a sharper consciouness of ineluctable reality, and with it a sense of the need of action. She looked at herself in the glass, and saw her face, white in the autumn dawn, with pinched cheeks and dark-ringed eyes, and all the marks of her state that she herself would never have noticed, but that Dr. Merkle's diagnosis had made plain to her. She could not hope that those signs would escape the watchful village; even before her figure lost its shape she knew her face would betray her.

Leaning from her window she looked out on the dark and empty scene; the ashen houses with shuttered windows, the gray road climbing the slope to the hemlock belt above the cemetery, and the heavy mass of the Mountain black against a rainy sky. To the east a space of light was broadening above the forest; but over that also the clouds hung. Slowly her gaze traveled across the fields to the rugged curve of the hills. She had looked out so often on that lifeless circle, and wondered if anything could ever happen to anyone who was enclosed in it. . . .

Almost without conscious thought her decision had been reached; as her eyes had followed the circle of the hills her mind had also traveled the old round. She supposed it was something in her blood that made the Mountain the only answer to her questioning, the inevitable escape from all that hemmed her in and beset her. At any rate it began to loom in her now as it loomed against the rainy dawn; and the longer she looked at it the more clearly she understood that now at last she was really going there.

# ——16——

THE RAIN held off, and an hour later, when she started, wild gleams of sunlight were blowing across the fields.

After Harney's departure she had returned her bicycle to its owner at Creston, and she was not sure of being able to walk all the way to the Mountain. The deserted house was on the road; but the idea of spending the night there was unendurable, and she meant to try to push on to Hamblin, where she could sleep under a woodshed if her strength should fail her. Her preparations had been made with quiet forethought. Before starting she had forced herself to swallow a glass of milk and eat a piece of bread; and she had put in her canvas satchel a little packet of the chocolate that Harney always carried in his bicycle bag. She wanted above all to keep up her strength, and reach her destination without attracting notice. . . .

Mile by mile she retraced the road over which she had so often flown to her lover. When she reached the turn where the wood road branched off from the Creston highway she remembered the Gospel tent—long since folded up and transplanted—and her start of involuntary terror when the fat evangelist had said: "Your Savior knows everything. Come and confess your guilt." There was no sense of guilt in her now, but only a desperate desire to defend her secret from irreverent eyes, and begin life again among people to whom the harsh code of the village was unknown. The impulse did not shape itself in thought: she only knew she must save her baby, and hide herself with it somewhere where no one would ever come to trouble them.

She walked on and on, growing more heavy-footed as the day advanced. It seemed a cruel chance that compelled her to retrace every step of the way to the deserted house; and when she came in sight of the orchard, and the silver-gray roof slanting crookedly through the laden branches, her strength failed her and she sat down by the roadside. She sat there a long time, trying to gather the courage to start again, and walk past the broken gate and the untrimmed rosebushes strung with scarlet hips. A few drops of rain were falling, and she thought of the warm evenings when she and Harney had sat embraced in the shadowy room, and the noise of summer showers on the roof had rustled through their kisses. At length she understood that if she stayed any longer the rain might compel her take shelter in the house overnight, and she got up and walked on, averting her eyes as she came abreast of the white gate and the tangled garden.

The hours wore on, and she walked more and more slowly, pausing now and then to rest, and to eat a little bread and an apple picked up from the roadside. Her body seemed to grow heavier with every yard of the way, and she wondered how she would be able to carry her child later, if already he laid such a burden on her. . . . A fresh wind had sprung up, scattering the rain and blowing down keenly from the mountain. Presently the clouds lowered again, and a few white darts struck her in the face: it was the first snow falling over Hamblin. The roofs of the lonely village were only half a mile ahead, and she was resolved to push beyond it, and try to reach the Mountain that night. She had no clear plan of action, except that, once in the settlement, she meant to look for Liff Hyatt, and get him to take her to her mother. She herself had been born as her own baby was going to be born; and whatever her mother's subsequent life had been, she could hardly help remembering the past, and receiving a daughter who was facing the trouble she had known.

Suddenly the deadly faintness came over her once more and she sat down on the bank and leaned her head against a tree trunk. The long road and the cloudy landscape vanished from her eyes, and for a time she seemed to be circling about in some terrible wheeling darkness. Then that too faded.

She opened her eyes, and saw a buggy drawn up beside her, and a man who had jumped down from it and was gazing at her with a puzzled face. Slowly consciousness came back, and she saw that the man was Liff Hyatt.

She was dimly aware that he was asking her something, and she looked at him in silence, trying to find strength to speak. At length her voice stirred in her throat, and she said in a whisper: "I'm going up the Mountain."

"Up the Mountain?" he repeated, drawing aside a little; and as he moved she saw behind him, in the buggy, a heavily coated figure with a familiar pink face and gold spectacles on the bridge of a Grecian nose.

"Charity! What on earth are you doing here?" Mr. Miles exclaimed, throwing the reins on the horse's back and scrambling down from the buggy.

She lifted her heavy eyes to his. "I'm going to see my mother."

The two men glanced at each other, and for a moment neither of them spoke.

Then Mr. Miles said: "You look ill, my dear, and it's a long way. Do you think it's wise?"

Charity stood up. "I've got to go to her."

A vague mirthless grin contracted Liff Hyatt's face, and Mr. Miles again spoke uncertainly. "You know, then—you'd been told?"

She stared at him. "I don't know what you mean. I want to go to her."

Mr. Miles was examining her thoughtfully. She fancied she saw a change in his expression, and the blood rushed to her forehead. "I just want to go to her," she repeated.

He laid his hand on her arm. "My child, your mother is dying. Liff Hyatt came down to fetch me. . . . Get in and come with us."

He helped her up to the seat at his side, Liff Hyatt clambered in at the back, and they drove off toward Hamblin. At first Charity had hardly grasped what Mr. Miles was saying; the physical relief of finding herself seated in the buggy, and securely on her road to the Mountain, effaced the impression of his words. But as her head cleared she began to understand. She knew the Mountain had but the most infrequent intercourse with the valleys; she had often enough heard it said that no one ever went up there except the minister, when someone was dying. And now it was her mother who was dying . . . and she would find herself as much alone on the Mountain as anywhere else in the world. The sense of unescapable isolation was all she could feel for the moment; then she began to wonder at the strangeness of its being Mr. Miles who had undertaken to perform this grim errand. He did not seem in the least like the kind of man who would care to go up the Mountain. But here he was at her side, guiding the horse with a firm hand, and bending on her the kindly gleam of his spectacles, as if there were nothing unusual in their being together in such circumstances.

For a while she found it impossible to speak, and he seemed to understand this, and made no attempt to question her. But presently she felt her tears rise and flow down over her drawn cheeks; and he must have seen them too, for he laid his hand on hers, and said in a low voice: "Won't you tell me what is troubling you?"

She shook her head, and he did not insist: but after a while he said, in the same low tone, so that they should not be overheard: "Charity, what do you know of your childhood, before you came down to North Dormer?"

She controlled herself, and answered: "Nothing, only what I heard Mr. Royall say one day. He said he brought me down because my father went to prison."

"And you've never been up there since?"

"Never."

Mr. Miles was silent again, then he said: "I'm glad you're coming with me now. Perhaps we may find your mother alive, and she may know that you have come."

They had reached Hamblin, where the snow flurry had left white patches in the rough grass on the roadside, and in the angles of the roofs facing north. It was a poor bleak village under the granite flank of the Mountain, and as soon as they left it they began to climb. The road was steep and full of ruts, and the horse settled down to a walk while they mounted and mounted, the world dropping away below them in great mottled stretches of forest and field, and stormy dark blue distances.

Charity had often had visions of this ascent of the Mountain but she had not known it would reveal so wide a country, and the sight of those strange lands reaching away on every side gave her a new sense of Harney's remoteness. She knew he must be miles and miles beyond the last range of hills that seemed to be the outmost verge of things, and she wondered how she had ever dreamed of going to New York to find him. . . .

As the road mounted the country grew bleaker, and they drove across fields of faded mountain grass bleached by long months beneath the snow. In the hollows a few white birches trembled, or a mountain ash lit its scarlet clusters; but only a scant growth of pines darkened the granite ledges. The wind was blowing fiercely across the open slopes; the horse faced it with bent head and straining flanks, and now and then the buggy swayed so that Charity had to clutch its side.

Mr. Miles had not spoken again; he seemed to understand that she wanted to be left alone. After a while the track they were following forked, and he pulled up the horse, as if uncertain of the way. Liff Hyatt craned his head around from the back, and shouted against the wind: "Left—" and they turned into a stunted pine wood and began to drive down the other side of the Mountain.

A mile or two farther on they came out on a clearing where two or three low houses lay in stony fields, crouching among the rocks as if to brace themselves against the wind. They were hardly more than sheds, built of logs and rough boards, with tin stovepipes sticking out of their roofs. The sun was setting, and dusk had already fallen on the lower world, but a yellow glare still lay on the lonely hillside and the crouching houses. The next moment it faded and left the landscape in dark autumn twilight.

"Over there," Liff called out, stretching his long arm over Mr. Miles's shoulder. The clergyman turned to the left, across a bit of bare ground overgrown with docks and nettles, and stopped before the most ruinous of the sheds. A stovepipe reached its crooked arm out of one window, and the broken panes of the other were stuffed with rags and paper. In contrast to such a dwelling the brown house in the swamp might have stood for the home of plenty.

As the buggy drew up two or three mongrel dogs jumped out of the twilight with a great barking, and a young man slouched to the door and stood there staring. In the twilight Charity saw that his face had the same sodden look as Bash Hyatt's, the day she had seen him sleeping by the stove. He made no effort to silence the dogs, but leaned in the door, as if roused from a drunken lethargy, while Mr. Miles got out of the buggy.

"Is it here?" the clergyman asked Liff in a low voice; and Liff nodded.

Mr. Miles turned to Charity. "Just hold the horse a minute, my dear: I'll go in first," he said, putting the reins in her hands. She took them passively, and sat staring straight ahead of her at the darkening scene while Mr. Miles and Liff Hyatt went up to the house. They stood a few minutes talking with the man in the door, and then Mr. Miles came back. As he came close, Charity saw that his smooth pink face wore a frightened solemn look.

"Your mother is dead, Charity; you'd better come with me," he said.

She got down and followed him while Liff led the horse away. As she approached the door she said to herself: "This is where I was born . . . this is where I belong. . . ." She had said it to herself often enough as she looked across the sunlit valleys at the Mountain; but it had meant nothing then, and now it had become a reality. Mr. Miles took her gently by the arm, and they entered what appeared to be the only room in the house. It was so dark that she could just discern a group of a dozen people sitting or sprawling about a table made of boards laid across two barrels. They looked up listlessly as Mr. Miles and Charity came in, and a woman's thick voice said: "Here's the preacher." But no one moved.

Mr. Miles paused and looked about him; then he turned to the young man who had met them at the door.

"Is the body here?" he asked.

The young man, instead of answering, turned his head toward the group. "Where's the candle? I tole yer to bring a candle," he said with sudden harshness to a girl who was lolling against the table. She did not answer, but another man got up and took from some corner a candle stuck into a bottle.

"How'll I light it? The stove's out," the girl grumbled.

Mr. Miles fumbled under his heavy wrappings and drew out a matchbox. He held a match to the candle, and in a moment or two a faint circle of light fell on the pale aguish heads that started out of the shadow like the heads of nocturnal animals.

"Mary's over there," someone said; and Mr. Miles, taking the bottle in his hand, passed behind the table. Charity followed him, and they stood before a mattress on the floor in a corner of the room. A woman lay on it, but she did not look like a dead woman; she seemed to have fallen across her squalid bed in a drunken sleep, and to have been left lying where she fell, in her ragged disordered clothes. One arm was flung above her head, one leg drawn up under a torn skirt that left the other bare to the knee: a swollen glistening leg with a ragged stocking rolled down about the ankle. The woman lay on her back, her eyes staring up unblinkingly at the candle that trembled in Mr. Miles's hand.

"She jus' dropped off," a woman said, over the shoulder of the others; and the young man added: "I jus' come in and found her."

An elderly man with lank hair and a feeble grin pushed between them. "It was like this: I says to her on'y the night before: if you don't take and quit, I says to her . . ."

Someone pulled him back and sent him reeling against a bench along the wall, where he dropped down muttering his unheeded narrative.

There was a silence; then the young woman who had been lolling against the table suddenly parted the group, and stood in front of Charity. She was healthier and robuster looking than the others, and her weather-beaten face had a certain sullen beauty.

"Who's the girl? Who brought her here?" she said, fixing her eyes mistrustfully on the young man who had rebuked her for not having a candle ready.

Mr. Miles spoke. "I brought her; she is Mary Hyatt's daughter."

"What? Her too?" the girl sneered; and the young man turned on her with an oath. "Shut your mouth, damn you, or get out of here," he said; then he relapsed into his former apathy, and dropped down on the bench, leaning his head against the wall.

Mr. Miles had set the candle on the floor and taken off his heavy coat. He turned to Charity. "Come and help me," he said.

He knelt down by the mattress, and pressed the lids over the dead woman's eyes. Charity, trembling and sick, knelt beside him, and tried to compose her mother's body. She drew the stocking over the dreadful glistening leg, and pulled the skirt down to the battered upturned boots. As she did so, she looked at her mother's face, thin yet swollen, with lips parted in a frozen gasp above the broken teeth. There was no sign in it of anything human: she lay there like a dead dog in a ditch. Charity's hands grew cold as they touched her.

Mr. Miles drew the woman's arms across her breast and laid his coat over her. Then he covered her face with his handkerchief, and placed the bottle with the candle in it at her head. Having done this he stood up.

"Is there no coffin?" he asked, turning to the group behind him.

There was a moment of bewildered silence; then the fierce girl spoke up. "You'd oughter brought it with you. Where'd we get one here, I'd like ter know?"

Mr. Miles, looking at the others, repeated: "Is it possible you have no coffin ready?"

"That's what I say: them that has it sleeps better," an old woman murmured. "But then she never had no bed. . . ."

"And the stove warn't hers," said the lank-haired man, on the defensive.

Mr. Miles turned away from them and moved a few steps apart. He had drawn a book from his pocket, and after a pause he opened it and began to read, holding the book at arm's length and low down, so that the pages caught the feeble light. Charity had remained on her knees by the mattress: now that her mother's face was covered it was easier to stay near her, and avoid the sight of the living faces which too horribly showed by what stages hers had lapsed into death.

"I am the Resurrection and the Life," Mr. Miles began; "he that believeth in me, though he were dead, yet shall he live. . . . Though after my skin worms destroy my body, yet in my flesh shall I see God. . . ."

*In my flesh shall I see God!* Charity thought of the gaping mouth and stony eyes under the handkerchief, and of the glistening leg over which she had drawn the stocking. . . .

"We brought nothing into this world and we shall take nothing out of it—"

There was a sudden muttering and a scuffle at the back of the group. "I brought the stove," said the elderly man with lank hair, pushing his way between the others. "I wen' down to Creston'n bought it . . . n' I got a right to take it outer here . . . n' I'll lick any feller says I ain't. . . ."

"Sit down, damn you!" shouted the tall youth who had been drowsing on the bench against the wall.

"For man walketh in a vain shadow, and disquieteth himself in vain; he heapeth up riches and cannot tell who shall gather them . . ."

"Well, it *are* his," a woman in the background interjected in a frightened whine.

The tall youth staggered to his feet. "If you don't hold your mouths I'll turn you all out o' here, the whole lot of you," he cried with many oaths. "G'wan, minister . . . don't let 'em faze you. . . ."

"Now is Christ risen from the dead and become the first-fruits of them that slept. . . . Behold, I show you a mystery. We shall not all sleep, but we shall all be changed, in a moment, in the twinkling of an eye, at the last trump. . . . For this corruptible must put on incorruption and this mortal must put on immortality. So when this corruption shall have put on incorruption, and when this mortal shall have put on immortality, then shall be brought to pass the saying that is written, Death is swallowed up in Victory. . . ."

One by one the mighty words fell on Charity's bowed head, soothing the horror, subduing the tumult, mastering her as they mastered the drink-dazed creatures at her back. Mr. Miles read to the last word, and then closed the book.

"Is the grave ready?" he asked.

Liff Hyatt, who had come in while he was reading, nodded a "Yes," and pushed forward to the side of the mattress. The young man on the bench, who seemed to assert some sort of right of kinship with the dead woman, got to his feet again, and the proprietor of the stove joined him. Between them they raised up the mattress; but their movements were unsteady, and the coat slipped to the floor, revealing the poor body in its helpless misery. Charity, picking up the coat, covered her mother once more. Liff had brought a lantern, and the old woman who had already spoken took it up, and opened the door to let the little procession pass out. The wind had dropped, and the night was very dark and bitterly cold. The old woman walked ahead, the lantern shaking in her hand and spreading out before her a pale patch of dead grass and coarse-leaved weeds enclosed in an immensity of blackness.

Mr. Miles took Charity by the arm, and side by side they walked behind the mattress. At length the old woman with the lantern stopped, and Charity saw the light fall on the stooping shoulders of the bearers and on a ridge of upheaved earth over which they were bending. Mr. Miles released her arm and approached the hollow on the other side of the ridge; and while the men stooped down, lowering the mattress into the grave, he began to speak again.

"Man that is born of woman hath but a short time to live and is full of misery. . . . He cometh up and is cut down . . . he fleeth as it were a shadow. . . . Yet, O Lord God most holy, O Lord most mighty, O holy and merciful Savior, deliver us not into the bitter pains of eternal death . . ."

"Easy there . . . is she down?" piped the claimant to the stove; and the young man called over his shoulder: "Lift the light there, can't you?"

There was a pause, during which the light floated uncertainly over the open grave. Someone bent over and pulled out Mr. Miles's coat—("No, no—leave the handkerchief," he interposed)—and then Liff Hyatt, coming forward with a spade, began to shovel in the earth.

"Forasmuch as it hath pleased Almighty God of His great mercy to take unto Himself the soul of our dear sister here departed, we therefore commit her body to the ground; earth to earth, ashes to ashes, dust to dust . . ." Liff's gaunt shoulders rose and bent in the lantern light as he dashed the clods of earth into the grave. "God—it's froze a'ready," he muttered, spitting into his palm and passing his ragged shirtsleeve across his perspiring face.

"Through our Lord Jesus Christ, who shall change our vile body that it may be like unto His glorious body, according to the mighty working, whereby He is able to subdue all things unto Himself . . ." The last spadeful of earth fell on the vile body of Mary Hyatt, and Liff rested on his spade, his shoulder blades still heaving with the effort.

"Lord, have mercy upon us, Christ have mercy upon us, Lord have mercy upon us. . . ."

Mr. Miles took the lantern from the old woman's hand and swept its light across the circle of bleared faces. "Now kneel down, all of you," he commanded, in a voice of authority that Charity had never heard. She knelt down at the edge of the grave, and the others, stiffly and hesitatingly, got to their knees beside her. Mr. Miles knelt, too. "And now pray with me—you know this prayer," he said, and he began: "Our Father which art in Heaven . . ." One or two of the women falteringly took the words up, and when he ended, the lank-haired man flung himself on the neck of the tall youth. "It was this way," he said. "I tole her the night before, I says to her . . ." The reminiscence ended in a sob.

Mr. Miles had been getting into his coat again. He came up to Charity, who had remained passively kneeling by the rough mound of earth.

"My child, you must come. It's very late."

She lifted her eyes to his face: he seemed to speak out of another world.

"I ain't coming: I'm going to stay here."

"Here? Where? What do you mean?"

"These are my folks. I'm going to stay with them."

Mr. Miles lowered his voice. "But it's not possible—you don't know what you are doing. You can't stay among these people: you must come with me."

She shook her head and rose from her knees. The group about the grave had scattered in the darkness, but the old woman with the lantern stood waiting. Her mournful withered face was not unkind, and Charity went up to her.

"Have you got a place where I can lie down for the night?" she asked. Liff came up, leading the buggy out of the night. He looked from one to the other with his feeble smile. "She's my mother. She'll take you home," he said; and he added, raising his voice to speak to the old woman: "It's the girl from lawyer Royall's—Mary's girl . . . you remember. . . ."

The woman nodded and raised her sad old eyes to Charity's. When Mr. Miles and Liff clambered into the buggy she went ahead with the lantern to show them the track they were to follow; then she turned back, and in silence she and Charity walked away together through the night.

# ——17——

CHARITY LAY on the floor on a mattress, as her dead mother's body had lain. The room in which she lay was cold and dark and low-ceilinged, and even poorer and barer than the scene of Mary Hyatt's earthly pilgrimage. On the other side of the fireless stove Liff Hyatt's mother slept on a blanket, with two children—her grandchildren, she said—rolled up against her like sleeping puppies. They had their thin clothes spread over them, having given the only other blanket to their guest.

Through the small square of glass in the opposite wall Charity saw a deep funnel of sky, so black, so remote, so palpitating with frosty stars that her very soul seemed to be sucked up into it. Up there somewhere, she supposed, the God whom Mr. Miles had invoked was waiting for Mary Hyatt to appear. What a long flight it was! And what would she have to say when she reached Him?

Charity's bewildered brain labored with the attempt to picture her mother's past, and to relate it in any way to the designs of a just but merciful God; but it was impossible to imagine any link between them. She herself felt as remote from the poor creature she had seen lowered into her hastily dug grave as if the height of the heavens had divided them. She had seen poverty and misfortune in her life; but in a community where poor thrifty Mrs. Hawes and the industrious Ally represented the nearest approach to destitution there was nothing to suggest the savage misery of the Mountain farmers.

As she lay there, half-stunned by her tragic initiation, Charity vainly tried to think herself into the life about her. But she could not even make out what relationship these people bore to each other, or to her dead mother; they seemed to be herded together in a sort of passive promiscuity in which their common misery was the strongest link. She tried to picture to herself what her life would have been if she had grown up on the Mountain, running wild in rags, sleeping on the floor curled up against her mother, like the pale-faced children huddled against old Mrs. Hyatt, and turning into a fierce bewildered creature like the girl who had apostrophized her in such strange words. She was frightened by the secret affinity she had felt with this girl, and by the light it threw on her own beginnings. Then she remembered what Mr. Royall had said in telling her story to Lucius Harney: "Yes, there was a mother; but she was glad to have the child go. She'd have given her to anybody. . . ."

Well! After all, was her mother so much to blame? Charity, since that day, had always thought of her as destitute of all human feeling; now she seemed merely pitiful. What mother would not want to save her child from such a life? Charity thought of the future of her own child, and tears welled into her aching eyes, and ran down over her face. If she had been less exhausted, less burdened with his weight, she would have sprung up then and there and fled away. . . .

The grim hours of the night dragged themselves slowly by, and at last the sky paled and dawn threw a cold blue beam into the room. She lay in her corner staring at the dirty floor, the clothesline hung with decaying rags, the old woman huddled against the cold stove, and the light gradually spreading across the wintry world, and bringing with it a new day in which she would have to live, to choose, to act, to make herself a place among these people—or to go back to the life she had left. A mortal lassitude weighed on her. There were moments when she felt that all she asked was to go on lying there unnoticed; then her mind revolted at the thought of becoming one of the miserable herd from which she sprang, and it seemed as though, to save her child from such a fate, she would find strength to travel any distance, and bear any burden life might put on her.

Vague thoughts of Nettleton flitted through her mind. She said to herself that she would find some quiet place where she could bear her child, and give it to decent people to keep; and then she would go out like Julia Hawes and earn its living and hers. She knew that girls of that kind sometimes made enough to have their children nicely cared for; and every other consideration disappeared in the vision of her baby, cleaned and combed and rosy, and hidden away somewhere where she could run in and kiss it, and bring it pretty things to wear. Anything, anything was better than to add another life to the nest of misery on the Mountain. . . .

The old woman and the children were still sleeping when Charity rose from her mattress. Her body was stiff with cold and fatigue, and she moved slowly lest her heavy steps should rouse them. She was faint with hunger, and had nothing left in her satchel; but on the table she saw the half of a stale loaf. No doubt it was to serve as the breakfast of old Mrs. Hyatt and the children; but Charity did not care; she had her own baby to think of. She broke off a piece of the bread and ate it greedily; then her glance fell on the thin faces of the sleeping children, and filled with compunction she rummaged in her satchel for something with which to pay for what she had taken. She found one of the pretty chemises that Ally had made for her, with a blue ribbon run through its edging. It was one of the dainty things on which she had squandered her savings, and as she looked at it the blood rushed to her forehead. She laid the chemise on the table, and stealing across the floor lifted the latch and went out. . . .

The morning was icy cold and a pale sun was just rising above the eastern shoulder of the Mountain. The houses scattered on the hillside lay cold and smokeless under the sun-flecked clouds, and not a human being was in sight. Charity paused on the threshold and tried to discover the road by which she had come the night before. Across the field surrounding Mrs. Hyatt's shanty she saw the tumble-down house in which she supposed the funeral service had taken place. The trail ran across the ground between the two houses and disappeared in the pine wood on the flank of the Mountain; and a little way to the right, under a wind-beaten thorn, a mound of fresh earth made a dark spot on the fawn-colored stubble. Charity walked across the field to the mound. As she approached it she heard a bird's note in the still air, and looking up she saw a brown song sparrow perched in an upper branch of the thorn above the grave. She stood a minute listening to his small solitary song; then she rejoined the trail and began to mount the hill to the pine wood.

Thus far she had been impelled by the blind instinct of flight; but each step seemed to bring her nearer to the realities of which her feverish vigil had given only a shadowy image. Now that she walked again in a daylight world, on the way back to familiar things, her imagination moved more soberly. On one point she was still decided: she could not remain at North Dormer, and the sooner she got away from it the better. But everything beyond was darkness.

As she continued to climb the air grew keener, and when she passed from the shelter of the pines to the open grassy roof of the Mountain the cold wind of the night before sprang out on her. She bent her shoulders and struggled on against it for a while; but presently her breath failed, and she sat down under a ledge of rock overhung by shivering birches. From where she sat she saw the trail wandering across the bleached grass in the direction of Hamblin, and the granite wall of the Mountain falling away to infinite distances. On that side of the ridge the valley still lay in wintry shadow; but in the plain beyond the sun was touching village roofs and steeples, and gilding the haze of smoke over far-off invisible towns.

Charity felt herself a mere speck in the lonely circle of the sky. The events of the last two days seemed to have divided her forever from her short dream of bliss. Even Harney's image had been blurred by that crushing experience: she thought of him as so remote from her that he seemed hardly more than a memory. In her fagged and floating mind only one sensation had the weight of reality; it was the bodily burden of her child. But for it she would have felt as rootless as the whiffs of thistledown the wind blew past her. Her child was like a load that held her down, and yet like a hand that pulled her to her feet. She said to herself that she must get up and struggle on. . . .

Her eyes turned back to the trail across the top of the Mountain, and in the distance she saw a buggy against the sky. She knew its antique outline, and the gaunt build of the old horse pressing forward with lowered head; and after a moment she recognized the heavy bulk of the man who held the reins. The buggy was following the trail and making straight for the pine wood through which she had climbed; and she knew at once that the driver was in search of her. Her first impulse was to crouch down under the ledge till he had passed; but the instinct of concealment was overruled by the relief of feeling that someone was near her in the awful emptiness. She stood up and walked toward the buggy.

Mr. Royall saw her, and touched the horse with the whip. A minute or two later he was abreast of Charity; their eyes met, and without speaking he leaned over and helped her up into the buggy. She tried to speak, to stammer out some explanation, but no words came to her; and as he drew the cover over her knees he simply said: "The minister told me he'd left you up here, so I come up for you."

He turned the horse's head, and they began to jog back toward Hamblin. Charity sat speechless, staring straight ahead of her, and Mr. Royall occasionally uttered a word of encouragement to the horse: "Get along there, Dan. . . . I gave him a rest at Hamblin; but I brought him along pretty quick, and it's a stiff pull up here against the wind."

As he spoke it occurred to her for the first time that to reach the top of the Mountain so early he must have left North Dormer at the coldest hour of the night, and have traveled steadily but for the halt at Hamblin; and she felt a softness at her heart which no act of his had ever produced since he had brought her the Crimson Rambler because she had given up boarding school to stay with him.

After an interval he began again: "It was a day just like this, only spitting snow, when I come up here for you the first time." Then, as if fearing that she might take his remark as a reminder of past benefits, he added quickly: "I dunno's you think it was such a good job, either."

"Yes, I do," she murmured, looking straight ahead of her.

"Well," he said, "I tried—"

He did not finish the sentence, and she could think of nothing more to say.

"Ho, there, Dan, step out," he muttered, jerking the bridle. "We ain't home yet. You cold?" he asked abruptly.

She shook her head, but he drew the cover higher up, and stooped to tuck it in about the ankles. She continued to look straight ahead. Tears of weariness and weakness were dimming her eyes and beginning to run over, but she dared not wipe them away lest he should observe the gesture.

They drove in silence, following the long loops of the descent upon Hamblin, and Mr. Royall did not speak again till they reached the outskirts of the village. Then he let the reins droop on the dashboard and drew out his watch.

"Charity," he said, "you look fair done up, and North Dormer's a goodish way off. I've figured out that we'd do better to stop here long enough for you to get a mouthful of breakfast and then drive down to Creston and take the train."

She roused herself from her apathetic musing. "The train—what train?"

Mr. Royall, without answering, let the horse jog on till they reached the door of the first house in the village. "This is old Mrs. Hobart's place," he said. "She'll give us something hot to drink."

Charity, half unconsciously, found herself getting out of the buggy and following him in at the open door. They entered a decent kitchen with a fire crackling in the stove. An old woman with a kindly face was setting out cups and saucers on the table. She looked up and nodded as they came in, and Mr. Royall advanced to the stove, clapping his numb hands together.

"Well, Mrs. Hobart, you got any breakfast for this young lady? You can see she's cold and hungry."

Mrs. Hobart smiled on Charity and took a tin coffeepot from the fire. "My, you do look pretty mean," she said compassionately.

Charity reddened, and sat down at the table. A feeling of complete passiveness had once more come over her, and she was conscious only of the pleasant animal sensations of warmth and rest.

Mrs. Hobart put bread and milk on the table, and then went out of the house: Charity saw her leading the horse away to the barn across the yard. She did not come back, and Mr. Royall and Charity sat alone at the table with the smoking coffee between them. He poured out a cup for her, and put a piece of bread in the saucer, and she began to eat.

As the warmth of the coffee flowed through her veins her thoughts cleared and she began to feel like a living being again; but the return to life was so painful that the food choked in her throat and she sat staring down at the table in silent anguish.

After a while Mr. Royall pushed back his chair. "Now, then," he said, "if you're a mind to go along—" She did not move, and he continued: "We can pick up the noon train for Nettleton if you say so."

The words sent the blood rushing to her face, and she raised her startled eyes to his. He was standing on the other side of the table looking at her kindly and gravely; and suddenly she understood what he was going to say. She continued to sit motionless, a leaden weight upon her lips.

"You and me have spoke some hard things to each other in our time, Charity; and there's no good that I can see in any more talking now. But I'll never feel any way but one about you; and if you say so we'll drive down in time to catch that train, and go straight to the minister's house; and when you come back home you'll come as Mrs. Royall."

His voice had the grave persuasive accent that had moved his hearers at the Home Week festival; she had a sense of depths of mournful tolerance under that easy tone. Her whole body began to tremble with the dread of her own weakness.

"Oh, I can't—" she burst out desperately.

"Can't what?"

She herself did not know: she was not sure if she was rejecting what he offered, or already struggling against the temptation of taking what she no longer had a right to. She stood up, shaking and bewildered, and began to speak:

"I know I ain't been fair to you always; but I want to be now. . . . I want you to know . . . I want . . ." Her voice failed her and she stopped.

Mr. Royall leaned against the wall. He was paler than usual, but his face was composed and kindly and her agitation did not appear to perturb him.

"What's all this about wanting?" he said as she paused. "Do you know what you really want? I'll tell you. You want to be took home and took care of. And I guess that's all there is to say."

"No . . . it's not all. . . ."

"Ain't it?" He looked at his watch. "Well, I'll tell you another thing. All *I* want is to know if you'll marry me. If there was anything else, I'd tell you so; but there ain't. Come to my age, a man knows the things that matter and the things that don't; that's about the only good turn life does us."

His tone was so strong and resolute that it was like a supporting arm about her. She felt her resistance melting, her strength slipping away from her as he spoke.

"Don't cry, Charity," he exclaimed in a shaken voice. She looked up, startled at his emotion, and their eyes met.

"See here," he said gently, "old Dan's come a long distance, and we've got to let him take it easy the rest of the way. . . ."

He picked up the cloak that had slipped to her chair and laid it about her shoulders. She followed him out of the house, and they walked across the yard to the shed, where the horse was tied. Mr. Royall unblanketed him and led him out into the road. Charity got into the buggy and he drew the cover about her and shook out the reins with a cluck. When they reached the end of the village he turned the horse's head toward Creston.

# ——18——

THEY BEGAN to jog down the winding road to the valley at old Dan's languid pace. Charity felt herself sinking into deeper depths of weariness, and as they descended through the bare woods there were moments when she lost the exact sense of things, and seemed to be sitting beside her lover with the leafy arch of summer bending over them. But this illusion was faint and transitory. For the most part she had only a confused sensation of slipping down a smooth irresistible current; and she abandoned herself to the feeling as a refuge from the torment of thought.

Mr. Royall seldom spoke, but his silent presence gave her, for the first time, a sense of peace and security. She knew that where he was there would be warmth, rest, silence; and for the moment they were all she wanted. She shut her eyes, and even these things grew dim to her. . . .

In the train, during the short run from Creston to Nettleton, the warmth aroused her, and the consciousness of being under strange eyes gave her a momentary energy. She sat upright, facing Mr. Royall, and stared out of the window at the denuded country. Forty-eight hours earlier, when she had last traversed it, many of the trees still held their leaves; but the high wind of the last two nights had stripped them, and the lines of the landscape were as finely penciled as in December. A few days of autumn cold had wiped out all trace of the rich fields and languid groves through which she had passed on the Fourth of July; and with the fading of the landscape those fervid hours had faded too. She could no longer believe that she was the being who had lived them; she was someone to whom something irreparable and overwhelming had happened, but the traces of the steps leading up to it had almost vanished.

When the train reached Nettleton and she walked out into the square at Mr. Royall's side the sense of unreality grew more over-

powering. The physical strain of the night and day had left no
room in her mind for new sensations and she followed Mr. Royall
as passively as a tired child. As in a confused dream she presently
found herself sitting with him in a pleasant room, at a table with a
red and white tablecloth on which hot food and tea were placed.
He filled her cup and plate and whenever she lifted her eyes from
them she found his resting on her with the same steady tranquil
gaze that had reassured and strengthened her when they had
faced each other in old Mrs. Hobart's kitchen. As everything else
in her consciousness grew more and more confused and immate-
rial, became more and more like the universal shimmer that dis-
solves the world to failing eyes, Mr. Royall's presence began to
detach itself with rocky firmness from this elusive background.
She had always thought of him—when she thought of him at all—
as of someone hateful and obstructive, but whom she could outwit
and dominate when she chose to make the effort. Only once, on
the day of the Old Home Week celebration, while the stray fragments of his address drifted across her troubled mind, had she
caught a glimpse of another being, a being so different from the
dull-witted enemy with whom she had supposed herself to be
living that even through the burning mist of her own dreams he
had stood out with startling distinctness. For a moment, then,
what he said—and something in his way of saying it—had made
her see why he had always struck her as such a lonely man. But
the mist of her dreams had hidden him again, and she had forgotten that fugitive impression.

It came back to her now, as they sat at the table, and gave her,
through her own immeasurable desolation, a sudden sense of
their nearness to each other. But all these feelings were only brief
streaks of light in the gray blur of her physical weakness.
Through it she was aware that Mr. Royall presently left her sitting
by the table in the warm room, and came back after an interval
with a carriage from the station—a closed "hack" with sunburned
blue silk blinds—in which they drove together to a house covered
with creepers and standing next to a church with a carpet of turf
before it. They got out at this house, and the carriage waited
while they walked up the path and entered a wainscoted hall and
then a room full of books. In this room a clergyman whom Charity had never seen received them pleasantly, and asked them

to be seated for a few minutes while witnesses were being summoned.

Charity sat down obediently, and Mr. Royall, his hands behind his back, paced slowly up and down the room. As he turned and faced Charity, she noticed that his lips were twitching a little; but the look in his eyes was grave and calm. Once he paused before her and said timidly: "Your hair's got kinder loose with the wind," and she lifted her hands and tried to smooth back the locks that had escaped from her braid. There was a looking glass in a carved frame on the wall, but she was ashamed to look at herself in it, and she sat with her hands folded on her knee till the clergyman returned. Then they went out again, along a sort of arcaded passage, and into a low vaulted room with a cross on an altar, and rows of benches. The clergyman, who had left them at the door, presently reappeared before the altar in a surplice, and a lady who was probably his wife, and a man in a blue shirt who had been raking dead leaves on the lawn, came in and sat on one of the benches.

The clergyman opened a book and signed to Charity and Mr. Royall to approach. Mr. Royall advanced a few steps, and Charity followed him as she had followed him to the buggy when they went out of Mrs. Hobart's kitchen; she had the feeling that if she ceased to keep close to him, and do what he told her to do, the world would slip away from beneath her feet.

The clergyman began to read, and on her dazed mind there rose the memory of Mr. Miles, standing the night before in the desolate house of the Mountain, and reading out of the same book words that had the same dread sound of finality:

"I require and charge you both, as ye will answer at the dreadful day of judgment when the secrets of all hearts shall be disclosed, that if either of you know any impediment whereby ye may not be lawfully joined together . . ."

Charity raised her eyes and met Mr. Royall's. They were still looking at her kindly and steadily. "I will!" she heard him say a moment later, after another interval of words that she had failed to catch. She was so busy trying to understand the gestures the clergyman was signaling to her to make that she no longer heard what was being said. After another interval the lady on the bench stood up, and taking her hand put it in Mr. Royall's. It lay enclosed in his strong palm and she felt a ring that was too long for her being slipped onto her thin finger. She understood then that she was married. . . .

Late that afternoon Charity sat alone in a bedroom of the fashionable hotel where she and Harney had vainly sought a table on the Fourth of July. She had never before been in so handsomely furnished a room. The mirror above the dressing table reflected the high headboard and fluted pillow slips of the double bed, and a bedspread so spotlessly white that she had hesitated to lay her hat and jacket on it. The humming radiator diffused an atmosphere of drowsy warmth, and through a half-open door she saw the glitter of the nickel taps above twin marble basins.

For a while the long turmoil of the night and day had slipped away from her and she sat with closed eyes, surrendering herself to the spell of warmth and silence. But presently this merciful apathy was succeeded by the sudden acuteness of vision with which sick people sometimes wake out of a heavy sleep. As she opened her eyes they rested on the picture that hung above the bed. It was a large engraving with a dazzling white margin enclosed in a wide frame of bird's-eye maple with an inner scroll of gold. The engraving represented a young man in a boat on a lake overhung with trees. He was leaning over to gather water lilies for the girl in a light dress who lay among the cushions in the stern. The scene was full of a drowsy midsummer radiance, and Charity averted her eyes from it and, rising from her chair, began to wander restlessly about the room.

It was on the fifth floor, and its broad window of plate glass looked over the roofs of the town. Beyond them stretched a wooded landscape in which the last fires of sunset were picking out a steely gleam. Charity gazed at the gleam with startled eyes. Even through the gathering twilight she recognized the contour of the soft hills encircling it, and the way the meadows sloped to its edge. It was Nettleton Lake that she was looking at.

She stood a long time in the window staring out at the fading water. The sight of it had roused her for the first time to a realization of what she had done. Even the feeling of the ring on her hand had not brought her this sharp sense of the irretrievable. For an instant the old impulse of flight swept through her; but it was only the lift of a broken wing. She heard the door open behind her, and Mr. Royall came in.

He had gone to the barber's to be shaved, and his shaggy gray hair had been trimmed and smoothed. He moved strongly and quickly, squaring his shoulders and carrying his head high, as if he did not want to pass unnoticed.

"What are you doing in the dark?" he called out in a cheerful voice. Charity made no answer. He went up to the window to draw down the blind, and putting his finger on the wall flooded the room with a blaze of light from the central chandelier. In this unfamiliar illumination husband and wife faced each other awkwardly for a moment; then Mr. Royall said: "We'll step down and have some supper, if you say so."

The thought of food filled her with repugnance; but not daring to confess it she smoothed her hair and followed him to the lift.

An hour later, coming out of the glare of the dining room, she waited in the marble-paneled hall while Mr. Royall, before the brass lattice of one of the corner counters, selected a cigar and bought an evening paper. Men were lounging in rocking chairs under the blazing chandeliers, travelers coming and going, bells ringing, porters shuffling by with luggage. Over Mr. Royall's shoulder, as he leaned against the counter, a girl with her hair puffed high smirked and nodded at a dapper drummer who was getting his key at the desk across the hall.

Charity stood among these cross-currents of life as motionless and inert as if she had been one of the tables screwed to the marble floor. All her soul was gathered up into one sick sense of coming doom, and she watched Mr. Royall in fascinated terror while he pinched the cigars in successive boxes and unfolded his evening paper with a steady hand.

Presently he turned and joined her. "You go right along up to bed—I'm going to sit down here and have my smoke," he said. He spoke as easily and naturally as if they had been an old couple, long used to each other's ways, and her contracted heart gave a flutter of relief. She followed him to the lift, and he put her in and enjoined the buttoned and braided boy to show her to her room.

She groped her way in through the darkness, forgetting where the electric button was, and not knowing how to manipulate it. But a white autumn moon had risen, and the illuminated sky put a pale light in the room. By it she undressed, and after folding up the ruffled pillow slips crept timidly under the spotless counterpane. She had never felt such smooth sheets or such light warm blankets; but the softness of the bed did not soothe her. She lay there trembling with a fear that ran through her veins like ice. "What have I done? Oh, what have I done?" she whispered, shuddering to her pillow; and pressing her face against it to shut out the pale landscape beyond the window she lay in the darkness straining her ears, and shaking at every footstep that approached. . . .

Suddenly she sat up and pressed her hands against her frightened heart. A faint sound had told her that someone was in the room; but she must have slept in the interval, for she had heard no one enter. The moon was setting beyond the opposite roofs, and in the darkness, outlined against the gray square of the window, she saw a figure seated in the rocking chair. The figure did not move: it was sunk deep in the chair, with bowed head and folded arms, and she saw that it was Mr. Royall who sat there. He had not undressed, but had taken the blanket from the foot of the bed and laid it across his knees. Trembling and holding her breath she watched him, fearing that he had been roused by her movement; but he did not stir, and she concluded that he wished her to think he was asleep.

As she continued to watch him ineffable relief stole slowly over her, relaxing her strained nerves and exhausted body. He knew, then . . . he knew . . . it was because he knew that he had married her, and that he sat there in the darkness to show her she was safe with him. A stir of something deeper than she had ever felt in thinking of him flitted through her tired brain, and cautiously, noiselessly, she let her head sink on the pillow. . . .

When she woke the room was full of morning light, and her first glance showed her that she was alone in it. She got up and dressed, and as she was fastening her dress the door opened, and Mr. Royall came in. He looked old and tired in the bright daylight, but his face wore the same expression of grave friendliness that had reassured her on the Mountain. It was as if all the dark spirits had gone out of him.

They went downstairs to the dining room for breakfast, and after breakfast he told her he had some insurance business to attend to. "I guess while I'm doing it you better step out and buy yourself whatever you need." He smiled, and added with an embarrassed laugh: "You know I always wanted you to beat all the other girls." He drew something from his pocket, and pushed it across the table to her; and she saw that he had given her two twenty-dollar bills. "If it ain't enough there's more where that come from—I want you to beat 'em all hollow," he repeated.

She flushed and tried to stammer out her thanks, but he had pushed back his chair and was leading the way out of the dining room. In the hall he paused a minute to say that if it suited her they would take the three o'clock train back to North Dormer; then he took his hat and coat from the rack and went out.

A few minutes later Charity went out too. She had watched to see in what direction he was going, and she took the opposite way and walked quickly down the main street to the brick building on the corner of Lake Avenue. There she paused to look cautiously up and down the thoroughfare, and then climbed the brassbound stairs to Dr. Merkle's door. The same bushy-headed mulatto girl admitted her, and after the same interval of waiting in the red plush parlor she was once more summoned to Dr. Merkle's office. The doctor received her without surprise, and led her into the inner plush sanctuary.

"I thought you'd be back, but you've come a mite too soon: I told you to be patient and not fret," she observed, after a pause of penetrating scrutiny.

Charity drew the money from her breast. "I've come to get my blue brooch," she said, flushing.

"Your brooch?" Dr. Merkle appeared not to remember. "My, yes—I get so many things of that kind. Well, my dear, you'll have to wait while I get it out of the safe. I don't leave valuables like that laying round like the newspaper."

She disappeared for a moment, and returned with a bit of twisted-up tissue paper from which she unwrapped the brooch.

Charity, as she looked at it, felt a stir of warmth at her heart. She held out an eager hand.

"Have you got the change?" she asked a little breathlessly, laying one of the twenty-dollar bills on the table.

"Change? What'd I want to have change for? I only see two twenties there," Dr. Merkle answered brightly.

Charity paused, disconcerted. "I thought . . . you said it was five dollars a visit. . . ."

"For *you,* as a favor—I did. But how about the responsibility— *and* the insurance? I don't s'pose you ever thought of that? This pin's worth a hundred dollars easy. If it had got lost or stole, where'd I been when you come to claim it?"

Charity remained silent, puzzled and half-convinced by the argument, and Dr. Merkle promptly followed up her advantage. "I didn't ask you for your brooch, my dear. I'd a good deal ruther folks paid me my regular charge than have 'em put me to all this trouble."

She paused, and Charity, seized with a desperate longing to escape, rose to her feet and held out one of the bills.

"Will you take that?" she asked.

"No, I won't take that, my dear; but I'll take it with its mate, and hand you over a signed receipt if you don't trust me."

"Oh, but I can't—it's all I've got," Charity exclaimed.

Dr. Merkle looked up at her pleasantly from the plush sofa. "It seems you got married yesterday, up to the 'Piscopal church; I heard all about the wedding from the minister's chore man. It would be a pity, wouldn't it, to let Mr. Royall know you had an account running here? I just put it to you as your own mother might."

Anger flamed up in Charity, and for an instant she thought of abandoning the brooch and letting Dr. Merkle do her worst. But how could she leave her only treasure with that evil woman? She wanted it for her baby: she meant it, in some mysterious way, to be a link between Harney's child and its unknown father. Trembling and hating herself while she did it, she laid Mr. Royall's money on the table, and catching up on the brooch fled out of the room and the house. . . .

In the street she stood still, dazed by this last adventure. But the brooch lay in her bosom like a talisman, and she felt a secret lightness of heart. It gave her strength, after a moment, to walk on slowly in the direction of the post office, and go in through the swinging doors. At one of the windows she bought a sheet of letter paper, an envelope, and a stamp; then she sat down at a table and

dipped the rusty post office pen in ink. She had come there possessed with a fear which had haunted her ever since she had felt
Mr. Royall's ring on her finger: the fear that Harney might, after
all, free himself and come back to her. It was a possibility which
had never occurred to her during the dreadful hours after she
had received his letter; only when the decisive step she had taken
made longing turn to apprehension did such a contigency seem
conceivable. She addressed the envelope, and on the sheet of
paper she wrote:

I'm married to Mr. Royall. I'll always remember you.

CHARITY

The last words were not in the least what she had meant to
write; they had flowed from her pen irresistibly. She had not had
the strength to complete her sacrifice; but, after all, what did it
matter? Now that there was no chance of ever seeing Harney
again, why should she not tell him the truth?

When she had put the letter in the box she went out into the
busy sunlit street and began to walk to the hotel. Behind the
plate-glass windows of the department stores she noticed the
tempting display of dresses and dress materials that had fired her
imagination on the day when she and Harney had looked in at
them together. They reminded her of Mr. Royall's injunction to
go out and buy all she needed. She looked down at her shabby
dress, and wondered what she should say when he saw her coming back empty-handed. As she drew near the hotel she saw him
waiting on the doorstep, and her heart began to beat with apprehension.

He nodded and waved his hand at her approach, and they
walked through the hall and went upstairs to collect their posses-
sions, so that Mr. Royall might give up the key of the room when
they went down again for their midday dinner. In the bedroom,
while she was thrusting back into the satchel the few things she
had brought away with her, she suddenly felt that his eyes were
on her and that he was going to speak. She stood still, her half-
folded nightgown in her hand, while the blood rushed up to her
drawn cheeks.

"Well, did you rig yourself out handsomely? I haven't seen any bundles round," he said jocosely.

"Oh, I'd rather let Ally Hawes make the few things I want," she answered.

"That so?" He looked at her thoughtfully for a moment and his eyebrows projected in a scowl. Then his face grew friendly again. "Well, I wanted you to go back looking stylisher than any of them, but I guess you're right. You're a good girl, Charity."

Their eyes met, and something rose in his that she had never seen there: a look that made her feel ashamed and yet secure.

"I guess you're good, too," she said, shyly and quickly. He smiled without answering, and they went out of the room together and dropped down to the hall in the glittering lift.

Late that evening, in the cold autumn moonlight, they drove up to the door of the red house.

# Madame
# de Treymes

# 1

JOHN DURHAM, while he waited for Madame de Malrive to draw on her gloves, stood in the hotel doorway looking out across the Rue de Rivoli at the afternoon brightness of the Tuileries gardens.

His European visits were infrequent enough to have kept unimpaired the freshness of his eye, and he was always struck anew by the vast and consummately ordered spectacle of Paris: by its look of having been boldly and deliberately planned as a background for the enjoyment of life, instead of being forced into grudging concessions to the festive instincts, or barricading itself against them in unenlightened ugliness, like his own lamentable New York.

But today, if the scene had never presented itself more alluringly, in that moist spring bloom between showers, when the horse chestnuts dome themselves in unreal green against a gauzy sky, and the very dust of the pavement seems the fragrance of lilac made visible—today for the first time the sense of a personal stake in it all, of having to reckon individually with its effects and influences, kept Durham from an unrestrained yielding to the spell. Paris might still be—to the unimplicated it doubless still was—the most beautiful city in the world; but whether it were the most lovable or the most detestable depended for him, in the last analysis, on the buttoning of the white glove over which Fanny de Malrive still lingered.

The mere fact of her having forgotten to draw on her gloves as they were descending in the hotel lift from his mother's drawing room was, in this connection, charged with significance to Durham. She was the kind of woman who always presents herself to the mind's eye as completely equipped, as made up of exquisitely cared for and finely related details; and that the heat of her parting with his family should have left her unconscious that she was

emerging gloveless into Paris, seemed, on the whole, to speak
hopefully for Durham's future opinion of the city.

Even now, he could detect a certain confusion, a desire to draw
breath and catch up with life, in the way she dawdled over the last
buttons in the dimness of the porte cochère, while her footman,
outside, hung on her retarded signal.

When at length they emerged, it was to learn from that func-
tionary that Madame la Marquise's carriage had been obliged to
yield its place at the door, but was at the moment in the act of
regaining it. Madame de Malrive cut the explanation short. "I
shall walk home. The carriage this evening at eight."

As the footman turned away, she raised her eyes for the first
time to Durham's.

"Will you walk with me? Let us cross the Tuileries. I should like
to sit a moment on the terrace."

She spoke quite easily and naturally, as if it were the most
commonplace thing in the world for them to be straying afoot
together over Paris; but even his vague knowledge of the world
she lived in—a knowledge mainly acquired through the perusal
of yellow-backed fiction—gave a thrilling significance to her naturalness. Durham, indeed, was beginning to find that one of the
charms of a sophisticated society is that it lends point and perspective to the slightest contact between the sexes. If, in the old
unrestricted New York days, Fanny Frisbee, from a brownstone
doorstep, had proposed that they should take a walk in the park,
the idea would have presented itself to her companion as agreeable but unimportant; whereas Fanny de Malrive's suggestion
that they should stroll across the Tuileries was obviously fraught
with unspecified possibilities.

He was so throbbing with the sense of these possibilities that he
walked beside her without speaking down the length of the wide
alley which follows the line of the Rue de Rivoli, suffering her
even, when they reached its farthest end, to direct him in silence
up the steps to the terrace of the Feuillants. For, after all, the
possibilities were double-faced, and her bold departure from custom might simply mean that what she had to say was so dreadful
that it needed all the tenderest mitigation of circumstance.

There was apparently nothing embarrassing to her in his silence: it was a part of her long European discipline that she had

learned to manage pauses with ease. In her Frisbee days she might have packed this one with a random fluency; now she was content to let it widen slowly before them like the spacious prospect opening at their feet. The complicated beauty of this prospect, as they moved toward it between the symmetrically clipped limes of the lateral terrace, touched him anew through her nearness, as with the hint of some vast impersonal power, controlling and regulating her life in ways he could not guess, putting between himself and her the whole width of the civilization into which her marriage had absorbed her. And there was such fear in the thought—he read such derision of what he had to offer in the splendor of the great avenues tapering upward to the sunset glories of the Arch—that all he had meant to say when he finally spoke compressed itself at last into an abrupt unmitigated: "Well?"

She answered at once—as though she had only awaited the call of the national interrogation—"I don't know when I have been so happy."

"So happy?" The suddenness of his joy flushed up through his fair skin.

"As I was just now—taking tea with your mother and sisters."

Durham's "Oh!" of surprise betrayed also a note of disillusionment, which she met only by the reconciling murmur: "Shall we sit down?"

He found two of the springy yellow chairs indigenous to the spot, and placed them under the tree near which they had paused, saying reluctantly, as he did so: "Of course it was an immense pleasure to *them* to see you again."

"Oh, not in the same way. I mean—" she paused, sinking into the chair, and betraying, for the first time, a momentary inability to deal becomingly with the situation. "I mean," she resumed, smiling, "that it was not an event for them, as it was for me."

"An event?"—he caught her up again, eagerly; for what, in the language of any civilization, could that word mean but just the one thing he most wished it to?

"To be with dear, good, sweet, simple, real Americans again!" she burst out, heaping up her epithets with reckless prodigality.

Durham's smile once more faded to impersonality, as he rejoined, just a shade on the defensive: "If it's merely our Americanism you enjoyed—I've no doubt we can give you all you want in that line."

"Yes, it's just that! But if you knew what the word means to me! It means—it means—" she paused as if to assure herself that they were sufficiently isolated from the desultory groups beneath the other trees—"it means that I'm *safe* with them: as safe as in a bank!"

Durham felt a sudden warmth behind his eyes and in his throat. "I think I do know—"

"No, you don't, really; you can't know how dear and strange and familiar it all sounded: the old New York names that kept coming up in your mother's talk, and her charming quaint ideas about Europe—their all regarding it as a great big innocent pleasure ground and shop for Americans; and your mother's missing the homemade bread and preferring the American asparagus— I'm so tired of Americans who despise even their own asparagus! And then your married sister's spending her summers at—where is it?—the Kittawittany House on Lake Pohunk—"

A vision of earnest women in Shetland shawls, with spectacles and thin knobs of hair, eating blueberry pie at unwholesome hours in a shingled dining room on a bare New England hilltop, rose pallidly between Durham and the verdant brightness of the Champs Elysées, and he protested with a slight smile: "Oh, but my married sister is the black sheep of the family—the rest of us never sank as low as that."

"Low? I think it's beautiful—fresh and innocent and simple. I remember going to such a place once. They have early dinner— rather late—and go off in buckboards over terrible roads, and bring back goldenrod and autumn leaves, and read nature books aloud on the piazza; and there is always one shy young man in flannels—only one—who has come to see the prettiest girl (though how he can choose among so many!) and who takes her off in a buggy for hours and hours—" She paused and summed up with a long sigh: "It is fifteen years since I was in America."

"And you're still so good an American."

"Oh, a better and better one every day!"

He hesitated. "Then why did you never come back?"

Her face altered instantly, exchanging its retrospective light for the look of slightly shadowed watchfulness which he had known as most habitual to it.

"It was impossible—it has always been so. My husband would not go; and since—since our separation—there have been family reasons."

Durham sighed impatiently. "Why do you talk of reasons? The truth is, you have made your life here. You could never give all this up!" He made a discouraged gesture in the direction of the Place de la Concorde.

"Give it up! I would go tomorrow! But it could never, now, be for more than a visit. I must live in France on account of my boy."

Durham's heart gave a quick beat. At last the talk had neared the point toward which his whole mind was straining, and he began to feel a personal application in her words. But that made him all the more cautious about choosing his own.

"It is an agreement—about the boy?" he ventured.

"I gave my word. They knew that was enough," she said proudly; adding, as if to put him in full possession of her reasons: "It would have been much more difficult for me to obtain complete control of my son if it had not been understood that I was to live in France."

"That seems fair," Durham assented after a moment's reflection: it was his instinct, even in the heat of personal endeavor, to pause a moment on the question of "fairness." The personal claim reasserted itself as he added tentatively: "But when he *is* brought up—when he's grown up: then you would feel freer?"

She received this with a start, as a possibility too remote to have entered into her view of the future. "He is only eight years old!" she objected.

"Ah, of course it would be a long way off?"

"A long way off, thank heaven! French mothers part late with their sons, and in that one respect I mean to be a French mother."

"Of course—naturally—since he has only you," Durham again assented.

He was eager to show how fully he took her point of view, if only to dispose her to the reciprocal fairness of taking his when the time came to present it. And he began to think that the time had now come; that their walk would not have thus resolved itself, without excuse or pretext, into a tranquil session beneath the trees, for any purpose less important than that of giving him his opportunity.

He took it, characteristically, without seeking a transition. "When I spoke to you, the other day, about myself—about what I felt for you—I said nothing of the future, because, for the moment, my mind refused to travel beyond its immediate hope of happiness. But I felt, of course, even then, that the hope involved various difficulties—that we can't, as we might once have done, come together without any thought but for ourselves; and whatever your answer is to be, I want to tell you now that I am ready to accept my share of the difficulties." He paused, and then added explicitly: "If there's the least chance of your listening to me, I'm willing to live over here as long as you can keep your boy with you."

# —— 2 ——

❧ WHATEVER Madame de Malrive's answer was to be, there could be no doubt as to her readiness to listen. She received Durham's words without sign of resistance, and took time to ponder them gently before she answered, in a voice touched by emotion: "You are very generous—very unselfish; but when you fix a limit—no matter how remote—to my remaining here, I see how wrong it is to let myself consider for a moment such possibilities as we have been talking of."

"Wrong? Why should it be wrong?"

"Because I shall want to keep my boy always! Not, of course, in the sense of living with him, or even forming an important part of his life; I am not deluded enough to think that possible. But I do believe it possible never to pass wholly out of his life; and while there is a hope of that, how can I leave him?" She paused, and turned on him a new face, a face in which the past of which he was still so ignorant showed itself like a shadow suddenly darkening a clear pane. "How can I make you understand?" she went on urgently. "It is not only because of my love for him—not only, I mean, because of my own happiness in being with him—that I can't, in imagination, surrender even the remotest hour of his future. It is because, the moment he passes out of my influence, he passes under that other—the influence I have been fighting against every hour since he was born!—I don't mean, you know," she added, as Durham, with bent head, continued to offer her the silent fixity of his attention, "I don't mean the special personal influence—except inasmuch as it represents something wider, more general, something that encloses and circulates through the whole world in which he belongs. That is what I meant when I said you could never understand! There is nothing in your experience—in any American experience—to correspond with that far-reaching family organization, which is itself a part of the larger system, and which encloses a young man of my son's position in a

447

network of accepted prejudices and opinions. Everything is prepared in advance—his political and religious convictions, his
judgments of people, his sense of honor, his ideas of women, his
whole view of life. He is taught to see vileness and corruption in
everyone not of his own way of thinking, and in every idea
that does not directly serve the religious and political purposes of
his class. The truth isn't a fixed thing: it's not used to test
actions by, it's tested by them, and made to fit in with them.
And this forming of the mind begins with the child's first consciousness; it's in his nursery stories, his baby prayers, his very
games with his playmates! Already he is only half mine, because
the Church has the other half, and will be reaching out for my
share as soon as his education begins. But that other half is still
mine, and I mean to make it the strongest and most living half of
the two, so that, when the inevitable conflict begins, the energy
and the truth and the endurance shall be on my side and not on
theirs!"

She paused, flushing with the represed fervor of her utterance,
though her voice had not been raised beyond its usual discreet
modulations; and Durham felt himself tingling with the transmit-
ted force of her resolve. Whatever shock her words brought to his
personal hope, he was grateful to her for speaking them so
clearly, for having so sure a grasp of her purpose.

Her decision strengthened his own, and after a pause of deliberation he said quietly: "There might be a good deal to urge on
the other side—the ineffectualness of your sacrifice, the probability that when your son marries he will inevitably be absorbed back
into the life of his class and his people; but I can't look at it in that
way, because if I were in your place I believe I should feel just as
you do about it. As long as there was a fighting chance I should
want to keep hold of my half, no matter how much the struggle
cost me. And one reason why I understand your feeling about
your boy is that I have the same feeling about *you:* as long as
there's a fighting chance of keeping my half of you—the half he is
willing to spare me—I don't see how I can ever give it up." He
waited again, and then brought out firmly: "If you'll marry me,
I'll agree to live out here as long as you want, and we'll be two
instead of one to keep hold of your half of him."

He raised his eyes as he ended, and saw that hers met them through a quick clouding of tears.

"Ah, I am glad to have had this said to me! But I could never accept such an offer."

He caught instantly at the distinction. "That doesn't mean that you could never accept *me?*"

"Under such conditions—"

"But if I am satisfied with the conditions? Don't think I am speaking rashly, under the influence of the moment. I have expected something of this sort, and I have thought out my side of the case. As far as material circumstances go, I have worked long enough and successfully enough to take my ease and take it where I choose. I mention that because the life I offer you is offered to your boy as well." He let this sink into her mind before summing up gravely: "The offer I make is made deliberately, and at least I have a right to a direct answer."

She was silent again, and then lifted a cleared gaze to his. "My direct answer then is: if I were still Fanny Frisbee I would marry you."

He bent toward her persuasively. "But you will be—when the divorce is pronounced."

"Ah, the divorce—" She flushed deeply, with an instinctive shrinking back of her whole person which made him straighten himself in his chair.

"Do you so dislike the idea?"

"The idea of divorce? No—not in my case. I should like anything that would do away with the past—obliterate it all—make everything new in my life!"

"Then what—?" he began again, waiting with the patience of a wooer on the uneasy circling of her tormented mind.

"Oh, don't ask me; I don't know; I am frightened."

Durham gave a deep sigh of discouragement. "I thought your coming here with me today—and above all your going with me just now to see my mother—was a sign that you were *not* frightened!"

"Well, I was not when I was with your mother. She made everything seem easy and natural. She took me back into that clear American air where there are no obscurities, no mysteries—"

"What obscurities, what mysteries, are you afraid of?"

She looked about her with a faint shiver. "I am afraid of every-thing!" she said.

"That's because you are alone; because you've no one to turn to. I'll clear the air for you fast enough if you'll let me."

He looked forth defiantly, as if flinging his challenge at the great city which had come to typify the powers contending with him for her possession.

"You say that so easily! But you don't know; none of you know."

"Know what?"

"The difficulties—"

"I told you I was ready to take my share of the difficulties—and my share naturally includes yours. You know Americans are great hands at getting over difficulties." He drew himself up confi-dently. "Just leave that to me—only tell me exactly what you're afraid of."

She paused again, and then said: "The divorce, to begin with—they will never consent to it."

He noticed that she spoke as though the interests of the whole clan, rather than her husband's individual claim, were to be con-sidered; and the use of the plural pronoun shocked his free indi-vidualism like a glimpse of some dark feudal survival.

"But you are absolutely certain of your divorce! I've con-sulted—of course without mentioning names—"

She interrupted him, with a melancholy smile: "Ah, so have I. The divorce would be easy enough to get, if they ever let it come into the courts."

"How on earth can they prevent that?"

"I don't know; my never knowing how they will do things is one of the secrets of their power."

"Their power? What power?" he broke in with irrepressible contempt. "Who are these bogeys whose machinations are going to arrest the course of justice in a—comparatively—civilized country? You've told me yourself that Monsieur de Malrive is the least likely to give you trouble; and the others are his uncle the abbé, his mother, and sister. That kind of a syndicate doesn't scare me much. A priest and two women *contra mundum!*"

She shook her head. "Not *contra mundum,* but with it, their whole world is behind them. It's that mysterious solidarity that you can't understand. One doesn't know how far they may reach, or in how many directions. I have never known. They have always cropped up where I least expected them."

Before this persistency of negation Durham's buoyancy began to flag, but his determination grew the more fixed.

"Well, then, supposing them to possess these supernatural powers; do you think it's to people of that kind that I'll ever consent to give you up?"

She raised a half-smiling glance of protest. "Oh, they're not wantonly wicked. They'll leave me alone as long as—"

"As I do?" he interrupted. "Do you want me to leave you alone? Was that what you brought me here to tell me?"

The directness of the challenge seemed to gather up the scattered strands of her hesitation, and lifting her head she turned on him a look in which, but for its underlying shadow, he might have recovered the full free beam of Fanny Frisbee's gaze.

"I don't know why I brought you here," she said gently, "except from the wish to prolong a little the illusion of being once more an American among Americans. Just now, sitting there with your mother and Katy and Nannie, the difficulties seemed to vanish; the problems grew as trivial to me as they are to you. And I wanted them to remain so a little longer; I wanted to put off going back to them. But it was of no use—they were waiting for me here. They are over there now in that house across the river." She indicated the gray skyline of the Faubourg, shining in the splintered radiance of the sunset beyond the long sweep of the quays. "They are a part of me—I belong to them. I must go back to them!" she sighed.

She rose slowly to her feet, as though her metaphor had expressed an actual fact and she felt herself bodily drawn from his side by the influences of which she spoke.

Durham had risen too. "Then I go back with you!" he exclaimed energetically; and as she paused, wavering a little under the shock of his resolve: "I don't mean into your house—but into your life!" he said.

She suffered him, at any rate, to accompany her to the door of the house, and allowed their debate to prolong itself through the almost monastic quiet of the quarter which led thither. On the way, he succeeded in wresting from her the confession that, if it were possible to ascertain in advance that her husband's family would not oppose her action, she might decide to apply for a divorce. Short of a positive assurance on this point, she made it clear that she would never move in the matter; there must be no scandal, no *retentissement,* nothing which her boy, necessarily brought up in the French tradition of scrupulously preserved appearances, could afterward regard as the faintest blur on his much-quartered escutcheon. But even this partial concession again raised fresh obstacles; for there seemed to be no one to whom she could entrust so delicate an investigation, and to apply directly to the Marquis de Malrive or his relatives appeared, in the light of her past experience, the last way of learning their intentions.

"But," Durham objected, beginning to suspect a morbid fixity of idea in her perpetual attitude of distrust—"but surely you have told me that your husband's sister—what is her name? Madame de Treymes?—was the most powerful member of the group, and that she has always been on your side."

She hesitated. "Yes, Christiane has been on my side. She dislikes her brother. But it would not do to ask her."

"But could no one else ask her? Who are her friends?"

"She has a great many; and some, of course, are mine. But in a case like this they would be all hers; they wouldn't hesitate a moment between us."

"Why should it be necessary to hesitate between you? Suppose Madame de Treymes sees the reasonableness of what you ask; suppose, at any rate, she sees the hopelessness of opposing you? Why should she make a mystery of your opinion?"

"It's not that; it is that, if I went to her friends, I should never get her real opinion from them. At least I should never know if it *was* her real opinion; and therefore I should be no farther advanced. Don't you see?"

Durham struggled between the sentimental impulse to soothe her, and the practical instinct that it was a moment for unmitigated frankness.

"I'm not sure that I do; but if you can't find out what Madame de Treymes thinks, I'll see what I can do myself."

"Oh—*you!*" broke from her in mingled terror and admiration; and pausing on her doorstep to lay her hand in his before she touched the bell, she added with a half-whimsical flash of regret: "Why didn't this happen to Fanny Frisbee?"

# 3

Why had it not happened to Fanny Frisbee?

Durham put the question to himself as he walked back along the quays, in a state of inner commotion which left him, for once, insensible to the ordered beauty of his surroundings. Propinquity had not been lacking: he had known Miss Frisbee since his college days. In unsophisticated circles, one family is apt to quote another; and the Durham ladies had always quoted the Frisbees. The Frisbees were bold, experienced, enterprising: they had what the novelists of the day called "dash." The beautiful Fanny was especially dashing; she had the showiest national attributes, tempered only by a native grace of softness, as the beam of her eyes was subdued by the length of their lashes. And yet young Durham, though not unsusceptible to such charms, had remained content to enjoy them from a safe distance of good fellowship. If he had been asked why, he could not have told; but the Durham of forty understood. It was because there were, with minor modifications, many other Fanny Frisbees; whereas never before, within his ken, had there been a Fanny de Malrive.

He had felt it in a flash, when, the autumn before, he had run across her one evening in the dining room of the Beaurivage at Ouchy; when, after a furtive exchange of glances, they had simultaneously arrived at recognition, followed by an eager pressure of hands, and a long evening of reminiscence on the starlit terrace. She was the same, but so mysteriously changed! And it was the mystery, the sense of unprobed depths of initiation, which drew him to her as her freshness had never drawn him. He had not hitherto attempted to define the nature of the change: it remained for his sister Nannie to do that when, on his return to the Rue de Rivoli, where the family were still sitting in conclave upon their recent visitor, Miss Durham summed up their groping comments in the phrase: "I never saw anything so French!"

Durham, understanding what his sister's use of the epithet im-

plied, recognized it instantly as the explanation of his own feelings. Yes, it was the finish, the modeling, which Madame de
Malrive's experience had given her that set her apart from the
fresh uncomplicated personalities of which she had once been
simply the most charming type. The influences that had lowered
her voice, regulated her gestures, toned her down to harmony
with the warm dim background of a long social past—these influences had lent to her natural fineness of perception a command
of expression adapted to complex conditions. She had moved in
surroundings through which one could hardly bounce and bang
on the genial American plan without knocking the angles off a
number of sacred institutions; and her acquired dexterity of
movement seemed to Durham a crowning grace. It was a shock,
now that he knew at what cost the dexterity had been acquired, to
acknowledge this even to himself; he hated to think that she could
owe anything to such conditions as she had been placed in. And it
gave him a sense of the tremendous strength of the organization
into which she had been absorbed, that in spite of her horror, her
moral revolt, she had not reacted against its external forms. She
might abhor her husband, her marriage, and the world to which
it had introduced her, but she had become a product of that
world in its outward expression, and no better proof of the fact
was needed than her exotic enjoyment of Americanism.

The sense of the distance to which her American past had been
removed was never more present to him than when, a day or two
later, he went with his mother and sisters to return her visit. The
region beyond the river existed, for the Durham ladies, only as
the unmapped environment of the Bon Marché; and Nannie
Durham's exclamation on the pokiness of the streets and the dullness of the houses showed Durham, with a start, how far he had
already traveled from the family point of view.

"Well, if this is all she got by marrying a marquis!" the young
lady summed up as they paused before the small sober hotel in its
high-walled court; and Katy, following her mother through the
stone-vaulted and stone-floored vestibule, murmured: "It must
be simply freezing in winter."

In the softly faded drawing room, with its old pastels in old
frames, its windows looking on the damp green twilight of a garden sunk deep in blackened walls, the American ladies might

have been even more conscious of the insufficiency of their friend's compensations, had not the warmth of her welcome precluded all other reflections. It was not till she had gathered them about her in the corner beside the tea table, that Durham identified the slender dark lady loitering negligently in the background, and introduced in a comprehensive murmur to the American group, as the redoubtable sister-in-law to whom he had declared himself ready to throw down his challenge.

There was nothing very redoubtable about Madame de Treymes, except perhaps the kindly yet critical observation which she bestowed on her sister-in-law's visitors: the unblinking attention of a civilized spectator observing an encampment of aborigines. He had heard of her as a beauty, and was surprised to find her, as Nannie afterward put it, a mere stick to hang clothes on (but they *did* hang!), with a small brown glancing face, like that of a charming little inquisitive animal. Yet before she had addressed ten words to him—nibbling at the hard English consonants like nuts—he owned the justice of the epithet. She was a beauty, if beauty, instead of being restricted to the cast of the face, is a pervasive attribute informing the hands, the voice, the gestures, the very fall of a flounce and tilt of a feather. In this impalpable *aura* of grace Madame de Treymes's dark meager presence unmistakably moved, like a thin flame in a wide quiver of light. And as he realized that she looked much handsomer than she was, so, while they talked, he felt that she understood a great deal more than she betrayed. It was not through the groping speech which formed their apparent medium of communication that she imbibed her information: she found it in the air, she extracted it from Durham's look and manner, she caught it in the turn of her sister-in-law's defenseless eyes—for in her presence Madame de Malrive became Fanny Frisbee again!—she put it together, in short, out of just such unconsidered indescribable trifles as differentiated the quiet felicity of her dress from Nannie and Katy's "handsome" haphazard clothes.

Her actual converse with Durham moved, meanwhile, strictly in the conventional ruts: had he been long in Paris, which of the new plays did he like best, was it true that American *jeunes filles* were sometimes taken to the Boulevard theaters? And she threw an interrogative glance at the young ladies beside the tea table. To

Durham's reply that it depended how much French they knew, she shrugged and smiled, replying that his compatriots all spoke French like Parisians, inquiring, after a moment's thought, if they learned it, *là bas, des nègres,* and laughing heartily when Durham's astonishment revealed her blunder.

When at length she had taken leave—enveloping the Durham ladies in a last puzzled penetrating look—Madame de Malrive turned to Mrs. Durham with a faintly embarrassed smile.

"My sister-in-law was much interested; I believe you are the first Americans she has ever known."

"Good gracious!" ejaculated Nannie, as though such social darkness required immediate missionary action on someone's part.

"Well, she knows *us,*" said Durham, catching, in Madame de Malrive's rapid glance, a startled assent to his point.

"After all," reflected the accurate Katy, as though seeking an excuse for Madame de Treymes's unenlightenment, "*we* don't know many French people, either."

To which Nannie promptly if obscurely retorted: "Ah! but we couldn't and *she* could!"

# 4

⚜ MADAME DE TREYMES'S friendly observation of her sister-in-law's visitors resulted in no expression on her part of a desire to renew her study of them. To all appearances, she passed out of their lives when Madame de Malrive's door closed on her; and Durham felt that the arduous task of making her acquaintance was still to be begun.

He felt also, more than ever, the necessity of attempting it; and in his determination to lose no time, and his perplexity how to set most speedily about the business, he bethought himself of applying to his cousin Mrs. Boykin.

Mrs. Elmer Boykin was a small plump woman, to whose vague prettiness the lines of middle age had given no meaning: as though whatever had happened to her had merely added to the sum total of her inexperience. After a Parisian residence of twenty-five years, spent in a state of feverish servitude to the great artists of the Rue de la Paix, her dress and hair still retained a certain rigidity in keeping with the directness of her gaze and the unmodulated candor of her voice. Her very drawing room had the hard bright atmosphere of her native skies, and one felt that she was still true at heart to the national ideals in electric lighting and plumbing.

She and her husband had left America owing to the impossibility of living there with the finish and decorum which the Boykin standard demanded; but in the isolation of their exile they had created about them a kind of phantom America, where the national prejudices continued to flourish unchecked by the national progressiveness: a little world sparsely peopled by compatriots in the same attitude of chronic opposition toward a society chronically unaware of them. In this uncontaminated air Mr. and Mrs. Boykin had preserved the purity of simpler conditions, and Elmer Boykin, returning rakishly from a Sunday's racing at Chantilly, betrayed, under his "knowing" coat and the racing glasses slung ostentatiously across his shoulder, the unmistakable cut of the American businessman coming "uptown" after a long day in the office.

It was a part of the Boykins' uncomfortable but determined attitude—and perhaps a last expression of their latent patriotism—to live in active disapproval of the world about them, fixing in memory with little stabs of reprobation innumerable instances of what the abominable foreigner was doing; so that they reminded Durham of persons peacefully following the course of a horrible war by pricking red pins in a map. To Mrs. Durham, with her gentle tourist's view of the European continent as a vast museum in which the human multitudes simply furnished the element of costume, the Boykins seemed abysmally instructed, and darkly expert in forbidden things; and her son, without sharing her simple faith in their omniscience, credited them with an ample supply of the kind of information of which he was in search.

Mrs. Boykin, from the corner of an intensely modern Gobelin sofa, studied her cousin as he balanced himself insecurely on one of the small gilt chairs which always look surprised at being sat in.

"Fanny de Malrive? Oh, of course: I remember you were all very intimate with the Frisbees when they lived in West Thirty-third Street. But she has dropped all her American friends since her marriage. The excuse was that de Malrive didn't like them; but as she's been separated for five or six years, I can't see—. You say she's been very nice to your mother and the girls? Well, I daresay she is beginning to feel the need of friends she can really trust; for as for her French relations—! That Malrive set is the worst in the Faubourg. Of course you know what *he* is; even the family, for decency's sake, had to back her up, and urge her to get a separation. And Christiane de Treymes—"

Durham seized his opportunity. "Is she so very reprehensible too?"

Mrs. Boykin pursed up her small colorless mouth. "I can't speak from personal experience. I know Madame de Treymes slightly—I have met her at Fanny's—but she never remembers the fact except when she wants me to go to one of her *ventes de charité*. They all remember us then; and some American women are silly enough to ruin themselves at the smart bazaars, and fancy they will get invitations in return. They say Mrs. Addison G. Pack followed Madame d'Alglade around for a whole winter, and spent a hundred thousand francs at her stalls; and at the end of the season Madame d'Alglade asked her to tea, and when she got there she found *that* was for a charity too, and she had to pay a hundred francs to get in."

Mrs. Boykin paused with a smile of compassion. "That is not *my* way," she continued. "Personally I have no desire to thrust myself into French society—I can't see how any American woman can do so without loss of self-respect. But anyone can tell you about Madame de Treymes."

"I wish you would, then," Durham suggested.

"Well, I think Elmer had better," said his wife mysteriously, as Mr. Boykin, at this point, advanced across the wide expanse of Aubusson on which his wife and Durham were islanded in a state of propinquity without privacy.

"What's that, Bessy? Hah, Durham, how are you? Didn't see you at Auteuil this afternoon. You don't race? Busy sight-seeing, I suppose? What was that my wife was telling you? Oh, about Madame de Treymes."

He stroked his pepper-and-salt mustache with a gesture intended rather to indicate than to conceal the smile of experience beneath it. "Well, Madame de Treymes has not been like a happy country—she's had a history: several of 'em. Someone said she constituted the *feuilleton* of the Faubourg daily news. *La suite au prochain numéro*—you see the point? Not that I speak from personal knowledge. Bessy and I have never cared to force our way"—he paused, reflecting that his wife had probably anticipated him in the expression of this familiar sentiment, and added with a significant nod: "Of course you know the Prince d'Armillac by sight? No? I'm surprised at that. Well, he's one of the choicest ornaments of the Jockey Club: very fascinating to the ladies, I believe, but the deuce and all at baccarat. Ruined his mother and a couple of maiden aunts already—and now Madame de Treymes has put the family pearls up the spout, and is wearing imitation for love of him."

"I had that straight from my maid's cousin, who is employed

by Madame d'Armillac's jeweler," said Mrs. Boykin with conscious pride.

"Oh, it's straight enough—more than *she* is!" retorted her husband, who was slightly jealous of having his facts reinforced by any information not of his own gleaning.

"Be careful of what you say, Elmer," Mrs. Boykin interposed with archness. "I suspect John of being seriously smitten by the lady."

Durham let this pass unchallenged, submitting with a good grace to his host's low whistle of amusement, and the sardonic inquiry: "Ever do anything with the foils? D'Armillac is what they call over here a *fine lame*."

"Oh, I don't mean to resort to bloodshed unless it's absolutely necessary; but I mean to make the lady's acquaintance," said Durham, falling into his key.

Mrs. Boykin's lips tightened to the vanishing point. "I am afraid you must apply for an introduction to more fashionable people than *we* are. Elmer and I so thoroughly disapprove of French society that we have always declined to take any part in it. But why should not Fanny de Malrive arrange a meeting for you?"

Durham hesitated. "I don't think she is on very intimate terms with her husband's family—"

"You mean that she's not allowed to introduce *her* friends to them," Mrs. Boykin interjected sarcastically; while her husband added, with an air of portentous initiation: "Ah, my dear fellow, the way they treat the Americans over here—that's another chapter, you know."

"How some people can *stand* it!" Mrs. Boykin chimed in; and as the footman, entering at that moment, tendered her a large coroneted envelope, she held it up as if in illustration of the indignities to which her countrymen were subjected.

"Look at that, my dear John," she exclaimed—"another card to one of their everlasting bazaars! Why, it's at Madame d'Armillac's, the Prince's mother. Madame de Treymes must have sent it, of course. The brazen way in which they combine religion and immorality! Fifty francs admission—*rien que cela!*—to see some of the most disreputable people in Europe. And if you're an American, you're expected to leave at least a thousand behind you. Their own people naturally get off cheaper." She tossed over the card to her cousin.

"There's your opportunity to see Madame de Treymes."

"Make it two thousand, and she'll ask you to tea," Mr. Boykin scathingly added.

# ─── 5 ───

🌿 IN THE MONUMENTAL drawing room of the Hotel de Malrive—it had been a surprise to the American to read the name of the house emblazoned on black marble over its still more monumental gateway—Durham found himself surrounded by a buzz of feminine tea-sipping oddly out of keeping with the wigged and cuirassed portraits frowning high on the walls, the majestic attitude of the furniture, the rigidity of great gilt consoles drawn up like lords-in-waiting against the tarnished panels.

It was the old Marquise de Malrive's "day," and Madame de Treymes, who lived with her mother, had admitted Durham to the heart of the enemy's country by inviting him, after his prodigal disbursements at the charity bazaar, to come in to tea on a Thursday. Whether, in thus fulfilling Mr. Boykin's prediction, she had been aware of Durham's purpose, and had her own reasons for falling in with it; or whether she simply wished to reward his lavishness at the fair, and permit herself another glimpse of an American so picturesquely embodying the type familiar to French fiction—on these points Durham was still in doubt.

Meanwhile, Madame de Treymes being engaged with a venerable Duchess in a black shawl—all the older ladies present had the sloping shoulders of a generation of shawlwearers—her American visitor, left in the isolation of his unimportance, was using it as a shelter for a rapid survey of the scene.

He had begun his study of Fanny de Malrive's situation without any real understanding of her fears. He knew the repugnance to divorce existing in the French Catholic world, but since the French laws sanctioned it, and in a case so flagrant as his injured friend's, would inevitably accord it with the least possible delay and exposure, he could not take seriously any risk of opposition on the part of the husband's family. Madame de Malrive had not become a Catholic, and since her religious scruples could not be played on, the only weapon remaining to the enemy—the threat

463

of fighting the divorce—was one they could not wield without self-injury. Certainly, if the chief object were to avoid scandal, common sense must counsel Monsieur de Malrive and his friends not to give the courts an opportunity of exploring his past; and since the echo of such explorations, and their ultimate transmission to her son, were what Madame de Malrive most dreaded, the opposing parties seemed to have a common ground for agreement, and Durham could not but regard his friend's fears as the result of overtaxed sensibilities. All this had seemed evident enough to him as he entered the austere portals of the Hotel de Malrive and passed, between the faded liveries of old family servants, to the presence of the dreaded dowager above. But he had not been ten minutes in that presence before he had arrived at a faint intuition of what poor Fanny meant. It was not in the exquisite mildness of the old marquise, a little gray-haired bunch of a woman in dowdy mourning, or in the small neat presence of the priestly uncle, the abbé who had so obviously just stepped down from one of the picture frames overhead: it was not in the aspect of these chief protagonists, so outwardly unformidable, that Durham read an occult danger to his friend. It was rather in their setting, their surroundings, the little company of elderly and dowdy persons—so uniformly clad in weeping blacks and purples that they might have been assembled for some mortuary anniversary—it was in the remoteness and the solidarity of this little group that Durham had his first glimpse of the social force of which Fanny de Malrive had spoken. All these amiably chatting visitors, who mostly bore the stamp of personal insignificance on their mildly sloping or aristocratically beaked faces, hung together in a visible closeness of tradition, dress, attitude and manner, as different as possible from the loose aggregation of a roomful of his own countrymen. Durham felt, as he observed them, that he had never before known what "society" meant; nor understood that, in an organized and inherited system, it exists full-fledged where two or three of its members are assembled.

Upon this state of bewilderment, this sense of having entered a room in which the lights had suddenly been turned out, even Madame de Treymes's intensely modern presence threw no illumination. He was conscious, as she smilingly rejoined him, not of her points of difference from the others, but of the myriad invisible threads by which she held to them; he even recognized the audacious slant of her little brown profile in the portrait of a powdered ancestress beneath which she had paused a moment in advancing. She was simply one particular facet of the solid, glittering, impenetrable body which he had thought to turn in his hands and look through like a crystal; and when she said, in her clear staccato English, "Perhaps you will like to see the other rooms," he felt like crying out in his blindness: "If I could only be sure of seeing *anything* here!" Was she conscious of his blindness, and was he as remote and unintelligible to her as she was to him? This possibility, as he followed her through the nobly unfolding rooms of the great house, gave him his first hope of recoverable advantage. For, after all, he had some vague traditional lights on her world and its antecedents; whereas to her he was a wholly new phenomenon, as unexplained as a fragment of meteorite dropped at her feet on the smooth gravel of the garden path they were pacing.

She had led him down into the garden, in response to his admiring exclamation, and perhaps also because she was sure that, in the chill spring afternoon, they would have its embowered privacies to themselves. The garden was small, but intensely rich and deep—one of those wells of verdure and fragrance which everywhere sweeten the air of Paris by wafts blown above old walls on quiet streets; and as Madame de Treymes paused against the ivy bank masking its farther boundary, Durham felt more than ever removed from the normal bearings of life.

His sense of strangeness was increased by the surprise of his companion's next speech.

"You wish to marry my sister-in-law?" she asked abruptly; and Durham's start of wonder was followed by an immediate feeling of relief. He had expected the preliminaries of their interview to be as complicated as the bargaining in an Eastern bazaar, and had feared to lose himself at the first turn in a labyrinth of "foreign" intrigue.

"Yes, I do," he said with equal directness; and they smiled together at the sharp report of question and answer.

The smile put Durham more completely at his ease, and after waiting for her to speak, he added with deliberation: "So far, however, the wishing is entirely on my side." His scrupulous conscience felt itself justified in this reserve by the conditional nature of Madame de Malrive's consent.

"I understand; but you have been given reason to hope—"

"Every man in my position gives himself his own reasons for hoping," he interposed with a smile.

"I understand that too," Madame de Treymes assented. "But still—you spent a great deal of money the other day at our bazaar."

"Yes. I wanted to have a talk with you, and it was the readiest—if not the most distinguished—means of attracting your attention."

"I understand," she once more reiterated, with a gleam of amusement.

"It is because I suspect you of understanding everything that I have been so anxious for this opportunity."

She bowed her acknowledgment, and said: "Shall we sit a moment?" adding, as he drew their chairs under a tree: "You permit me, then, to say that I believe I understand also a little of our good Fanny's mind?"

"On that point I have no authority to speak. I am here only to listen."

"Listen, then: you have persuaded her that there would be no harm in divorcing my brother—since I believe your religion does not forbid divorce?"

"Madame de Malrive's religion sanctions divorce in such a case as—"

"As my brother has furnished? Yes, I have heard that your race is stricter in judging such *écarts*. But you must not think," she added, "that I defend my brother. Fanny must have told you that we have always given her our sympathy."

"She has let me infer it from her way of speaking of you."

Madame de Treymes arched her dramatic eyebrows. "How cautious you are! I am so straightforward that I shall have no chance with you."

"You will be quite safe, unless you are so straightforward that you put me on my guard."

She met this with a low note of amusement.

"At this rate we shall never get any farther; and in two minutes I must go back to my mother's visitors. Why should we go on fencing? The situation is really quite simple. Tell me just what you wish to know. I have always been Fanny's friend, and that disposes me to be yours."

Durham, during this appeal, had had time to steady his thoughts; and the result of his deliberation was that he said, with a return to his former directness: "Well, then, what I wish to know is, what position your family would take if Madame de Malrive should sue for a divorce." He added, without giving her time to reply: "I naturally wish to be clear on this point before urging my cause with your sister-in-law."

Madame de Treymes seemed in no haste to answer; but after a pause of reflection she said, not unkindly: "My poor Fanny might have asked me that herself."

"I beg you to believe that I am not acting as her spokesman," Durham hastily interposed. "I merely wish to clear up the situation before speaking to her in my own behalf."

"You are the most delicate of suitors! But I understand your feeling. Fanny also is extremely delicate: it was a great surprise to us at first. Still, in this case—" Madame de Treymes paused—"since she has no religious scruples, and she had no difficulty in obtaining a separation, why should she fear any in demanding a divorce?"

"I don't know that she does: but the mere fact of possible opposition might be enough to alarm the delicacy you have observed in her."

"Ah—yes: on her boy's account."

"Partly, doubtless, on her boy's account."

"So that, if my brother objects to a divorce, all he has to do is to announce his objection? But, my dear sir, you are giving your case into my hands!" She flashed an amused smile on him.

"Since you say you are Madame de Malrive's friend, could there be a better place for it?"

As she turned her eyes on him he seemed to see, under the flitting lightness of her glance, the sudden concentrated expression of the ancestral will. "I am Fanny's friend, certainly. But with us family considerations are paramount. And our religion forbids divorce."

"So that, inevitably, your brother will oppose it?"

She rose from her seat, and stood fretting with her slender boot tip the minute red pebbles of the path.

"I must really go in: my mother will never forgive me for deserting her."

"But surely you owe me an answer?" Durham protested, rising also.

"In return for your purchases at my stall?"

"No, in return for the trust I have placed in you."

She mused on this, moving slowly a step or two toward the house.

"Certainly I wish to see you again; you interest me," she said smiling. "But it is so difficult to arrange. If I were to ask you to come here again, my mother and uncle would be surprised. And at Fanny's—"

"Oh, not there!" he exclaimed.

"Where then? Is there any other house where we are likely to meet?"

Durham hesitated; but he was goaded by the flight of the precious minutes. "Not unless you'll come and dine with me," he said boldly.

"Dine with you? *Au cabaret*? Ah, that would be diverting—but impossible!"

"Well, dine with my cousin, then—I have a cousin, an American lady, who lives here," said Durham, with suddenly soaring audacity.

She paused with puzzled brows. "An American lady whom I know?"

"By name, at any rate. You send her cards for all your charity bazaars."

She received the thrust with a laugh. "We do exploit your compatriots."

"Oh, I don't think she has ever gone to the bazaars."

"But she might if I dined with her?"

"Still less, I imagine."

She reflected on this, and then said with acuteness: "I like that, and I accept—but what is the lady's name?"

# 6

ON THE WAY home, in the first drop of his exaltation, Durham had said to himself: "But why on earth should Bessy invite her?"

He had, naturally, no very cogent reasons to give Mrs. Boykin in support of his astonishing request, and could only, marveling at his own growth in duplicity, suffer her to infer that he was really, shamelessly "smitten" with the lady he thus proposed to thrust upon her hospitality. But, to his surprise, Mrs. Boykin hardly gave herself time to pause upon his reasons. They were swallowed up in the fact that Madame de Treymes wished to dine with her, as the lesser luminaries vanish in the blaze of the sun.

"I am not surprised," she declared, with a faint smile intended to check her husband's unruly wonder. "I wonder *you* are, Elmer. Didn't you tell me that Armillac went out of his way to speak to you the other day at the races? And at Madame d'Alglade's sale— yes, I went there after all, just for a minute, because I found Katy and Nannie were so anxious to be taken—well, that day I noticed that Madame de Treymes was quite *empressée* when we went up to her stall. Oh, I didn't buy anything: I merely waited while the girls chose some lampshades. They thought it would be interesting to take home something painted by a real marquise, and of course I didn't tell them that those women *never* make the things they sell at their stalls. But I repeat I'm not surprised: I suspected that Madame de Treymes had heard of our little dinners. You know they're really horribly bored in that poky old Faubourg. My poor John, I see now why she's been making up to you! But on one point I am quite determined, Elmer; whatever you say, I shall *not* invite the Prince d'Armillac."

Elmer, as far as Durham could observe, did not say much; but, like his wife, he continued in a state of pleasantly agitated activity till the momentous evening of the dinner.

The festivity in question was restricted in numbers, either

owing to the difficulty of securing suitable guests, or from a desire not to have it appear that Madame de Treymes's hosts attached any special importance to her presence; but the smallness of the company was counterbalanced by the multiplicity of the courses.

The national determination not to be "downed" by the despised foreigner, to show a wealth of material resource obscurely felt to compensate for the possible lack of other distinctions—this resolve had taken, in Mrs. Boykin's case, the shape—or rather the multiple shapes—of a series of culinary feats, of gastronomic combinations, which would have commanded her deep respect had she seen them on any other table, and which she naturally relied on to produce the same effect on her guest. Whether or not the desired result was achieved, Madame de Treymes's manner did not specifically declare; but it showed a general complaisance, a charming willingnes to be amused, which made Mr. Boykin, for months afterward, allude to her among his compatriots as "an old friend of my wife's—takes potluck with us, you know. Of course there's not a word of truth in any of those ridiculous stories."

It was only when, to Durham's intense surprise, Mr. Boykin hazarded to his neighbor the regret that they had not been so lucky as to "secure the Prince"—it was then only that the lady showed, not indeed anything so simple and unprepared as embarrassment, but a faint play of wonder, an underflicker of amusement, as though recognizing that, by some odd law of social compensation, the crudity of the talk might account for the complexity of the dishes.

But Mr. Boykin was tremulously alive to hints, and the conversation at once slid to safer topics, easy generalizations which left Madame de Treymes ample time to explore the table, to use her narrowed gaze like a knife slitting open the unsuspicious personalities about her. Nannie and Katy Durham, who, after much discussion (to which their hostess candidly admitted them), had been included in the feast, were the special objects of Madame de Treymes's observation. During dinner she ignored in their favor the other carefully selected guests—the fashionable art critic, the old Legitimist general, the beauty from the English Embassy, the whole impressive marshaling of Mrs. Boykin's social resources—and when the men returned to the drawing room, Durham found her still fanning in his sisters the flame of an easily kindled enthusiasm. Since she could hardly have been held by the intrinsic interest of their converse, the sight gave him another swift intuition of the working of those hidden forces with which Fanny de Malrive felt herself encompassed. But when Madame de Treymes, at his approach, let him see that it was for him she had been reserving herself, he felt that so graceful an impulse needed no special explanation. She had the art of making it seem quite natural that they should move away together to the remotest of Mrs. Boykin's far-drawn salons, and that there, in a glaring privacy of brocade and ormolu, she should turn to him with a smile which avowed her intentional quest of seclusion.

"Confess that I have done a great deal for you!" she exclaimed, making room for him on a sofa judiciously screened from the observation of the other rooms.

"In coming to dine with my cousin?" he inquired, answering her smile.

"Let us say, in giving you this half hour."

"For that I am duly grateful—and shall be still more so when I know what it contains for me."

"Ah, I am not sure. You will not like what I am going to say."

"Shall I not?" he rejoined, changing color.

She raised her eyes from the thoughtful contemplation of her painted fan. "You appear to have no idea of the difficulties."

"Should I have asked your help if I had not had an idea of them?"

"But you are still confident that with my help you can surmount them?"

"I can't believe you have come here to take that confidence from me?"

She leaned back, smiling at him through her lashes. "And all this I am to do for your *beaux yeux?*"

"No—for your own: that you may see with them what happiness you are conferring."

"You are extremely clever, and I like you." She paused, and then brought out with lingering emphasis: "But my family will not hear of a divorce."

She threw into her voice such an accent of finality that Durham, for the moment, felt himself brought up against an insurmountable barrier, but, almost at once, his fear was mitigated by the conviction that she would not have put herself out so much to say so little.

"When you speak of your family, do you include yourself?" he suggested.

She threw a surprised glance at him. "I thought you understood that I am simply their mouthpiece."

At this he rose quietly to his feet with a gesture of acceptance. "I have only to thank you, then, for not keeping me longer in suspense."

His air of wishing to put an immediate end to the conversation seemed to surprise her. "Sit down a moment longer," she commanded him kindly; and as he leaned against the back of his chair, without appearing to hear her request, she added in a low voice: "I am very sorry for you and Fanny—but you are not the only persons to be pitied."

"The only persons?"

"In our unhappy family." She touched her breast with a sudden tragic gesture. "I, for instance, whose help you ask—if you could guess how I need help myself!"

She had dropped her light manner as she might have tossed aside her fan, and he was startled at the intimacy of misery to which her look and movement abruptly admitted him. Perhaps no Anglo-Saxon fully understands the fluency in self-revelation which centuries of the confessional have given to the Latin races, and to Durham, at any rate, Madame de Treymes's sudden avowal gave the shock of a physical abandonment.

"I am so sorry," he stammered—"is there any way in which I can be of use to you?"

She sat before him with her hands clasped, her eyes fixed on his in a terrible intensity of appeal. "If you would—if you would! Oh, there is nothing I would not do for you. I have still a great deal of influence with my mother, and what my mother commands we all do. I could help you—I am sure I could help you; but not if my own situation were known. And if nothing can be done it must be known in a few days."

Durham had reseated himself at her side. "Tell me what I can do," he said in a low tone, forgetting his own preoccupations in his genuine concern for her distress.

She looked up at him through tears. "How dare I? Your race is so cautious, so self-controlled—you have so little indulgence for the extravagances of the heart. And my folly has been incredible—and unrewarded." She paused, and as Durham waited in a silence which she guessed to be compassionate, she brought out below her breath: "I have lent money—my husband's, my brother's—money that was not mine, and now I have nothing to repay it with."

Durham gazed at her in genuine astonishment. The turn the conversation had taken led quite beyond his uncomplicated experiences with the other sex. She saw his surprise, and extended her hands in deprecation and entreaty. "Alas, what must you think of me? How can I explain my humiliating myself before a stranger? Only by telling you the whole truth—the fact that I am not alone in this disaster, that I could not confess my situation to my family without ruining myself, and involving in my ruin someone who, however undeservedly, has been as dear to me as—as you are to—"

Durham pushed his chair back with a sharp exclamation.

"Ah, even that does not move you!" she said.

The cry restored him to his senses by the long shaft of light it sent down the dark windings of the situation. He seemed suddenly to know Madame de Treymes as if he had been brought up with her in the inscrutable shades of the Hotel de Malrive.

She, on her side, appeared to have a startled but uncomprehending sense of the fact that his silence was no longer completely sympathetic, that her touch called forth no answering vibration; and she made a desperate clutch at the one chord she could be certain of sounding.

"You have asked a great deal of me—much more than you can guess. Do you mean to give me nothing—not even your sympathy—in return? Is it because you have heard horrors of me? When are they not said of a woman who is married unhappily? Perhaps not in your fortunate country, where she may seek liberation without dishonor. But here—! You who have seen the consequences of our disastrous marriages—you who may yet be the victim of our cruel and abominable system; have you no pity for one who has suffered in the same way, and without the possibility of release?" She paused, laying her hand on his arm with a smile of deprecating irony. "It is not because you are not rich. At such times the crudest way is the shortest, and I don't pretend to deny that I know I am asking you a trifle. You Americans, when you want a thing, always pay ten times what it is worth, and I am giving you the wonderful chance to get what you most want at a bargain."

Durham sat silent, her little gloved hand burning his coat sleeve as if it had been a hot iron. His brain was tingling with the shock of her confession. She wanted money, a great deal of money: that was clear, but it was not the point. She was ready to sell her influence, and he fancied she could be counted on to fulfill her side of the bargain. The fact that he could so trust her seemed only to make her more terrible to him—more supernaturally dauntless and baleful. For what was it that she exacted of him? She had said she must have money to pay her debts; but he knew that was only a pretext which she scarcely expected him to believe. She wanted the money for someone else; that was what her allusion to a fellow victim meant. She wanted it to pay the Prince's gambling debts—it was at that price that Durham was to buy the right to marry Fanny de Malrive.

Once the situation had worked itself out in his mind, he found himself unexpectedly relieved of the necessity of weighing the arguments for and against it. All the traditional forces of his blood were in revolt, and he could only surrender himself to their pressure, without thought of compromise or parley.

He stood up in silence, and the abruptness of his movement caused Madame de Treymes's hand to slip from his arm.

"You refuse?" she exclaimed, and he answered with a bow: "Only because of the return you propose to make me."

She stood staring at him, in a perplexity so genuine and profound that he could almost have smiled at it through his disgust.

"Ah, you are all incredible," she murmured at last, stooping to repossess herself of her fan; and as she moved past him to rejoin the group in the farther room, she added in an incisive undertone: "You are quite at liberty to repeat our conversation to your friend!"

## —— 7 ——

🌿 DURHAM did not take advantage of the permission thus strangely flung at him. Of his talk with her sister-in-law he gave to Madame de Malrive only that part which concerned her.

Presenting himself for this purpose, the day after Mrs. Boykin's dinner, he found his friend alone with her son; and the sight of the child had the effect of dispelling whatever illusive hopes had attended him to the threshold. Even after the governess's descent upon the scene had left Madame de Malrive and her visitor alone, the little boy's presence seemed to hover admonishingly between them, reducing to a bare statement of fact Durham's confession of the total failure of his errand.

Madame de Malrive heard the confession calmly; she had been too prepared for it not to have prepared a countenance to receive it. Her first comment was: "I have never known them to declare themselves so plainly—" and Durham's baffled hopes fastened themselves eagerly on the words. Had she not always warned him that there was nothing so misleading as their plainness? And might it not be that, in spite of his advisedness, he had suffered too easy a rebuff? But second thoughts reminded him that the refusal had not been as unconditional as his necessary reservations made it seem in the repetition; and that, furthermore, it was his own act, and not that of his opponents, which had determined it. The impossibility of revealing this to Madame de Malrive only made the difficulty shut in more darkly around him, and in the completeness of his discouragement he scarcely needed her reminder of his promise to regard the subject as closed when once the other side had defined its position.

He was secretly confirmed in this acceptance of his fate by the knowledge that it was really he who had defined the position. Even now that he was alone with Madame de Malrive, and subtly aware of the struggle under her composure, he felt no temptation to abate his stand by a jot. He had not yet formulated a reason for his resistance: he simply went on feeling, more and more strongly with every precious sign of her participation in his unhappiness, that he could neither owe his escape from it to such a transaction, nor suffer her, innocently, to owe hers.

The only mitigating effect of his determination was in an increase of helpless tenderness toward her; so that, when she exclaimed, in answer to his announcement that he meant to leave Paris the next night: "Oh give me a day or two longer!" he at once resigned himself to saying: "If I can be of the least use, I'll give you a hundred."

She answered sadly that all he could do would be to let her feel that he was there—just for a day or two, till she had readjusted herself to the idea of going on in the old way; and on this note of renunciation they parted.

But Durham, however pledged to the passive part, could not long sustain it without rebellion. To "hang round" the shut door of his hopes seemed, after two long days, more than even his passion required of him; and on the third he despatched a note of good-bye to his friend. He was going off for a few weeks, he explained—his mother and sisters wished to be taken to the Italian lakes: but he would return to Paris, and say his real farewell to her, before sailing for America in July.

He had not intended his note to act as an ultimatum: he had no wish to surprise Madame de Malrive into unconsidered surrender. When, almost immediately, his own messenger returned with a reply from her, he even felt a pang of disappointment, a momentary fear lest she should have stooped a little from the high place where his passion had preferred to leave her; but her first words turned his fear into rejoicing.

"Let me see you before you go: something extraordinary has happened," she wrote.

What had happened, as he heard from her a few hours later—finding her in a tremor of frightened gladness, with her door boldly closed to all the world but himself—was nothing less extraordinary than a visit from Madame de Treymes, who had come, officially delegated by the family, to announce that Monsieur de Malrive had decided not to oppose his wife's suit for divorce. Durham, at the news, was almost afraid to show himself too amazed; but his small signs of alarm and wonder were swallowed up in the flush of Madame de Malrive's incredulous joy.

"It's the long habit, you know, of not believing them—of looking for the truth always in what they *don't* say. It took me hours and hours to convince myself that there's no trick under it, that there can't be any," she explained.

"Then you *are* convinced now?" escaped from Durham, but the shadow of his question lingered no more than the flit of a wing across her face.

"I am convinced because the facts are there to reassure me. Christiane tells me that Monsieur de Malrive has consulted his lawyers, and that they have advised him to free me. Maître Enguerrand has been instructed to see my lawyer whenever I wish it. They quite understand that I never should have taken the step in face of any opposition on their part—I am so thankful to you for making that perfectly clear to them!—and I suppose this is the return their pride makes to mine. For they *can* be proud collectively—" She broke off, and added, with happy hands outstretched: "And I owe it all to you—Christiane said it was your talk with her that had convinced them."

Durham, at this statement, had to repress a fresh sound of amazement; but with her hands in his, and, a moment after, her whole self drawn to him in the first yielding of her lips, doubt perforce gave way to the lover's happy conviction that such love was after all too strong for the powers of darkness.

It was only when they sat again in the blissful after-calm of their understanding, that he felt the pricking of an unappeased distrust.

"Did Madame de Treymes give you any reason for this change of front?" he risked asking, when he found the distrust was not otherwise to be quelled.

"Oh, yes: just what I've said. It was really her admiration of *you*—of your attitude—your delicacy. She said that at first she hadn't believed in it: they're always looking for a hidden motive. And when she found that yours was staring at her in the actual words you said: that you really respected my scruples, and would never, never try to coerce or entrap me—something in her—poor Christiane!—answered to it, she told me, and she wanted to prove to us that she was capable of understanding us too. If you knew her history you'd find it wonderful and pathetic that she can!"

Durham thought he knew enough of it to infer that Madame de Treymes had not been the object of many conscientious scruples on the part of the opposite sex; but this increased rather his sense of the strangeness than of the pathos of her action. Yet Madame de Malrive, whom he had once inwardly taxed with the morbid raising of obstacles, seemed to see none now; and he could only infer that her sister-in-law's actual words had carried more conviction than reached him in the repetition of them. The mere fact that he had so much to gain by leaving his friend's faith undisturbed was no doubt stirring his own suspicions to unnatural activity; and this sense gradually reasoned him back into acceptance of her view, as the most normal as well as the pleasantest he could take.

# ——— 8 ———

🍃 THE UNEASINESS thus temporarily repressed slipped into the final disguise of hoping he should not again meet Madame de Treymes; and in this wish he was seconded by the decision, in which Madame de Malrive concurred, that it would be well for him to leave Paris while the preliminary negotiations were going on. He committed her interests to the best professional care, and his mother, resigning her dream of the lakes, remained to fortify Madame de Malrive by her mild unimaginative view of the transaction, as an uncomfortable but commonplace necessity, like housecleaning or dentistry. Mrs. Durham would doubtless have preferred that her only son, even with his hair turning gray, should have chosen a Fanny Frisbee rather than a Fanny de Malrive; but it was a part of her acceptance of life on a general basis of innocence and kindliness, that she entered generously into his dream of rescue and renewal, and devoted herself without afterthought to keeping up Fanny's courage with so little to spare for herself.

The process, the lawyers declared, would not be a long one, since Monsieur de Malrive's acquiescence reduced it to a formality; and when, at the end of June, Durham returned from Italy with Katy and Nannie, there seemed no reason why he should not stop in Paris long enough to learn what progress had been made.

But before he could learn this he was to hear, on entering Madame de Malrive's presence, news more immediate if less personal. He found her, in spite of her gladness in his return, so evidently preoccupied and distressed that his first thought was one of fear for their own future. But she read and dispelled this by saying, before he could put his question: "Poor Christiane is here. She is very unhappy. You have seen in the papers—?"

"I have seen no papers since we left Turin. What has happened?"

"The Prince d'Armillac has come to grief. There has been some terrible scandal about money and he has been obliged to leave France to escape arrest."

"And Madame de Treymes has left her husband?"

"Ah, no, poor creature: they don't leave their husbands—they can't. But de Treymes has gone down to their place in Brittany, and as my mother-in-law is with another daughter in Auvergne, Christiane came here for a few days. With me, you see, she need not pretend—she can cry her eyes out."

"And that is what she is doing?"

It was so unlike his conception of the way in which, under the most adverse circumstances, Madame de Treymes would be likely to occupy her time, that Durham was conscious of a note of scepticism in his query.

"Poor thing—if you saw her you would feel nothing but pity. She is suffering so horribly that I reproach myself for being happy under the same roof."

Durham met this with a tender pressure of her hand; then he said, after a pause of reflection: "I should like to see her."

He hardly knew what prompted him to utter the wish, unless it were a sudden stir of compunction at the memory of his own dealings with Madame de Treymes. Had he not sacrificed the poor creature to a purely fantastic conception of conduct? She had said that she knew she was asking a trifle of him; and the fact that, materially, it would have been a trifle, had seemed at the moment only an added reason for steeling himself in his moral resistance to it. But now that he had gained his point—and through her own generosity, as it still appeared—the largeness of her attitude made his own seem cramped and petty. Since conduct, in the last resort, must be judged by its enlarging or diminishing effect on character, might it not be that the zealous weighing of the moral anise and cumin was less important than the unconsidered lavishing of the precious ointment? At any rate, he could enjoy no peace of mind under the burden of Madame de Treymes's magnanimity, and when he had assured himself that his own affairs were progressing favorably, he once more, at the risk of surprising his betrothed, brought up the possibility of seeing her relative.

Madame de Malrive evinced no surprise. "It is natural, knowing what she has done for us, that you should want to show her your sympathy. The difficulty is that it is just the one thing you *can't* show her. You can thank her, of course, for ourselves, but even that at the moment—"

"Would seem brutal? Yes, I recognize that I should have to choose my words," he admitted, guiltily conscious that his capability of dealing with Madame de Treymes extended far beyond her sister-in-law's conjecture.

Madame de Malrive still hesitated. "I can tell her; and when you come back tomorrow—"

It had been decided that, in the interests of discretion—the interests, in other words, of the poor little future Marquis de Malrive—Durham was to remain but two days in Paris, withdrawing then with his family till the conclusion of the divorce proceedings permitted him to return in the acknowledged character of Madame de Malrive's future husband. Even on this occasion, he had not come to her alone; Nannie Durham, in the adjoining room, was chatting conspicuously with the little marquis, whom she could with difficulty be restrained from teaching to call her "Aunt Nannie." Durham thought her voice had risen unduly once or twice during his visit, and when, on taking leave, he went to summon her from the inner room, he found the higher note of ectasy had been evoked by the appearance of Madame de Treymes, and that the little boy, himself absorbed in a new toy of Durham's bringing, was being bent over by an actual as well as a potential aunt.

Madame de Treymes raised herself with a slight start at Durham's approach: she had her hat on, and had evidently paused a moment on her way out to speak with Nannie, without expecting to be surprised by her sister-in-law's other visitor. But her surprises never wore the awkward form of embarrassment, and she smiled beautifully on Durham as he took her extended hand.

The smile was made the more appealing by the way in which it lit up the ruin of her small dark face, which looked seared and hollowed as by a flame that might have spread over it from her fevered eyes. Durham, accustomed to the pale inward grief of the inexpressive races, was positively startled by the way in which she seemed to have been openly stretched on the pyre; he almost felt an indelicacy in the ravages so tragically confessed.

The sight caused an involuntary readjustment of his whole view of the situation, and made him, as far as his own share in it went, more than ever inclined to extremities of self-disgust. With him such sensations required, for his own relief, some immediate penitential escape, and as Madame de Treymes turned toward the door he addressed a glance of entreaty to his betrothed.

Madame de Malrive, whose intelligence could be counted on at such moments, responded by laying a detaining hand on her sister-in-law's arm.

"Dear Christiane, may I leave Mr. Durham in your charge for two minutes? I have promised Nannie that she shall see the boy put to bed."

Madame de Treymes made no audible response to this request, but when the door had closed on the other ladies she said, looking quietly at Durham: "I don't think that, in this house, your time will hang so heavy that you need my help in supporting it."

Durham met her glance frankly. "It was not for that reason that Madame de Malrive asked you to remain with me."

"Why, then? Surely not in the interest of preserving appearances, since she is safely upstairs with your sister?"

"No, but simply because I asked her to. I told her I wanted to speak to you."

"How you arrange things! And what reason can you have for wanting to speak to me?"

He paused a moment. "Can't you imagine? The desire to thank you for what you have done."

She stirred restlessly, turning to adjust her hat before the glass above the mantelpiece.

"Oh, as for what I have done—!"

"Don't speak as if you regretted it," he interposed.

She turned back to him with a flash of laughter lighting up the haggardness of her face. "Regret working for the happiness of two such excellent persons? Can't you fancy what a charming change it is for me to do something so innocent and beneficent?"

He moved across the room and went up to her, drawing down the hand which still flitted experimentally about her hat.

"Don't talk in that way, however much one of the persons of whom you speak may have deserved it."

"One of the persons? Do you mean me?"

He released her hand, but continued to face her resolutely. "I mean myself, as you know. You have been generous—extraordinarily generous."

"Ah, but I was doing good in a good cause. You have made me see that there is a distinction."

He flushed to the forehead. "I am here to let you say whatever you choose to me."

"Whatever I choose?" She made a slight gesture of deprecation. "Has it never occurred to you that I may conceivably choose to say nothing?"

Durham paused, conscious of the increasing difficulty of the advance. She met him, parried him, at every turn: he had to take his baffled purpose back to another point of attack.

"Quite conceivably," he said. "So much so that I am aware I must make the most of this opportunity, because I am not likely to get another."

"But what remains of your opportunity, if it isn't one to me?"

"It still remains, for me, an occasion to abase myself—" He broke off, conscious of a grossness of allusion that seemed, on a closer approach, the real obstacle to full expression. But the moments were flying, and for his self-esteem's sake he must find some way of making her share the burden of his repentance.

"There is only one thinkable pretext for detaining you: it is that I may still show my sense of what you have done for me."

Madame de Treymes, who had moved toward the door, paused at this and faced him, resting her thin brown hands on a slender sofa back.

"How do you propose to show that sense?" she inquired.

Durham colored still more deeply: he saw that she was determined to save her pride by making what he had to say of the utmost difficulty. Well! He would let his expiation take that form, then—it was as if her slender hands held out to him the fool's cap he was condemned to press down on his own ears.

"By offering in return—in any form, and to the utmost—any service you are forgiving enough to ask of me."

She received this with a low sound of laughter that scarcely rose to her lips. "You are princely. But, my dear sir, does it not occur to you that I may, meanwhile, have taken my own way of repaying myself for any service I have been fortunate enough to render you?"

Durham, at the question, or still more, perhaps, at the tone in which it was put, felt, through his compunction, a vague faint chill of apprehension. Was she threatening him or only mocking him? Or was this barbed swiftness of retort only the wounded creature's way of defending the privacy of her own pain? He looked at her again, and read his answer in the last conjecture.

"I don't know how you can have repaid yourself for anything so disinterested—but I am sure, at least, that you have given me no chance of recognizing, ever so slightly, what you have done."

She shook her head, with the flicker of a smile on her melancholy lips. "Don't be too sure! You have given me a chance and I have taken it—taken it to the full. So fully," she continued, keeping her eyes fixed on his, "that if I were to accept any farther service you might choose to offer, I should simply be robbing you—robbing you shamelessly." She paused, and added in an undefinable voice: "I was entitled, wasn't I, to take something in return for the service I had the happiness of doing you?"

Durham could not tell whether the irony of her tone was self-directed or addressed to himself—perhaps it comprehended them both. At any rate, he chose to overlook his own share in it in replying earnestly: "So much so, that I can't see how you can have left me nothing to add to what you say you have taken."

"Ah, but you don't know what that is!" She continued to smile, elusively, ambiguously. "And what's more, you wouldn't believe me if I told you."

"How do you know?" he rejoined.

"You didn't believe me once before; and this is so much more incredible."

He took the taunt full in the face. "I shall go away unhappy unless you tell me—but then perhaps I have deserved to," he confessed.

She shook her head again, advancing toward the door with the evident intention of bringing their conference to a close; but on the threshold she paused to launch her reply.

"I can't send you away unhappy, since it is in the contemplation of your happiness that I have found my reward."

# —— 9 ——

THE NEXT DAY Durham left with his family for England with the intention of not returning till after the divorce should have been pronounced in September.

To say that he left with a quiet heart would be to overstate the case: the fact that he could not communicate to Madame de Malrive the substance of his talk with her sister-in-law still hung upon him uneasily. But of definite apprehensions the lapse of time gradually freed him, and Madame de Malrive's letters, addressed more frequently to his mother and sisters than to himself, reflected, in their reassuring serenity, the undisturbed course of events.

There was to Durham something peculiarly touching—as of an involuntary confession of almost unbearable loneliness—in the way she had regained, with her reentry into the clear air of American associations, her own fresh trustfulness of view. Once she had accustomed herself to the surprise of finding her divorce unopposed, she had been as it now seemed to Durham, in almost too great haste to renounce the habit of weighing motives and calculating chances. It was as though her coming liberation had already freed her from the garb of a mental slavery, as though she could not too soon or too conspicuously cast off the ugly badge of suspicion. The fact that Durham's cleverness had achieved so easy a victory over forces apparently impregnable, merely raised her estimate of that cleverness to the point of letting her feel that she could rest in it without farther demur. He had even noticed in her, during his few hours in Paris, a tendency to reproach herself for her lack of charity, and a desire, almost as fervent as his own, to expiate it by exaggerated recognition of the disinterestedness of her opponents—if opponents they could still be called. This sudden change in her attitude was peculiarly moving to Durham. He knew she would hazard herself lightly enough wherever her heart called her; but that, with the precious freight of her child's future weighing her down, she should commit herself so blindly to his hand stirred in him the depths of tenderness. Indeed, had the actual course of events been less auspiciously regular, Madame de Malrive's confidence would have gone far toward unsettling his own; but with the process of law going on unimpeded, and the other side making no sign of open or covert resistance, the fresh air of good faith gradually swept through the inmost recesses of his distrust.

It was expected that the decision in the suit would be reached by mid-September; and it was arranged that Durham and his family should remain in England till a decent interval after the conclusion of the proceedings. Early in the month, however, it became necessary for Durham to go to France to confer with a business associate who was in Paris for a few days, and on the point of sailing for Cherbourg. The most zealous observance of appearances could hardly forbid Durham's return for such a purpose; but it had been agreed between himself and Madame de Malrive—who had once more been left alone by Madame de Treymes's return to her family—that, so close to the fruition of their wishes, they would propitiate fate by a scrupulous adherence to usage, and communicate only, during his hasty visit, by a daily interchange of notes.

The ingenuity of Madame d Malrive's tenderness found, however, the day after his arrival, a means of tempering their privation. "Christiane," she wrote, "is passing through Paris on her way from Trouville, and has promised to see you for me if you will call on her today. She thinks there is no reason why you should not go to the Hotel de Malrive, as you will find her there alone, the family having gone to Auvergne. She is really our friend and understands us."

In obedience to this request—though perhaps inwardly regretting that it should have been made—Durham that afternoon presented himself at the proud old house beyond the Seine. More than ever, in the semi-abandonment of the *morte saison* with reduced service, and shutters closed to the silence of the high-walled court, did it strike the American as the incorruptible custodian of old prejudices and strange social survivals. The thought of what he must represent to the almost human consciousness which such old houses seem to possess, made him feel like a barbarian desecrating the silence of a temple of the earlier faith. Not that there was anything venerable in the attestations of the Hotel de Malrive, except insofar as, to a sensitive imagination, every concrete embodiment of a past order of things testifies to real convictions once suffered for. Durham, at any rate, always alive in practical issues to the view of the other side, had enough sympathy left over to spend it sometimes, whimsically, on such perceptions of difference. Today, especially, the assurance of success—the sense of entering like a victorious beleaguerer receiving the keys of the stronghold—disposed him to a sentimental perception of what the other side might have to say for itself, in the language of old portraits, old relics, old usages dumbly outraged by his mere presence.

On the appearance of Madame de Treymes, however, such considerations gave way to the immediate act of wondering how she meant to carry off her share of the adventure. Durham had not forgotten the note on which their last conversation had closed: the lapse of time serving only to give more precision and perspective to the impression he had then received.

Madame de Treymes's first words implied a recognition of what was in his thoughts.

"It is extraordinary, my receiving you here, but *que voulez vous?* There was no other place, and I would do more than this for our dear Fanny."

Durham bowed. "It seems to me that you are also doing a great deal for me."

"Perhaps you will see later that I have my reasons," she returned, smiling. "But before speaking for myself I must speak for Fanny."

She signed to him to take a chair near the sofa corner in which she had installed herself, and he listened in silence while she delivered Madame de Malrive's message, and her own report of the progress of affairs.

"You have put me still more deeply in your debt," he said as she concluded. "I wish you would make the expression of this feeling a large part of the message I send back to Madame de Malrive."

She brushed this aside with one of her light gestures of deprecation. "Oh, I told you I had my reasons. And since you are here—and the mere sight of you assures me that you are as well as Fanny charged me to find you—with all these preliminaries disposed of, I am going to relieve you, in a small measure, of the weight of your obligation."

Durham raised his head quickly. "By letting me do something in return?"

She made an assenting motion. "By asking you to answer a question."

"That seems very little to do."

"Don't be so sure! It is never very little to your race." She leaned back, studying him through half-dropped lids.

"Well, try me," he protested.

She did not immediately respond; and when she spoke, her first words were explanatory rather than interrogative.

"I want to begin by saying that I believe I once did you an injustice, to the extent of misunderstanding your motive for a certain action."

Durham's uneasy flush confessed his recognition of her meaning. "Ah, if we must go back to *that*—"

"You withdraw your assent to my request?"

"By no means, but nothing consolatory you can find to say on that point can really make any difference."

"Will not the difference in my view of you perhaps make a difference in your own?"

She looked at him earnestly, without a trace of irony in her eyes or on her lips. "It is really I who have an *amende* to make, as I now understand the situation. I once turned to you for help in a painful extremity, and I have only now learned to understand your reasons for refusing to help me."

"Oh, my reasons—" groaned Durham.

"I have learned to understand them," she persisted, "by being so much, lately, with Fanny."

"But I never told her!" he broke in.

"Exactly. That was what told *me*. I understood you through her, and through your dealings with her. There she was—the woman you adored and longed to save; and you would not lift a finger to make her yours by means which would have seemed—I see it now—a desecration of your feeling for each other." She paused, as if to find the exact words for meanings she had never before had occasion to formulate. "It came to me first—a light on your attitude—when I found you had never breathed to her a word of our talk together. She had confidently commissioned you to find a way for her, as the medieval lady sent a prayer to her knight to deliver her from captivity, and you came back, confessing you had failed, but never justifying yourself by so much as a hint of the reason why. And when I had lived a little in Fanny's intimacy—at a moment when circumstances helped to bring us extraordinarily close—I understood why you had done this; why you had let her take what view she pleased of your failure, your passive acceptance of defeat, rather than let her suspect the alternative offered you. You couldn't, even with my permission, betray to anyone a hint of my miserable secret, and you couldn't, for your life's happiness, pay the particular price that I asked." She leaned toward him in the intense, almost childlike, effort at full expression. "Oh, we are of different races with a different point of honor; but I understand, I see, that you are good people—just simply, courageously *good!*"

She paused, and then said slowly: "Have I understood you? Have I put my hand on your motive?"

Durham sat speechless, subdued by the rush of emotion which her words set free.

"That, you understand, is my question," she concluded with a faint smile; and he answered hesitatingly: "What can it matter, when the upshot is something I infinitely regret?"

"Having refused me? Don't!" She spoke with deep seriousness, bending her eyes full on his: "Ah, I have suffered—suffered! But I have learned also—my life has been enlarged. You see how I have understood you both. And that is something I should have been incapable of a few months ago."

Durham returned her look. "I can't think that you can ever have been incapable of any generous interpretation."

She uttered a slight exclamation, which resolved itself into a laugh of self-directed irony.

"If you knew into what language I have always translated life! But that," she broke off, "is not what you are here to learn."

"I think," he returned gravely, "that I am here to learn the measure of Christian charity."

She threw him a new, odd look. "Ah, no—but to show it!" she exclaimed.

"To show it? And to whom?"

She paused for a moment, and then rejoined, instead of answering: "Do you remember that day I talked with you at Fanny's? The day after you came back from Italy?"

He made a motion of assent, and she went on: "You asked me then what return I expected for my service to you, as you called it; and I answered, the contemplation of your happiness. Well, do you know what that meant in my old language—the language I was still speaking then? It meant that I knew there was horrible misery in store for you, and that I was waiting to feast my eyes on it: that's all!"

She had flung out the words with one of her quick bursts of self-abandonment, like a fevered sufferer stripping the bandage from a wound. Durham received them with a face blanching to the pallor of her own.

"What misery do you mean?" he exclaimed.

She leaned forward, laying her hand on his with just such a gesture as she had used to enforce her appeal in Mrs. Boykin's boudoir. The remembrance made him shrink slightly from her touch, and she drew back with a smile.

"Have you never asked yourself," she inquired, "why our family consented so readily to a divorce?"

"Yes, often," he replied, all his unformed fears gathering in a dark throng about him. "But Fanny was so reassured, so convinced that we owed it to your good offices—"

She broke into a laugh. "My good offices! Will you never, you Americans, learn that we do not act individually in such cases? That we are all obedient to a common principle of authority?"

"Then it was not you—"

She made an impatient shrugging motion. "Oh, you are too confiding—it is the other side of your beautiful good faith!"

"The side you have taken advantage of, it appears?"

"I—we—all of us. I especially!" she confessed.

# —10—

THERE WAS another pause, during which Durham tried to steady himself against the shock of the impending revelation. It was an odd circumstance of the case, that though Madame de Treymes's avowal of duplicity was fresh in his ears, he did not for a moment believe that she would deceive him again. Whatever passed between them now would go to the root of the matter.

The first thing that passed was the long look they exchanged: searching on his part, tender, sad, undefinable on hers. As the result of it he said: "Why, then, did you consent to the divorce?"

"To get the boy back," she answered instantly; and while he sat stunned by the unexpectedness of the retort, she went on: "Is it possible you never suspected? It has been our whole thought from the first. Everything was planned with that object."

He drew a sharp breath of alarm. "But the divorce—how could that give him back to you?"

"It was the only thing that could. We trembled lest the idea should occur to you. But we were reasonably safe, for there has only been one other case of the same kind before the courts." She leaned back, the sight of his perplexity checking her quick rush of words. "You didn't know," she began again, "that in that case, on the remarriage of the mother, the courts instantly restored the child to the father, though he had—well, given as much cause for divorce as my unfortunate brother?"

Durham gave an ironic laugh. "Your French justice takes a grammar and dictionary to understand."

She smiled. "*We* understand it—and it isn't necessary that you should."

"So it would appear!" he exclaimed bitterly.

"Don't judge us too harshly—or not, at least, till you have taken the trouble to learn our point of view. You consider the individual—we think only of the family."

"Why don't you take care to preserve it, then?"

491

"Ah, that's what we do; in spite of every aberration of the individual. And so, when we saw it was impossible that my brother and his wife should live together, we simply transferred our allegiance to the child—we constituted *him* the family."

"A precious kindness you did him! If the result is to give him back to his father."

"That, I admit, is to be deplored; but his father is only a fraction of the whole. What we really do is to give him back to his race, his religion, his true place in the order of things."

"His mother never tried to deprive him of any of those inestimable advantages!"

Madame de Treymes unclasped her hands with a slight gesture of deprecation.

"Not consciously, perhaps; but silences and reserves can teach so much. His mother has another point of view—"

"Thank heaven!" Durham interjected.

"Thank heaven for *her*—yes—perhaps, but it would not have done for the boy."

Durham squared his shoulders with the sudden resolve of a man breaking through a throng of ugly phantoms.

"You haven't yet convinced me that it won't have to do for him. At the time of Madame de Malrive's separation, the court made no difficulty about giving her the custody of her son; and you must pardon me for reminding you that the father's unfitness was the reason alleged."

Madame de Treymes shrugged her shoulders. "And my poor brother, you would add, has not changed; but the circumstances have, and that proves precisely what I have been trying to show you: that, in such cases, the general course of events is considered, rather than the action of any one person."

"Then why is Madame de Malrive's action to be considered?"

"Because it breaks up the unity of the family."

"*Unity*—!" broke from Durham, and Madame de Treymes gently suffered his smile.

"Of the family tradition, I mean: it introduces new elements. You are a new element."

"Thank heaven!" said Durham again.

She looked at him singularly. "Yes—you may thank heaven. Why isn't it enough to satisfy Fanny?"

"Why isn't what enough?"

"Your being, as I say, a new element; taking her so completely into a better air. Why shouldn't she be content to begin a new life with you, without wanting to keep the boy too?"

Durham stared at her dumbly. "I don't know what you mean," he said at length.

"I mean that in her place—" she broke off, dropping her eyes. "She may have another son—the son of the man she adores."

Durham rose from his seat and took a quick turn through the room. She sat motionless, following his steps through her lowered lashes, which she raised again slowly as he stood before her.

"Your idea, then, is that I should tell her nothing?" he said.

"Tell her *now*? But, my poor friend, you would be ruined!"

"Exactly." He paused. "Then why have you told *me*?"

Under her dark skin he saw the faint color stealing. "We see things so differently—but can't you conceive that, after all that has passed, I felt it a kind of loyalty not to leave you in ignorance?"

"And you feel no such loyalty to her?"

"Ah, I leave her to you," she murmured, looking down again.

Durham continued to stand before her, grappling slowly with his perplexity, which loomed larger and darker as it closed in on him.

"You don't leave her to me; you take her from me at a stroke! I suppose," he added painfully, "I ought to thank you for doing it before it's too late."

She stared. "I take her from you? I simply prevent your going to her unprepared. Knowing Fanny as I do, it seemed to me necessary that you should find a way in advance—a way of tiding over the first moment. That, of course, is what we had planned that you shouldn't have. We meant to let you marry, and then—. Oh, there is no question about the result: we are certain of our case—our measures have been taken *de loin*." She broke off, as if oppressed by his stricken silence. "You will think me stupid, but my warning you of this is the only return I know how to make for your generosity. I could not bear to have you say afterward that I had deceived you twice."

"Twice?" he looked at her perplexedly, and her color rose.

"I deceived you once—that night at your cousin's, when I tried to get you to bribe me. Even then we meant to consent to the divorce—it was decided the first day that I saw you." He was silent, and she added, with one of her mocking gestures: "You see from what a *milieu* you are taking her!"

Durham groaned. "She will never give up her son!"

"How can she help it? After you are married there will be no choice."

"No—but there is one now."

*"Now?"* She sprang to her feet, clasping her hands in dismay. "Haven't I made it clear to you? Haven't I shown you your course?" She paused, and then brought out with emphasis: "I love Fanny, and I am ready to trust her happiness to you."

"I shall have nothing to do with her happiness," he repeated doggedly.

She stood close to him, with a look intently fixed on his face. "Are you afraid?" she asked with one of her mocking flashes.

"Afraid?"

"Of not being able to make it up to her—?"

Their eyes met, and he returned her look steadily.

"No, if I had the chance, I believe I could."

"I know you could!" she exclaimed.

"That's the worst of it," he said with a cheerless laugh.

"The worst—?"

"Don't you see that I can't deceive her? Can't trick her into marrying me now?"

Madame de Treymes continued to hold his eyes for a puzzled moment after he had spoken; then she broke out despairingly: "Is happiness never more to you, then, than this abstract standard of truth?"

Durham reflected. "I don't know—it's an instinct. There doesn't seem to be any choice."

"Then I am a miserable wretch for not holding my tongue!"

He shook his head sadly. "That would not have helped me, and it would have been a thousand times worse for her."

"Nothing can be as bad for her as losing you! Aren't you moved by seeing her need?"

"Horribly—are not *you?*" he said, lifting his eyes to hers suddenly.

She started under his look. "You mean, why don't I help you? Why don't I use my influence? Ah, if you knew how I have tried!"

"And you are sure that nothing can be done?"

"Nothing, nothing: what arguments can I use? We abhor divorce—we go against our religion in consenting to it—and nothing short of recovering the boy could possibly justify us."

Durham turned slowly away. "Then there is nothing to be done," he said, speaking more to himself than to her.

He felt her light touch on his arm. "Wait! There is one thing more—" She stood close to him, with entreaty written on her small passionate face. "There is one thing more" she repeated. "And that is, to believe that I am deceiving you again."

He stopped short with a bewildered stare. "That you are deceiving me—about the boy?"

"Yes—yes; why shouldn't I? You're so credulous—the temptation is irresistible."

"Ah, it would be too easy to find out—"

"Don't try, then! Go on as if nothing had happened. I have been lying to you," she declared with vehemence.

"Do you give me your word of honor?" he rejoined.

"A liar's? I haven't any! Take the logic of the facts instead. What reason have you to believe any good of me? And what reason have I to do any to you? Why on earth should I betray my family for your benefit? Ah, don't let yourself be deceived to the end!" She sparkled up at him, her eyes suffused with mockery; but on the lashes he saw a tear.

He shook his head sadly. "I should first have to find a reason for your deceiving me."

"Why, I gave it to you long ago. I wanted to punish you—and now I've punished you enough."

"Yes, you've punished me enough," he conceded.

The tear gathered and fell down her thin cheek. "It's you who are punishing me now. I tell you I'm false to the core. Look back and see what I've done to you!"

He stood silent, with his eyes fixed on the ground. Then he took one of her hands and raised it to his lips.

"You poor, good woman!" he said gravely.

Her hand trembled as she drew it away. "You're going to her—straight from here?"

"Yes—straight from here."

"To tell her everything—to renounce your hope?"

"That is what it amounts to, I suppose."

She watched him cross the room and lay his hand on the door.

"Ah, you poor, good man!" she said with a sob.